Beauty, Fury, and Lies

(Belle's Revenge Series Book One)

Victoria Helen Rose

ISBN: 978-0-9906141-0-4

August 2014

Table of Contents

Prologue

Chapter One: Beauty

Chapter Two: Alphabet Soup

Chapter Three: Fury

Chapter Four: Truths and Lies

Chapter Five: The Uniform

Chapter Six: Evolution

Chapter Seven: Homeland Insecurity

Chapter Eight: Friends and Foes

Chapter Nine: Rage

Chapter Ten: Operation Waldo

Chapter Eleven: Cast the Net

Chapter Twelve: Bloody Hands

For my kind knight and my kickass sister

Prologue

I don't know what it says about me that my biggest accomplishments in life involved hunting down and killing people.

Today's history books may record the biggest, messiest, most regret-inducing mistake in history as that made by two men: Osama Bin Laden and his silent and far deadlier partner Omar Al-Zahrani. They grew up together in the same neighborhood in Saudi Arabia. Everyone in the world wanted Bin Laden after the attacks but I became far more interested in the silent mastermind.

The biggest mistake in history was taking credit for the murders of my mother and then my brother: she was in the towers and he was killed in action. Grief ignited fury. Fury drove me to rampage across the terror centers of the world leaving a trail of blood and confused intelligence agencies. Fury drove me to my greatest life accomplishments: earning the respect of some and the fear of many.

I never intended to keep Belle Jones as my identity. It was my first *nomme de guerre* and I intended to dump Isabelle Jones from Ohio as I got entrenched. Like most names, however, mine was established by another person. Early in my career I came across an Algerian terror cell that had a warning about me on their dining room wall with my picture and the term *belle dangereuse,* with a red bolded *FATALE* under it.

That was fine by me; let them know me as the deadly woman, the dangerous beauty, the *belle fatale*. After all: that is exactly what I am.

Chapter 1: Beauty

August 2010
France

There is something delightful about the abandoned châteaux in the French countryside, particularly those with any kind of modern plumbing installed. I had holed up in that haven before and knew the area well; it was far enough away from Cannes to avoid pesky tourists. I had been there for two nights and as dawn came I decided I couldn't put it off any longer and shuffled into the bathroom. I peed on a thick white stick and left it to cure on a dusty lighting niche before forcing myself to go out and check my stock and weaponry.

My third sat-phone rang and for a second there I seriously considered throwing up on it. "As-salamu alaykum," I greeted my client and listened as he inquired about a job. I sauntered back to the elegant bathroom as he spoke. "Yes, they are at the drop site," I replied in the same Arabic the caller used.

"Beauty, you are the best. Any changes with the fee arrangement?" the caller inquired.

I peeked at the seven-inch-long stick of destiny and lost my breath. My client had to repeat my name a few times. "Khalid, my apologies," I sank down to sit against the beautifully decorated cold tile of the wall. "Something has come up. Can we alter our arrangement, trading money for something a little less conventional? I need to be somewhere."

"I think we can arrange something. Speed will depend on the destination. If you are going back to Afghanistan," he replied.

"No, I'm afraid not this time. Can you get me to America?"

There was silence for a moment. "I hope all is well with your family. I've never known you to go there."

"Can you get me there?"

"Of course. Will you need weapons? My cousin knows a man," Khalid replied.

"Thank you, but I am well equipped."

"Of this I am certain," he replied and agreed to call me after *Dhuhr*, or midday prayers. Khalid was a lot of things, but mostly he was rare. I met him years ago when we were both trying to off an explosives trader for different reasons.

In my line of business I avoid terms like 'good' or 'bad'; they're almost all relative. There's only one person I consider truly 'bad', and it was well past time for me to end this. First, however, I needed to a make a detour to the place every pregnant global freelance intelligence operative assassin goes: Washington D.C.

*****

A week after my phone call with Khalid I had returned to my homeland and took a midnight walk to an unpopular destination. My slim body was neatly encased in my favorite black jumpsuit with bulges for weapons; my long brown hair was contained in a bun. I almost look like a dominatrix when I'm working.

Outside it was pitch black and the streets of DC were taking a breath of cool night air while radiating the day's heat. DC is miserable in the third week of August.

"God I am so tired," I hooked my harness onto a very handy railing and stepped silently through the marble halls. It's a beautiful building with a spiraling staircase through the center wrapped around a sky-high foyer. The halls were empty and dimly lit but there are always some lights on; the living dislike approaching the dead in the dark. I stopped in front of the slot I sought.

"Hello Mickey," I greeted Mikhail's stone. "I miss you, you old bastard." I set my gloved hand on the cold stone and stared at his brassy name plate.

In the near distance I heard a series of car doors slamming. *Time to go.* I ran down the hall and hooked myself expertly into the harness attached to the staircase's railing. I lowered one floor and then I held my breath and my position as men with large guns ran in. *Hello boys.* I was unseen in the shadows above them. *I can beat them to the roof. Let's go. Wait!* A man walked into the building and changed the entire situation. It was George. He was here for me.

"Belle!" he called out into the building. "Belle, this is Agent George Tomopolis, I want to help you," he called.

I glanced above me but suddenly I didn't want to beat them to the roof.

"Belle?" George shouted in the wrong direction.

I pushed off and lowered myself quickly and quietly to the ground. I had unclipped myself before anyone saw me.

"Show me your hands, right now!" Someone ordered and half a dozen guns pointed my direction. George ran up with his gun out.

"Hello George," I greeted him calmly and traced my breast as though I was surprised. George is six foot two with spiky brown hair, high cheek bones, and brown eyes. He looks exactly like the FBI agents you see on television complete with the suit, tie, and large gun.

5

"Hello Belle Jones, or should I say Alexis?" George greeted while aiming right at my head. I profiled him ages ago; he likes head shots.

"Belle is good enough for the rest of the world," I offered.

"Get your hands up and get on the gr-,"

I interrupted, "Reel it in George," I looked him straight in the eye as I whipped out a .38 from my breast holster and pressed it against my jaw, ready to fire. I almost enjoyed the jerk reaction this caused by the seven men in my lines of sight. "Why should I trust you?"

"Alexis, get that gun away from your head right now; you are way too good for that," George ordered paternally. "I came to bring you home with me; we'll put you somewhere safe. Think about it," he tried to coax while still holding his weapon ready to fire.

"Convince me."

"Come with me. You'll be with me and my friends. There's so much we need to talk about. Just put the gun down. Belle,"

I swung my thumb and unloaded the gun and kicked the cartridge to my left. I'll admit my hands were shaking a little as I hit my knees, slid the gun toward George, and lowered myself to my stomach.

Other people's hands, knees, and boots were everywhere and I was smothered. I noticed that they put plastic cuffs and metal handcuffs on me; clearly they had learned from others' experiences. They stood me up and found the pocket knife in my bra. For the first time in years I felt vulnerable and exposed but George clapped his hand on my shoulder after they pulled me up.

"You're okay. Take a deep breath."

I did and looked at him again. "You missed one," I told him and lifted my right boot. "The sole has a knife in it." I felt someone grab the ankle, unlacing the boot and jerking it off before they released that leg and grabbed the other as soon as my sock hit the marble. Then the hands started petting me again as others crushed my arms in their grip.

"Okay. Agent Powell will put you in my car. Be nice, you'll be okay," he told me. "You too," he told the man behind me. I was marched out of the building in my socks and put into an SUV.

"Okay, got her," a female agent reported as I was placed next to her in the SUV. She fenced me in. We sat in silence for a few minutes.

"Are you on George's team?" I asked. She didn't verbally respond but her eyes betrayed her thoughts. I answered her face, "Someone hunts you, you learn about them. There was no firefight."

"It seemed pretty quiet. Did you know?"

"Yeah. How far along are you?"

"Excuse me?"

"I profiled you too: well, everything I could get from hacking the FBI. You're a FBI sniper and a damn good one. If I was going after me, I'd bring the best snipers I had. I see no rifle so,"

"Thank you," she clearly couldn't think of anything else to say.

"I'll tell you more: that's why I didn't shoot myself. I never could kill in cold blood. I'm not...George would know."

"First trimester; they don't know yet," she admitted very quietly.

"I think I may be about nine weeks. It's exhausting."

7

Doors swung open. "Ready ladies?" George entered. "If you've already picked your cuffs, don't forget your seat belt." The she-agent immediately checked my intact cuffs. We were on our way.

We drove forever, then they blindfolded me and we drove some more. A few hours later, I had been x-rayed, searched, put into what appeared to be pajamas or scrubs with fuzzy slippers, questioned for an hour or so, read my rights, photographed, finger, hand and foot-printed and given a six by eight gray, sterile cell with a bathroom stall and a camera. It was four a.m. when I fell asleep on the cot.

A loud banging on the door woke me at 0830.

"Prisoner X one-twenty-eight, breakfast," a speaker on the wall informed and someone shoved a bagel through the door slot. Next came the mesh bag with a towel and shower essentials. I took the hint. An opaque curtain barely shielded me from the camera. The minute I reappeared the door opened.

"Prisoner X128, step out!" a soldier instructed and held the door. "Face the wall," he instructed in the same tone and handcuffed me again. He transported me to a room many floors up and a building over. He released me and left me in a plush furnished sitting room; a pleasant woman a few decades older than I was entered and smiled.

We spent the entire morning together. She got me some mint tea and we had cookies. It was wonderful. We took a break and some kind of medic looked me over, took a blood test, and confirmed my pregnancy. I started shaking again. I was taken to yet another building and into an interview room with George.

"Alright, go!" I sat, ready for a torrent of questions. He was silent for a moment.

"Have you any idea how lucky you are that my men and I had orders to bring you in alive? Had any other target tried anything like you did," he paused to fume silently before returning his attention. "Are you hungry?"

"No, I'm pregnant. I'm just tired."

"Okay. Question one — why did you send these?" He laid out pictures of letters, and other intel I had sent.

"There are levels of right and wrong, you know? It's all true. What they did was wrong — very wrong. So I guess I tattled. I knew every rat I sold was a nail in my coffin — a live trace through the underworld. I didn't care. It felt good, really good when they arrested Moley. Al-Khazim got shot; Dirt Man's car blew up: all the bad guys were catching karma. So I wrote."

"A counterfeiter, arms dealer, human trafficker, armed burglars, more than one filthy politician," George summed.

"Did they get caught?"

"Most. Some slipped away. Some disappeared. Most are in one prison or another. Okay. Here," he handed me a cold diet soda, which I took appreciatively. "No energy shots with the baby."

I smiled to myself. "How long have you been studying me?"

"Nineteen months, but of course we got a good history. I assume you know the father?"

"Who taught you how to interrogate?" I exclaimed and drank the soda. I shook my head.

"Well I'm being a lot nicer than you were in Lebanon."

"He was trying to blow up a bunch of U.S. soldiers!" I defended.

"So you're a patriot?"

"Well I'm not a traitor. There are some things you just don't do."

9

"Why did you let us catch you last night? What on earth were you doing in a memorial building?" he leaned forward and I leaned back.

"It was an accident," I replied.

"Bull, you don't have accidents."

"Clearly you missed the whole pregnant thing," I muttered, "Getting in: I just fell into it all. There is no way out."

"You were getting set up for a major operation," he led.

"Reel it in, George. Ask what you want to ask."

"You did notice that you're a prisoner, right? I could and should chuck you into the nearest women's facility," he replied saucily.

Hilarious. "Knock yourself out. I'm sure you'd love me to educate the population on some of my finer capabilities," I dared.

"Like how to take out cops after being handcuffed? That was cute."

"It is easier without the cuffs, but whatever."

"What have you been up to in Saudi Arabia?"

"Spain, London, Germany, France, New York," I led him.

"You hate terrorism," he misunderstood.

"A little henna stain on the face and hands, everyone looks the same in a burqa. It wasn't a hit. It wasn't Mossad, or any political entity. I retrieved something, procured something, and placed something. Three visits in all. Hottest damn place on earth." I drank again.

"You went to get something? For a client?"

"Sure. But while I was there, I uncovered something. I got interested. Have you searched my hotel room yet?"

He wasn't going to answer.

10

"Check the front cover of the bible. There is a list there, between the binding and the book. It's a very important list," I divulged. "My client wanted something delivered to Saudi Arabia, illegal goods. So, I took the opportunity to deliver some crack and porn and take a little walk in the moonlight. It is slightly less hotter-than-hell in the evenings," I drank and my stomach growled.

"Is the chip going to destroy the computer we put it in?"

"No! That would be pointless," I knew his people had found it.

"What do I find?"

"You find all the answers as to why I surrendered."

"You are pregnant."

"He's a good man. Where am I? FBI, therapists, the military police, a medical office? Underground holding cells?"

"It's better than Gitmo." He pushed back from the table and I set the empty bottle on the surface. "How do you feel?" He was clearly relaying a message from his earpiece.

I glared at him with meaning.

"Right. Well we'll talk later."

"Read the chip," I instructed. A guard touched my shoulder and I stopped my reflex just fast enough to not harm myself or others.

"Good girl," George praised as I lowered my arms to my side and stood up. The MP gently held my wrists with one hand and clipped the cuffs on with the other.

"I was visiting someone," I called over my shoulder as they turned me away.

"Friend? Family?" George inquired, "Victim?"

How do I describe Mickey? Friend of the not-quite-family? Avuncular buddy? Now you're showing off, Ali. Oh, answer him! "You know I've never killed on U.S. soil. He's not important

11

to you." The guards walked me out and the lady sniper was waiting in the hallway.

"Hello again," she greeted and fell in with us.

"How's it going?" I asked casually.

"Giving George a hard time?"

"Old habits die hard," I said as we exited an elevator and got into a golf cart with its very own armed guard. "Seriously, where am I going?" I commented, mostly to myself. This was a three fence, barbed wire, guarded perimeter with radar kind of place.

"No offense, but you're fairly dangerous."

"Back at you, sweetie," I smiled at the sniper and we arrived.

"How are you feeling?" she asked in the elevator to doom.

"Why's everyone so curious?"

"Belle, we've been working on this case for a long time. We feel like we know you. Well, Isabelle Jones, anyway," she shrugged it off as we cleared the third security gate. I counted guards from habit, and noted that they were equipped with shock guns. Agent Sniper stepped back as one man opened my cell door. The smell of warm chicken soup mixed with the smell of chocolate, which totally distracted me. The guard had to repeat the order for me to face the room before he un-cuffed me.

"Get some sleep," she called and I was totally fascinated by the TV dinner tray and stool which held chicken soup and a warm chocolate chip cookie. I inhaled it and fell back on the cot.

The lights had been dimmed when I woke up. As I sat up and stepped over to the restroom, they returned to normal brightness. I reappeared and the door opened for the lady agent.

"Can I come in?" she asked before she entered and the door shut.

"What time is it?"

"It's about six-thirty," she perched on the stool and I sat to face her on the cot. "Someone wants to meet you."

"NSA?"

"Close."

"You read the chip."

"Someone did. George is waiting."

I stood up and we exited. This time they cuffed me in front instead of behind my back. It's a significant improvement. We stayed in the same building, went through two elevators, and ended up in an interrogation room. The seats were much nicer, and it actually had a window. I sat and they attached my cuffs to the table. George entered following a middle aged man with a belly and balding head.

"Prisoner X128. Who the hell are you, lady? It's like Mata Hari meets Jason Bourne!" he entered dramatically and sat.

"That was one hell of a chip," George lauded me in his own way. I nodded recognition. "We're still working on the password to that one file."

"Why password-protect that file?" the fat bald man asked.

"Do you ever ask good questions?" I rebuffed.

"Hey, I can make those chains come off," he answered.

"Turn your back for two seconds and so can I," I replied testily. "They're slightly annoying," I turned my attention to George. "File A was a full directory of terrorists living in London. The second page was Paris, the third Madrid, and so on. File B is everything I have on each and every one of them. The PDFs were trade routes, drug routes and vessels. I'm sure you know who the pictures include, and where," I watched his eyes as he mentally cracked the code to the protected file.

"Saudi," he said.

"Saudi," I confirmed.

"She is smart." The bumble blustery act was replaced by cool consciousness. "Miss Belle, I'm interested in what you might have been up to recently. I'm your buddy George's CIA counterpart, I have ties. I let him track you. Now I know exactly why. You were an adequate spy. Really excellent fighting skills; you learn languages like people learn to breathe; you keep cool and you're one hell of a shot. In a way, you're a con artist, a black widow and a James Bond all in one. And you're American. Interpol wants you for a half a dozen crimes, but I don't think you're really a criminal at heart. I think you're more than that."

He looked at someone over my shoulder and I was released. "I can remove you from the pile of shit you have fallen into."

"What kind of shit have I fallen into?"

"You're under arrest for espionage, murder, arson, drugs charges, international violations, we can go on," he answered.

"I never took an American life."

"Exactly. You cooperate with us, you get perks. The more cooperation, the more perks. I'm not read in on all the details of whatever operation you may have had going when we caught you, but think about it," he got up and left me with George.

"I thought it was a very organized presentation," George commented to break the silence.

"I know someone who knows how to get their hands on bank routing numbers of some of these characters," I offered and leaned back in the chair.

"What do you want?"

"George, there is no way out of this business. So I let myself get arrested; it beats the alternative."

"You weren't going to up and quit this Saudi case."

"Well the timing did suck. I thought the CIA could help," I admitted. "Maybe MI-6 would have been a better choice."

"I'll talk to some people. Belle, tell me: what was the Saudi gig?"

"It was not for a client. I used my clients to get there; to have a cover. I planted two bugs, one of which will be found and traced to a misnomer. Never use your own material when dealing with the big dogs. The bug transmits via a special kind of wireless frequency. It's very difficult to detect unless you know exactly what you are doing. Frequency was going to be set up to be received and fed into an internet based program."

"Yeah, CIA's gonna want to talk to you about that."

That and about fifty other things, "So, have I cooperated myself into a bed with sheets, a little lotion and some chap-stick?"

"It will have to be a twin bed."

"A little Sprite® would be great."

"That all sounds pretty agreeable. I'll see what I can do. Are you depressed?"

"Maybe a little, but I am in the middle of a life-quake." The wheels in my head turned. "You people think I'm suicidal!"

"Are you?"

I got up and headed for the window. "No! I don't know! Hello, Life-quake!" a tear leaked from my right eye. "God I hate being a woman!" I smacked the cinderblock wall with my left hand: half the hand has nerve damage or is covered in scar tissue. Sometimes I hit stuff just to feel something in my hand.

"Belle, the Marine is about two seconds from -" George started to say and I turned to face the guard, who had stepped forward. He was about 185 lbs., six foot two, standard Corps chiseling. "Belle, don't even think about it," George warned.

I took three steps back to my seat and leaned my arms on the table, toward George. "He has a weak left knee. I can't not think about it. I can choose to not act. Like I did earlier. Like I did last night. Do you appreciate what I'm doing?"

"Belle, you blow me away. Not like you did that Algerian guy: that was messy. People like you don't happen. Yes, we appreciate it. You could be covered in blood and bruises and chained like a death row rebel, do you appreciate it?"

"They found pieces of him on the next floor up," I recalled. "And across the street: it was definitely messy. Look: I'm nice to you, you're nice to me. You get all authoritarian dictator on me, it could get a bit messy. You should know my bottom line: end of the day, I'm American. If that guy was stationed at certain places in the last five years, I've probably saved his life or his friends. What I do, what I did for clients wasn't always kosher, but it opened doors for me, and there are a few very bad people who aren't around anymore. Half of what I do is tit-for-tat intelligence trading. The Palestinians are probably pretty pissed at me but I don't see the Mossad on the list of people who want my head."

"You done?" he asked, unimpressed by my emotional ramble.

"Yes," I took a breath.

"Great. Let's have dinner," he fiddled with his phone for a minute. "So essentially, you like being an inmate."

"No one here is trying to kill me and all of my information is secure. The handcuffs and cell with camera is less than pleasant, but I feel like I'm actively in the middle of something."

Someone entered and set down two trays. It smelled fairly good and lids revealed hamburgers and mixed vegetables.

"Thank you," I said from habit. We made awkward small talk as we ate. As I finished my plate off, I turned the conversation back to normal. "Yes, the CIA will want to speak with me. The question for you is, before or after you see the Saudi file."

"I have two very good people trying to crack your coding."

"I wrote it around password software; they could go all night. If you were to choose a very small core team, like you and your boss, in a secure viewing room, and gave me my laptop,"

"It's that impressive?" George asked skeptically.

"We can wait until tomorrow morning when your geeks are tired," I offered.

"You want us to see it," George read, "It's so obvious. It's probably stupid."

"Alright. Goodnight," I replied and held my wrists together in the air.

"I'll make some calls," he stood and I knew I had won. George left me with the guard.

"I like Marines; they don't whine," I turned slightly to face him. It was like talking to a Beefeater. "The military wouldn't have taken me. I'm kinda psycho," I turned back because he wasn't interested.

17

George returned. "One of my geeks congratulates your cyber skill: said that the hard drive had a fail-secure system that he just barely avoided tripping. He says you may have modified a Japanese system."

"Right after I stole it, yes."

"John is coming back and the geek in question, Agent Kmetz, is going to be with us and the laptop. Let's go."

I stood and the guard saw that my wrists were firmly secured in steel. "Padded handcuffs. That's the next perk I want."

I think George really wanted to laugh, but he resisted.

Chapter 2: Alphabet Soup

The look on the computer tech's face when we entered the appropriate viewing room was priceless. "She's the super spy?" the boy, who appeared to be fresh out of high school, gaped at me.

"That's why no one ever caught me," I smiled at him as the cuffs released. "Belle Jones," I introduced myself.

"Seriously?" he blinked at me. "I've been working on the password for four hours."

"Should have called me," I shrugged and took the seat I was directed to. "Is he old enough to see what's on this file?" I asked George just before John entered.

"Wait for us outside," George instructed my guard. "Alright, let's see it."

Kmetz pulled the screen up and got it projected onto a larger screen. I took my place and felt the keyboard lightly. Thirty-nine characters later the computer let us in. I clicked on the photo file first, let them get a peek, and then switched off for an Excel file. I left it on the screen and let it sink in.

"I believe he is still on everyone's most wanted list," I said quietly after a few minutes and took my original seat.

"Did you plant the bug in his house, the mosque?" John asked.

"The one they won't find is in his house."

"You were in his house," George gawked.

"Last trip in early May; security is very high."

"What was your objective, what did the client want?"

"Oh, the client was unrelated. This is all me. I hadn't decided exactly what to do: I want him dead, but the general radical Islamist jihad movement would have a major spike if he was 'martyred'. I needed to investigate the Saudi government a little more."

"God, I could kiss you," John said, staring at the screen like it was Christmas.

"I don't recommend it," George advised. He was contemplating the screen. "This is all solid?" he checked with me.

"Would I lie to you?" I replied. "I didn't think he was in Afghanistan. Really, I found it because of a client: they wanted someone's communications monitored. I noticed a discrepancy and followed it until I found the tell-tale rat's nest: someone purposefully trying to disguise input and output of calls and internet connections. Omar Al-Zahrani and Bin Laden should have hired a better geek."

"How long ago?"

"First inkling was about ten months ago. It took me nine weeks to hack the Saudi system: it's not easy to be online invisible in Europe. I got it from Cyprus, and went through two very talented programming gurus. Talented in computers, not in bed. Highly effective," I winked at the kid. "May I have some mint tea or coke please?"

"Yeah," John said blankly, still trying to capture it.

George texted someone. "Give us a few minutes. I was not expecting this. You hacked Saudi Arabia?"

"Just the internet service provider of a small region," I clarified and took a breath. Everything was unfolding before me: all of my work, my dedication, just handed to these guys. "China does shit like this all the time. Bin Laden and Al-Zahrani killed my mother in 9/11. His spawn killed someone else in Afghanistan. I want him dead. I wanted his entire network dead. But if you pull a weed you gotta get the roots." My soda arrived and I re-caffeinated. I sat back and let them review the file for the next hour.

"Most people blame Bin Laden for that," John stated with reservation.

"You have a thousand people searching for him and they're not wrong: Bin Laden was definitely involved and unlike Al-Zahrani, he was willing to shout to the world that he was the mastermind. O.Z is different."

"What do you already know about Al-Zahrani?" George asked.

"Look, I started in after Bin Laden, but during my stay in Israel I came across some information about a quiet man with a heart of pure evil. Al-Zahrani was Osama's childhood best friend and next door neighbor. Both wealthy families, both Saudi Arabian; they separated and then sometime in the late eighties they got back together. That's when shit really kicked up for Bin Laden. The sudden explosion in influence? Al-Zahrani has brains, people skills, and he is wicked good at manipulating organized intelligence. British and French operatives very nearly took each other out in 2006 because of his treachery. Everyone is so focused on UBL they're missing the real trouble."

"I don't suppose you found Bin Laden?" George asked hopefully.

"Of course I fucking found Bin Laden. But here's my deal: you help me get Ozzie and then I'll point you to the striped rat. They are intimately connected; never far from each other."

"Ozzie?" George asked with amusement.

"Omar Al-Zahrani. O.Z. I ran out of wizard jokes a long time ago," I replied. "Look, I have his address. I cloned his phone. I'll give you Bin Laden's phone number if you need something for upstairs."

"We have his phone number!" John finally exclaimed.

"Want to crank-call him? Find out if his refrigerator is running?" I asked. "A word of caution: I suspect he has friends here in D.C. I try not to operate here unless it's absolutely necessary, so I don't have anything on locals."

"Alexis, why did you turn yourself in?" John asked, penetrating my eyes.

"Because I couldn't send you Al-Zahrani via UPS?" I offered. "My options were to fake my own death or get caught, and the dead don't send people mail. I get a kick out of helping you guys," he continued to look. "Okay, let's say that in the world I found myself in, it was all about greed and money and revenge. Let's say I discovered that I missed life in the real world, that I was getting tired of sleeping with a gun under my pillow and blowing things up and stealing information and arranging things to happen," I took a breath, "and hacking Al-Zahrani and sending in bits of intelligence via mail to someone who I didn't know for certain was reading them. Then I discovered George. The information got juicier but my sleep got worse. I was obsessed with Al-Zahrani; eventually it would have caught someone's attention. Like he caught mine. I was torn between wanting everything and wanting it all to be gone. Last night happened and I do appreciate not being shot, it hurts a lot. We're here now."

"Tell you what, Belle, you keep working with me, we're going to improve your quality of life here," John decided and looked at his phone. "They're setting up the bed right now. George and I need to have a few minutes. You want to chat here with Kmetz?"

"Sure," I yawned. The screen went off-projection and the two men left and the guard came back in.

"What did they arrest you for?" the geek said.

"Seriously? I'm wanted for everything from murder to transporting stolen goods, not to mention stealing said goods, plus hacking everything in sight," I informed him. "No one walking on the right side of the street would have ever found these bastards."

"What's the Algerian?" he asked.

"I strongly disapprove of human trafficking. People steal or sell their kids to these people, and the children become slaves, or worse. He had a little girl in his room. I got her out of there before he went boom."

"So you know a lot of computer stuff," he opened. "Good thing I was the one who discovered the trip wire."

"Did you extract that sequence before you copied the hard drive? If not, your whole lab could go off," I warned.

"You know, you're really helpful for a master criminal," Kmetz the kid looked at me suspiciously. "You're right, but it's just kind of odd."

"I prefer to think of myself as someone who did what had to be done."

The door flew open. "Belle, we need to get you out of here," George entered and I stood. "You're going to go with Agent Starr," the guard grabbed my elbow and whipped my arms behind me to cuff. We walked briskly down the hall until Agent Starr, the female agent sniper, met us and fell in. George disappeared. We got into the elevator and she pressed the button for the first basement floor — not my floor.

Agent Starr was around my age- somewhere between twenty-five and thirty years old and she had a Nordic beauty: natural blond hair, cold gray eyes and a little nob on the tip of her nose. Her face was oval and she was an inch or two taller than me.

"Well, whatever happened must have been productive," she commented. "We're just going to sit down, recap a few things. This way please," she led down the hall and into a small sitting area. We sat.

"I'll be brief, because I know you're tired. First, I have to warn you that the guards are very protective of the agents, especially the female ones. For your own protection, please be careful," she made eye contact and meant it. "Next, how did you like the therapist you spoke with today?"

"I liked her," I answered carefully.

"Good to hear. You'll meet with her at least once a day."

"Until she decides I'm no longer a threat to myself," I concluded. Starr just shook her head.

"She is read in on this case, but she's not interested in extracting information. Your depression is worth monitoring," I tuned her out after that, preferring to undress the guard with my eyes.

"Hey," she snapped her fingers in front of my face twice. "This part's important. This isn't a standard prison. It's not even Gitmo. We don't have the kind of red tape bureaucratic fetters a normal detainment site has. We straight up don't exist. I am asking you as someone who cares; please be good. Be careful, be nice, because if we don't exist,"

"It's easy to make me disappear too." I finished her sentence.

She handed me a legal pad and a felt tipped pen and eventually I was taken back to the cell, which now had a proper bed with sterile white sheets. I laid awake long after they dimmed the lights, trying to make up my mind.

The next morning the bagel shot through my door again. Hours passed without anything. I showered, arranged my toiletries, made my bed, and when they brought me some scrubs-like clothes I put them on and washed my own in the sink.

Okay. Think think think think. God I want to hit something. Are they even taking me seriously? We should have been up all night with this. This is fucking Omar al Fucking Zahrani! God, I even look like a prisoner. That's it! They're going to move me! Clearly, not to Gitmo because I'd kill half the population. Ha, half. Right. Give me an energy shot and a tired guard and they're all dead. I am going to hurt the next guard that bruises me. This is ridiculous. I stared at the red lines on my wrists. *There was no call for that. I'm the good guy, remember? Does anyone freaking remember me? Hello! Oh God I think I'm going to puke.* I went over to the door.

"Hey, pregnant and about to puke here! What do I have to do to get a ginger ale?" I called and walked back to the bed. The camera followed me. A minute later someone slid a Sprite® through a hatch at the bottom of the door. "Thanks," I called insincerely.

This is what I was looking for? A concrete and steel cell; bruises on my wrists and people who have no idea what I'm capable of? It makes me so mad.

They slid a grilled cheese sandwich through the slot. Apparently it was lunch time. I finished it quickly and started to count the tiles on the wall.

"Step out." The door opened and I sauntered over. "Face the wall."

"Just, be gentle please. The guy yesterday -," a cuff whacked the bruise, "Ow. Not so tight!" I admonished. I could tell it made a difference: not. He got me settled back into the interrogation room from the night before just as someone poked their head in to say we were in the wrong place. Again, I cautioned him about my wrists.

He didn't listen so I pulled a very cute maneuver. To be specific, I knocked him on his ass, rolled over the table and landed on my feet. The guard who ran in didn't have the fastest reflexes: I hopped onto a chair and fan-kicked him in the neck. The first guy was up by then and had my shoulders, so I forward rolled him off once I got a foot on the floor. A third man came in and threw me across the room as I popped up: I hit the wall hard enough to not-quite knock me out but still disorient me and I fell down. I think they picked me up and one of them got me in a headlock; we moved like that to the second location.

Once we were there a new man arrived with a kind of belt that strapped my legs together once I was in the chair. One of the guards firmly placed my face against the table with the butt of his hand rimming my orbital ridge, effectively blocking my view of anything. They changed the cuffs to bind in front and then locked me to the table. A second strap went under my breasts to lock me to the chair like a seat belt before the gloved hand was removed from my face. George walked in, saw me as the guards finished, and walked out again. I took a deep breath and released it slowly.

"I'm sorry if I hurt you," I said sincerely of the man whose jugular I had taken a shin to. No answer.

"That was unexpected," John entered and I almost smiled. "Thank you gentlemen, we'll take it from here. What brought this on?" The men left.

"He pissed me off," I replied evenly. "I was being nice, he was being mean, so I kicked his ass a little. The rest was just reflex."

"Hell of a reflex," John replied, amused. "I saw the video tape," he pressed a rag to my face and unlocked my one of my wrists. "Anyway, we've been up all night with your very exciting news. It will take some time, but eventually this could be very helpful. How did you know he wasn't in Afghanistan?"

"He's ad Arab," I replied stuffily while pinching my nose: it wasn't broken, just bleeding. "Doe self-resptheking Arab would live in Athganistan."

"Good conclusion, as it turns out. Now, about these other files,"

George entered. "What the hell did you do?"

"I kicked someone's ass," I informed bluntly. "They bruised my wrists yesterday!" I defended, removing the rag, "I asked very politely for him to be gentle with them today, and he didn't listen. Then we did the whole thing again in that room and I swear he actually did it harder. So I knocked him on his ass. You don't get it, do you? You think I'm all sweet and tame and waiting to do whatever you want, but I'm a real person, I have done some really amazing things. Most were illegal, but they're still worth respect! I give you Al-Zahrani on a silver tray and you leave me in my room for hours and hours and give me prison clothes?! I have more than half a mind to shoot my way the hell out of here. It just really pisses me off. They should be alright. The first guy might have a sore back, but the guy I wind-piped is probably worse off. It's a fast recover wound." The blood ebbed as I searched for a clean part of the rag.

"Belle, they didn't forget who they were dealing with," George pointed and took a seat opposite me.

"They're bruising my wrists so that I can give you information and cooperate with you," I replied venomously and swore at him in Hebrew.

"Tell me about the undercover work you did in Saudi Arabia," John led, "henna stains?"

"Yes; if you take the plant fresh and prepare it like they do for henna tattoos, then smear it over your face and hands and get under a tanning light. Tan for about an hour; spray some lemon juice or vinegar, and slip gloves on to sleep. The next morning the crud will have fallen off. You get back under the lamp for an hour; do any touch-ups with brown foundation cream, pencil in the eyebrows, and -"

"Medical team," someone called outside the door before coming in.

"Did you take care of the guy I kicked in the throat?" I asked while someone un-cuffed the other hand.

"They're fine," the attendant replied as he looked me over. "She really should be fully restrained." He was a smaller guy but he looked plenty spry, especially for his age.

I then noted the guard who had slipped in. "I'm still tied to the chair. I'll be good; I'm usually well behaved," I replied apologetically and showed him my wrists rings.

"Hands flat on the table. You make one move and he's going to stun the hell out of you," the medical man replied and the guard showed a stun gun before taking a position behind me.

"Thank you," I replied as he set to washing off my face, neck and chest, "I hit the wall with this part of my face; I think I spared the nose."

"Yeah, I can tell where the wall was. Excuse me," he pulled my shirt out and looked down. "Do you think you hit a rib?" He got out of my shirt and started feeling along the cage.

"Ow-ow-ow-ow yes, I think they're bruised. I can breathe without the usual broken-rib pains, so I think they're just -"

He cut me off, "This is going to sting, just remember: guy with a stun gun." He put a butterfly suture on my head;

apparently I had cut it. "Ice pack," he handed it to me and turned to my wrists. For all of his lack of charm, he was gentle and wrapped the wrists carefully. "Here are some NSAIDs; your face is going to look like that for a while. I advise not fighting with the guards again," he packed up and left.

"I'll give you a whole pot of tea if you tell me who your contact in Saudi Arabia is," John offered.

"That's easy. The CIA has a man there named Abrahim Al-Himin. He's a native informant. We weren't entangled, but he helped me get around a little. At first he was going to kill me because I could break his cover, but ultimately he saw sense," I earned my tea with stevia and took the pain killers. "That reminds me, there's a reason Bin Laden was tied to the poppy fields. He was shot in the leg a dozen years ago, heroin keeps the pain down."

"Interesting," John noted. "We sent your information on London to the British this morning."

"Would you like me to hack their system and see what they're doing with it?" I asked. "What? I'm bored."

"Frequency of the transmitter?" George handed me a piece of paper and a pen.

I wrote it down with its coordinates.

"What have you done in Iran?" John asked.

"Iran? Closest I ever got to Iran is procuring some supplies for the insurgency against Khamenei. We made the deal in Afghanistan. God, you wouldn't believe Afghanistan if you saw it. Rampant chaos, warlords, Sharia justice, criminal activity coming right left and sideways. It's not the Wild West; it's the first circle of hell."

"I feel like you're holding back something," George analyzed.

"I'm sure you'll figure it out. There's really no need for it right now, you have more than you know what to do with."

"There's another disc," John inferred. I gave a noncommittal nod.

"Is it secure?" George asked.

"Very," I assured.

"Alright," George moved on. "What did you get from the Algerian before he exploded?"

"A little girl named Nela. She was dressed in a woman's teddy and handcuffed to the bed. He was in the shower. I picked her lock, planted the bomb, and lowered us to safety before he walked in and it detonated. I placed her in a good home; I still send money so she can eat good food and go to school. You should know, George: nothing infuriates me like an abuser of women and children."

"Then who is the Indian family you send money to?"

"Their father died in my arms; an Indian policeman. A cohort killed him, not me. Those kids would be on the street because a man got trigger-happy. I was involved, so I took the responsibility for those kids and that woman. Oh, and I also stole the Algerian's laptop. Full of porn and not even the vanilla kind."

"Lebanon?" John led.

"Hamas, second degree leader: I shot him to hell with an Israeli gun. The Hezbollah arms suppliers mysteriously dropped dead from blue-ringed octopus poison about the same time. Some stupid 'jihad without a God' morons beheaded a friend of mine. I hadn't decided how to murder them when their bodies showed up naked on street corners, branded and hanging by a foot. It was gruesome, even by my standards."

"Syria?" George added.

"Drugs," I shrugged. "They also have a black market for human organs there, if you're interested."

"Israel?" George prompted.

"No comment," I smiled to myself. The game continued until I had to use a restroom. The guard unlocked me from the chair and escorted me there and back with slightly less cold indifference. The shocker was looking in the mirror; I hadn't looked like that since the last time someone detonated a building I was occupying. I returned to find John gone.

"We're done for now, it's time for you to go see the therapist. I wonder what she'll make of your Xena imitation," George pondered.

"Point of order," I said as the guard handcuffed me carefully "thank you! Point of order, I'm real, she wasn't. See you later," I called as the guard and I walked out.

I walked into the room and waited as the nice guard released me and the woman tried not to stare.

"Now I know why they asked for an ice pack," she observed. "Would you like to talk about it?"

"He cuffed my bruised wrists too hard. Twice. I got mad and knocked him on his butt. Twice. And his friend. Then someone threw me into a wall," I summed. "I guess it's not good to lash out at others, but it's been very effective. And I did restrain myself," I defended and the hour long session began. We ended with breathing exercises and a suggestion that I ask for colored pencils and some paper for my dead time.

An agent I didn't know picked me up from there and we went to the third building. We were indoors before I recognized him.

"You're the K-9 specialist," I said calmly and appreciatively. "You have some very talented dogs. I assumed they were bomb sniffers. I know, you're probably not allowed to talk to me."

"How long have you been studying us?" he asked.

"Two days for most of you, others I have worked with for months."

"I heard that you talk to everyone," he replied as we entered an elevator.

"Pretty much. At this point I have nothing to hide, and I think I've experienced enough to have something in common with everyone."

"Just keep the martial arts to yourself, that's all I ask."

"What—did a bulletin go out?" I rolled my eyes

"We all watched the video on our lunch breaks. It would have been awesome if it hadn't been our guys."

"I woulda laughed," the MP said and I pressed the ice pack to my face.

"It was definitely not funny in person," I informed. "I could have hurt those guys."

"Did I break anything?" We rounded a corner to find MP number three.

"Nope," I replied but removed my ice pack.

"Lighter than I thought," he explained to the others.

We didn't have any more time to compare war stories because I was guided into a room, unchained, placed in a chair and flanked by the two guards.

"You will be able to read the input on the screen," the agent explained. "Please type back your responses. If you are truthful and cooperate, you get rewards."

"So I'm texting a conference. Okay," I pulled up the keyboard.

"Are you ready?" the screen asked.

"Yes," I replied. There was a lull.

"When did you realize you had found Omar Al-Zahrani?" the screen asked.

"Well, I realized about nine months ago that I had discovered someone who wanted to be unseen. There was an excess of false wiring in the telephone records and a company's lines list had been hacked many times. There are electric signatures for those," I submitted. "I did not realize who the person was until I had traced some of the lines to major Al-Qaida leaders and operatives."

"Are you trained in cyber activity?" The next question came.

"I am trained in computers, network systems, hacking, cyber-attacks and programming," I replied.

There was a longer lull. "We understand you went to Saudi Arabia three times and planted a bug in his house. How did you manage this?"

"I was able to disguise myself as a native. I speak Arabic, although I rarely spoke in that country. Using a CIA contact, I was able to get around in the country. Once I knew exactly where I was going, I used a stealthy approach involving a burqa and my skills in conflict avoidance. I could not linger there."

"Why did you go after him?"

"I have a personal vendetta against OZ. I also feel strongly about terrorism in general."

"What kind of criminal are you? White collar, blue collar?"

"Technically, I was a contractor. I performed various acts from industrial espionage to drug transporting and the occasional hit. Realistically, I'm a criminal with a conscience. I've probably saved as many lives as I have harmed."

"Please tell the truth."

I glared at the screen. "This is not going to end well for them," I took a breath and typed. "I went after human traffickers and rescued children from them. I stopped an attack on a Marine base. I helped the insurgency in Iran," I submitted and took a deep breath only to feel my battered ribs.

"Retracted," the screen said. There was a long lull. "Did you turn yourself in, or were you arrested?"

"Both. I could have escaped but I chose not to."

"Are people trying to kill you?"

"Yes."

"Who have you spied for?"

"There are many countries, including the United States," I typed back. "Also, certain organizations."

"Did you ever spy for an enemy of the United States? N Korea, Iran, Somalia, Hezbollah, Hamas?"

"Never for. Sometimes against, especially terrorist-linked organizations."

"How much of a threat are you to American interests?"

"Not at all and quite a lot. I am very loyal to my homeland and when I am treated like the expert I am, I have been very useful to United States Intelligence and Counterterrorism. But the threat is only neutralized because I neutralized it. I have escaped Spanish and Belgian custody before, and I am, after all, an international spy."

"Are you secure?"

"Extremely," I wrote back. "There are two seasoned MPs in here with me, and they could wipe the floor with me," We giggled a little at that one. "I acknowledge that I have revealed too much information in interrogations to successfully evade notice if I did escape."

"Are you a man or a woman?"

"I find the question irrelevant," I answered truthfully.

"Answer the question."

I looked at the guys behind me and the agent in the room.

"I am an adult human being who is capable of engaging in combat and who is extremely intelligent. If you'd like to have a pissing match with me, you should bring an umbrella," I hit 'send' a little too soon on that one.

"You must answer the question."

"I am a female."

"Age?"

"25," I wrote back, "-ish," I muttered to myself.

"Do you have children?"

"No," I typed.

"Why did you send intelligence to the FBI?"

"I needed my mail read. I knew someone at the FBI knew about my existence."

"Last question—how long have you been in custody?"

"Two days,"

"Have you been abused?"

"Thought that was your last question," I muttered. "No," I typed. "Can I have more aspirin for my face?" I asked the agent who was locking the computer.

"Yup," he reached into his bag and produced a large bottle of water and a packet. "Water and pain killer. Let's go back to the block."

"High five," the guard from earlier said and I made the touchdown sign. "Nice and easy," he clipped me very carefully. "She's very particular."

"Good job Belle!" Agent K-9 said. We ended up in the base building in a room similar to the one Agent Starr had used.

"Very good Belle," George entered. "That went pretty well. God, you look like hell."

I laughed.

"Tonight you get to have dinner with Agent Starr—Chinese or Italian?"

"Italian," I chose.

"Angel hair pasta with Bolognese sauce?"

"You have definitely been on this case too long."

"Yes I have. Give me a moment," he stepped out and back in again. "Okay. So from here you can go back to your cell, see your benefits, rest, ice your face for about an hour. Then, dinner and a movie."

"Wow. You must be really happy."

"Well, someone is."

I returned to my cell to find a pad and colored pencils, a stuffed dolphin and a sanitized stripped laptop with Open Office, games, and a media player. I was very happy. There was also a beer cooler with water and soda, as well as ice packs. I was just settling in when urgent pounding came on my door.

"Prisoner X128, step out, hands behind please," he snapped them on quickly and we hustled upstairs. I immediately knew this wasn't a dinner date. We went to the top level and through doors which were held open for us.

"Tell me they are en route!" a woman's upset voice demanded. We went through the door and a woman in her late fifties with short cropped brown hair and half-moon glasses took me in visually. Her face turned from storm to sweet aunt in a blink. "Remove, please," she instructed and stared at my wrists. "Have a seat please."

I sat, finding the aura of the room.

"Hello dear. Have you had medical attention for," she waved her hand.

"Yes ma'am. It was my fault."

"Do you understand your Miranda rights?" and she read them to me again.

"Ma'am, I'm an international spy. I just knocked two MPs on their butts. I was mad because the handcuffs hurt," I explained.

"So I've heard. What happened?"

"Got thrown into a wall."

"And you are willing to cooperate with this FBI-CIA joint effort?"

"Yes."

"I want to see her: visually, my eyes on her face in person," she told George and John, "Once a week. And you," she turned back to me, "cooperate with them, but every week I want to see every bruise, scratch, scrape, burn, paper-cut, everything. Am I clear?"

"Yes ma'am," The three of us said in unison.

"Show me your wrist," she ordered and I unwrapped the gauze and tape on one hand. "Alright. Thank you. You may go."

The guard cuffed me in front of her. We left; I was still shell-shocked when we got to a B1 waiting room with TV and pasta waiting, along with Agent Starr. *Excellent.*

As I looked around my cell that night, laptop charging atop my stool, dolphin in my bed, guards outside with a supply of weird painkillers; life was good.

Chapter 3: Fury

The next day was Saturday. I still met with the therapist but most everyone else was off. The guards fed me and gave me painkiller and my cooler was restocked. I lay in bed and played with the laptop, eventually getting back to 'work' by recording my experiences in France and then Great Britain. I drew a picture of my dolphin and colored it.

On Sunday I received a set of underwear in my size sufficient for the next week. I immediately changed and looked around for a place to keep all this underwear. My problem was solved when a box with mostly green or brown clothes arrived. I hid my bras and panties underneath. I had just settled down to eat soup and the speaker spoke.

"Miss Jones?"

"Yes?"

"You have a meeting in thirty minutes."

"Okay. Thanks," I said to the camera. I was clean and neat when the guard took me up and out. To my great surprise, we got off the golf cart and I was put in an SUV with the guard.

"Blindfold on please," the driver said and cloth covered my eyes. "Just a little field trip."

They took me out still blindfolded and guided me into a building and into an elevator.

"Just a few more minutes, Belle," my guard said quietly.

"I don't like this."

"Think about the dolphin," he whispered.

"I'm getting dizzy." The elevator dinged and we stepped out.

"This is your superspy?" a man scoffed. He was a smoker.

"Can I punch him?" I asked my guard. He pulled my blind off.

"Banged up and barefoot, just like I like them," he looked like a redneck too.

"Sir, can I please hit him?" I asked the guard, who had a firm grip on my arm.

"No."

"How bad could it be?" The redneck asked as we turned away.

"No hitting, kicking, spitting, stomping, flying, defenestration, using chains as brass knuckles, choking, mauling or murder," the guard led me quickly.

What about outing him to my contacts? "Fine," I grumbled. We entered a conference room and I appraised the man and woman sitting there. I hadn't made a decision when John walked in.

"Belle Jones?" the man said. "Have a seat please."

The woman handed me a bottle of water. "We understand your case involves some very unusual circumstances and some highly lucrative information."

"She has been very cooperative," John said, sitting a seat down from me.

"What caused your bruises?" The man asked politely.

"Handcuffs and a wall," I replied. "How long have you been following me?"

"You caught our attention in Algeria."

"Two years ago?" I remembered. "Was I interesting?"

"Odd," the woman replied. "We kept looking to see if you were black ops."

"But I sent the intelligence to the FBI, not the CIA or anyone else."

"We have questions for you," the man led.

"Fire at will," I sat back and enjoyed it. I had to make three bathroom breaks for my newly baby-squished bladder in two hours.

"I sat in on the meeting yesterday," the woman eventually said. "Did you feel adequately rewarded?"

"I was very pleased. The items make life in a cell a little more pleasant."

"I'm curious; did you want to be in the general population of the nearest women's facility?"

"God no. I have way too much work to do which can't be done there, and besides, I wouldn't be in the general population long. I know too many tricks," I said and popped the cuff off my right hand. The tiny piece I had jammed in there landed on the table. "Ask the MPs. I'm a complete pain in the ass." I tapped the band on the table to make sure I had completely cleared it before I snapped the band shut, sans wrist and checked the strength. I then held it up in the air for the guard.

"High five," he decided and I offered the temporarily-freed hand. He promptly zipped me up in plastic zip-cuffs.

"Thank you, officer. You can escort her back to her main building now," the man said and we returned to the hallway.

The redneck poked his head out again and I rolled my eyes. "You're a skinny lil' thing aren't you?" He stretched an arm out to touch me.

"Please do not touch the prisoner," the MP and I stepped back a little.

"You want to save that for your own? Lessee," he grabbed my arm. The MP went for his radio.

"Remove your arm, or I will break it," I pulled out of his grasp and he grabbed my shirt and pushed me against the wall. The MP tased him the second after I kneed his groin and threw him away from me.

"Well done. Let's go," John caught up to us the same time the elevator came.

"I haven't broken his arm yet!" I mentioned but stepped into the elevator as my guard's backup arrived.

"Good job, Belle," John praised and handed me a blindfold. "Do you like the goodies?"

"Very much. That woman I saw on Friday, is she the boss behind this? She was pissed."

"She's in the loop," he said lightly as I applied the sleeping mask. "You look like a domestic abuse victim who got hit by a train," John informed as we started walking. "Okay, we're at the door. Step up…"

I blindly felt for the door and the floor until I found them. I felt a strap and realized it was a seat belt.

"Alright. They're going to take you back now Belle. I'm going to go see if Ray is still on the floor," I heard the door slam shut and the SUV started. I laid my head back and had a rest. When I stirred we were back and I could take the blindfold off again.

"May I have some more medication for my face please?" I requested as we reached my level and started going through the doors.

"We'll check your chart," the MP said patiently. For the first time I noticed that there was a chart on the wall for every time I was given medication. "It went well," he informed the guys at my cell.

"He tased a hick," I added as the door was opened. "And I never did get to break his arm."

"He grabbed her and threw her against the wall. She did a nutcracker and I neutralized the threat. Hand out," he instructed as I entered the cell and I presented my palm for the two pills. They clipped the cuffs off and gave me the drugs.

"Thank you," I said as I backed up and the door slammed shut. "I so should have broken his arm," I said to myself and waved at the camera. A few minutes later, I was flopped on the bed, telling my dolphin all about it. I must have fallen asleep, because the guard woke me up with dinner.

The rest of the evening was uneventful, as was life until the next morning. Breakfast was not slid under the door; it was carried in by Agent Starr.

"I have a problem," she handed me the plate. "They heard about the skin-dyeing stuff and they think it's brilliant."

"So you want me to show you how?" I perched on the bed and she pulled the stool over. She nodded. "The best results are from the actual plant. They sell powder too, but you can never tell exactly how old it is. From the powder, which is crushed leaves, you add an acidic liquid. I use eucalyptus oil and lemon juice. It's a mixture. Stir it up, leave it alone, come back and get leathered up," I explained.

"How do you crush the leaves?"

"Easiest way? Coffee grinder. After that I'd say crunch them up with your hands and use a pepper grinder, a stone mill, whatever you have. If you can get the ingredients, I'll go through the whole process with you. All I ask is a shaving razor: I'm going to die if I don't shave."

She smiled awkwardly. "That's going to be awkward. You can have the cream, but they have to keep the razor outside. Until the shrink certifies that you're not a danger to yourself."

"Is that why they keep the drugs out there?" I exclaimed. "Okay, okay, your house, your rules. Razor first. Then you'll need these," I wrote down a list on the notepad she had given me. She gave me the cream and razor, and I had a very nice shower. I then returned my razor and received a bottle of lotion. I had just finished breakfast when they were ready for me.

Soon I was in an interrogation room with Agent Starr looking at the improvised science lab before us.

"Alright, welcome to espionage 101, lesson one; chemically based disguises," I joked. "We have both powdered henna and the actual plant, which is excellent. Let's take our electric hotplate, which can be replaced by a glass object and a flame, and heat our eucalyptus oil a little," I poured some oil into a container and let it heat. "Mix with the henna powder until you have a consistency of ready-to-bake bread. Then we cut it with about a tablespoon of lemon juice, work that in, and pour in the oil until it's more like toothpaste. Then we seal it up, let it sit overnight in at least room temperature," I explained.

"Middle East room temperature?" she asked.

"About 85 degrees seems to work, for about 10 hours. We should be able to use it this evening if you're around."

"Now, what do we do with the plant?"

The leaves were nice and crumply. "This is perfect. It was picked 48-72 hours ago," I cracked the flower open. "Looks Israeli."

"Plants have nationalities?"

"This one has explosive residue in it. Someone blew something up within flying distance."

"It's from Iraq," she informed.

"Okay," I peeked into the box and pulled out a few more plants. "We're going to pluck the leaves, don't be shy," I smiled at her and she smiled back. Together we crushed the leaves with a stone mill and then a coffee grinder. "See how that's a little rougher? It's like sea salt instead of table salt. We use a little more lemon juice. Brewing a really strong tea is also a great ingredient. It's all about the acid releasing the dye. Don't worry; this is all perfectly pregnancy safe."

"I know," she dabbed a piece of something off of her hand. "So we do the same thing, with the oil and the lemon juice?"

"Yeah, we can pour in about two spoons of lemon juice. There's no measurement in the field. A little more oil then beat it with that spoon," It became a greenish-brownish paste. "Perfect. We'll let it stew for a while. Now, when henna is used to make those designs, they use a very thin tube or hollow reed with a bag attached. The best tool I've found is a flat piece of bamboo or a Popsicle stick with a piece of cotton wrapped around the end. Part of a shirt, a rag, anything, just nice and tight. It protects you from splinters and keeps the henna spread evenly."

"So are you willing to come back in nine hours and demonstrate the application technique?" she asked.

"Absolutely, as long as the CIA doesn't let that hick near me again. I owe him a broken arm."

"Off of the top of your head," she sat in one of the seats so I sat next to her. "What else do you think you could teach me?"

"Well, you already know how to shoot," I joked. "Concealing goods and weapons: men and women have different strengths for that. I could do a seduction 101: it is a valuable tool for interrogation. Blending in with the natives: Americans are so easy to spot because of the clothes, the attitude, and the body language. We are the slouchiest people in the world. We also have different haircuts and body hair styles. You can use different deodorants which can get the job done without smelling like an American.

Forgery, but you all probably don't care about that one," I listed. "Oh, and there is the heart to heart interrogation technique, but you've already learned that one."

"You have to admit, it's more pleasant than good cop bad cop," she replied.

"And it almost exclusively only works with women," I revealed. "But yes, it is effective. Women have a host of techniques that aren't available to men. Men automatically discount the ability of women and they like to think they're protecting us. We can get in faster, get out easier, and by the time they realize what happened, we have disappeared."

"So they must have tested you for STDs," she inferred.

"I'm negative. I always use a condom, except for the one I made love to."

"So you do know the father."

"Of course!"

"You made your own passports? Do you have any idea how difficult that should have been?"

"Yes," I replied and someone opened the door.

"I have chocolate," K-9 guy said.

"You have my attention."

"Let's step into the next room," he replied and the guard just held my arm for the puddle-jump. "First, here's some chocolate. This," he handed me a caramel filled-bar, "is for being so cooperative this morning. This," he showed me something nutty, "is my bargaining chip. I need to know what happened yesterday which resulted in an MP using his stun gun."

I bit into the chocolate and he gave me a moment of bliss.

"I also have Sprite®," he mentioned.

"Okay, so, we went to the CIA for the interview," I began and retold the story of Sunday's events. "Hick grabbed my arm first and the MP radioed something. I was warning the guy off. Then he grabbed me by the shirt, here," I gestured, "and slammed me into the wall. I noticed what the MP was doing and I knocked him in the crowbar and shoved back. Then the MP tased him. He had warned him not to touch me, I warned him not to touch me or I would break his arm. I still owe him a broken arm."

"After that?" he set the soda on the table.

"We got into the elevator. John, the MP, and I. I want it to be clear that if the threat hadn't been neutralized, he would have escalated. He was armed and a moron. I would have killed him." I returned my attention to the candy bar in my mouth.

"The crowbar is the male genitals?" he checked as he was writing.

"Yes,"

"Did he leave any marks on you?"

"Just this," I pulled my collar over to show the small slightly pink blotch. "He was wearing knuckle busters: a huge ring on the first or second finger. In his case, the first. When he shoved, the ring got shoved too. You can hardly see it," I let him take a few pictures of my chest.

"Any other scrapes, scratches, bruises?" he asked.

"No. Armed and stupid is a very bad combination."

"In your opinion, did the guard act appropriately, act too late with too little, or overacted?"

I thought about it. "It happened very fast. I'd say he acted appropriately. He neutralized an aggressor."

"My next question isn't in procedure, but I'm curious. Why did you let him slam you like that?"

"I knew I could very easily take him," I replied evenly and finished off the chocolate bar. "He didn't hurt me."

From there I went to therapy, where I argued with the therapist as to whether I was a threat to myself or not. It accomplished nothing, but I felt a little better inside. She assigned me homework. After dinner, I rejoined Starr in the lab-interview room and found a small audience of volunteers. I drew sketches for recommended techniques of application, and then helped the two victims/volunteers: very pale man and woman, to smooth over the slime.

"That's right. Get it up as close as you can, but not to the lash line," I instructed the man. The woman needed less help. "All the way up on the forehead, yup. Looks good," I encouraged. They each painted one half of their face: the woman used the rougher henna. It took about an hour to get them all slimed up, including their left hands, and it was kind of fun. Making a squeeze tube out of a glove and drawing a design on my upper forearm was fun too. Our guinea pigs left and Starr produced some liquid makeup foundation.

"These seemed the darkest," she excused.

"Great. I used two, to blend it. No one is actually one color."

"This was fun."

"I'm a fun person," I joked and someone tapped on the other side of the mirror.

"I'll see you later," she said apologetically and left. The woman from the other night walked in.

"Hello," she said. "This was a fun little experiment. Where did you come up with the idea?"

"Israel," I replied.

"Mossad," she concluded.

"Wedding, actually," I corrected.

"I spoke to someone at the Mossad today. They were pleased you were under my care and not somewhere worse. May I see your chest?"

I was wearing a sports bra so I pulled off my shirt.

"Alright, there's the ring mark; that must be the time you were shot in the chest," she analyzed.

"Grazed me," I shrugged at the mark that had entered at an extreme angle and exited harmlessly through my armpit. The only damage was to a layer of muscle. It had been three years and I had regained full range of motion and strength. I showed off my other bullet mark: one that could have killed me if it had been two inches to the right. It went into my hip. Fortunately, there are enough shootings in the area I was in that no one asked how I got shot when they performed surgery.

"Thank you. You can put your shirt back on. Have a seat Belle."

I sat, she did not.

"You're twenty-four and you've been to at least twenty-seven nations. You speak English, French, and Arabic, as well as some Hebrew, Russian, and Pashtun. You possess great resources and abilities from experience in the world of intelligence. The CIA is funding a program centered on extracting the most possible information from you for both agencies. The FBI is ensuring your rights as an American citizen and a collaborator are not violated. Military police are charged with containment because you are legally both an enemy force and a domestic issue. From what I've seen and heard, you showed restraint at the CIA building when you knocked that man 'in the crowbar' instead of, oh say, taking his gun and killing him. The CIA is quirky to work with. They know what you have in your head, and they want it. Agent Tomopolis and John have convinced the necessary people that their way of extraction will be greatly beneficial, and psychoanalysis and profiling backs them up. As does the bruise on your face: people get tough, you get tougher."

"That sounds about right," I submitted.

"On paper, I need to ensure no one tortures you and the information we get is of value. In reality," she pulled up a chair and sat facing me. "I see a pregnant young woman, essentially alone in this world, which is a one in a million opportune resource. You're not greedy. You're honest. Tell me what you need: you can tell any agent. Tell us what you want: no guarantees, but it's good to know. Capische?"

"Yes ma'am."

"Does this henna thing actually work?"

"Absolutely. I'll need maybe an hour tomorrow to apply the needed touches. I gave Agent Starr a list of needed supplies. Nothing makes you think outside the box better than not having a box in the first place."

"Would you mind if I had a little fun with you?" She suddenly looked impish. I was intrigued.

"I'm all yours."

"They are bringing a foreign combatant in for interrogation. I'd like you to convince him to cooperate."

"Limitations?"

"Don't break any bones. This is an off-camera event."

"I like it. I'll need a costume change."

"We'll take you to the restroom. You can change there and get prepared. Any time you're ready, come on out."

The idea seemed incredible. "Is my shrink watching through the glass?"

"I doubt she's up this late. He was captured trying to blow up U.S. and British soldiers. I want to know where his father was born."

"Anything else?"

"You know what to do," she said frankly.

"Yes I do," I grabbed one of the foundations and a bronzer off of the table.

Twenty minutes later, I was a different person. It was such an incredible release. I wore boots, black pants, and a blouse with a vest. I was also a different color thanks to a little stain technique, a little henna, and some CoverGirl®. I pulled my hair up into a bun, dusted off my Arabic, and was set. I could barely keep from grinning ear to ear.

The guard was stone-faced. The prisoner was trying to look unimpressed.

"Relax," I greeted him in Arabic. "The monkey does not speak this tongue."

"And the camera does?" he replied cynically.

"This won't be recorded," I perched on the table in front of him by about three feet and looked him over. "What are you, fifteen, sixteen?"

"Seventeen now. I am mujahedeen."

"This is all the holy war has to offer?" I was visibly not impressed.

"Allah makes me tough."

"Allah saw to your capture and detainment by American pigs. What did you do, what sin caused this downfall?"

"You know nothing."

"I know everything!" I corrected and laughed a little. We went from there. At one point, he rose from his seat in anger and the otherwise stoic guard slammed him back down. Toward the end of his usefulness, he lunged forward again and I popped him back into his seat and gave his neck a squeeze. He called me a golden whore, I called him a street rat and he gave us enough information to be very useful. Apparently there is a sewer system in a city we did not

50

know about. I blew him a kiss and told him we'd talk later before I strutted out.

The door slammed behind me and I was directed into the viewing room next door. There was a Marine Colonel there along with the woman.

"Young lady that was well done," the colonel said as I pulled a baby wipe and started changing ethnicities.

"I trust the information was useful?" I asked in my normal voice and language.

"You speak like a native," he stated. The woman's eyes directed me to say nothing. I obeyed.

"Very good. Any observations for future sessions?" she inquired.

"Yes ma'am. If I interrogate him again, I should wear tighter clothing. He hasn't been with a woman in a long time and he will respond. I believe he has very little knowledge of Al-Qaida; he seems to be from a street cell in Turkey. He has no pride in accomplishment and he could be a good tool. Did everything translate well?"

"Yes. You may go home now," she nodded and I left the room, was walked to the restroom, changed back into prison clothes, and returned to the restrained life. I couldn't help smirking to myself, proud of what I had done. My candy bar was waiting for me in my cell, and I slept very soundly.

I could smell the bacon before my lights came on to wake me. I could smell it, coming down the hall, pausing outside my door and sliding into my room. Bacon. The best food in the world.

Breakfast was eaten quickly and then I waited until they were ready for me. I was excited knowing that I would soon be playing with make-up and proving my point. Different people react differently to henna, so I was impatient to see what my subjects looked like. Finally my door opened.

I was giddy as I saw the now-stained portions of the two people in the interrogation room. I was giddy even before the cuffs came off. I was even giddy when I had to pause and throw up the bacon. It's about the only food I know that still tastes good the second time.

"I am so sorry," I apologized once I had wiped my mouth off. "Here," I closed the plastic liner of the trash can I had puked in and double-bagged it. "Okay, now, you look great. Next we take the foundations. Pour them in your hand together and mix until you find about the right color. Darker than the stain is ideal," I sipped water as my body readjusted itself. "Take this eyebrow pencil and this eye liner pencil and fill in the rest," I pointed and made the agents do the hard work. "Alright let's see. You're fine," I told the male. "A little powder, but other than that, you're good. Take a look. You can use hairspray to keep the foundation from smudging."

"You look Pakistani," the man told the woman.

"You appear Egyptian, if I had to guess," she replied.

"Belle," An agent called from the hallway and I knew I was being summoned. The guard already had the restraints out. I often wonder if these guys don't get off on handcuffs. Anyway, he took my water, restrained me, and we went outside to the golf carts. Soon we were in the third building: much larger than mine from the ground up. A nicely furnished sitting room or an informal conference room held George and John. They were not pleased with each other.

"Well we'll find out then won't we?" John snipped a little as I entered. "What happened last night?"

"Ah, well, we made this henna blend to demonstrate," I started.

"With Elsa Goode," he interrupted.

"Who is that?"

"The woman, the woman on the top floor who was all upset last week, her," John described.

"I'm supervised every minute, I couldn't have done anything!" I pointed.

"Did you meet a military man last night?" George asked calmly.

"I saw one," I offered.

"John is upset because the FBI moved forward without letting the CIA know you were going to interrogate that foreign combatant," George explained. "Would you like some Sprite®?"

"Yes please, I got sick earlier," I replied.

"I understand you did very well," John added, forcibly calming himself.

"I do know how to do it," I said. "Listen, I don't know what kind of interagency guy-machismo is going on here, but get it straightened out."

"Was the interrogation in Arabic?"

"Exclusively. I also changed my clothes and wore a dark makeup to change my identity."

"The information?" John asked.

"I don't know if I can tell you. Whose boss is the woman?"

"Both of ours, at the moment. You can tell us, she wants us to hear it from you," George said.

"I was asked for his father's name and birthplace. I gave her and Colonel Comb-Over his origin, nationality, combat team, purpose, age, intention, weapons, and a description of an underground system we didn't know about. I know you didn't know because I didn't know and I've been there," I answered and held my head.

"Are you alright?" John examined me with his eyes.

"I'm experiencing the joy of morning sickness combined with a Marx Brothers' routine. Look: you don't share with him. He doesn't share with you. This is why people like me can run rampant for so damn long. Communicate, people! Work with me or I'm defecting to Canada."

George and John suppressed giggles long enough for it to be funny and laughter broke out.

"Did you really bruise that guy's nuts?" George finally asked.

"He required it. I wanted to kill him, but the Marines got in the way."

"She did well," John remarked.

"Here," George opened his briefcase and produced a bag of Oyster crackers in a sealable bag. "My wife found out that you were pregnant. I have oyster crackers and ginger snaps: that's what she said."

"I love your wife," I took the offered food and broke into the ginger cookies. They were heavenly. "Okay, what did you want to know?"

"I want you to make a list for me," John said gently.

"List of what?" I popped another cookie.

"A little list of things you want, things we can exchange for information. So far we've been working off of George's profile, but he has better things to do than answer the phone to tell people what kind of chocolate you would like."

"What do you want, John?" I smiled knowingly.

"Director Goode would like you to interrogate that same man again this afternoon."

"I would be extremely amused by it," George added.

"I would like grilled cheese, cheerios and Coke Zero® for lunch, and I would like at least a small mirror in my cell so I can see myself," I posed.

"Two percent?" John asked and I nodded.

"What else would she like to know?"

"Everything, but I think she's looking for drug smuggling routes," John replied.

"I like pickles on my grilled cheese," I informed.

"Preferably the sliced dill," George added to himself.

"Are you going to watch?" I stood with my cookies and crackers.

"Maybe," George said nonchalantly and handed me the bag for the stuff. "Bon appétit."

"Merci," I replied as the soldier took me back into custody. I was returned to my room and I promptly fell asleep with my dolphin. The scent of food woke me again and I yawned to find lunch waiting for me in the tray. I set it on the table and satisfied my craving for cheerios and grilled cheese. They also slipped a hand mirror and the same ingredients I had used the night before through the slot. I took my time using the henna and then smoothing the dark matte foundation over my face, neck, chest, hands, and arms, anything he might see. A little eyeliner and some lipstick, sandalwood deodorant and a tight black and red outfit they handed me: I was ready.

The guards released me and I took a moment just outside the door. I could hear someone questioning him in English: it was an intimidation routine which I considered completely passé. I took a breath and stormed in.

"Thank you," I dismissed the interrogator.

"What are we going soft?" he barked back at me.

"Get out or I'll shoot you," I said in character. He left. I came and sat on the table, keeping my knees slightly apart. "So," I switched to Arabic, "how was your sleep?"

"They are torturing me with sleep deprivation. Every few minutes, bang, crash," he reported.

"All prisons are loud," I said mildly. "Tell me, do you hate the British or the Americans more?"

"Same beast, different heads," he replied. "I don't know who dropped the bomb that killed my father on a business trip, but it was Americans, British, or Israel. Probably Israel. You're Israeli, aren't you? Filthy Jew."

I slapped him across the face and resumed my seat. "I am from the true country, Arab Palestine."

"Then where is your headscarf, you prostitute?"

"The Americans don't know. They think I'm from Israel. That's why I don't let them tape or have an interpreter in the room: I give them some small stuff and take the rest for my own purposes."

He bought it and we continued to chat for a period of time until I decided to press forward.

"Using the sewers was not easy, but we endure all for the most merciful Allah," he stated.

"It sounds so…exciting! The saints that you must have worked with, toiling down in the foulest places, using the city itself to fight the invaders," I stroked his arm. "I know some people who would greatly aid the jihad if they knew this kind of thing was possible. Can you draw me a map to show them?"

"You will show it to the Americans."

"I took that into account, and made a second map. It's just behind this one, so I give them the fake map," I turned to the guard in English, "please remove the necessary shackles so he can write."

The right hand was freed and I gave him a pencil and paper. He started drawing, and was most of the way through the upper sewer when a speaker whined.

"Filthy liar!" he picked up quickly and leapt to stab me in the chest as I stood by his side. I blocked with a hard

56

swing of my right arm; diverted by returning to his side, and when he moved in reaction I flipped him onto the table and broke his arm.

I heard the sound of a stun gun firing up; as well as the words "get her out of here!" I panted for breath as men ran in and the original guard slammed the prisoner on the floor. A MP grabbed my knees and shoulders and got me out of there and shuttled me into the next room, which monitored an empty cell.

"Damn it!" I swore as I fully absorbed the situation. I then noted that my arm was bruised and bleeding lightly. George entered with concern. "I guess that ends the interrogation," I tried to joke. "That damn speaker had to pop."

"That was awesome!" George said as he lifted my damaged arm and set the baby wipes he was carrying on the table.

"I don't think it's broken, just banged. I must have caught his chain at some point."

"Medical team is on their way. I'm pretty sure you did break his arm."

"Considering that he tried to kill me, I don't think I'll cry about it." I finished wiping my face, neck and chest and turned to my arms. They were functional but the right ulna was definitely bruised. Finally I was white again. "My clothes!" I realized, "I have to change."

An awkward moment passed as I attempted to change into the prison garb using only one arm in the presence of two males.

"What did you do this time?" The medic entered with sarcasm.

"Another prisoner attacked her in an attempt to escape custody," George informed coolly. "She acted heroically and stopped him. He's in the next room."

"He's going to need a medic," I added.

"I see," he looked embarrassed. "So what hurts?"

I lifted my right arm for inspection. "I slammed his arms away from me. I must have caught a chain along the way."

"Martial arts background," he drew his own conclusion. "Your face looks much better, by the way," he examined me briefly. "I need an X-ray, Susan!" he cleaned the wound with peroxide. "Susan is going to take you to the medical center, we're going to X-ray your arm and see if it's broken."

"I'm going with you," George told me.

The medic called for a gurney and returned with an arm splint. "Try to keep it still."

The guard wrapped his arm around me in an odd fashion so he could walk, control, and support me at the same time. The four of us went to the medical center, where I donned as much protective equipment as possible to keep the fetus safe from X-rays. While we waited George and I sat down.

"You were very good in there. I had forgotten what you looked like fighting."

"You like to forget the juicier side of me," I replied.

"Hard to do when you change clothes in front of me."

"You do what you have to," I informed. "Your boss lady seemed to want this private."

"We appreciate your discretion."

The blond lady doctor appeared. "The bone has bruising on it, but the ulna is not broken. May I ask when you broke your fifth phalanges?"

"It wasn't broken so much as severed," I held my hand out so he could see where the blade had sliced through the skin and slowly pushed through the bone. "It was a long time ago; it healed very well."

"Yes, it did." She held the image up to the light, "It was set perfectly."

"So she's not broken. Alright, now what?" George asked.

"Follow me please," Susan the medic said and led us out and into a small examination room. "I need to properly clean the wound, then I'll bandage it again and we'll be able to put an air cast on this for a week or so, just to make sure the bone gets rest and avoids new trauma," she was mostly talking to George. "So, you overpowered a bad guy, huh?" she said conversationally to me as she scrubbed the abrasion.

"You tell me," I replied as I watched them reel in the man through the crack in the door. He couldn't see me, and wouldn't have cared. "I fractured his radius and ulna: at least that was my intention."

"Why isn't she restrained?" she asked George and the guard.

"She's well behaved," the guard answered, "and she knows I'll shock her if she merits it."

"And it really, really hurts," I added. "I believe their stunners are set at a lower voltage because of the baby. It's like sticking a fork into a wall socket."

She slid the air cast on with my palm facing up. "How far along are you?"

"Nine or ten weeks," I saw concern in her eyes. "Look, I'm fine. My uterus was untouched by the conflict. I still feel nauseated, so clearly I'm fine."

"Thank you Susan. Let's go," George decided.

"High five," the guard said and I offered my arms. The steel actually did fit over the cast.

"I want you to meet someone," George said in the cart as we whizzed back to the main building. "Are you tired?"

"Nothing a soda wouldn't fix," I replied, suspicious.

"Good. He's a fan," George said cryptically as we entered the building and got off at an interrogation floor. "In here."

"Who's watching this time?" I called as I entered and immediately recognized the interrogator from a few hours ago. "Hello," the handcuffs were removed and I forced myself to step forward.

"Hi," he smiled. It was freaky. "I thought that chop might have broken something."

"You watched," I gathered and sat across from him.

"Miss the chance to watch an expert on a return visit? Never." He was soft; not just his voice, his whole personality seemed like it might be squishy.

"You were a soldier," I sorted from my impressions. "Army, infantry but you wanted to go into intelligence. You are new in the field of interrogation, or you do it by the book."

"No interrogating," he replied drolly.

"First rule: no questions means no interrogation. There is intelligence gathering, and then there is interrogation. What did you want to learn from me?"

"I just wanted to meet the famous Belle Jones. I was in one of the units you saved. Liberia."

"The odds are just a little quirky on this, so I'll assume this afternoon was a set up."

"You saved my life," he looked me in the eye.

"Once. And the pleasure was all mine. I have always been an American at heart."

"Did you break it?" he looked at my cast.

"Just a little bruise. She thinks it will need protection to heal, for some reason," I joked.

"I really thought he had you."

"No chance. The guard speaks Arabic, or he had a feed," I replied.

"Is it true that you're pregnant?"

"Yes," I replied.

"Your martial arts skills are remarkable," he leaned back relaxed in his chair. "Did you have special forces training?"

"In a way, but not in the US," I mentally flashed to my weeks of training at the hands of Israeli intelligence for a mission.

"I just read the file and it said you carried a Marine knife."

"They're the best for my purposes," I smiled at him and leaned forward. "Have *you* ever killed someone?"

"Yes, yes I have. How do you handle it?"

"The same way you did, probably," I took a slight at his intimation that it was different for women.

"I didn't take it so well."

"In that case, better than you did," I confided smoothly. "But I really hated most of them. I think it's harder when you set things up but don't actually execute in person. I don't know why. It should be easier, right? Just press the button, and it's over. But not for me."

"So I'm guessing you have no issue with blood."

"Brain matter was worse. And body goo: the stuff that flies everywhere when someone's been hit hard and fast. That's gross because you don't know what it is, but you do."

"They're going to drag you away in a minute, but I wanted one more question," he said and I raised eyebrows permissively. "Why?"

"Modern intelligence and law enforcement simply isn't as effectively designed as the underworld. Other countries have known this for years. Think of it as an exercise in anger expression."

"Would you please teach me how to do those martial things you did, you do," he asked abruptly as someone knocked on the door. He had already stood, and I stood to face him over the table. I hadn't gotten a word out when I felt a hand on my shoulder, thumb lightly pressing the pressure point on my neck.

I pulled my arms back in response, peacefully allowing the guard full access to snap iron from behind. "I should be able to practice for several weeks. Before we begin, you should get permission, a place with mats and the guards will have to trust me to not kill you. Good luck with that one, considering that I sent a man to the hospital earlier."

"If I thought you wanted me dead, I wouldn't have asked," he replied and stepped in front of me.

"We've been here for ten minutes. If I wanted you dead, you would be dead," I replied frankly but without malice.

"Let's go see the nice lady," the man holding the door open said.

"I don't want to go to therapy," I stated but walked as directed.

"Hold on," the former Marine interrogator said. "New orders. I just got clearance to continue," he instructed the others and I was returned and released. I was also given some ginger ale and acetaminophen.

When we were alone with the guard again he came to my side of the table. "What would you do to me if I let you?"

"Who said you would let me?" I replied cockily. "What do you want from me?"

"I want," he pulled out the pair of handcuffs from their home over his back pocket, "I want to know what it feels like to be touched by Belle Jones."

"I'm sure you do," I replied evenly. Nowhere he was going to go with this would turn out well.

"I do," he took he cuffs and attached one to my wounded arm and one to one of his arms.

"Good theory, but no," I realized what he was trying to do. "This is not the place. There are hard floors and hard tables and corners and I'm supposed to be good to this arm."

"Just do it. You act or I act."

"You need to stop," I retorted and he grabbed my throat firmly.

I tucked my chin and did a controlled fall backwards, bringing him down on top and freeing my neck. We rolled quickly so I was on top and I placed the cast against his collar bone. He pulled it away via the chain and I whirled into an inverted crucifix, placing my foot carefully on his jaw. His chained arm was beneath me and I clutched his waistband.

"Are you done, or would you prefer a little incentive?" I asked, wiggling my toes.

"This is lovely. You could break my neck, play with my jewels, fracture the larynx," he listed.

"There's a way out, but not while we're cuffed. So if you'd like to behave like an officer and a gentleman, let's get off of the floor. I can teach you more when I don't have bruised bones," I looked up, "and a man pointing a Taser at me."

We scrambled to our feet and I requested that the adjoining metal be removed from one or both of us.

"Sir, you need to leave," the MP directed. "Sit," he said to me and I did: plotzing on the floor with injured arm held high. He clicked the restraint off of me and the man left shortly. "Good job, let's get into the chair."

I switched seats and returned to my beverage when I remembered something. I pulled it out of my bra and set it on the table. "He'll want those at some point," I informed the guard regarding the man's car keys. "And he'll definitely want these now," I loosened the cast and produced a set of handcuff keys. The guard was dying to laugh.

"Stand up, take your shoes off," he said as seriously as possible and he searched me for other concealed goodies. He didn't find anything, but it was nice to be touched by a man with strong hands. He probably took my smirk as a reaction to having stolen the agent's keys; he would have been wrong. I returned to my seat and refastened the cast carefully. My arm did hurt, as did my ribs. My face was mostly brown, green and yellow, which was a good sign.

Agent Starr poked her head in. "Did you kick his ass?" she asked in a non-condemning tone. She took me back to my cell.

Days passed: I tried to keep track of what the date was but they hoarded all information like my orientation was a dangerous thing. I could sort of guess that it was Labor Day weekend when things wound down a bit for three days. They would come get me and take me to the therapist almost every day and sometimes to interrogation for quick question and answer sessions. One day they took me to a conference room and set out a dozen maps with the request that I track my whereabouts over my career. As I had cautioned them this took more than one day. I tried to map out the last nine years of my life for the better part of three days and there were still some unresolved periods.

A morning came with French toast sticks instead of a bagel or cereal and I suspected that it would be a special day. I was correct: the boring morning bled into a very exciting afternoon.

The guards took me to an interrogation room and John and a somewhat familiar looking man in a gray suit came in. "Is that arm broken?" he asked and sat adjacent to me. His friend sat opposite.

"No, they're just protecting it," I replied and eyed the man.

"This is a liaison from the Mossad," John informed me but I knew the beast behind those gray eyes.

"I thought you were dead," the man said in Arabic.

"Likewise," I replied in the same. I recognized the man as the same Israeli agent who had shot me, almost fatally. "You never could keep your eyes off my ass."

"Better dead than to look like you do now," he retorted calmly, still in Arabic.

"I've sent more people to the hospital in the last month than you have in the last year."

"My marks go to the morgue."

"Your marks walk away waving their hands bye-bye," I insulted.

"English," John requested.

"Your friend is a hit man. My hip was his miss," I informed John calmly. "He's supposed to be Mossad, but his orders come from terrorists."

"It took three hours to make those up," he said in English before switching back to Arabic. "They sent me here to kill you."

"Then you have come to die," I replied in Arabic and he pulled a gun on me and aimed. I shoved the table at him, the shot went into the ceiling, and John was on top of him in seconds, as were the agent and MP who came running in. My MP guided me up and against the wall next to him, shielded by an arm.

As the scuffle ended, John stood up. "Well done, Belle. Good reflexes."

The others led the man out and away, and he was yelling insults.

"And I also think you look better than a dead person," John added.

"You speak Arabic," I realized.

"My reflexes are good, but not that good. My gun was,"

"Already out," I finished for him. "Well done John. I'd like to go back to my cell now."

Director Goode burst into the door with her storm face on. "Please take Miss Jones to my office, Natalie is expecting her. Now; use the back way. Thank you," she told the MP and turned to John.

I do not want to see this. I thought as the Marine secured my arm and we snuck into the woman's office. A young woman, probably younger than me, was waiting nervously in the office.

The girl reminded me of a rabbit or a Chihuahua; she was so timid she almost shook. "I'm Natalie," she said a second time. Natalie was probably about twenty pounds overweight but her round face made it hard to tell. She wore her dark blond hair in a long bob with what wanted to be side-swept bangs.

"Hi Natalie. I'm Belle," I said softly.

"Ms. Belle, I mean, Director Goode, wants you to be as comfortable as possible. She said it may be a while," her eyes darted to the back exit as two more guards came in, one carrying a moderately large gun. "Can I…can I get you anything? You're welcome to use the couch and take a nap if you want."

"Do you like ginger snaps?" I asked. "I happen to have some ginger snaps in my room, I'm sure Agent Starr wouldn't mind getting them for us," I sat on the couch.

"That's a great idea," Natalie agreed and went to make the call. "Would you like a pillow? I have a pillow and some blankets here," she brought them anyway. "The restroom is right there."

"So I'm in lockdown," I said aloud.

"Yep," Agent Starr entered with the bag of cookies. "Do you want anything else from your room? Your dolphin?"

"No thanks, I'm okay. I think I'm just going to rest for a while. Natalie, why don't you have a seat? You look like you're about to collapse."

"You have my number," Agent Starr said as she exited.

I ate some snaps, used the restroom, and decided that a nap was in order. I was asleep in maybe two minutes. I woke an hour later, Natalie was speaking quietly on the phone with her back turned.

"Yes ma'am, she's sleeping…two. Well she has a cast on her arm and she walked a little stiff…right. DVDs, no TV. What time do you think…7, right. Yes ma'am."

I'm comfy, I rolled over a little and adjusted the blanket before returned to sleep.

Sometime later the lights got brighter and I stirred. *Where the hell am I?* "Oh," I sat up slowly.

"Hi. You're supposed to stay here," Natalie explained, slightly calmer than previously. "Agent Tomopolis should be here soon. Would you like a cheeseburger?"

"What happened?" I asked as the first wafts of cheeseburger came to my nostrils. Natalie gawked.

"That guy, almost killed you?"

"He's a lousy shot," I said with a note of sarcasm. I took the cheeseburger.

"So, does your arm hurt?" Natalie nervously attempted conversation, sitting a safe distance away.

"Only a little. Do you know why you're babysitting me?"

"I don't know, but those guys don't come up here very often. Are we in danger?"

I smiled at her naivety. "No, I don't think so. Do you have any idea who I am?"

"Belle Jones," she replied quickly. "That's about it. Sorry."

"So the TV there must plug into the system. Do you speak Arabic?" I asked casually.

"No," she looked at me like I was nuts.

"It's a valuable language," I smiled as I saw George coming. The guards let him in and he came straight to me.

"Alexis, are you alright?"

"Sure, that guy always has been a lousy shot. Did we get him?"

"In a way," he said with measured enthusiasm. "I see you got some sleep."

"Gotta get my beauty rest," I finished my burger. "You know John speaks Arabic?"

"I know ben-Adat didn't know," he offered.

"He probably didn't know he was being televised either. Did your friend ever get his keys back?"

"He will think twice before attacking again."

"He grabbed my throat: you're lucky I didn't kill him," I informed bluntly. "Care for a snooze? It's a comfy couch," I offered.

"It is," he agreed and sat next to me. "I haven't been sleeping so well."

"I'm sleeping pretty well, but it is actually strange to sleep without a gun under my pillow."

"The .38?"

"Forty. I like the grip better. Didn't matter where I was, I always slept with a gun or two. The twenty-two fit inside my bra, my underwear, or a thigh strap. I liked to keep the .38 or .357 on my ankle and my forty in the waistband, right where a tramp-stamp would be. Got me out of Spain."

"And that's why we disarmed you first," George replied. I got up and walked around a little.

"Let me take him," I requested after a moment.

"No way," George stated. "Not going to happen. The agency."

"The agency put him in the room with me with a gun on him," I pointed with raw emotion showing. "I'm not asking you to arm me, just leave us in a room together. Preferably without restraints, but I can make it work."

"Belle, try a jog down logic lane. How does his body help us? Mossad knows he's here."

"Hamas knows he's here. Bloody Al -Qaida knows he's here."

"What did he say to you?"

"He thought I was dead, I looked horrible, he said it took him three hours to forge the papers that link him to Hezbollah to cover his trail, he said his marks go to the morgue, I insulted his marksmanship and he said, "I'm here to kill you", and pulled the gun out. Hey, how's the Turk doing?"

"Natalie, I want a VTC for that number I gave you. Now is good," Deputy Director Elsa Goode entered slightly out of breath. "Alexis, would you like to talk to the Mossad?"

"Yes, yes I would," I replied honestly.

She directed me off camera and told me to wait for her cue. I knew the bit well, so I sat patiently in the dark as a familiar face appeared on the screen. She was stern but not hostile as she explained the situation. It took them a good twenty minutes to get to me.

"You have Beauty?" he repeated in English. Goode gave me a nod and I walked onto the screen.

"Shalom, Abba," I greeted in Hebrew. "If I was going to betray you, you'd be dead by now," I said in English and sat as directed. "So, is Ben-Adat yours or someone else's?"

"Why do you ask about him?" he seemed genuinely confused.

"He's dead. If he's yours I'll send him back. If not, I'm thinking warehouse fire."

"Ben-Adat is on a list of ours. Number eight, actually."

I switched to Hebrew. "You can pull that with them, but don't start raking the coals for me."

"I know you beauty," he replied in Hebrew. "You say he's dead, he's dead or as good as. Well done and I approve, either way. How did the Americans catch you?"

"American prisons are nicer than yours," I replied. "I keep my word."

"I'm beginning to believe you."

"So the next assassin you send better be yourself," I warned him calmly.

"Please send Ben-Adat back with my agent, in Mossad custody," he spoke to Director Goode. "Or his body, if needed. You look good, Beauty. Did he do that?"

"No," I smiled.

"All the way?" he asked in Arabic.

"All the way to the border," I replied.

"As always," he replied in English and looked at Director Goode. "She has always been a Yankee. Good night." The screen blanked.

"Belle, why don't you and Natalie go to the kitchen and see if there's still ice cream in the fridge. Help yourselves," Goode essentially ordered and I grabbed the ginger snaps and let the guard with the slightly smaller gun lead the way.

Once we were in the kitchenette, Natalie and I found ourselves in opposite corners. She was afraid of me.

"So, do you want a cookie?" I offered quietly.

"You're an international shalom-talking, terrorist fighting, gun-shooting, guy-killing, bomb-making," she ran out of words and tried to breathe.

"Kid-saving, scum scrubbing, data stealing," I picked up for her, "you know the rest. Please breathe. Okay, look at him. Look at him. Now look at me. Feel better?"

"A little," she said, still pressed against the wall.

"Here," I slid down to the floor and sat Indian-style. "I'm just sitting here, eating my cookies. It's been a long month for me. Morning sickness is a pain in the ass, men with bad judgment attacked me three times, I bruised a bone and a dude tried to shoot me."

"That sounds pretty scary," she edged toward a chair, still several feet from me.

"I've had a lot worse. Like actually getting shot, blown up, or nearly decapitated."

"Where were you shot?" she was interested.

"Israeli territory, through the hip, and North Africa in the chest," I told her and pulled my collar so she could see the scar.

"That's pretty cool. I have a tattoo," she shared. "On my hip."

"Did it hurt?"

71

"Probably not as much as getting shot," she judged.

I heard the order over the guards' radio. Mr. Big gun grabbed my good elbow and took me back to the office, which had cleared. She was behind her desk, thinking.

"I like you. You're tough," she finally said. "Life throws a wall at you, you bounce. Life slams a door, you shoot it down. You did something important today. You uncovered one thing and recovered another, and you came out alive. That man was proud of you."

"Yes ma'am. He made me who I am, how I am. Tough," I answered.

"We have a bigger mission; to find Bin Laden and Omar Al-Zahrani. I should not have wasted your time with the interrogations."

"You gained valuable intel!" I defended. "Our soldiers needed that information."

"We have made progress. Are you still on board?"

"All the way to hell and back. Ma'am, if it were my decision I would not send Ben-Adat back. If he was sent to kill me, there's a chance Mossad knows something about what I've been doing."

"Mossad should approve our actions," she reflected.

"Everything could be unrelated," I admitted.

"Ben-Adat is not an operative," she informed me. "Secure the prisoner and return to base two," she told the guard without a hint of warmth.

He yanked me up and started 'securing' me, but I was facing her. "Ma'am, what happened to the Turk? To Assam Ali?" I asked. I hadn't actually spoken with her since that night and no one tells me anything.

"No longer my concern," she said with a stone face.

The guard pulled me around and forced me out. "Nice and easy, Belle," he coaxed with a soft voice and hard arms.

"He's dead," I told him. "He's a god-damn kid," I said as we came off of the elevator.

"He was a god-damn terrorist," John stepped out of the shadows in the hall we had to cross to get to the elevator that went to the dungeons.

"Is that what you call a man who tries to get people killed by foreign assassins?" I snapped at him.

"He's behind bars," John pointed.

"Move it," the guard said and pushed me through the corridor.

I heard George's voice behind me as the elevators dinged. "What the hell?!" he exclaimed.

"I HATE THIS!" I screamed and the silence of the elevator contained me. We walked in tense silence, and I felt someone put their hand on my back as the cuffs were removed.

"Step in," a female voice ordered and I obediently turned 90 degrees and entered my cell. The door slammed behind me and I heard the bolts. I climbed into my bed, covered myself with the sheets and blanket, and hid from the world. The straw that broke the camel's back was the newspaper I had caught a glimpse of in the kitchen upstairs. I finally had a date. I had guessed that it was a weekend day but had no idea that it was September 11th.

Chapter 4: Truths and Lies

They slid breakfast in and banged to wake me, but I had no desire to eat and I chose to remain huddled under the blankets. My arm throbbed, my ribs ached, and nausea made me feel dizzy. Eventually I heard a voice through the speaker.

"Belle? This is Agent Starr. The henna project was a huge hit. Are you there?"

"Nope," I called from under the blankets.

"Um, well, Agent Kmetz, one of our computer technicians? He needs a little help with some stuff you brought in."

"Will the CIA be there?" I poked my head out.

"No, just you and Agent Kmetz and maybe another agent. He said he's having problems coordinating the trans-interfacing of the net systemic...I don't know. Techie-techie geek-geek," she sounded honest. I got out of bed.

"Tell the guards: I'll be ready in five minutes," I replied and pulled a cold soda out of the beer cooler.

A few minutes later I was in the room with Kmetz the geek and an agent who had martial arts training. I can tell by the way someone shakes my hand if they can break it. She had a graceful, willowy beauty and I guessed that she had one Chinese parent and one Caucasian from her bone structure and features.

"Don't you people have better things to do on a Sunday morning?" I greeted grumpily.

"It's Monday morning, frankly that's bad enough on its own," Kmetz informed and I realized that the paper was old.

"Are you read in, Agent Won?" I asked the Asian agent.

"I am. We have found the information given to us very helpful."

"We're not picking up the feed as well as we think you could," Agent Kmetz said and showed me the computer.

"Pull up the terrain layout: I placed a signal magnifier on an appropriate altitude so I could pull the feeds received by a satellite," he pulled up a fairly modern map derived from IM-INT. "Good. There. Focus the beam in that direction and tune it to this frequency range," I sat back as he typed furiously to someone.

"We should know in a few minutes," he stared at his screen. "Thank you."

"What else do we have? I planned to plant a second feed on a traffic camera nearby: they are not serviced regularly, so a parasite cam would be effective."

"It seems that you had this operation carefully planned and organized," Won complimented.

"It is important to me to harm him greatly," I replied. "Have you succeeded in hacking the Saudi government yet?"

"We cannot do that," Agent Won replied.

"One of the princes is going to meet with an ambassador of the United States soon," Kmetz offered.

"Can we observe the event through the ambassador's connection?" I tried again.

"The FBI cannot operate in an illegal operation, nor could it break faith with another country," Won stated.

"Well could someone provide me with a dual-use machine capable of withstanding firewall attacks and providing penetration codes and false-front techniques?"

"What legal reason would we use to give you that computer?" Agent Won was interested.

I thought for a moment. "Agent Kmetz, do you believe that I have the skills to encrypt further information in a hidden file on the chip which was associated with my laptop?"

"Information which might be engineered to dissolve if a highly complex code was entered improperly?" His face lit up. "That is plausible."

"How complex was the most complex thing you found, Agent Kmetz?" Agent Won asked.

"Extremely. The Saudi file was password-protected beyond our code technology and the entire chip and computer was on a hair-trigger fail-safe code which nearly destroyed everything. She definitely is capable of doing this," he replied.

"Sounds like probable cause to me," Won said and Kmetz's computer dinged.

"Long and strong. Well done, Miss Jones," Kmetz congratulated and returned to being absorbed by his computer.

"I heard your hand to hand combat was well developed," Agent Won sat next to me.

"What are you trained in?" I asked and she told me. "You don't want to spar with me today. I'm pissed off."

"I would like to not spar with you ever; so I will not grab you by the throat."

"Or attempt to stab me with a pen," I added, lifting my casted arm.

"Broken?"

"Just a little bruising, maybe a micro-fracture or two. I think it hit a chain."

"How many ribs have you cracked?"

"About half, in total. Some worse than others. You?"

"Four badly, four not so badly," she replied. "It's always the upper body, isn't it?"

I related. "Some reason, it doesn't hurt as bad to be kicked in the ribs."

"Unless you're down."

"You got bigger problems at that point. In my world, you're damn near dead at that point."

"Very true. We're cool. But if you hurt one of my geeklings,"

"I like geeks," I cut her off. "I'm not going to hurt your people. If I do, feel free to kick my ass, just remember the baby."

The door beeped and Agent Tomopolis entered. "Alexis,"

"George," I greeted him with a subtly masked fury.

"Would you please come with me to go to the doctor regarding your pregnancy and the recent trauma?" It was a reasonable request.

"Yes," I stood and said goodbye to the techies. George handed me a coat; the September rain was in full force as the cart took us to the medical building. George was quiet.

"I'm sorry," he finally said as we were waiting for the doctor to come into the room. "I want you to know that his death was not your fault."

"Head trauma?" I guessed and he just took a breath.

"The man who I took you to see will be disciplined. The man who shot at you is no longer in FBI custody, and I do not expect to see him again."

"He was not Mossad, I believe he may be working with Hamas or al-Qaeda," I mentioned just before the doctor walked in.

"Okay, from the top down, how is your face?"

"Almost healed up."

"Throat?"

"Nothing wrong,"

"Ribs?"

"Bruised, but not broken."

"Arm? Micro-fractures showed on the x-ray. The laceration looks good, as does your head injury."

We continued down the chain from there as he checked off a list of every injury I had sustained in the last week. Eventually he had me pick a sock from a bag, snip the end off, and slide it over my left hand and arm. Then he gently secured the handcuff attached to the bed to my wrist. We continued the exam alone from that point.

"Look me in the eye," he requested after gently helping me re-cover my abdomen. "Are you suicidal?"

"No. If I wanted to die, I would be without several of these bruises. Two different men tried to kill me yesterday. I want to recover the best life possible."

"The fetus is doing well. I'm giving you prenatal vitamins, a dietary plan and folic acid, and by you, I mean your custodians. We'll meet periodically to check on your progress and hopefully not on new injuries. Come in," he called to the door and the guard and a massive man in a suit came in. "Captain," he addressed the suit. "She's all yours. Take care of her." The doctor left.

"Do you read Arabic?" the captain asked. He looked like a retired football player.

"A little," I replied.

"Like you speak 'a little'?" he replied and the guard unlocked me from the bed.

"Fine, yes, I read it," I stood and pulled my coat on. "Do you need something translated?"

"More like verified; I'm the captain of the guards here, Jack Stover."

"Nice to meet you. I'm Belle. What does the head of security want with me?" The guard secured my wrists behind me and we started walking.

"Absolutely nothing, I just wanted to meet the girl who can operate against three men with her hands tied behind her back." We met up with a man I vaguely recognized. "Morning, Agent Powell."

"Good morning Captain Stover. Is she complacent?" he asked over my head.

"Would you like to read a transcript of a terrorist-issued guide to avoiding detection? It's quite a lot of reading."

"Seven thousand pages," I replied. "I only finished the first three thousand. Could I have English and Arabic versions, to detect any subtleties?"

"It can be arranged. I've been told to barter with you."

"I will need a pencil, an Arab-English dictionary, some paper, and a place to do the actual reading. My cell is unsuitable."

"We want the tips and contexts to hunt out 'undetectable' terrorists."

"I can write notes and then type them onto my laptop. It will take some time, and I need a well-lit, comfortable, quiet work place."

"Noted. I'll pass that information on. Agent," Stover greeted and left.

"This way please," Agent Powell indicated and we walked.

As we walked and rode, my mind wandered to that tiny little worm inside of my uterus, snuggled tightly to a part of me. I was giving it life. Without realizing it, I had started weeping silently. I honestly thought it was raining and water had sprayed on my face.

"And we're going to therapy," Powell stated.

"Huh?" I snapped back into reality. "No, I don't want to go to therapy."

"Don't care."

I was shuttled there anyway. I laid on the couch in Freudian fashion and stared at the ceiling.

"He's dead."

"Are you sure?" she asked.

"He tried to stab me, I flipped him onto the table and broke his arm: I mean, BROKE it. The angling was off and everything. They evacuated me, and then I saw him at the medics' place, where they x-rayed my arm. I wore lots of lead: I hope the baby didn't get x-rayed. Anyway, so I'm looking at this little squiggle on the lining of my uterus and I'm like, that thing is completely dependent on me. It is drinking my blood for survival."

"So when everyone was threatening you, how did it feel?"

I hate therapy. We ended up talking about 'feelings' and other mushy sentimental crap for a long time and I never got to express how mad I was at John. I think she got more out of it than I did.

"Take me back to the geeks. I like them," I told the guard as he collected me from therapy.

"Someone's cranky," Agent Powell said and placed me next to the guard's gun in the cart.

"Sit in an interrogation room and have someone try to assassinate you, see how cheery you get," I shot back.

"The Turk or the Lebanese?" he replied.

"The Lebanese: the kid never had a shot. The Lebanese took one. You're so damn busy," I said as we got out of the cart, guard securely holding my right arm, "keeping yourself safe from me, you leave me wide open territory for others."

80

"Law of the jungle," Powell replied as we came through the building's doors. I clicked the cuff on my right wrist open quickly, courtesy of a toothpick, grabbed him by the back of the shirt and a short scuffle ensued. Since the guard had a good grip on me, it was very short. I had given him a black eye on my knee before the MP nearly broke my arm and dropped me to the ground.

"Legs together, hand behind your head, on the ground flat," the guard ordered and I succumbed gracefully. "Call a medic, he pissed her off," he told the backup.

I laughed to myself a little even as I felt a heavy knee or large elbow pressing on my back and the familiar hand taking mine and zip-cording the appendages together. A soldier put his boot on my butt.

"Stay down or I'll shock you," he instructed calmly. I caught a reflection and could tell he had gun in hand. "Where's your pick?"

"Toothpick. It's on the floor," I replied.

"You can't pick handcuffs with a toothpick," the agent said, holding his face.

"Care to bet?"

"What happened?" A voice I might have recognized said.

"She snaked her cuffs and bashed my head in," Powell said.

"What'd she use?" the medic asked.

"My knee. It's not like I broke anything," I answered. "He's the one who claimed jungle law!" I pointed. "He doesn't give a damn about me and he pissed me off."

"He's not supposed to give a damn about you!" George entered. "Get that x-rayed. Alexis, they are federal agents. To them, you are a criminal. Up, get her up," he was very exasperated.

I was lifted and allowed to stand.

"What did you do?" He tried to calm.

"I popped the lock and knocked his head on my leg."

"Why?"

"Because confinement doesn't agree with me."

"Well you'll come to terms with it. Please take her back to her cell."

"John is trying to kill me!"

"Trust me, Belle; no one here is trying to kill you. We'd get along better if you'd stop trying to kill us."

I started to lose it. "I'm not trying to kill you, any of you! But he brought Ben-Adat into that room armed so what am I supposed to think?!"

"Okay, okay, I know. Come on; let the guards get you home, you'll watch some DVDs, take a nap, rest for the baby," he coaxed and we started walking.

"Face the door," the guard ordered a few minutes later and I stared at the battleship gray. "The pencils," he told his colleague.

"Rough day?" the woman asked.

"She gave Agent Powell a black eye," he reported, holding me in place. I felt the tip of his stunner in the middle of my shoulders. "Don't move!" a snap later and the nylon was gone. The dangling half of the handcuffs was also removed. "Hold out your right arm," he instructed and I stretched it out so they could check the cast for surprises. "Alright. Step to the left. One step. Two steps. Three steps."

SLAM!

To accompany the slamming noise, there came a sudden darkness as they cut the lights off entirely.

"Grand," I said to myself sarcastically. Not to be hindered by the darkness, my eyes adjusted to the faint light from the doorway and soon I was moving around. I opened my laptop and by its light I showered, dried off, and French-braided my hair. I left the cast on the floor on the hunch that nothing was going to encounter my arm any time soon. *I wonder if that camera has night vision technology. I know they're trying to punish me, or deprive me of stimulation which is nearly torture in and of itself.* I took a deep breath as the computer's sleep function kicked in. *Works for me. Okay, maybe I shouldn't have attacked the agent. I'm just really irritated. I really hate these hormones. Why are you so mean to me, little worm?* I stroked my abdomen lightly with my middle finger, tracing lines along the skin. *Oh Luc. You've got a little French-American spy-politician on the way. My little Luc-worm. No one's going to get to you, my little parasite.* I patted my stomach and then slid my hand over to gently test my tender ribs. My mind jumped to the incident that had just occurred and I smiled smugly. *Totally kicked his ass. They're not so tough.* I drifted off to sleep.

Someone flipped the lights on at some point and I woke up, groggy.

"Are you awake?" the speaker asked.

"Yes."

"Sit on the end of your bed, legs crossed underneath you, hands on your knees," the voice came back and I scrambled around in bed to comply. The door opened and a guard came in with a charged stun gun. "You stay where you are, understood?"

"Yes sir."

"You sit still, you keep your hands on your legs, or I'm going to aim low."

My eyes widened. "Do not hurt my baby," I replied firmly.

"You don't move, we have no problem," he replied. "Understand?"

"You hurt my baby and I will unleash hell," I replied. "Understood."

Another guard came in and stood calmly as Agent Starr came in and sat on her usual stool. I made my hands grab my knees.

"What part of 'don't hurt the agents' did you miss?"

"This isn't working for me," I flared back at her, assuming a Buddha-like position. "And why do they keep sending you down to talk to me? Are you even on this case?"

"They're men. They think anything with ovaries can bond," she fired back.

"Having ovaries would imply that I acted like a normal female! Do I look like Martha Stewart?! This is ludicrous; do you even know why they're keeping me? I was a spy and I uncovered something that they want very badly. I'm their information source, and they're treating me as though I was a serial killer!"

"You are responsible for dozens of deaths!"

"At least I've never shot an American."

"I do what the government tells me to do. You do whatever the hell you want."

"I do what has to be done. Do you know what the Mossad said to Director Goode? "She always has been a Yankee," a damned Yankee: red, white and blue blood and I have taken every opportunity to help U.S. forces abroad. I'm helping them right now, well not this moment because I'm in time-out with you yelling at me without taking a good look at the facts first and the Terminator trying to abort my fetus!" I was speaking quite loudly at that point. "So you just calm down or get out and you stop threatening my baby-machine!"

"I see this is going well," George came on the speaker.

"Go to hell, George, I'm drawing a line here," I said.

"And John," John said from the speaker.

"John, you're already on my shit list, are you trying for the hit list?" I growled.

One of the guards made a motion and Agent Starr got up and left, taking the guards with her.

"Ben-Adat was not John's fault," George said.

"George, this is not working for me."

"Do you want to catch him?"

"Yes, of course."

"Well, one of the analysts of some of the other information, the stuff that helped us catch and convict some of your former associates is here, and they want to thank you. Will you come up?"

The door opened and they gestured for me.

"It appears I will be there soon," I replied to the speaker box and strapped on my cast. I looked at the guard like 'yeah, what do you want here'.

"Your choice, Belle," a familiar guard said. "You want to play nice, we'll cuff you in front and you don't try anything. You want to be mean; we'll strap you into a straightjacket and carry you around like a duffel bag."

"I like it," I offered my wrists for the cuffs. Upstairs I was walked into a small conference room where George, John, and a pleasant looking man waited. The cuffs were left on. *Probably a good idea.*

"Hello," the man said. "I'm Tom McEwan."

"Hi. I'm your spy. He's trying to kill me," I smiled and pointed to John. I observed him for a few moments, and then I turned to George. "No."

"What do you mean, no?" he asked.

"He's a psychologist."

Tom laughed a little. "Yes, I am a psychologist. I'm also an analyst. I don't want to know about your feelings. John, we won't need you. Thanks."

John left and I leaned back in my seat.

"Now, I've been studying you for a month now, so it's a real pleasure to see you in person. You are a truly remarkable person," he wasn't lying. "You feel trapped right now, which I expect means flare-ups of temper and violence. Your mind is like a teapot: it gets under pressure and you slide into escape mode. I understand you are quite a lock pick."

"Trick of the trade," I replied, showing off my still intact cuffs.

"In your mind, you are choosing to be held here, doing us a service by helping find the target. I am very interested in your pregnancy mindset. I do know that you love the father enough to protect him. You are defensive of the child, and threatening to harm the child will lead to great violence on your part. I could see you blowing up this entire facility if you were driven to it."

I listened, mind wide open to him.

"You are also extremely intelligent and bold, cocky at times. Tell me about the guards."

"We had one little incident in the beginning, but I have nothing against them. They are not overly violent, and except for the one that threatened to aim low, we get along just fine. After that skirmish, we're balancing out pretty well. I meant to hurt the first, but not the second man, whom I believe I hurt worse."

"And the man who threw you into the wall?"

"We're cool. Same for the guy who gently took me down today. It seems perfectly logical to me that they do what they do."

"And the terrorist?"

"The guard..." I swallowed. "They do what they have to do. The threat was neutralized before I was removed, but that was my hand and my eye, not theirs."

"Why do you defend the guards?"

"They defend me. They're soldiers."

"You will do whatever it takes to protect American troops; that was already established," he noted aloud. "What if the terrorist had attacked the guard instead of you?"

"It would have been over quickly. I positioned myself to come before the guard, rotate-and-stab wise. I was ready to clamp-squat him if he turned his back on me. There is no way to know what would have happened."

"She would have killed him," he concluded to George.

"I didn't say that," I told George.

Tom set an Ipod on the table. "Would you listen to something for me, tell me what you think of it?" He unlocked one of my cuffs.

"Sure," I listened to the clip and then replayed it. "Cell phone tap, possibly French. The man is an Algerian who has been living in a pure Arab nation for a long time: he dropped most of his 'frarabic' terms, but not all. From the subject matter, they're probably really talking about financial movements: I recognized some sweet terms. The background noise indicates a pub or restaurant of some kind, or possibly an industrial building."

"Agent Tomopolis, we have the perfect spy tool. Counter espionage in a size six!"

"Excuse you, try size four!" I objected vainly.

"She's extremely dangerous."

"Give her a week without the handcuffs, see how it goes. She's rational; I recommend trying the program with her understanding that one violent attempt on anyone or anything and the cuffs will be back."

"She just gave Agent Powell a black eye."

"She's under pressure. Valve's gonna blow, or we can take the steam and power up the boat."

"Why did you call the Mossad agent 'daddy'?" George asked me suddenly.

"He took me under his wing, taught me quite a lot," I replied. "He is not my father."

"You think he has a hit on you?"

"You think Ben-Adat was here looking for directions to funky town? Paranoia is a skill, not an affliction. It keeps you going. You want me to level with you? Attach a device that shocks me like a bark collar, or shoot me with a real gun in the leg or arm. Stay away from my baby."

The phone buzzed.

"We have a problem," George looked grave. A guard ran in with his hand on his firearm.

"Secure in place," the guard said and locked the door, drawing the blind.

"Dead guard, missing Ben-Adat," George said aloud.

"How long?"

"Minutes."

"How long has he been on this base?"

"Never unsupervised, few days maybe?"

"He's in a uniform by now. Did he take the guard's side arm?"

"She knows how he operates," Tom pointed and George dialed a number.

"He's going to escape," I judged. "90% chance of that, 10% that he's coming for me," I listened hard to the hallway. Everything was tense and silent for four minutes, until I heard running footsteps.

"Orders, we need to secure her," I heard a man say, and the soldier inside drew his weapon. I drew George's back-up gun from his leg as he ducked me under the table.

Ben-Adat fired two shots after breaking in the door before I shot him through the chin and the guard fired several rounds into his chest. I stood up and we all just stood there, guns in hand on standby trying to make sense of it.

"Anyone hit?"

"I ducked," Tom said and I saw the shattered window.

"Gun! Put the gun on the table," the guard was aiming for my heart now, and I casually set it in front of George. "On the ground, hands on your head," he ordered and I obeyed. Another guard came in and assisted.

"Give me this hand," the second man said, taking my left hand and pulling it back to loop it into a plastic cuff. "Now give me this hand," he did the same with the right and he searched me before we stood up. "Come here, sit down."

I did, staring at the body as the blood spill spread. "Bastard had bad aim."

George stood behind me, reassuring arms on my shoulders. "I guess now we know. I have a feeling I know what the autopsy is going to say."

"I had to borrow your back-up," I was shaken. "I wasn't going to hurt any of our guys. Just him."

"I know," George answered his phone. "Yes, we have a body, suspect escaped custody; opened fire on agents, guard and prisoner. No casualties to report here. Yes ma'am," he put the phone on the table and it went to speakerphone.

"Belle, are you there?" The lady director inquired.

"Yes ma'am."

"Are you hurt?"

"No ma'am. I was under the table, where I procured a weapon and shot the bastard dead when he busted the door in and opened fire."

"Everyone else alright?"

"Agent Tomopolis, code green," George said and the rest of the room followed suit. The guard outside the door was splattered in blood spray, but he was fine.

"He shot the seat here," Tom said of my chair, which sported a bullet hole. "You shot with your left hand?"

"I'm ambidextrous," I replied and took yet another deep breath. "Who is dead?"

The head guard from earlier, Stover, came in, slightly red in the head. "You got him."

"Yes sir," the Marine said.

"Standard code Charlie Echo 569," he said and I had no idea what he meant. "Sirs, we need to return her for her own safety while we run a sweep and assessment. I have a man down."

"Belle, we're going to be doing paperwork most of the rest of the day," George said apologetically.

"I understand," I told him. "I'm sorry I just ruined your theory by stealing a gun and killing the hit man," I told Tom and stood.

"She saved our lives, along with the guard," Tom told Captain Stover. Stover looked at the body.

"I fired three times sir. Shoulder, double tap," the guard reported.

"Well, he's dead," my voice cracked a little. "I'm ready to cooperate."

"Captain," guy number three from my first skirmish came in. He stepped over the body.

"Take her home, gently," he instructed. The two guards walked with me in silence until we were in the elevator.

"That was a hell of a shot," the first man said. "From under the table."

"I've spent a lot of time learning how to shoot from beneath because in my profession it is your last chance to stay alive," I revealed. "You have great technique, by the way."

"She shot him?" wall guard said as we transferred elevators.

"He opened fire; I had no choice." We passed a guard with a large gun into the smaller elevator.

"So what, now you're a hero?" Wall-guard said.

"No, just alive," I replied and we finished the trip in silence. They did not slam the door so hard this time, and the lights remained on. Two DVDs were on my bed, and I set one playing on my laptop before burying my face into my dolphin.

Dinner came and I ate because I hadn't really eaten all day and I was dizzy. I got dessert too: mint chocolate chip ice cream. It was really yummy. Sometime after dinner, the intercom beeped at me.

"Miss Jones?" Natalie asked apprehensively.

"Yes dear?" I replied with a smile.

"Um, Director Goode wanted you to know that the kill shot was the 22. That's what she said."

"Does she want to see me?"

"Tomorrow morning, maybe. She asked how you felt."

"I don't have a response for that," I replied to the box.

"Oh, okay...um, would it be okay if I came down and saw you in person?"

"She wants a report, right?" I guessed.

"Yeah. I mean, I'm coming down, but I wanted to ask first."

"Come on down, join the party," I invited. The door opened and the intercom clicked. I blinked in surprise as I saw Agent Starr, looking slightly contrite.

"I brought chocolate," she said apologetically.

"Come on in," I turned the DVD off.

"I know all about today, and how you saved lives, and that you're working with the counter-terrorism team, and the cyber-terrorism team, and a few other things I didn't know about before," she sat on the stool.

"Hey, never apologize unless you're lying about it," I sat on the end of the bed and we both ignored the guard standing next to the door.

"Are you…okay?" she asked.

"You know, every time I kill someone, I feel one or two things. Either I feel a deep hollow sense of a loss of humanity, or I feel a moment of smug satisfaction immediately followed by the deep hollow sense of loss of humanity," I revealed. "I mean, there's a balance to it. The Algerian, it was like a 70-30 deal. With others more like 5-95. I won't know about Ben-Adat until I've subconsciously come to terms."

"I was also going to say that you're one hell of a shot," she smiled a little.

"Was anyone else hurt? Besides the dead guard."

She seemed confused. "The guard isn't dead; but I bet we thought he was. No, he was unconscious and shot several times, but they're in surgery now."

I felt relieved. "Wow."

"Okay, civilian coming in," the guard said. The door opened and the very nervous Natalie stepped in, staring at me, the cell, and Agent Starr at the same time.

"This is where you live?" she squeaked. "Uh, sorry."

"Good God, calm down already," I said warmly. "Want some chocolate?"

She laughed a little and took a breath. "Um, I need you to stand up please and take the cast off please."

I complied, making no sudden movements.

"Nat, just give me the guidelines and we'll make this short and sweet," Agent Starr said and she was given the index card. "Okay, hands front and back."

I showed them off.

"Arms? Neck, face, wrists, lower right ribs," Starr read off and I showed Natalie the places she needed to see.

"I'm sorry, what's that on your collar bone?" Natalie noted the small pink spot.

"Shell," Starr knew. "Extreme angle, left hand, it hit you right in the clavicle."

"Bingo. I hadn't noticed it."

"Okay, I guess that's all I need…" Natalie looked at me again, and then scurried out.

"So you're not even a little mad at me?" Agent Starr returned to her intentions.

"You came in and yelled at me for hurting the agent. So, no. The guard with you, hell yeah, but only because he threatened my wiggle-worm!" I replied.

"So, you think Ben-Adat was Al-Qaida?"

"Probably Hezbollah or Hamas-hired. Al-Qaida is too vague these days. Not Egyptian…Egypt. That guy was in Egypt. I need to get a message to Agent Tom…God what's his face."

"Morrow? McEwan?" she caught my excitement.

"McEwen. His tape is a conversation tapped in France and the person speaking was in Egypt."

She pulled out her cell phone and dialed a number. "It's Agent Starr. Sorry to bother you at home, but Belle Jones wanted you to know that the message was in Egypt."

"It was tapped in France, so he was in Egypt talking to someone in France," I said loudly and she held the phone out.

"Did you catch that?" she asked. "She's fine. We were just chatting. Uh-huh same to you," she hung up, "I should get going." Her phone rang. "Yes ma'am," she stood up. "Right away ma'am. We're coming now." She pocketed the phone. "Quick, cast, shoes, let's go."

They cuffed me in back again and I knew where we were going. A few minutes later, I eavesdropped on a call through Director Goode's door.

"I said before that when Beauty says a man is dead, he is," my Mossad man was saying.

"Inside," the guard said and I swept in and was released.

"Damn straight he is," I replied to the screen in English. "I thought I had made it clear: very, very clear, of the consequences of touching those under my protection," I was fury on fire, and Director Goode was amused.

"You cannot pretend to protect everyone," he replied, unmoved.

"Allow me to clarify then: if they're in an American uniform, they have my protection. If they carry an American badge, mine. If there is an American child or innocent, they're mine."

"Beauty, you are their prisoner!"

"I am still a fully functioning warrior, and Ben-Adat would testify to that if I hadn't blown his brains out. You know damn well I can't be contained or filed away. The consequences of your hit man were mild, and I think the Americans might be able to curb my wrath, but if not, I will dismantle your organization man by man. Your computers will explode, your servers will fry, your people stranded across the world until they are eaten up by the beasts they hunted. You will witness the wrath of the House of Angels, and then I will mail your head to the Knesset so they will know that it is over," I switched to Arabic. "Tell me I lie."

He looked acutely uncomfortable. "You mean it," he replied in Hebrew.

"You know only some of what I am capable of," I replied in Hebrew.

"You make a good point," he said in English, wary of his image. I walked off-camera. "I trust you will ensure that she is retained in custody?" he said to Director Goode.

"I may require incentive," she said bluntly. "We will finish our investigations here and send the body to you."

"We will arrange a pick-up time for my agent there, perhaps off-base would be best, at this time," he agreed and hung up.

She looked at her screen. "So what does that last line mean? Only some of that which I can do?"

"It refers to the same incident as the beginning of the dialogue addressed," I replied.

"Threat, or reminder?" she asked coyly.

"Yes," I replied.

"Aside from what you did to Agent Powell, I am pleased with you today."

"After we catch Al-Zahrani, I would like to hack the Mossad to see what they have on me," I told her.

"He's scared of you, at the moment," she was amused. "It has been a very long day. I can recommend removal of restraints only after a week of no violent activity. Start tomorrow, and a week from tomorrow we'll start the experiment under the guidelines proposed by Agent

95

McEwen. And, as a bonus, on the condition that you not attack any more agents, we'll use the 'incentive' money the Mossad gives us to construct a better living area for you."

"Thank you, ma'am."

"Under no conditions are you to attack an agent or guard, to pick your own locks, or 'borrow' someone's side arm. You know only some of that which I can do," she quoted the translation of my own words to me.

"Understood ma'am. May I ask a question regarding?" she consented. "What if one of them goes rogue and starts killing people? I have seen it happen."

"No conditions," she repeated.

"The guard that was severely injured, is he going to be alright?"

"I don't know. Marine!" she called and I stood up as the guard approached. He cuffed me quickly and we were out of there within a minute.

There was chatter in the hallway as we got off of the second elevator. All male voices seemed to relate to whatever they were discussing. We turned the corner and I saw the group, which included the guard who had also shot Ben-Adat.

"He-Hay!" they called in friendly tones.

"She's gonna teach us all how to shoot like that," one man joked and I smiled to the group.

"Gentlemen," I greeted.

"We got you some puzzle books and pretzels," his name tag read 'Benzion'; he was the guard who also shot the terrorist. "Kind of a thanks for killing him before he killed us."

"My pleasure, sir. Thanks for not shooting me," I faced the door and patiently let my current guard unlock me.

"Hell of a shot," I heard someone say as I entered my cell and the door slammed shut. I saw the puzzles and pretzels and also a new dolphin blanket on my bed. It was incredibly soft and I knew it would be warm.

"Thank you," I shouted in the direction of the door. *Now what?*

Chapter 5: The Uniform

The days immediately following were peaceful: I spent most of the time trying to sift out clues from the seven thousand page manuscript for terrorists. They set me up in a nice little reading nook: it was probably once an office. The guard stood outside and I sipped tea and muttered to myself. No one tried to interrogate me for three straight days, and I turned my notes over to Captain Stover at the end of each day. News finally came that the injured guard was now in critical condition, but looked like he would live.

It must have been Monday when Tom McEwen requested a second meeting with me; this time he came to my 'office'.

"Well, this is quite a set up," he entered and surveyed the room.

"They frosted the one window over there so I couldn't see the compound, and therein no one could see me. I like it," I replied. "I'm going over the last four thousand pages first; then I'll go back to what I've already read."

"You seem to be having a good week."

"Well, I haven't hurt anyone, so I suppose so. It's all about finding the balance."

"*Exactement*," he replied knowingly. "You took the cast off."

"It was annoying," I shrugged.

"I heard you told the Mossad assistant director to go to hell."

"I told him to back off or I would send him to hell," I replied as he took a seat. "And it felt really good."

"As good as shooting the shooter?"

"That didn't really feel 'good'. Maybe at some point it will, but right now it just feels like I took another man down. I feel no guilt about it," I clarified for him, "I just didn't receive any emotional satisfaction."

"You were correct about the tape," he changed the subject. "And the cyber team is still working on logistics. The meeting starts tomorrow, on a US ship in the gulf."

"Crap. I hate hacking the Navy."

"I'll let them figure things out with you," he laughed a little. "Director Goode is impressed, and pleased with this project. Your friend George is going to benefit from his unconventional partnership with you. So will you. Plus, we might actually catch the striped rat."

"Sometimes I think I should have shot him when I had the chance," I said wistfully.

"We'll get him."

"Ironically, he's not really the one we're after," I observed. "Others have risen, people who don't answer to him. Abram Khalifsa, for example. Could I have a whiteboard or something like it in here?"

"I'll see if I can arrange it. Anything else?"

"No, life is perfect. I'm going about three hundred pages a day."

"In Arabic?"

"It's repetitive," I replied.

"So, I'll admit I'm curious. How exactly did you scare the Mossad?"

"I threatened them with something they believe I would and could do," I replied simply and re-opened the book.

"But they're the Mossad!"

"They would not be, for long," I said lightly. "I can take them down in three weeks, like flies."

"Shooting all the agents? Explosions?"

"My trade, my secrets," I replied, "Ask yourself what the worst thing that could happen to an agent in the field is. Then, let others do the knife-work."

"That's brilliant."

"Well, it's an establishment I know from the inside."

He smiled and we began to become comfortable. He left after a while and I continued with my work. I thought it would be lunch, but it was John at the door.

"Well done, Miss Jones. What do you have on the Mossad's people?"

"I shot the hit man," I warned and set the paper down. The guard stepped into the room.

"I will buy your forgiveness."

"With?"

"Come with me."

The guard already had the restraints out, so I decided to humor him. We went up to the penthouse and sat to watch the screen, which showed a night-vision event of some kind. The camera was shaky. The view changed and zoomed in quickly.

"Oh my God," I recognized the scene.

"This was strapped onto a Saudi chopper, making a routine flight," Director Goode said.

"That's the mosque, there. Then there are the apartment buildings," we watched, "Just a little north of here," I pointed. The camera zoomed out and cleared up. I heard sounds like a camera snapping and the chopper moved on. The printer produced the picture and I drew a blue circle around Al-Zahrani's home.

"Well done, Miss Jones," John repeated. Someone flipped the lights on and I saw George standing in the back. "George," John was surprised.

"Hey, if she's going to kick your ass, I'm not going to miss it."

"Boys," Director Goode put an end to that.

"We've got it," John stared at the page.

"Technically, we've got it," Director Goode pointed.

"Our feed,"

"Our girl," she returned.

"Our money,"

"Not to the Mossad," she played.

"That's it," John surprised me and tossed me over his shoulder. He moved to walk out.

"Ma'am?" I looked for permission.

"Whoa, okay, okay, putting the girl down," John said: something changed his mind. I was soon on the ground again and I saw the two real guns the guards were aiming.

"Alexis," George called to me and I stepped toward him. "Our girl," he restated.

"Joking, ah, hell. Money's in your inbox. Can I put my hands down now?"

"Welcome to my world," I laughed. We all had a good laugh about it.

"So, we did well with the Mossad?" I asked.

"Between that and this," George judged and looked to his boss.

"We did well. You should get some rest."

"Yes, I'm tired," I picked up the cue. "Ma'am, if he does that whole wench-grabbing thing again...?"

"No."

I caught the guard Samuel's face and smirked because he knew exactly what I was thinking.

"You gotta admit that I had you," John smirked.

"Oh honey, you'll never have me," I replied and turned my back and arms to the guard, who obliged me.

"Then how did we capture you?"

"He asked nicely. So do they."

"May I have Al-Zahrani's head on a platter, please?" Goode asked.

"Silver, gold, or platinum?" I smiled wickedly.

At 8 p.m. that night they finally left me alone in the closet with the computer. I took a breath and began. It was three hours before I called, "Prep for impact," to Kmetz.

"They're firing," he replied.

"Hang tight," I penetrated the first wall. "You with me?"

"Three more walls and I'll take the Navy," he called back.

I leaned forward and thoroughly enjoyed myself. At two a.m. I was through to the Navy wall. Kmetz swept those aside and we rode the router for the next hour.

"You're bolstering us, right?" I asked.

"Hell yeah. You tired?"

"Exhausted. We're in though."

"We have a live feed," he sounded impressed.

"Three, actually," I informed. I wrote the coordinates of the location of my two back feeds. "I fucking love your technology here. Now I need to check the background lapse of these," I said.

"I'll take it from here," Agent Won entered the closet. She didn't look tired at all. "Great technique."

"You've been watching?"

"Only since midnight. That's my shift. You do good work."

"K. Goodnight." My legs felt like pasta and my stomach growled. "Can I have some cereal?" I asked the guard as she cuffed me.

"Yes, if you're nice and quiet," she replied and we practically tip-toed back to the sub-sub-basement. True to her word, I was given Cheerios and milk before I crawled into bed and they turned out the lights.

They woke me up by turning on the lights around eleven. The shower helped; so did lunch. They took me to the office but I fell asleep reading. George knocked on the door and woke me up.

"Dull reading?" His expression told me everything I needed to know. The hack had been successful, and was probably gathering information as we spoke. He was pleased. George sat opposite me and I placed the two books I had been cuddling on the table. "Okay, the following conversation is between you and me. No record, no wire, nothing."

"Deal," my senses rose a little.

"Whatever you said to Mossad induced a good deal of money. We're building you a little…apartment of sorts. You'll still be in the sub-sub-sub-basement, but it's going to be considerably nicer. "

"Well they can't have me walking around out there knocking off agents," I explained.

"I also wanted to say, completely off the record, that you have done better here than I ever thought you would. Never have you ceased to amaze me, but, really, you're awesome. Cyber thinks you're awesome, Assistant Deputy Director Goode thinks you're awesome, and the CIA is beginning to fear and distrust you, which is their version of awesome."

I laughed because it was true.

"How do you like Tom?"

"As a shrink, not bad at all. He's mostly right: I am a boiling kettle. And I do feel better now that I've made up my mind about killing that man."

"Did it help to know he died almost instantly?"

Of course he did. "Not much: it had to be done. You think I'm doing well?"

"For what we're doing? It's like I hit the jackpot. How are you doing?"

"Well, my little parasite here is sucking away my life force, but I keep going."

"How'd you like the hack closet?"

"It was nice. That kid and I sat up all night and he just let me drill until I hit the Navy. I left around 3 a.m., I think. I was wiped out."

"You did a good thing. John was astounded."

"He's a twit."

"He's not as bad as he seems. The little baby package was from him: the 'expecting' book and the medications, along with the pajamas."

"Oh," I really liked those. "So he's not a jerk?"

"Nope, just a little awkward," he leaned back. "He hasn't been chasing you as long as I have. He found you by accident: he was hunting a chem dealer named Roshad."

"Ah yes, the one they never found," I remembered it fondly.

"What did you do with him anyway?"

"Chemicals? Hello? It did not smell nice. Aron knocked him dead; so we got creative. I left the rest to a third party," I caught myself just in time. "Those who attempt to traffic chemicals for chemical warfare tend to get knocked off."

"And dissolved."

"It's not as barbaric as it sounds. It's better than what the Iranian terrorists were going to do with them. I use the same standard you use: if they're a really bad guy threatening the wrong people, it's open game."

He thought about it for a moment and mentally agreed. "Government makes it 'right'."

"Maybe to your God, but not to mine."

"We have an encryption code we can't crack," he read off of his phone.

"Beta 781R4ZQ?" I asked and he blinked. "Right. Beam me up Scotty."

"We're waiting for a staff meeting so we can sneak you back into the closet. Agent Won will call me."

"She won't be missed at the staff meeting?"

"Agent Won isn't FBI."

"Great. Another Company girl."

"Nope. She's DIA."

"You're kidding me."

"No: they're in this mess too."

"Makes sense," I said as the phone rang. *Okay, so that means that the DIA is under the FBI because she talked like they were bound by FBI regulations. We may need to get that altered because we're going to need CIA flexibility to get anything done.* I was back in my closet staring at the screen and scribbling on a sheet of paper within five minutes. "Oooh, mutation," I muttered to myself.

Agent Won climbed into the closet with me and shut the door.

"It's a mutated Beta 781-R4ZQ protective sealant code," I greeted.

"Those are usually built to fry in case of emergency," she said.

"Yes, they are. Fortunately, I know the sequencing on this one."

"How?"

"Ask Agent Kmetz about my laptop sometime," I hit 'enter' and waited. DENIED the screen read. "Excellent. But you already knew what it was."

"Sure, but not how to crack it."

"Alright, here we go," I started typing methodically. "The code is wired for commands, not just keys, and it feeds in three intervals. Exclamation point... good."

The screen did exactly what it was supposed to: it flashed "DENIED!" before slowly melting the words away. I waited for the screen before I began again.

"What if you make a mistake?" Won asked.

"I hit escape, back up, come from another portal and start from scratch. If I had the machine, I would force a shut down," I typed another sequence in and waited. "Perfect."

"Genius," Won said and I realized that she smelled of cherry blossoms. "So, last layer right?"

"Pretend you didn't see this," I said and I typed a very precise sequence which had government coding and hacking codes interwoven. "And make sure these get changed."

"Where did you get those?" Won demanded.

"The French. They got it from China," I replied honestly and watched the last layer of wall melt away. "All yours."

"Thank you," she said insincerely and motioned me out, her face frozen and her cell phone dialing.

"What time is it?" I asked as a guard appeared from behind a door. It was almost dark outside and my stomach was ready for food.

"You've been in there for about five hours."

"Wow," I let them cuff me in front. "So she's working a twenty-four hour shift?"

"No idea." John appeared from around the corner. "Those guys are crazy. Shall we eat?" He joined us and we returned to my office space, where hot roast beef sandwiches awaited. "Area rugs are going to cover most of the floor. You'll have a mini fridge for drinks, and a bathroom area where you don't have to move the TP to shower. Double bed, monitor to watch DVDs with, little table with two chairs…" he led and I was impressed.

"In the jail cell."

"Think of it as a protective custody unit. There's a little chest with drawers and stuff for your clothes and hooks to hang things on. It's going to be the sweetest unit ever made."

"It sounds nice."

"Oh, and did I mention it's 2.5 times bigger than your current cell?"

"Very nice." *For a jail cell with no window.*

"You'll have light controls," he pitched, "and, this is so cool. I am jealous. You're getting, courtesy of a very uncomfortable Israeli, this completely awesome fake window. It has daylight equivalent and everything. It's programmable!"

"Sweep it for bugs if it's coming from Israel," I replied, slightly less bitterly.

"Think of this as a little prize for finding and helping us find 'Waldo'," he said as I finished my dinner. "So, do I still suck eggs?"

I laughed. "George already had that talk with me. Perhaps not. I do wish you had been there when I shot Ben-Adat with George's gun from under the table. It was a sweet shot, and you would never have tried to 'kidnap' me."

"I should have known from the incident at the other building," he brushed it aside. "I think Ray's still walking a little funny."

"I think lessons were learned," I concluded.

"I was thinking of painting it a nice mellow yellow," he sat back and sipped a cup of tea.

"I would like that," I said, drowsy.

"You should get some rest. Do you think you might want to interrogate a prisoner again?"

I nodded without thinking about it. "I'll need my ethnic kit, and dying my hair black wouldn't be a bad idea."

"Okay. He speaks French better than Arabic."

"So, am I going to be French?"

"Can you pull off Quebecois?"

"I don't know: I've never done it. Sure. Same set up as before?"

"I'll have to check: we'll have the outfit and everything ready for you in a changing room; then you can watch him for a few minutes through the viewing room before you go in. This time, I do know, he will be completely secured."

"What did he do?"

"Agent McEwen will tell you tomorrow," he replied and I knew.

"How did we get him?"

"He was tracked to Afghanistan. The rest is classified."

"What is his wire name?"

"I don't remember," he lied. "We'll wake you up in time."

"Good. It has definitely been a long day."

I was fast asleep when the lights came on suddenly and the door opened.

"Sorry," it was Agent Won. Now she looked tired, and she closed the door behind her. "We have a chance to get an agent into the Saudi government's system if we can write a one-shot program virus in the next three hours," she explained.

"Well I can't do it on that thing, let's go," I glanced at my laptop and slid my shoes on. I covered my pajamas with my coat and we slunk into the closet.

"I have the main body written," she explained as she closed the door. "The problem is we don't know what kind of system we're facing."

"Norton, last I checked," I replied and pulled my hair back. "Alright, I'm thinking about inserting a key into the start-up sequence to transmit in real-time the computer's actions and transactions."

"We need it to feed to other computers," she pulled up a chair and started typing.

"So we'll put a present in the transactions. Email okay?" I read the screen and started typing. "I'll make it invisible, you make the sequence."

"Deal," she said and no words were exchanged for the next thirty minutes.

I sat back. "Feed it in," I said and we connected our computers to place the virus into her candy coating. "Can you detect-code?"

"Only European and Asian programs."

"You write those, I'll do American and Middle Eastern knock-off programs. I want to set it," I stopped talking as I typed faster and faster.

"So it can ping and only attack once," she finished for me. Cyber war is not exciting: it's mostly a lot of geeks typing stuff over and over again. That's part of why I love it.

She finished first, but only by a minute. "Forty minutes to go."

"Okay," I attached and smoothed over the package. "Slip that into a zip and e-mail that puppy off to the Navy."

"You are awesome," she said as she sent it off.

"You're not half bad either," I replied as she signaled for the door to be opened.

"He got it," she said as she joined me in the hall. "It's four a.m.; sorry to drag you out of bed."

"Like that's the first time I've done that," I brushed it aside and yawned. "I hope the interrogation session isn't too early."

"Sleep as long as you like: he's not going anywhere," she offered her hand and I shook it before the guard escorted me, sans cuffs, back to bed.

I got a solid 6 hours more sleep and woke up feeling great. My fingers were a little cramped, but otherwise I was in top condition.

"Go Canada, eh?" I greeted George outside the changing room.

"You look good for a vampire."

"Merci," I slipped into the room and switched clothes quickly, tousling my hair.

"In here," George gestured and we stepped into a viewing room. I watched as a rapid fire interrogation in French, then English, produced moderately dissimilar results.

"You don't need me for this one," I reported.

"I know, but it is fun," George replied. I rolled my eyes. "We'd like the name of his associate in Egypt."

"The Algerian," I confirmed. "No problem," I went in and kicked out the current interrogator. I then performed a technique called fawning doe: it was quite a lot of fun to sexually stimulate and tease the man while thinking about whom all was watching. It's a sympathetic character, and it won't work in every situation, but it was like stealing candy from a baby in this case. I got the name, the towns, an associate, and the person he was going to meet in

110

Afghanistan. It was a cake walk. I took everything I felt I could take and I walked out. I strolled into the viewing room to find an open-mouthed colonel and a grinning George.

"Good morning sir," I greeted the colonel.

"That was effective," he stated.

"Did everything come through on audio alright?" I asked George.

"Yes, yes it did," he fought his urge to laugh. "I'm going to bring in a masseuse and a beautician and give you a spa day."

"Excellent."

"And a chocolate chip cookie," he added and I smiled.

"Now you're going to spoil me."

"I'll give you a dozen chocolate chip cookies if you tell me where you came from," Colonel Comb-Over upped the ante.

I looked to George.

"Colonel Wyatt, this is the black swan. The non-attack in Liberia was her doing, as was the intelligence on several other issues."

He considered it for a moment. "She is responsible for the deaths of the six terrorists who intended to blow up the base?"

"At the least," George replied.

"She from the company?" he asked in a quieter tone.

"She's a part of this joint operation," he replied.

"What else do you speak, so I'm not surprised next time?"

"Whatever I have needed to. I'm sorry colonel, but surprise is my best friend," I stated calmly.

"She saved a few more lives the other day when there was a major security breach. Stole a gun, plugged an assassin," George said, almost proudly.

"Excuse me," the colonel touched my shirt's neckline; clearly he had glimpsed the scar. I watched his eyes as they found it, realized it, and drew a conclusion. He pulled his hand back quickly. "What is this? You're the angel. Soldier!" he yelled and my guard came in. "Whoever you are, you're under arrest for espionage, murder, and anything else that's out on you. Don't make any sudden movements."

"Colonel Wyatt, I'm already arrested," I informed as carefully as possible. "I've been a prisoner for weeks," I let him digest that information. "And you're very welcome for murdering those six men to keep your men alive."

"Samuels," George said and the MP stepped up and I left with him.

I changed clothes, as usual, and Samuels was right there when I opened the door again. "Come on, sir, contain the prisoner," I said bitterly.

"This way," Samuels said warmly. He opened a door and we entered an interrogation room. He left me there alone and unrestrained.

I took a deep breath and mulled around a little. *What an imbecile. Ungrateful imbecile, to be specific. Hey, thanks for being the best around, and by the way, you're under arrest. Moron. Breathe, just breathe. Stress isn't good for the baby. Ohm....Ohmmmm.* I hopped onto the stainless steel table and swung my legs. Ten, fifteen minutes passed and I sighed. I lay back on the cool steel and relaxed, refusing to allow their games to affect me.

The door opened; it was the colonel. He brought Samuels in with him.

"Do I understand that you gave yourself up and have switched sides?" he asked.

"Essentially, yes," I replied.

"And you claim that you were not a U.S. sponsored operative during the time in which you supplied information and took actions to aid and shelter American interests and troops?"

"I do," I replied clearly.

"Is it true that you were under no pressure to do so?"

"Does patriotism count?"

"You passed a psychiatric evaluation regarding perception, delusion, and morality."

"So I'm not crazy, so what makes me different?" I skipped ahead. He took a seat and I slid off of the table and into a chair.

"Interrogating is not my job. I understand that you have acclimated to your guards, even putting yourself at risk for them and agents. I do not dislike you."

"As a man of the military, you should. I am the very best argument against the policy of not allowing women into combat zones," I replied and he stood.

"My dear, I have always known that the female of the species is deadlier than the male." He smiled and exited after exchanging salutes with the MP.

"Colonel," I heard a voice greet in the hall and Tom strolled in. "That was the best interrogation he's ever had," he joked.

"It's a carefully crafted maneuver, and a lot of fun at parties," I returned with a smirk.

His phone rang. "Yes Natalie...Why upstairs? ... If that's the purpose, why don't you bring one down so she can...Right. No, I wouldn't forget. See you soon." He hung up. "The girl needs sedation. They have created a new uniform so you're slightly less conspicuous running around the building. Something that looks professional, but it's comfortable."

Good luck with that one.

"And warmer. It comes with a special strap around your ankle. Allegedly, it can't be removed without a special tool. I know you, so I say 'allegedly'. Don't pick the lock or they'll go all cave-man shackles and chains on you."

I laughed a little and someone knocked. Upon being shown the outfit, I just stared for a moment. "How is something straight out of *Madeleine* less conspicuous?" I asked of the black pants with an elastic waist and a long, trim gray top that was like a dress without waistline. The top had short sleeves which were compensated for by a jacket that had a strange seal on it. Samuels took me to the restroom and I put the costume on without a fight. I returned to Tom unamused.

"This is a joke, right?"

"Is it comfortable?" he asked.

"Well, yeah, but I look ridiculous!"

"It comes with shoes!"

"If it comes with a hat, someone is going to die," I replied sternly.

"Look, we need you on the floor without actually letting people know you're you, there," he explained. "This is a modified version of what someone around here might wear."

"American fashion has gotten that bad?" I shoved the jacket on. It was a nice fit, and had that nice fuzzy cotton lining.

"Table," Tom directed and Samuels approached with the black strap. It looked a little like a watch, but the casing was all inside the strap. He fit it onto my left ankle and I discovered it had a limited flexibility.

"Belle, we're going to test it on its lowest frequency. Sorry," Samuel said and pushed a button on his control set. It was like accidentally messing with a lamp which was still plugged in: a short, unpleasant jolt with no long term numbness.

"Let's not find out if it works at full blast," I resolved and Tom seemed pleased. I slid the shoes on. "Anyone tries to put a ribbon in my hair, they die."

He snickered as the three of us wound the halls and stairs and elevators up to the top. I caught a glimpse of myself in a huge mirror and was taken aback: I actually looked like I was genuinely a normal human being. Probably an intern here, a jellyfish in a sea of tuna. The guard cleared his throat and we continued. I found myself adopting the character, as I did with all of my characters.

We entered the main office, passing Natalie, who looked pretty fish-like for a moment. I stood quietly, flanked by the men, with perfect posture before her desk. Her eyebrows said more than anything else could.

"Yes, that's acceptable," Director Goode said. "And the device?"

"Has been tested, ma'am," I replied.

"A beautician is coming tonight to cut your hair and see to your eyebrows, nails, and toenails. You may have tweezers in your cell, and you will have supervised access to a set of nail scissors for your normal repairs," she informed as though she were reading it off of a screen. "The device is wired to do two things: to keep you under control if necessary, and to give you all hell if you try to remove or manipulate it. It has levels, guards have guidelines, this is an option which seemed to me to benefit you from your perspective. Questions?"

"Yes ma'am. Two things regarding the device: water and swelling. I bathe, and at some point I expect my ankles will swell."

"We'll adjust it when that time comes, and as for the water, don't tamper with it and you'll be fine. Other questions?"

"Will anyone else be trying to kill me this week?"

"Have a seat, let's start our weekly meeting," she replied. "I think it only fair to tell you that your cyber efforts have yielded a positive result," she said and Natalie brought in tea for the three of us. "As has the information you attained for us regarding Afghanistan. You have become the best source of intelligence either agency has ever had," she paused to sip the tea. "I have been told that the worst part of imprisonment was the boredom, which I can certainly understand. We are limited in what we can provide you with for security purposes, but we also seem to be keeping you busy."

I nodded in agreement.

"You can always refuse to perform an interrogation, or to pull guidelines out of a terrorism 101 book, or even to hack. You would not be penalized. These are chances to do something you enjoy and to be rewarded for it," she explained calmly and slowly and I felt myself relax. "You can always request things. You can always request to see me, to see the doctor and the therapist. You can request to go from your cell to the office. Sometimes the answer will be no, but we may surprise you," she stopped talking and looked at me.

"Will my new room have a camera in it?"

"Yes, but it will be set on the door."

"I won't apologize for killing Ben-Adat," I reported.

"I won't apologize if a guard has to zap you," she replied without hostility. "They are doing their job."

"Yes ma'am. So am I."

"What kind of mattress do you like?" she asked.

"Firm with foam padding: that's how my bed used to be at home."

"Show me every bruise, scrape, and assorted," she decided and I started with the wrists, as usual. Tom, gentlemen that he was, turned his back as I began adjusting clothing. "I would like," she started as I showed off my perfect shins, "for you to spend the next few days observing interrogations of several black listed guests. You'll work with Agent McEwen here to assess the most effective strategies and likely results."

"So we'll just watch from the control room, ma'am?" I asked and placed the strapped ankle on the table for her inspection.

"Correct. Technique is everything in an interrogation, but you know that." We both sat back down. Tom was still standing. She glanced at her computer. "Just a moment, please. The head of the CIA task force wants to talk to me, and I can really only dodge him so long."

"Sir, you," I heard Natalie say and we all spun to face the door as a large man in his mid-fifties walked through the door with a briefcase.

"Leon."

"Elsa," he greeted with the charm of sandpaper. "What the hell kind of bullshit are you trying to pull in here, you slimy sneaky bitch?"

Within ten seconds he was in a chair, in a headlock involving his own right arm, and my left leg was wrapped around him to secure his other limbs.

"You can apologize now," I stated and ignored the sharp pain in my ankle, creeping up my leg. She made a hand motion and the pain stopped. "Well?" I pulled lightly on the top of his right ear.

"Let the man go," Tom ordered.

"Alexis," Director Goode said and I released his arm and removed my leg. The guard slapped some speed cuffs on me.

"I should not have called you a bitch," Leon said. "But then again, I did not expect to be attacked by an intern."

"I'm Belle Jones, and I get offended easily," I retorted.

"You're Jones. I have a bullet with your name all over it."

"I hope the engraver thought to remove the powder first. I've seen those things explode," I fired back.

He reached into his coat pocket and retrieved a slug in an evidence cylinder.

"Twenty two, impacted," I observed aloud.

"Straight through the aorta, and it's not even one of your favorites," he replied. "I want her," he directed to Goode. "As a citizen of France, she is no longer American. She's mine."

My heartbeat increased rapidly.

"She's American," Goode replied with certainty. "If you can find 'Vitoria Rose DeBlase', take her. This is Alexis Lisbeth Johnston, and we have the DNA to prove it. Nice try though."

"When you attain an identity through fraud and deception, it is technically null and void," I added, shaking my left leg.

"It really stings, doesn't it?" Director Goode asked.

"Yes ma'am," I replied ruefully. "But no one calls you that and gets away with it."

"I think I understand that situation with Israel a little better now," Leon said.

"It was epic," she replied with a little warmth in her voice. "Officer, please," she said and the cuffs were unlocked. I was thinking some terrible things but contained my emotions.

I picked up the evidence jar with the bullet and examined it. "It must have been embedded in the ceiling," I observed, "looks like it got part way through."

"She's a forensics technician too?" Leon asked Director Goode.

"No, I just know a lot about killing people," I replied and handed him the jar.

"Clearly," he acknowledged. "Is she being cooperative?" he asked Director Goode.

"Extremely," she replied.

"You have no idea," I told him.

"We've been very successful," Tom added.

I shook my left leg like a dog with an itch. "I don't like this thing," I told Tom.

"Don't attack people," he replied with no sympathy.

I felt hormones mess with my head. "I need to leave now," I stated.

"Go sit outside for a while," Director Goode said and I stepped out to where Natalie stopped what she was doing and stared at me. I slumped against the wall in a corner and started to cry.

It was a release I needed; hormones do terrible things in the right conditions. Natalie went into female caregiver mode almost instantly. I sobbed, caught my breath, hardened a little resolve, and got back into the game. With my nose cleared and tears dried, I stormed back into the room.

"You each rose through ranks and achieved your positions by hard work and playing with people's heads; well you're done playing with mine," I announced and interrupted their conversation. "You will never recover the second chip, which contains information vital to homeland security. You will never catch al-Zahrani if you go in through conventional means. And if you want any information drawn out of hostile foreign combatants, you're going to have a hell of a time explaining the need to torture to the president because you pissed off the best method at your disposal. No, I should probably not have pinned you for calling her a bitch," I told the CIA man, "but I sure would hate to miss an opportunity to put the CIA in a headlock.

"I am beginning to realize that the very core of my belief system and ethics code is based on very shaky ground; and you're beginning to lose the driving force behind my cooperation, collaboration, and generally nice demeanor. Yes, I'm an international superspy. I buy, steal, and sell industrial and military secrets! I know the drug and arms routes through most of the world and I did not meet the people I know through the Red Hat Society. Normally, the people who piss me off really regret it.

"So if you want to play your games, have at it. If you'd like to do business in an environment where I'm a respected human intelligence resource it would be best to speak up soon because my very thin patience is slimming away to nothing. If you want me, I'll be in my cell. For now," I turned around and walked back out before the guards had a chance to tackle me. Samuels trailed me closely, but wisely did not touch.

Chapter 6: Evolution

No one bothered me for the rest of the day. I was given meals and the doctor's pills and I watched movies and entertained myself. When I went to bed they lowered the lights, as usual, and when I rose the next morning they raised them again. Later in the morning, I asked to go to my office and they obliged and did not cuff me.

After lunch, which was served in the office while I worked on my notes for Captain Stover, Agent K-9 appeared in the doorway.

"You want to get your hair done?" he asked.

"Sure," I set down my materials.

"You going to hit me?" he asked again.

"No," I replied after a little thought.

"Good, because it might freak the lady out if you show up all chained," he said as he led me out of the room and through the hallways. "Women's showers," he explained as we entered a Ladies room marked 'Closed for Repairs'.

"Ground rules?" I inquired.

"You can talk to her about hair, nails, hands, and feet. Everything will be recorded. I'll be here the whole time, along with your guard, who has strict instructions regarding use of the zapper," he explained. "You behave or I'll sic one of my dogs on you when you least expect it," Agent K-9 added.

"Understood, sir," I replied and they let the woman in with her suitcase. She was all warm, bubbly, and smiley and would not shut up as she sprayed down and cut my hair, cleaned up my feet, and polished all of my nails. When she was done, I thanked her, replaced my shoes and went with the guard as directed by Sully.

"Where are we going?" I asked as we climbed into the elevator.

"Home or office?" he replied.

"Office please; I need to finish that report for the captain," I decided and there we went. I had just settled when I heard someone in the doorway.

"Wow," Agent Won complimented with genuine expression. I finished typing my sentence and set it aside. "You know, I've seen pictures of you with all sorts of different styles and colors; you really have played the whole board, but seeing a transformation like that in person…it's different."

"Once you've transformed a few dozen times, you'll discover that you can't be surprised anymore," I replied. "I've changed races before, so a haircut and a little manicure doesn't really rank."

"You're very pretty," she replied and took a seat. "But I'm sure you've heard that before. You're also extremely useful to my agency. Can I ask you a purely hypothetical question?"

"Why not?"

"What would you do if you found out that a second nation was beginning to close in on "Waldo", perhaps to the extent that they could disrupt your operations?"

"Wait; is "Waldo" Bin Laden or Al-Zahrani?"

"I tend to think of Waldo as Bin Laden. After all, that is the main search focus even though you never stop shouting about Ozzie."

"What's our real goal here? To kill Bin Laden or to capture the real issue?" I demanded.

"Both. First Waldo," George announced and entered. "So, second player?"

"Well, I have never done diplomacy. This has actually come up more than once before; you have to really work at the situation. Sometimes it's great; parasite information and resources are good. Other times you make the call that the fight's not worth it and you back off. If the fight is worth it, you do whatever it takes. Plant false information, send them on a wild goose chase, give them all food poisoning, take down the leader, or in extreme cases do what you have to," I took a breath and Agent Won offered a bottle of water. "In this case, with Waldo, I would need to know more about the second player. Why do they want him? What will they do with him? Whose face will it blow up in? Do we get anything from their actions? These are the important questions. There are many, many states Waldo has committed crimes against. From a personal perspective, I'd like to know how this second player caught wind of Waldo, and if I left footprints. Does that help at all?"

"Yes. Food poisoning?" George asked.

"Salmonella rocks my socks. It's easy to breed and easier to distribute."

"Fighting dirty," Won commented.

"I'm clean, the world is dirty," I replied. "If the second player is Canada, I'd pat them on the head and assure them it was under control. Great Britain might be alliance-worthy; other than that, knock them out of the ballpark. It's only going to mean trouble. Go get some facts, I can take a look and tell you how to take them down. Chances are I've dealt with them." Something clicked inside of my head.

"What?"

"The tunnels. There are two sets of tunnels!" I jumped to my feet. "We need to go to the closet."

"Little more please?"

"There are two sets of tunnels under the city; the old and the really old. I was waiting for a drug dealer in an entrance once and when he didn't show, I discovered the first set of tunnels. They map the area. Half the time they're filled with water; that's probably the only way they survive. Kandahar is old."

"Kandahar in Afghanistan?" Agent Won realized and we started walking.

"You know another one? It's nowhere near mountains and well north of the desert, but the irrigation system was well designed. Where there's an irrigation system…"

She slid her card and we entered the geek section. We looked around surreptitiously before she and the guard joined me in the closet. She took the first seat. "Can you think of a way to clear the tunnels?" she asked as she typed.

"Sure, sulfur, cicadas and mosquitoes; that will get anyone out of anywhere," I replied. "When the tunnels aren't wet they are very dry, just like the area. There is a trap door to the tunnels just north of the city in someone's backyard; that's how I got out. I was walking for a good three miles: first west then south and then around to the north. It was not pleasant. All I had was a pen-light and a cell phone, which I alternated in use."

"I would have been scared shitless," Agent Won pulled up a map of the area and I pointed to the cave where I entered and exited.

"The door in the ground, of which there are many in that area, is somewhere around here," I leaned over here and used the mouse. "I remember because I borrowed a bike to get me back to my safe house, which was in the western part of the city."

"Hang on a second," Won typed, clicked, and the computer beeped and the screen jumped and stalled, jumped, blacked-out, and a new program backlit in green appeared. "Hold onto your hat," she started clicking like mad. "Okay, here are the geographic and soil inputs, scanned by the satellite terrain and density and infrared." The density scans showed traces of the tunnels.

"Okay, so focus on the areas of this map which are cooler," I directed and she clicked-to.

"Wow," she commented.

"Damn. That was effective," I added.

"I need to get this to cartography," Won said as we stared at the screen. "You are the best!" she kissed my cheek as she passed in the tight space.

I wonder if the gate swings both ways. A brief but intense fantasy flashed through my head; the guard interrupted it as he took my arm and helped me out of the closet. "Okay," I said to no one in particular as I breathed open air again.

"This way," he kept a hand on me and we returned to my cell. Waiting for me in a sealed plastic bag was a dozen chocolate chip cookies. I lay on the bed and listened to the cell next door. A man was yelling in Frarabic. It was not polite. I crossed to the door and knocked.

"What's wrong?" The guard answered.

"May I tell him to shut up? He's on my nerves."

"If you can get him to shut up I will give you my candy bar," he replied and the door clicked open. I saw a strap and picked it up.

"We're being recorded right?" I checked outside the belligerent's door. The guard nodded the affirmative and opened the door. He watched and learned as the bull charged, was caught in the strap and thrown into the wall. The man was cuffed and we laid him on his mattress. I climbed on top and got the feel of the strap.

"What are you doing?" he asked in Arabic.

"Shhh…relax," I looped the strap gently around his neck. "It doesn't have to hurt."

"What do you want?!"

"It's okay," I said comfortingly and traced his carotid arteries. "We were going to wait, but since you seem to be out of answers and you're causing such noise," I told him in Arabic. He silenced immediately and started panting.

"Wait, wait, please love of God wait!"

"Well you're just not being honest with us! Why should I hold onto you?"

"Let me live; I will tell you things."

"What things? You don't know things."

"I do. I will give you my list; tell you where Ahan-din is!"

"All I ask is a little honesty," I replied in the same serial killer sing-song voice. "I could do good things for you," I stroked his jaw line. "All we want is the truth, some cooperation in exchange for your life. You could walk in the sun again," I leaned in close "fresh air," I seduced. "What do you think, sergeant?" I asked in English and popped off of him. "I can wait if you think it's worth it."

He picked up the game immediately. "One day won't hurt," he shrugged.

"Think hard, and stop that noise," I said in Arabic. "They'll talk to you. Don't make me come too soon," I gave him a sympathetic look and walked out to let the guard release him. In the hall, I waited as he strutted out and barred the door.

"Was that good for you, because it was good for me," I said as he opened my door. When he didn't reply I walked through and he closed me in. Then he opened the window so we could talk.

"I was not expecting that, but well done!"

"Did you think I would go in and kick his ass?"

"Yeah," he admitted after a few seconds.

"Were you going to help?" I asked with a friendly tone.

"Not my job," he replied professionally.

"Keep your candy; I have cookies from your colonel."

"We really shouldn't be talking."

"You're absolutely right. I would sway you with my charms, and Court Martials are fun to watch but not to play in," I backed up. "Besides, now I smell like him. Think I'll shower before dinner."

He shut the window and I rinsed off the smell of prison and the mountain of mousse. My hair was considerably easier to wash though.

"I want to talk to you," I recognized Agent McEwen's voice from behind the curtain and quickly covered myself as I dried off. I peeked, and it was only his voice.

"Well I'm here," I replied and got dressed, wrapping the towel as a turban.

"I want to know why you just did what you did."

"Shits and giggles," I replied. "Wait, which just did done are you talking about?"

"Going into that man's cell."

"Oh, that actually was shits and giggles. He was making a racket; I wanted to rest, so I shut him up. More accurately, I opened his vulnerability to interrogation while simultaneously satisfying my primal urge to mess with people."

"And before that?"

"Agent Won listens to me. Those who ask receive."

"And before that?"

"You know damn well what I would do to take out some of these terror cells. So if that includes transliteration of a tome large enough to serve as a dinner table, then it shall be. I'm not chattel here, it's more like employment."

"You are a prisoner, you get that, right?"

"Let's see, handcuffs, cell, uniform, guards with guns, stun device attached, yeah, I think I might have gotten that impression," I shook my hair out and toweled it again.

"Director Goode wants you to begin our surveillance project tomorrow morning."

"But you don't want to work with me anymore," I read from his tone.

"Quite the contrary. I just wanted to test your mental and emotional state."

"And how do they test?" I hung up the towel.

"Adequately. Very adequately. Would you like to have dinner?"

I grabbed a hair band and looped my tresses into a bun. "Sure."

"Then I'll meet you in your office," he said and a clicking noise sounded like he had hung up.

About ten minutes later, he joined me with two Styrofoam containers of food. It looked like a bastardized Mongolian dinner. It was good.

"So, what time are you escaping?" he asked as we finished up.

"You know, you insult your own intelligence when you ask questions like that," I replied dryly and opened my beverage.

"How?" he baited.

I didn't fall for it for a moment. "If you had done your homework, you would know that I already know enough about this facility to map it out. If you had any brains whatsoever, you would realize that I am fully capable of escaping if given the motivation. If you were mentally present yesterday...should I go on? Don't ask stupid questions."

"You can't escape."

"Correction: I can't escape without killing someone," I threw back at him with my coldest eyes.

"How did you feel when you shot Ben-Adat and he fell to the ground and died?"

Psychologists. I rolled my eyes. "My only concern was that the guard had already killed him and I wasn't doing any good," I replied. "That man tried at least twice to kill me. I didn't take it personally the first time around, but this time he could have killed a child, and I take that very personally."

"So how did you feel when you realized that you had done it?"

"Safer. It doesn't bother me at all," I changed my voice to mimic his, "And why doesn't it bother you, Belle?" I asked myself. "Because once I've made the decision and the declaration that someone is going to die, it is already done. He said he was here to kill me; I told him he was here to die. When we lied to Israel and I told him that Ben-Adat was dead, it was already in the making. His escape and stupid attempt to kill me in custody was convenient, and certainly not planned on my part. I'm not lying," I informed him because he seemed amused. "I don't lose sleep at night because of people I've killed. I lose sleep because of those I have not killed. No, you're not on the list."

"Good. Now, how do you feel when you're interrogating?"

"There is no 'feeling' during an interrogation. None. Ever. There is the point, the information, and how to get it and making sure it's good. Emotions kill interrogations

129

faster than acid on an ant hill. You know better," I admonished.

"You feel nothing during an interrogation," he restated.

"Correct."

"Nothing."

"Not as an interrogator, no. Could we skip the crap and get to the good stuff?"

"You got a hot date?" he asked.

"No, I've got a tunnel to start digging," I replied sarcastically and stood up. "Goodbye," I walked toward the door, halfway expecting it to work.

"We're not done here," he called and the soldier blocked the path.

"Why are you playing these childish games?" I demanded to know as I returned to him.

"I'm trying to provoke a temper tantrum to see what exactly sets you off," he said and he was being honest.

I laughed hard as I returned to my seat. As I caught my breath, I placed a hand on the table. "I'm sorry, that was so…pop! There it went. I love it. Okay, what sets me off…insulting something I'm vain about, for one," I listed and he started making notes. I let my mind empty and wander for a few minutes before returning to vigilance. He seemed pleased.

"You are the most fascinating person I know," he revealed.

"I really hate psychologists," I replied warmly.

"Hey, it's not like I'm asking about your childhood trauma or anything," he defended. "Alright, we're done. Go back to your cell," he stood up.

"It's my office!" I pointed. "I am allowed to be here."

"I'll see you tomorrow," Tom called to me. "Please take her back to her cell for the night," he told the Marine.

"You don't want to play power games with me, Agent McEwen," I stood up and called after him.

He stuck his shiny face back in the doorway. "I win," he ducked out again. I straightened my chair and scowled.

"Miss," the guard said.

"I know Sergeant. I'm coming," I replied and finished straightening the chairs.

"Would it be alright if I handcuffed you?" he asked as we met each other in the doorway.

"If you feel it is appropriate, sure, knock yourself out," I replied stoically. "I've certainly cuffed my share of people, although that was mostly for fun," I presented my arms, palms facing upward. He was busy talking to his radio. It must have said something interesting, because suddenly he grabbed one of my arms and we returned rapidly to the center of the room. The Sergeant whipped a set of handcuffs on me and the leg of the desk with remarkable speed, and soon I was pretty stationary in one of the wooden guest chairs.

"Sorry about that." Captain Stover walked in and assessed the situation. From the way he looked at me, the Sergeant, and me again, I could see the wheels turn.

"I told him that it was a good idea to take whatever measures," I excused. "Let's face it; I'm not a little girl."

The cuffs were removed within seconds.

"We are transferring the prisoner to an interrogative unit, now that he seems complacent." Captain Stover said.

"Can Agent McEwen order me back to my cell when I'm here?" I asked.

"Yes, I'm afraid that agents overrule you. My men have orders on those lines."

I nodded to myself. "I've never resisted your men, with one exception."

"Yes, relations seem good. I think everyone here knows who they're dealing with. I admire your maturity."

"Thank you, captain. I admire your security; you aren't afraid of me so you treat me better."

"So you wouldn't kill one to escape?"

"It would take a lot," I replied succinctly.

"What did you say to the Algerian?"

"I told him that if he made himself useful and told the truth I might not kill him."

"He bought that?"

"I can be extremely persuasive," I locked eyes with him for a moment.

"How long have you been doing this?"

My eyes closed and I sat back. "Long enough,"

"You disappeared off of the face of the planet when you were 16."

I said nothing, staring hard at his foot. I didn't realize I had stopped breathing until Stover had called my name and shaken my shoulder.

"Hey, breathe! Belle,"

I was vaguely aware as he moved and started shaking my back. I took a breath in a short gasp and my lungs rejected it and my body shook and I tried again.

"Come on Belle," Stover pleaded and lowered my head to my knees. I hyperventilated, making a lot of noise. Someone bared my arm; I felt a prick and realized the medic was there just before I blacked out.

I realized I was on the floor when I saw shoes in my direct line of vision. I heard men talking.

"What the hell happened?" Tom's voice asked.

"She just snapped. We were talking about how long she's been involved in her activities." Stover explained.

"Someone should stay with her for a while," the medic said as he took my pulse.

"What happened, Belle?" Tom asked and helped me sit up.

"I don't remember," my voice sounded odd. He leaned me against the wall and stepped outside with Captain Stover for a few minutes.

"You know, I'm starting to like you," the medic joked with me as my head cleared. I think I managed a weak smile for him. "Hey, just to make sure you don't go blue in the face, someone should hang out with you for a few hours. Got any ideas?"

"Agent Won," I replied groggily; the men returned.

"Alright, up we go," Tom said softly and helped me get on my feet. "Here we go."

"It might be a good idea to call Agent Won to stay with her," the guard suggested.

"Great idea," Tom replied and wrapped one of my arms around his shoulders. We walked awkwardly and slowly to my cell. The woman guard stayed with me until Won arrived, and she jumped right into the impromptu slumber party.

"What we need in here is a bean bag chair," she declared. "This will be so much better in your new rooms. I bet you'll be in there soon; the paint is drying."

"It sounds really cool. There is room here for you," I scooted over on the bed and she joined me.

"Really, this is one of the nicest cells I've ever been in."

"Thanks. Are your people happy?"

"My people are very happy." She touched my hair bun. I took it down and shook my mane out. Her eyes smiled at me and I felt like I might be blushing. "I like it shorter."

"It suits you nicely. I had my hair super short once."

"I think we've all done that at one stage," I laughed a little. We kept chatting until the door opened.

"Guess it's time to go. Goodnight," she said and tucked my hair behind my ear. I felt warm and fuzzy and sauntered over to the sink to brush my teeth.

A minute or two later I heard a knock on the door and flushed quickly before peeking around the curtain. The door clicked open.

"Friendly neighborhood medic!" the old wiry medic called before a guard entered with him. "How's it going?" he asked conversationally as I stared at the two men.

"Have a seat," the guard gestured to the stool and spoke calmly to me. I sauntered to the stool and sat apprehensively with my hands pulling at my shirt.

"I just want to talk," the medic said, "and give you a shot."

"I'm listening."

"First I want to listen to your heart," he said and stepped behind me to hear it from the rear. "I think I know what happened when you were a teenager."

I took a deep breath. "It's not what you think."

"You ran away to Canada, where you were admitted for treatment as a Jane Doe for lacerations indicative of being whipped by something sharp on your legs. Your arms indicated bondage, as did your ankles."

"No," I denied.

"You claimed they were the result of falling on a bale of barbed wire. We have the blood-soaked clothes the Canadians kept. We'll just match the DNA."

"I was not engaged in criminal activity at that time. It doesn't matter."

"You want them to get away with it?"

"Why not? I always did," I replied and shifted uncomfortably on the stool.

"You were sixteen and someone tortured you. The FBI is interested. Plus, some of the scars are still there."

"Take off my left shoe," I closed my eyes and felt him remove the shoe and sock. I lifted the foot.

"Cigar," he recognized it. I pulled up my shirt to expose my left ribs. "Light shrapnel," I dropped the shirt and pulled my pants down on the right side to expose the pelvis. "Cattle prod?"

"For goats," I conceded. "These are more recent and far more interesting, don't you think? Besides, whatever happened to me before I became who I am is unimportant. I am me," I took a deep breath and let it out. "Besides, the person is on American soil. He's out of my reach."

"Well he is well within ours," the guard said.

"Someone will talk about this with you tomorrow. I'm going to give you a shot to help you sleep and keep your heart rate under control."

I slid off of the stool and backed away. "I don't want to talk about it. There's nothing to talk about," I'll admit my tone was sharp.

"Nothing. I'm totally wrong?" he asked and I hit the wall.

"It's none of your fucking business!" I raised my voice. "Why the hell do you care? I didn't kill anyone back then; I was just another teenage girl with nowhere to go. So I went. And if you'll check your files you'd know I didn't just fall off the face of the earth: I made several attempts before I got it right," I was regaining ground inside myself. "What the hell do you care, nobody cared back then and I guarantee, all around the world, no one cares right now. Missing and exploited my ass; we were the only adults in the room. No

135

one misses us. Given the shot now, I can promise that I wouldn't miss them."

I came to within two feet of him and stared dead on. "You want to see my scars?" I turned my back to him and the guard, dropped my pants, and stripped off my long shirt until I was in my underwear. I let him have a good look before I turned around and lifted my right arm behind my head. "Glass bottle," I showed him. I pulled my hair up to expose a scar which was nearly gone. "Curling iron held to my head. Shrapnel, two bullets, and a car bomb. You come in here all pretentious and Doctor Phil and want to know my dark little secrets? Don't look at me like I'm some poor little kitty left in the rain. I've been blown up more times than a Jewish deli in Palestine!" I pulled my pants back on. "No one misses Ali Johnston. And there's at least one person who misses Belle Jones, who has never been missed or exploited in her entire life," I finished calmly, holding part of my weight on the stool.

The medic collapsed onto my bed. "Wow."

"You want to calm down?" The guard asked as I took a deep breath.

"Would you like to give me the shot?" I asked in a smaller voice and the medic stood back up.

He appeared to be visually examining me. "How old are you?"

"Twenty-four, unless it's after January."

"How many of them are still out there? The ones who did this to you."

He had these puppy dog eyes. I mentally counted from toe to head. "Dead, dead, took each other out, that one took care of himself but I riffed up their new shipments of explosives anyway; dead now, alive," I said of the goat-prod, "I think, anyway, died in the gutter, my personal favorite, he disappeared entirely," I pointed to the curling iron scar, "and this one was from falling out of a tree," I pointed to the very small scar on my eyebrow.

"So two men."

"Two men, one woman," I corrected, pointing at my behind and then my hip in order. "Most men don't do sadistic things on their own. Buddy system," I shrugged.

He gave me a shot and paused just before exiting. "Thank you," he said quietly. I sat on the stool until they slammed the door again.

"Fine," I said to myself and went to bed. "Stupid freaking psychologists," I tucked myself in and after a while they killed the lights. "I totally kicked his butt," I muttered to myself.

Morning came with lights and knocking and all its groggy glory.

"What?"

"Thirty minutes," he said and slid a hot breakfast in.

"Ooh, pancakes," I was coaxed out of bed and ate breakfast on the floor there. Thirty minutes later I met Tom in an observation room.

"Okay, go on in," Tom said into the speaker. On one of the monitors, an interrogator and interpreter entered the room. Tom turned up the sound and I sat and listened. It took all of four minutes for me.

"Native speaker needed, preferably an Arab. He separates himself too strongly from western culture and tradition. Is it possible to zoom in on his face?" I asked and the screen refocused. "What about his hands? There. See that? Chemical burns. That little pox mark on his left cheek was probably low quality shrapnel, like something exploded prematurely. He isn't going to say anything in this interview. He's totally isolated."

"I agree. You sure you never had formal training?"

"In what? People reading? Hola, I'm a spy?"

"Hola, right. What about this guy?" he switched screens. The man who I hadn't killed yesterday was writing quickly and nervously as a stone faced agent faced him silently.

"He thinks if he doesn't cooperate a lot, I may just kill him," I explained. "Noisy neighbor, so I may have psychologically tortured him a little. Emphasize that we only want the truth, nothing else."

"Alright. The third man isn't in for another few minutes, so it looks like we have some time. How are you feeling?"

"Fine. The medic saw me last night," I replied vaguely.

"And got an earful, from what I heard."

I shot him a 'you know better' look.

"I'm sorry all of that happened to you. I knew you had background trauma, but it always stings more to put facts in place of idea. I won't ask any questions, but if you ever want to talk about any of those incidents, my ears are yours," he offered paternally.

I looked away and realized that I couldn't breathe. I started taking shallow breaths and I reached out to touch him lightly.

"Okay, its okay, stay calm. Can you breathe at all?"

"What….s…..ha…" I uttered. He whipped out his phone and called it in while the guard lifted me from my chair to lie on the floor. Tom got my pulse and I knew my heart was racing.

"You're going to be okay. I believe this is an anxiety attack in a severe form. Try to relax, and don't worry: help is on the way."

"I'm…not…anxious!" I said between breaths.

"It's not about how you feel; it's what's going on in your brain," he explained quickly as Susan the medic came in. A lot of things happened very quickly, and suddenly I was on a gurney being hurtled down the hall with an oxygen supply up my nose and straps holding me down and one of those stupid beeping devices.

When I finally started to recognize my surroundings again, I was in a small white room with sticky hospital tags on my chest and arms and an EKG machine sitting in the odd corner. Susan walked in with a chart.

"Do you know where you are?"

"I'm guessing the clinic. Is something wrong with me?"

"Do you know what your name is?"

"Yes."

"Okay. I will be right back," she left and I realized that my arms had been soft-strapped to the bed. I could hear two men talking to each other, but I couldn't discern words. I closed my eyes and let my head rest.

"Belle?" Tom McEwen called from the foot of the bed.

"Oh, hi," I wiggled a little to prop my head up.

"Describe the scar on your hip," he requested.

"The bullet or the goat-prod?" I replied. "The bullet looks like a typical gunshot wound: the metal ripped through the flesh and part of the bone. They were able to retrieve it, so there are surgery marks as well as the actual circular," I tried to talk with my hands and found them restrained. "You know, bullet. The goat prod was a beaut to clean up. It's essentially a third degree burn, so I had to keep dressing the wound. I went to a friend and he cleaned it up a lot for me. It healed at a much better rate. It's hard to assess your own ass." We had a polite laugh.

"What about your hand?"

139

"Ninja star. How hokey is that? One actually killed someone that day, until Argo opened fire and mowed them down. Martial arts must meet metal. It healed fine."

"Right arm?"

"Glass bottle in the middle of a really interesting row. I was just collateral damage there. It bled a lot, but it seems to have recovered."

"The curling iron?"

"Excellent torture device, especially on men. This particular man was a chemical weapons smuggler who wanted to know what I knew. A third party intervened for their own purposes, and I have reason to believe he was dissolved in a very corrosive acid. What's wrong with me?"

"We're working on it. Tell me about the two men who shackled you and whipped your legs and butt."

"I told you not to go there," I said firmly. "Look kid, I've been tortured by professionals for information. I am very capable of keeping my mouth shut."

"So being incarcerated and losing control of some basic things of life doesn't increase your emotional pressure which has kept you alive up to this point?"

Reality hit me like a brick wall. "Oh."

He let me chew on that thought for a moment. "Everyone is mentally affected by incarceration. First you defied, then fought, then deceptively accepted, but your body was still on survival mode."

"Okay," I weighed the new information. "So…"

"I don't know. We're looking at a lot of things right now. I know that your heart is okay and the baby's heartbeat is audible and appears healthy. I have to go," he stood up and unstrapped my wrists, "because people are lining up to bore me to death. Right now I need you to stay here, stay calm, they need to observe you for a little while. I brought something for you."

He reached out of the door and produced a small bag. "These are copies of some of your tools and this is a GSA lock. Think you're up to it?"

"Is there a stethoscope in there?"

"It's a medical steth, but yes."

"Excellent," I rededicated myself to my new diversion. It was a difficult lock and I lost my place when Susan came in and did an airway strength test.

If there is anything that moves more slowly than time spent while bored, I don't know what it is, but it's probably dead. I had studied the tiles of the ceiling, examined each of my appendages to great length, braided my hair six different ways, and discovered that standing on the bed will get me the guard's attention. I decided I must be in the agent side of the clinic because the bathroom had a door and a toilet seat. They brought me lunch, and then dinner, and then my pajamas and dolphin.

I slept there that night, waking to the actual sunrise through the well-frosted window. The lock had been open since 9 the night before, and I hung it from my bed frame as a trophy. With breakfast I was given a coloring book and some crayons. For a person like me, death by boredom is entirely possible, so I started coloring. The lady medic came in and checked my vital signs and said I was doing really well and they were working on getting an anti-anxiety medication for preggos like me.

She left and in walked Tom McEwen. "Ready to get out of here?"

"Definitely," I commented and got into the golf cart. We went to the therapy building.

"You feel alright?"

"Yes," I replied as we entered the building only to take a left instead of a right.

"You're not going to therapy," he explained. "Well, not couch-and-tea therapy anyway." He led me through a series of halls and doorways and into a medium sized gymnasium with familiar mats. Agent Won was waiting dressed in traditional martial arts gear.

"Come on, get changed, we'll take a few laps around to warm up, and then you are going down," she greeted warmly.

I grabbed the offered clothes and dashed off quickly. I was changed and my hair was contained within a minute and a half. Ten minutes later after warming up and stretching, as well as donning light protective gear, we bowed to each other.

It was fast action, tense, certain, controlled, liquid, flying, rolling, pressing, folding, sweat-dripping into the eyes, heart-pumping combat. My skills were rusty at first, but I warmed up after a few tumbles. Tom called out "Time!" and we broke apart.

"You are out of practice!" Won said as we both got water.

"Hello, been sitting in a jail cell for a month or two?" I laughed. "They frown on it when I practice with the guards or agents. Remember the cracked ribs and meat face?" I sat down. "I know my balance is off."

"You are still very good. Your rhythm is intelligent."

"Thank you. I used to do stuff."

"Like?"

I put the water down and stepped onto the open mat. I did a simple double backflip and adjusted my mental balance before slipping into an old floor routine. Tom and Won clapped when I finished. I walked back.

"Okay, I'm dizzy."

"Good," Won did a hand-spring and landed directly in front of me. She tried an arm strike but I blocked, trapped, and threw her. She recovered quickly and waited for me to charge, so I didn't. We did a futile series of maneuvers, exchanged tosses, and broke apart by order of the guard.

"Alright, alright. Stop with the Kung Fu."

"I was doing Tai Kwando and Judo," Won replied.

"Mine was mostly Aikido and Jujitsu, mixed with a little Tai-Jutsu," I added.

"Kung Fu is totally different," Won stated.

"Whatever. Hit the showers; pris-," he stopped himself. "Belle, you have a set of clean clothes waiting in the showers."

Won entered the stall next to mine. "Good practice," she commented before turning her shower on.

"Yeah," I replied and hurried it along. The hot water felt good. "What's next?" I asked as I exited the locker room.

"Personally, it's time for me to spend an hour or so answering emails. I don't know what's on your schedule," she replied. "Thanks for the workout."

"This way," a guard poked his head around the corner. He was almost smiling. We went up two flights of stairs, and I was about to make a joke about watching my heart rate when a man with dark skin and blond hair opened the door for us. I recognized him as a fake bake and started to study him when I saw the other ten people in the room.

Three were shades of brown from Henna dye. Three were geeks, positing different programs. Two were attempting to do gymnastics wearing handcuffs. One looked perfectly normal, standing in front of a camera held by a natural-looking dyed man.

143

"Here we see the accumulative collaboration of the intelligence departments to confirm and apply lessons brought to us by the new asset. We've seen the variation in effectiveness of the henna dye techniques based on race and coloring. Here at the first station, we have thermo-graphic imaging running on specific areas of interest. This has led to a handful of discoveries listed in the report appendix F. At this station, we see scenarios running through a database."

"What do you think, Miss Belle?" The Aryan asked me.

"You need to dye your hair, brows, beard and body hair. It's possible. Then some colored contacts," I analyzed. "They," I turned to the two who had stopped fighting. "Need to learn to be one handed. It will help a lot. I used to tie one hand to my belt."

"Yeah, this is hard," one of the fighting men admitted as he unchained himself.

"Have a seat," the man in front of the camera said and directed me to a table where we sat on the same side. "So, we're here with the asset. Any comments?"

I stared at him for a moment. "Um."

"What does it feel like to see your work coming into play?" he asked me.

"Well, every piece of intelligence is worth something. I learned in the field, and that's where things really happen," I managed to say.

"In a way, you're somewhat of a hero to some of the men and women here; being able to give so much information about things we haven't had access to."

"I'm not a hero. I like to think of myself more as a "helper", kind of a guardian angel of the actual heroes."

"Tell me about your work in counterterrorism."

"Well the first thing about counterterrorism which everyone seems to forget is the mindset. You can't be afraid.

You can't be discouraged or deterred by bombs or threats. If you want to fight terrorism, you have to fight terror and the people who inflict it. I usually fight it with a round to the forehead," I said with a touch of dark humor. He looked amused and slightly intimidated. "It's like fighting devout gangs. Sometimes it can get very bloody. Sometimes you knock down the head and everything scatters like dust in the wind," I shared.

"What advice would you give to someone about to go into the field?"

"Know the area and watch the people. Watch how they move, how they talk, what their body looks like. Homemade bombs are usually heavy. I have greatly benefited from learning how to be silent; learning to listen."

"What about the years you've spent in the field, the personas and identities you've owned: what can you tell us about that?"

"Not much," I replied succinctly.

"Your fighting skills were primarily taught abroad, correct?"

"I learned from each experience," I answered.

"How old are you?"

"I'm twenty-four. I started learning Arabic with my mom when I was fourteen. She was killed in 9-11. I was always good with languages though. I learned French pretty well in seventh and eighth grade. I used programs like Rosetta Stone® to learn some other languages and dialects."

"Incredible," he said and apparently saw a cue I missed. "Thank you," he said and the man put the camera away. The camera man stayed; the interviewer left.

"I'm from the CIA, Agent Smith," he introduced.

"If you want to talk to me, you have to tell me who you are," I replied, seeing directly through the alias.

"CIA. Smith," he replied.

I shook my head. "Nope."

"I don't care if you believe me, that's who I am."

"Okay, fine. My name is Martha Washington. I'm from the Department of Agriculture," I replied.

"They said you might be annoying."

"Listen, Smithy; I'm touchy about people lying to me. You're clearly not CIA or you would have said DOD. That leaves DIA, Homeland Security, NIA or GOA, Secret Service, NSA. Oh, NSA. Fine. About time they got into this. I mean you, Mr. Smith."

"Alright, let's say I am not from the CIA, but I am involved in this project and I report to an Agency. Would that work?"

"Absolutely. Is there enough light for your camera-watch? You should wear that on your left wrist. I know you're not left-handed, or ambidextrous, so wearing it on your right wrist is a giveaway."

"Are you even trained in intelligence? Did you even graduate high school?"

"Yes. I whizzed my GED. Perfect score. If my father had been looking, he might have found me then, but I disappeared before anyone asked questions. Seven years actively doing what I'm doing and staying alive? That's worth at least a Masters in Espionage, counterterrorism, geography, and languages."

"You're very smart," he meant it as a compliment. "Do you know how many people can get a perfect score on the GED?"

"Less than one percent," I replied. "Would you like to check your recording?"

"I think we're breaking for lunch," he said and I smelled pizza. It made me extremely nauseous.

"Oh God," I covered my nose. "I can't...I'm going," I stuttered.

"Belle," The guard called and I practically ran out. We went to another floor and I took some breaths. "Would you like something to eat?"

"Yes. Baklava. Just not pizza."

"I have an apple," Agent Starr entered with a lunch box. "How's it going?"

"I can't take the smell of pizza, apparently."

"Who can?" She handed me the apple. "Did you say 'baklava'?"

"I first became addicted in Israel. It was a German bakery," I said.

"That sounds really good," she said and started texting. I bit into the apple. "What do you want to do next?"

"I'm a little tired," I said and she produced a soda. "Does cyber need anything?"

"Not at the moment. Oh!" her phone rang and she picked it up immediately. "Starr...yes ma'am. Building three, ma'am. Good condition. No ma'am, not yet. I'll ask her ma'am," she put the phone aside and said, "Chicken soup for lunch?" to me. I nodded. "Yes ma'am. I have it here. Understood," she hung up and I finished the apple. "Please take one of these," she handed me a little yellow pill.

"Can I wash the apple off of my face?" I requested as she gathered everything up.

"There's a restroom down the hall here," Starr offered. We used it together and walked briskly out of the building and into a golf cart with armed guard. We arrived at the primary building.

"You know why we're here, right?" she asked in the elevator.

"Director Goode," I replied.

"Right," she confirmed. The elevator dinged and we arrived. We walked briskly until I saw three men in suits and a strangely uniformed soldier. "Oy," Starr said and we stopped.

"Isabelle Jones," the tallest man said as he matched my face to a photograph. He pulled out a set of handcuffs and my guard stepped forward.

"Sir, you have negative access to this person," the guard said.

"Fuck access, I hunted for her for four years; I'm taking her," he said and his guard stepped toward me. Starr pulled out her weapon and the guard called a code. Foreign agent number three grabbed my forearm and yanked me toward him.

"Belle, don't kill," Starr directed and I nearly fractured the man's patella before tossing him on the ground. I assisted Starr with the guard, and lifted a gun. The struggle was short and ended with two men cuffed to each other, the guard shocked and tied, and the one man backing into a corner. Backup arrived late.

"On the ground!" a man ordered.

"Belle, put the gun down and get on the ground," one of my familiar guards said as he pointed a rifle at my head. A laser beam appeared on my breast.

I took a step back before lowering my weapon.

"Belle?" Sullivan asked as he continued to aim at me. I bent my knees until the gun touched the ground and then I slid it toward them.

"You got it, Sully," I replied and Agent Starr retrieved it.

"Down! On the ground!" he insisted and I put my hands on my head and put my other knee down. If they wanted me any lower, they'd have to help. As soon as I was down they hoisted me back up and frisked me.

"Great job. Everyone done being stupid? Alright then," Starr said. "Natalie, it's safe to come out from under your desk now."

"Who are you?" I re-cornered the lead man and I felt a hand on my shoulder. "CIA, DIA, NSA, MI-6? Trust me, if they give you to me, you will tell me things."

"Well done, Belle. Now back away from the man so I can have him," Captain Stover appeared and I followed his directions.

"Good god," Director Goode walked in to the spectacle and observed for a moment. "Right, you're cleaning this up, Captain? Good. Ladies, my office."

Starr, Natalie, and I went into the office, followed by the soldier on my detail. He shut the door behind him.

"Interagency Star Wars," Goode said as she plopped into her chair and took a deep breath. "Ms. Jones, you have the right to have that scrimmage out there explained to you. Were you hurt in combat?"

"No ma'am. Actually, it was rather fun," I replied and sat across from her. "No need to explain. I already have a pretty good idea."

"Alright. Things have been reported, analyzed, and approved regarding certain changes in your stay here. You have more respect, more privacy, and considerably better living conditions. You will need to yield to occasional mental examinations in addition to your routine physicals. We would like to bring you in on certain operations here, writhing through our technical and legal restraints. You will have the right to keep some foods in your room. We can't give you a newspaper or television, but if you want books or a general magazine, we can give you outdated but reasonably recent versions. You can have DVDs. If you would like to contact the father of the child, it can be arranged."

"He doesn't know," I replied, hanging tight to my secret lover. "He doesn't know."

"Alright. The soup should be here soon. Agent Starr, you will receive a message. Perhaps you could calm Natalie down. I need to go yell at people."

I stood with her. "Thank you, ma'am."

She smiled warmly to me and left.

Natalie looked less terrified than usual. "That was so cool!" she finally uttered with a squeak. "Can I do stuff like that?"

"Sure, I could teach you that thing I did with my elbow," I laughed a little at her enthusiasm. "When he grabbed me, he also blew his own center of gravity. You take that, you can take anyone down," I explained and stood up.

"No," the guard said and I sat right back down.

"Engage without making contact," Starr qualified and I stood again, cautiously.

"The male center of gravity is right here," I showed her as she came to face me. "So every time they pull, they lose that center. It works for them when they push. Girls' center is in our baby maker. No brainer, right? So," I struggled to teach without contact, "Say a man grabs your upper arm and pulls. You grab him by that arm and yank toward you, pull it toward your core. Do it very quickly. Then, with the other arm, pop! Chin, nose, mouth, throat, he will release your arm. So grab, snag, pop," I described and watched her perform the maneuver.

The soup arrived and I ate while Starr and Natalie chatted. It was very good.

"No baklava yet," Starr announced after a while. I had stretched out on the couch. "Now you've got me craving it."

It was worth a smirk, so I gave her one. "God this baby thing is going to kill me. I used to do," I caught myself "all kinds of really gross things and it never made me sick. Now I smell pizza and puke."

"What's the grossest thing you've ever done?" Natalie asked innocently.

"I performed surgery a few times. That's some nasty shit. Sometimes when you're out there, really out there, you get what you can. In this case, I helped a nurse stitch up where a man had been gored in the belly."

"That must have been really hard. Did he recover?"

"We'll never know. He was shot a few days later in a firefight."

"Were you?"

"Not in that fight," I gave her a motherly smile.

"Right. Sorry. Did you get the guys who killed him?"

"Yeah. I did. They got the nurse too, so that made it my fight."

"Sounds like a superhero comic or something."

"Trust me; it is not at all like a comic book. Blood sprays, teeth flying, metal flinging, guns firing, screams and shouts, and then sometimes all you can hear is your own breathing, and it is too loud, but you can't breathe any quieter, and the need for air really presses on you. Sometimes, in here, you need air. It feels like you just need air; space to think, time to decide, something actually giving when I push. They would keep me locked away until I die if I let them. I'm not finished yet," I nearly whispered. "I have work to do," I stated in my normal business voice. "Starr, can I go to the cyber closet?"

"No."

"I have a new coding idea."

"No."

"Can I talk to Agent Won then?"

"Yes. I'll give her a call," she dialed and spoke. "Really? Right, see you then," she said and waited for someone to knock. Agent Won walked in less than a minute after the call.

"There's still some blood spatter on the walls," she observed. "Well done."

"She would like to talk to you about some new coding idea," Starr replied professionally.

"I can't go to the closet right now," I explained.

"No, you can't. What's up?" She came over and we sat on the couch while I explained my idea.

"I think I can help design a program which would constantly decode encrypted messages, regardless of send-and-receive points."

"I've seen it," she said.

"But I can make it target-specific, if you know what I mean."

Her eyes lit up. "Really?"

"Really. All of those millions of things we intercept every minute, we can weed those out in a way which focuses on real threats or real networks."

"How?"

"Same way Israel sorts its mail."

"That would be brilliant. You're on lockdown but get some sleep. As soon as you're not locked down, we're gonna be up all night," she was excited. "I'll start with what we have."

"Remember the modeling I showed you? It's the only one that works."

"Right. Integrated beehive. You're a genius," Won almost ran out.

I flopped back onto the couch and closed my eyes. Calculations were running in my head, but they had nothing to do with the new analysis system.

Chapter 7: Homeland Insecurity

I woke up because someone rustled a paper. I saw Agent Tomopolis reading a newspaper on the chair next to me. Naturally I sat up a little to study him.

"I know what you're thinking," he informed me calmly as he slowly folded the paper closed, ever so careful with the creases. "And I don't know what to do about it."

"Please, continue," I smoothed my clothes and came to rights.

"You are ready, pinned, confined, still highly mobile and capable, and very, very smart. So naturally you're working on a plan to escape. I understand! It must be driving you batty that it's driven you, well, slightly batty, to say it comically."

I smiled. George understood me. *Well that's going to be a problem in the long run.*

"I want you to know two things. One, life is changing around here and it's changing immediately. Two, you have been deemed highly valued and extremely dangerous. Would you like it spelled out?"

"The guards have a shoot to kill order," I replied.

"If you attempt escape and short measures fail, yes. The government has decided that for the next six months, at least, you cannot be released. They're good shots."

"I know. They're Marines."

"We're introducing creative therapy techniques, giving you access to the gym at odd hours, and changing your living conditions. We would like to put you to work doing more of the same thing you have been doing. We are going to catch Al-Zahrani."

"Catch or kill?" I queried.

"Hopefully capture alive. Not my call, at any rate. If you had really wanted him dead, you had your chance," he pointed.

"I want the music from my old laptop. It's just music, let Kmetz comb through it if needed. It's just too...dead in there," I requested and took a deep breath. I caught his eyes in mine. "George, am I ever going to leave this place?"

"At some time you will be declassified, your threat to national security will be voided, and I hope to God it will be soon. Then I believe we'll relocate you, give you a new identity and some boundaries, and leave you and your son or daughter to live your lives out in peace." He was being honest. "Yes, you will keep the child. The new living quarters are infant-safe: air filters, water is pure, so on, you get the idea."

Tears started leaking. I ignored them in hopes they would scoot. "So first we get Al-Zahrani and the bastard," I stated.

"Alexis, you and I both know that you placed yourself in my hands," he handed me a tissue. "I've never seen anyone as talented as you are in this field, and I've never even heard of a compassionate blackguard. I'm going to do for you as you have done for the world. You just hang in there. Tell me if I'm lying: you would know."

"I know. You're not," I caught my breath and smiled. "You should have seen the guys whose asses I kicked earlier. It was classic."

"I heard," he gave me a fatherly smile. "Two of them need stitches. They should have just asked politely. Tea?"

He presented a thermos and two cups. "Earl Grey or lemon?"

"Lemon please," I replied and caught a scent. "Do I smell Baklava?"

"Oh that's what it is!" George exclaimed dramatically, "I thought it was a fly trap." He produced a large plate of Baklava. "That is way too much honey for me. Enjoy."

Starr and I descended on it like lionesses on a fresh kill. My face was covered in honey and pastry flakes when I pulled back.

"Wow. I know what I'm getting you for Chanukah," George joked.

"I'm not really Jewish," I replied on the way to the bathroom. I wondered what the director would think if she saw me like that, doused in honey and flakes. "So who were the men in black?"

"What men in black?" he replied and I rolled my eyes. The phone rang and George picked it up. He set it on speakerphone after a few words.

"Miss Jones, can you hear me?" a male voice said.

I looked at George, who gave me a 'go on' gesture. "Yes."

"Clearly, we aren't going to get our hands on you. Our intentions were good if badly delivered. I've spoken to my superiors, who urged me to offer an olive branch to you and the task force. I would like to speak with you in person, and Director Goode has given her permission for that to occur later today," he seemed to hesitate for a moment. "To be honest, half of us are in the hospital because of you."

"This is Agent George Tomopolis," George intervened.

"Yes Agent Tomopolis," Director Goode's voice replied.

"Is it the intention to secure assurance that the meeting will not put our guest in the hospital?"

I laughed silently, covering my face.

"It would help relations, yes," Director Goode answered.

"To be perfectly frank, I couldn't give you that promise," George replied, sitting back in his chair.

"I was afraid of that. She appears to be hard to contain."

"That's well put," I responded, "However...Director Goode, would you like this to happen?" I requested.

"I would prefer it to happen today, yes," she replied.

"Then I will give my word not to physically harm or otherwise threaten," I replied clearly.

"How good is her word?" The other man said, clearly failing to block the sound.

"A damn lot better than yours is," I replied.

"What she said," Director Goode relayed. "Pick up please, George."

He did, they exchanged a few words, and he hung up. "Thank you Agent Starr. I believe you're off shift now."

"Goodbye," she said and left.

"Let's go," George put his jacket back on and straightened his tie. I straightened my jacket and pulled my hair into a bun. It was a short walk to the conference room down the hall. The guard posted himself outside while George and I entered and sat. A few minutes later Director Goode and the man whose palms and pits were sweating profusely came in.

"Alright, all set in here? Good," Goode left and I slowly stood to meet the man. After a few awkward jitters, he reluctantly held his hand out. I sat down.

"I promised to not touch you," I excused calmly. He sat across from George.

"Jameson, Homeland Security," he introduced and tried to get a grip.

"I'm Jones, Belle Jones."

"International assassin, spy, and smuggler and a great intelligence resource, as well as a mole of sorts in the Eurasian underworld," he summed.

"And Africa. Don't forget Africa and the Middle East."

"So you admit to it?"

"No. I'm definitely not an international assassin. Name someone I've assassinated."

"October 18, 2007," he mentioned the date of the Algerian.

"Ah, the day bits and pieces of an international child trafficker flew around. Good day. You know, they found the pieces of that bomb, but they disappeared. Turns out, it was the same model used by…well, you know."

"Moving along," George interrupted.

"Is she read in on Operation Waldo?" he asked George.

"She wrote Operation Waldo," he replied.

"I found Waldo."

Suddenly he turned aggressive. "I'm not above recommending enhanced interrogation techniques to acquire information."

"I'm not above throwing your sorry ass out the window," I replied stone-faced.

"You are withholding information that is vital to national security!" he practically yelled and slammed his hands on the table.

"That doesn't really do much for me," I replied simply. "I am not withholding," I tried and he interrupted.

"Where is the second data chip?!"

"Have you checked up your ass? That's where I'd like to put it," I answered quickly.

Jameson reached over and grabbed my left forearm tightly. "When I'm done with you," he started to say, but he was interrupted when I jerked my arm back toward me hard and his face hit the table.

"You are done with her," George said and walked me out and back to Director Goode's office.

"In my defense, I promised not to touch him. I said nothing about him touching the table," I entered.

"You should teach me some of that sometime." Director Goode said, totally unaffected and staring at her computer. "I saw and heard everything. Well done. Go show her to her room please, Agent Tomopolis. If he attacks on the way out, Belle, you may kick his ass."

"Yes ma'am."

The conference room door was closed and the three of us got into the elevator quietly.

"You do not mix well with Homeland Security," George observed.

"The man is nuts," I replied calmly.

"Is everything good to go?" he asked the guard.

"Yes sir," he said as we stopped and stepped out on the transferring floor.

"Am I going to do anything interesting today?" I asked as we walked through the barren halls.

"I thought slamming that man's face was interesting," George replied and we entered the other elevator. I winked at the guard.

The guard with me pressed the wrong button. He set it to the level above where I was supposed to be. I went with it. We met Captain Stover as the doors opened.

"Did you really just put a DHS man's face in a table?" he tried to be serious.

"He may have lost his balance while trying to break my arm," I replied innocently.

Stover pointed the dad finger at me. "You're not going to try it with us."

"FBI, DIA, NSA, USMC, you're all in the do not touch book. You know that, sir."

"C'mere you," he gestured and we poured out of the elevator. He grabbed my right arm gently and held it up. He found where the errant hand had been quickly. "So you just," he moved his arm around a little, "huh. I'll remember that one."

"We're not putting her on report for a little gravity," George stated.

"Well, come on then," he moved aside and led us through a door; a checkpoint followed by another door; and down a hall which seemed extremely quiet. I stared at an overly obvious portal. It was electronically secured, metal locks with pick resistant technology, and an old fashioned bolt. It was taller than Stover, which was an accomplishment in itself.

"Great door," I had to admire. "I might have been able to get through the first three parts, but that damn bolt. Old fashioned sometimes works the best," I reached up and opened a window which had enforced glass.

"Care to see inside?" George asked and the seal was breached.

The first thing I noticed was the smell. It was pleasant: a very light scent of vanilla and lavender. In captivity it was extremely strange and soothing. The door opened with beeps and clicks and revealed a little burst of sunshine with yellow walls and the promised special lighting window which gave me a very nice 'view' of the Grand Canyon. The bathroom stall had walls up to about four feet and then opaque glass or plastic up to the ceiling. The door was opaque glass. Next to that was a small desk with my laptop,

160

paper, pencils, and other materials set up for me. Then came the round table for two with chairs, and the refrigerator; one like you would find in a dorm room. The bed was in the middle of the room. Considering what I had gotten used to, it was all magnificent. There was a little light attached to the bed frame, and some comic books set on the chest of three drawers which was right next to the bed. I pulled a drawer open and found my clothes.

"Do you want to hear my spiel now or later?" Captain Stover asked. I had forgotten everyone.

"Yes, sorry," I shook it off and turned to face him, walking around the bed.

He turned to someone in the hall. "Morgan?"

A female guard came in and Stover shut the door behind her. He pulled up a seat, I perched on the bed, and she stood. "This is a weird new situation for everyone. This used to be two cells, so we immobilized one door but left a food slot in it," he gestured behind him. "That's where the food comes from. There's a dead zone around it because we're not going to have a repeat of the Ben-Adat issue."

"Good. I'd hate to have to shoot myself in the heart," I said with a little humor.

He smiled. "This quadrant is designed for you. Comfort, resources, and high security. The door here has a privacy screen you can pull: all details become blurred. You control the lights in here. We can override that, but you do have an on-off switch. The rest of the stuff in here, you can figure out. Rules: no men without female personnel in here. You do your own cleaning: supplies are right outside you just check them out. The laundry comes on Tuesdays, strip your bed every other week to be washed, put it all in that bag hanging there. Ditto for the towels. If at any time we think you're self-endangering or engaging in shenanigans, we will bust in and end the party. Clear?"

"Clear sir. Where is my dolphin?"

"Your dolphin is being held hostage in cyber, ma'am," Officer Morgan said with a straight face.

"Request permission to go rescue the dolphin?" I asked Captain Stover.

"Yeah, I'm done here," Stover stood up and banged on the door. It opened and we poured into the hall. George was reading his newspaper.

"You going after the dolphin?" he asked casually.

"Of course. No one gets away with stealing my dolphin," I replied lightly and we went on our way. A few minutes later we walked into Cyber, where a three-D holographic machine was shooting lines everywhere. "Alright, hand over the dolphin and no one gets hurt," I called to the nearly empty room.

"She's over here," Agent Won called, spinning a chair around to reveal my dolphin and a pretty pink dolphin about the same size. "She has a friend now. I needed to get you up here, and they were just throwing stuff in a cart. I knew you would have wanted better for her. Make that work and they're both yours."

"I'm going to need a few things," I looked around the room, found or requested supplies and sat down to write and rewrite formulas. I was startled when she broke my silence.

"Do you like Thai food?"

"I love Thai food. Just not the beetles," I added. Through the blinds I realized it had gotten dark. "I think I've figured out the issue. Do we have something caffeinated here?" I yawned. George got up, walked across the room, and handed me a cold bottle. I blinked at him. "Have you been here?"

"Not the entire time. I came back around six. You're getting the cokes cut out pretty soon; prenatal hoo-ha."

"Do you need something? I get sucked into the computer stuff: it's hard to get out of once you're in it."

"No, I'm just hanging around."

"Okay," I turned to Won. "The primary issue is the integration of six levels of programmed sorters. Four are the common sorters used by intelligence agencies, governments, and spies like me. The fifth is something unique to Israel: I've been trying to reverse engineer it. The sixth layer is our new program, which will act as a primary and final layer of sorting. In the primary layer, it establishes the real IP source and location."

"Right, I have that part worked out," Won agreed.

"The final layer takes all of the previous six layers and is target specific with the information," I made a few changes to my notepad. I heard a voice and jumped right out of my seat.

"Oh my god this might actually be feasible," Kmetz said through a speakerphone.

"Sorry hon, he's in the other room with some other geeks."

"Don't do that!" I told the speakerphone.

"So we're reverse engineering something from Israel?" A new, young voice said.

"Yes. The only other way to get it would be to steal it from China, which got it from Iran through Russian tradesmen."

"How'd Iran get it? Aren't they enemies?" Kmetz said.

"Why else steal and sell someone's technology?" Won said. "The food should be here in 20 minutes. If you could give me a rough sketch of what we're looking at, the moles and owls can do something with it, maybe save you some work."

"I am going to need a bigger board."

She sat at a station. "You talk, I'll write."

George seemed to be perfectly comfortable. He even walked over to a station and played with a computer for a few minutes. I dictated, sketching out small sections as they happened and labeling them. It was tedious. It was painful. It was almost done when the food arrived. We continued and wrapped up about seven minutes later. The Thai Pad was seducing me, and I went for it as soon as I was done with the last sketch-model. Eventually George, Agent Won, and I sat at the small conference table there and attacked food with chopsticks.

"I love spring rolls," George observed as he sucked down the third one.

I laughed a little: I had never seen him like this. I liked it. We finished our meal and had a moment to chat at the table.

"You look exhausted," Agent Won told me.

"I am! I'm going to need way more caffeine to stay up all night and code this up."

"No, no, go to bed. Make the lab rats do some work. You know perfectly well what the next seven to ten hours are going to look like," she replied and I nodded.

"Yes, yes I do. I used to do this stuff all the time. But I really need to finish reverse engineering the Israeli program," I interrupted myself with a yawn. "Seriously, though, Agent Tomopolis, why are you here?" I turned to Agent Won, "Why is he here?"

"Agent Tomopolis is always welcome in my lab," Agent Won offered.

"I'm not here for you, super whiz, I'm hanging around the building for something to happen and I decided that observing you in the workplace is more interesting than watching FOX News or checking my email for the four hundred and fifteenth time."

That made sense. I finished off my bottle of soda and replaced it with a bottle of water. The minute I touched the water I needed to pee. After solving that dilemma, I returned to see George talking on his cell phone proactively. He hung up re-energized.

"Okay: you go to bed," he pointed at me. "You come with me please," he told Agent Won, "Kmetz, in here, start looking this over."

Won started grabbing materials, Kmetz came in, and I had only a moment to blink before the guard gestured that we were going.

"Oh, dolphins," I exclaimed as I nearly reached the door.

"Now, Belle," the guard stated.

I dashed over and grabbed the dolphins. He had the zapper in his hand but Agent Won stopped him as she rushed out.

"Yeah, don't hurt her, she's doing well," George commented as he followed her and then I was marching down hallways with a hand on my arm and two dolphins clutched tightly to my chest. I allowed resentment to bubble in my chest until we were in the elevator.

"We're on the same team, sir," I pointed, avoiding eye contact.

"Then learn to follow orders," he replied after a moment. The elevator dinged open. We walked briskly.

Let it go. Breathe. We stopped in front of my cell. Officer Morgan was on shift.

"Everything alright, Miss Jones?" she inquired. I shot a sideways look at the other guard and bit my tongue.

"Yes ma'am. Agent Tomopolis told me to come back. The dolphin has been rescued."

"No casualties?" she asked. I like her: she has a sense of humor.

"No ma'am. I gained ground from the enemy," I waved the pink dolphin. "We'll reengage tomorrow, I'm sure," I stepped into my new room.

"May I come in for a moment?" she surprised me by asking. "Branch, you can take over here. Thank you," she shut the door behind herself.

"Uh, sure. Would you like a seat, or is this a standing thing, or a rubber hoses kind of thing, I just like to keep tabs," I was suddenly nervous. How on earth this kind woman made me nervous when I routinely handle psychopaths is beyond me.

"Let's sit, here at your little nook table," Officer Morgan said, slightly friendly. She was on the shorter side for guards; probably around 5'5", with green eyes, freckles on her nose and medium brown hair contained in a French braid at all times. I joined her apprehensively. "I won't stay long, I know you're tired. I also know the whole situation here. So what's with Lieutenant Branch?"

"Oh. That obvious?" I asked and cleared my throat before briefly recounting the previous seven minutes. "Really, it's nothing unusual. Absolutely nothing to be worried about ma'am."

"Alright," she sat back in her chair slightly. "Not all of the guards know what you do, what you're doing for us. Even I'm not completely read in on the details. But from what I do know, I think you're pretty awesome. I know you protected American troops overseas multiple times without

166

credit or benefit. You are extremely dangerous but highly valuable. I was put on this detail to try to work those two together; to treat you nicely, but also keep you secure."

"Do you know about the project I'm on?"

"Yes, I know that you are hunting a highly valued target linked to the war on terror."

"Well I'm not going anywhere until that target has been reached and neutralized. I came here for this purpose: if you've read my case file you know full well I didn't get captured involuntarily. I traded my freedom at the price of many lives, and more to come."

"You're a master interrogator, a follower of trails, and a hell of a shot. You're also bloody brilliant. I believe you. I also watched what you did with a few interrogations just for laughs."

"I'm probably the prime source of entertainment here," I joked and we shared a smile.

She stood.

"You're also a trained interrogator, but not by the same people who trained me," I told her. "You're a good runner, and you know your way around a gun, but you've never taken a human life."

"How would you know, that last one?"

"I just do. It's like when a picture gets wet: it's never going to be exactly the same."

"Get some sleep," she tapped the table lightly with her hand. "Breakfast is set for 8 a.m. tomorrow. Its half past nine now," she exited and I heard the bleep-click gung-BOOM as the door was sealed. I found it oddly reassuring.

I spent the next fifteen minutes playing with the lights and fake window. I explored the bathroom, my new drawers, and the doors. It was like a kid in a hotel. Finally I changed into my pajamas, brushed my teeth, and set about making up my bed. I remembered the privacy screen and slid it over the observation window in the door.

As I snuggled into bed, I decided that this was a 200% improvement on my old cell. The bed was perfect, the air smelled better, and the carpeting helped keep the cell warmer. There was even a nightlight in the bathroom. I flipped off the last light and was asleep within ten minutes.

The problem with underground cells is that you can never tell what time it is. The fake window had some stars in a dark sky when I woke up, wide awake and ready to go. I flipped on my little light and walked over to the laptop. 4:30 a.m. *Seriously?* I took a breath, let it out, and blinked. *Yes, I'm up. Okay then. Israeli data processing through signal detection and identification.* I sat down at the little desk and started working again. Around six I decided to transfer to my bed, where I sat and sketched out things on a notepad for some time. At some point I fell asleep, because I woke up with the sunrise, just in time to scramble through the shower, dress, and braid my hair before breakfast. The overhead lights flipped on and someone knocked on the fixed door before sliding the tray onto the ledge.

"Thank you!" I called and sat down to eat.

"Could you move the screen please?" someone asked from outside.

"Oh, sure," I slid it aside and returned to eat. Captain Stover opened the door just after I returned the tray. "Morning. I need to get this to cyber," I tore the relevant pages out of the book.

"Did you sleep?"

"Very well sir. Just woke up and worked and then I fell asleep again. Are we going to cyber?"

"Not directly. I'll let them know they've got mail. I'll be right back." He shut the door again and I went and brushed my teeth. "It's these papers?" he called and I returned from the bathroom.

"Yes. That's pretty important, and it's private," I explained. "They'll know what it is."

"Agent Kmetz will meet us," he placed the papers in a black envelope. "Bring your jacket."

I grabbed the jacket and we were on our way. We had a very low-profile encounter with Kmetz: Stover handed the papers to him and I said nothing but drew a box with my fingers silently. Kmetz didn't say anything, but he saw my sign.

"Where are we going?" I asked as the Captain and I hopped into a golf cart. He sheltered me from the rain but didn't answer until we had ducked in out of the rain to another gray building.

"You're here to meet with Ms. Thoreau. She just wants to meet, have a cup of tea," he lied very subtly as we climbed the stairs a flight and he pointed me toward a room with an open door.

It didn't stay open once I stepped inside. The lighting was dim; from a single lamp on an end table. Someone's grandmother was sitting there reading a newspaper. She made mostly inconsequential small talk with me and eventually withdrew to be replaced by John.

"How is Operation Waldo coming?" he asked.

"Very well, I think Homeland Security has learned to back off. The DIA and FBI appear to work very well: the project would suffer considerably if Agent Won wasn't working with me. She is very astute in the areas involved."

"Good. You like your new quarters?" The old woman returned and appeared to have lost about two decades of age. It didn't surprise me; her character was good but not perfect incognito.

"I do, ma'am. The options available have eased the pains of captivity."

"Belle Jones, Greta Thoreau, my boss," John introduced.

"We've narrowed down the possible candidates for the paternity," she informed.

"Possibly to the last forty, but you would be wasting resources beyond that." I pretended not to care about how many men I had been with.

"You know the father?" she asked.

"Yes I do," I said confidently. "You read my medical report?"

"I have it," she replied.

"Alright then. More questions?"

"What exactly did you do to the Homeland Security man?" she asked and I told her what had happened. She nodded wisely. "Fine; alright, go back to what you were doing."

I stood up and suddenly felt exhausted. "Did you drug me?" I asked John.

"What's wrong?" his face told me the truth.

"I'm just completely exhausted!"

"Welcome to being pregnant," the woman said with an air of experience.

"Special Agent Starr is outside with Lt. Sullivan," John said and opened the door. I took the cue and walked out. "Might want to take her home," he mentioned to them during the transfer. "Good job," he said to me with a light pat on the back.

"Sorry, I'm just so incredibly tired all of a sudden," I greeted the soldier and agent.

"Hits you like an earthquake, doesn't it?" Starr said as we walked downstairs.

"More like a tsunami," I replied and got into the cart. In the elevator I leaned my head against the wall and dozed. I got disoriented and walked into the door while walking back through the layers of security. The guards made me sit in a chair outside my door while the wiry medic came jogging with his bag.

"Hey there princess. I'm just going to check your heart before you take a nap. Okay, thermometer…you're a little warm, but not bad. Here we go," He squeezed my arm with the blood pressure monitor while probing my chest with the stethoscope. "And stand up," he checked that pressure. "Okay. Say goodnight Gracie."

I yawned and shuffled into my cell. I turned off the lights and kicked off my shoes and I was in bed before the door finished sealing. I woke up feeling stiff and sore; lunch was waiting for me. I picked at it and opened a Sprite®.

"Belle?" Lt. Benzion called from the hall. "Can you come out for a minute?"

"Yeah," I said and placed my tray back on the slot. I padded over to the real door, which opened. I sat in the appropriate chair.

"Okay, just a second," Benzion stuck the thermometer in my ear again. I sneezed right after he took it out. I had covered my face with my shirt, and I think they were grateful. "102.1" he announced. "Agent Won wants to talk to you. She'll come down here. In the meantime, I'm going to report to the medic so we can see what's going on here. Agent Won will be here in a moment. Here, take these please," he dropped two Tylenol® in my hand and gave me a bottle of water. "Good job. You can go back in now."

"Mkay," I muttered and shuffled back inside. I went to the bathroom mirror and started self-diagnosing. "Freaking head cold," I decided. Someone knocked.

"Hey babe," Agent Won called and I reappeared. She was wearing a medical mask but I could tell she was smiling. "Brought you some tissues and throat lozenges: it's all we had lying around. These are the lotion tissues and these are just regular."

"Thanks. It's just a little cold," I joined her at the table. "Did you get my sketches?"

"Yes we did. The tech squad and I are still working on logistics: it's going to take a while to get the actual hardware and software in place. It's looking good though," she handed me a folder and I flipped through the pages.

"Oy," I chugged some tea. "Go figure I get sick after I get put into the really nice living quarters and not after spending weeks in a cold cell," I joked.

We chatted for several minutes as I reviewed the diagrams and equations. It was maybe twenty minutes later when Susan the medic knocked on the door. She was also wearing a mask. She examined me, took a blood sample and made me pee in a cup. I put the sample inside a paper bag so Agent Won wouldn't be grossed out.

"This looks like a cold. I'll give the guards some supplies and a list of other things you can have. Right now, fluids, rest, Tylenol®, and chicken soup. I'll check the lab work to rule out something more serious but I'm 99 percent sure this is just a bad case of the sniffles," she smiled sympathetically and left.

"Anything interesting happening in the real world?" I asked Won.

"The guy from Homeland had a snit fit, but it didn't get him anywhere. Now he's behind a desk," she informed.

"I'm guessing I got written up for that," I blew my nose.

"Actually, there were two copies. One told the man he shouldn't have attacked and he was lucky the guard didn't plug him. The other told the guards to give you ice cream for dessert for a week."

"Actually, that sounds really good. I guess I don't get it until dinner, but vanilla ice cream…it's these cravings."

"You up to eating it?" she asked.

"Yeah. Lunch wasn't all that edible."

"Prison food," she shrugged. "We'll get you healthy and back into the lab. Can you take a look at something for me?"

I was scratching notes on a spare piece of paper when I heard a 'clank'.

"Well look at that," Agent Won went to the dining tray and produced a large bowl of vanilla ice cream.

"Thank you!" I called to the food gods and descended on my prey. "Gah, brain freeze!" I admitted a moment later and slowed down.

"Thank you," Agent Won took my notes and files and exited.

I went back to bed shortly after that, licking the ice cream from my face.

I opened my eyes slowly. Something was off. The wall was battleship gray! I sat up violently and pushed against the bare cot. *What the hell! They moved me!* I looked around. It wasn't even my cell! The arrangement was off, and there was no curtain or shower, just a sink and a bare prison toilet.

"Hey!" I shouted in anger. *How could they do this to me? Why am I here? When did they move me? How did I get here?* "HEY!" I ran to the door and kicked it several times. Two strange men in uniform came in and violently cuffed me behind my back. One grabbed my head by my hair and held it toward the door.

The man from Homeland Security was standing there in a dark suit. "You stupid bitch," he said calmly. "Take her to *my* interrogation room. We'll get some answers PDQ."

"NO!" I yelled and threw one man down. I pushed my back to the wall, the stone cold battleship gray wall. "Get off! Get away from me! I'll kill you!"

The man laughed at me and some part of my brain realized something odd.

"Don't laugh at me."

"You silly little girl. You're going to scream, I can tell," Jameson smirked.

"Get off! You Bas—no! Don't touch me!" *The wall is soft. Push through!* My brain said and I pushed harder.

"Belle!" someone called but I couldn't see anyone but him.

PUSH! My brain said and I recoiled up in bed. I was covered in a cold sweat, my heart was racing, and the overhead lights were on. Officer Morgan and another Marine were in there with me.

"Belle? Can you hear me?" Officer Morgan practically climbed into bed with me.

I nodded. "Jameson wants to torture me," I uttered and gathered my thoughts.

"Okay. It was just a nightmare. It's okay. He's not going to get anywhere near you. No one is going to torture you," she handed me my dolphin and I hugged it tightly.

"Yeah," I laughed with a little embarrassment. "I feel kind of silly. Nightmare. Was I yelling? I don't usually. It was bad," I blew my nose.

"Okay. It's almost time for dinner. We need to take your temperature before that, so when you're ready, come on out for just a minute." She and the man exited and I put on shoes and my jacket. I had been sleeping in my clothes. The door opened, I took a seat and the tool beeped in my ear.

"101.2" the guard reported and Officer Morgan recorded it.

"Agent Tomopolis would like to meet with you upstairs," she informed.

"Can I just grab some tissues?" I asked before they closed my door. She handed me a few pills and I swallowed them before we went up.

George was in a small conference room with a military man with a ton of ribbons on his chest.

"General Jackson, this is Alexis, better known as Belle Jones."

"General," I greeted.

"I understand you've caught a bug."

"Yes sir, we're working very hard to isolate and extract information using programs that we're writing as we go. I've been able to incorporate," I stopped myself because George looked like he was going to laugh. "You were talking about me being sick," I realized.

The General smiled. "Please, have a seat," he gestured and I joined them at the table. "I've read the reports, heard the accounts and seen some of the footage. I like your approach to terrorists; and I understand your relationship with security has gotten a lot better. You're a tough woman. I wanted to meet you in person. Not too close though, I hear you have a fever."

I smiled back at him. I had placed a chair between myself and anyone else. "Thank you sir. I'm looking forward to getting over this silly cold so they'll let me go back to work," I heard myself and realized my voice had started fading. George handed me a cup and a thermos of lemon tea.

"You conduct interrogations?"

"Yes, a few. I'm pretty good at getting people to spill."

"You write software?"

"Yes, more like programs using existing software."

"You have firsthand experience in infiltration techniques, serious martial skills, and you're a sharp shooter?"

"Yes."

"You sent the FBI information on fugitives and terrorists before your capture?"

"Yes."

"Have you ever seen this man?" he asked and produced a 5x7 picture. I studied it.

"Possibly."

"He was assigned to take someone out. You beat him to the punch. Once he got over being upstaged, he started our file on you. Special Agent Tomopolis didn't even know about it. Every hacker leaves dust behind them. We never knew exactly what you were up to, but after the second trip to Saudi Arabia, we got a pretty good idea."

"I am not a terrorist," I stated.

"Not at all; you're a counter-terrorist. I want a battalion of men just like you."

"I'm guessing he doesn't mean 'knocked up and in military custody'" I joked lightly.

"No," he smiled warmly.

I caught George reading a text and rolled my eyes at him. "What now?"

"Nothing. We're going to do a quick strep test."

"Great," I said sarcastically.

"Can I come see you when you're well again?" The general asked.

"Of course. The Marines are guarding me, so I won't be going anywhere."

"My boss' men are guarding the Marines, but I'd prefer you use the telephone to contact me," he stood, nodded to me, shook George's hand, and left.

"Susan's going to come take a quick strep test and then you can go home."

"I want ice cream," I said quietly. Susan came in with her bag. It didn't take long for the results to show positive. She didn't really need the test; apparently there were white patches all across the back of my throat.

"Alright. Take these please," she handed me a large white pill and a smaller yellow one. "We'll kick-start the antibiotics and you'll be running around in a few days."

"72 hours," George said after I swallowed with some difficulty.

"Three days?" I squawked. "What on earth am I supposed to do in a cell for three days?"

"Type, draw, plot, watch movies, review files, go back to the terrorist handout, sleep, and eat ice cream."

"Yeah, okay." That didn't sound so bad.

Someone knocked on the door sharply. The General reappeared with Director Goode.

"Look who I found in the elevator," he greeted.

"She has strep throat," George announced and I sat back down.

"Sorry to hear that. How are the new quarters?" Director Goode inquired.

"Very nice ma'am."

"I know you must be tired, but could you stick around a little longer and chat with us?"

"I'll get some ice cream," George assured me and excused himself.

"I just wanted you to know that General Jackson has the same clearance and need-to-know that I and Agent

177

Tomopolis have on this case. He knows all about Operation Waldo," she told me with a gentle voice and a sympathetic look. "Now, general, did you have any questions you'd like to ask?"

"Well, I wouldn't mind knowing a little more about how she detected the terrorists in time to stop them from attacking the soldiers in Liberia."

I nodded, took a drink, and began my story. George arrived with a bowl full of ice cream which I ate while the general asked questions and made notes.

"Tunisia," I realized. "That's where I saw him. The man in the photograph: so the target must have been Ahmed al-Shad bin Qarid, AKA Sand Man."

The general chose to not acknowledge that.

"So you shot the Sandman?" Director Goode asked.

"That's what my man said," the general replied when I didn't.

"I can honestly say that I did not shoot that man," I said and sipped tea.

"Alright, she's too sick to continue," Director Goode declared.

"My man found him dead with no apparent cause," The general stated. "Only you could have managed that. Look we're not here to prosecute. Believe me, I'll give it to you in writing that you have full immunity given by the office of the President."

"That sounds reasonable," I said as the guard came in. I left with him, we went down to the cell alone and they took my temperature and fed me more Tylenol®. My fever was back up to 102.9, and I was feeling the effects. I changed into my pajamas and ate half a bowl of soup, set up a DVD of Bugs Bunny cartoons and crawled into bed.

I slept through the sunrise until the guards woke me up long enough to pump breakfast and drugs into me. I felt better after a shower. My fever was down to 100.9. Swallowing hurt like hell.

"Hey, can I have some pain killers? My throat really hurts," I tapped on the meal door. They set a cup with two ibuprofens and a bag of throat drops. My semi-miserable experience continued until the evening. I felt slightly better as I ate my chicken and dumplings and I ranked at only 99.9 degrees when they pulled me out that night.

"We have something for you, special delivery," Lt. Sullivan said from a short distance. He kept his distance and handed me an official looking envelope.

I read the seal on it, opened it and pulled out the starchy paper. I read through it twice, very carefully. "Total immunity," I mumbled to myself and checked the seal on the paper. "I don't escape and no one can charge me in the United States of America. Okay. Let's go talk to the president."

"You'll have to settle for the General," Sully informed and stood. I took the letter and envelope with me and we went upstairs to meet with General Jackson again in an interview room. Agents Won and Tomopolis joined us and Sully left once we were settled.

"We're all read in?" the General checked.

"Yes, we're all in the core team," George assured him.

"You are feeling better today?" General Jackson asked me.

"A little, sir," I replied.

"Alright. You have it in your hand. Full immunity and umbrella protection from extradition as an asset to national security."

"Yes sir."

"Sandman?"

"Tetrodotoxin; a strong dose injected into his shoulder. I put the needle into his flask afterwards to make sure no one else would die. I was in and out in less than two minutes, one minute on the ground."

"Brilliant."

"There are others. Seventeen others who I killed directly or likely killed in battle."

"None of whom were Americans," George stated.

"No. Two were French citizens, four were Israeli, and one was South African. The rest were of some variety or another of Afghani, Iranian, Iraqi, Pakistani, Lebanese, I think one may have been Syrian, and of course, North African countries. I only regret one or two of them: they were some very nasty characters. Wait, make that 18 if you count Ben-Adat."

"Methods varied, from our records," General Jackson said.

"I've used tetrodotoxin twice but I dislike poisons. I never got into the whole stabbing thing either: the one man I killed with a knife had it thrown at him. Methods varied with opportunity, resources, and on occasion, how much I hated the bastard."

"Algeria," everyone else said.

"He was raping and selling children. I was going to knock him over the head, but the bomb just sort of made itself useful. I rescued not only the little girl in his hotel room, but the twelve others she led me to."

"We know how that went, leaving them with a note at the door of the police chief's home."

"And bits of him all over Algiers."

"And his associate, who you ran down next?"

180

"More like ran over, pumped for information, and put him out of his misery by breaking his neck. I remember every single person I've killed. But it's the faces and sounds of those kids, the women at the markets, the men who can walk home at night without terrorists; those are the images I get at night. It's not like I enjoy carnage: but there is a greater cause to fight for. I'm not ashamed."

"You have nothing to be ashamed of," Agent Won spoke first.

"Every soldier I know would have loved to have been able to do what you did. Unfortunately we couldn't, or we would be Israel," Jackson said reassuringly. "Tell me about Ben-Adat."

"He came here to kill me. He told me so in interrogation. He tried to shoot me, he was detained, escaped and came after me again. He opened fire. Agent Tomopolis was there. I procured a gun and shot him from under the table. The guard shot him three times. Ben-Adat gave me the bullet wound in my hip."

"And the six men in Liberia?"

"I used a silencer. I got three outside before taking care of the three inside. I neutralized their weaponry, set the house on fire, and stole the truck. I drove it over a ledge into the lake: I didn't know how to disarm everything in time."

"Good thinking," Jackson complimented.

"Thank you, sir. What else would you like to know?" I asked.

"How did you get involved in Israel?"

"I shot a suicide bomber just in time in the streets. They picked me up and kept me for a while," I calmly stated.

He nodded and said nothing.

"How are you feeling?" Won asked with her kind eyes.

"I'm doing okay. My throat hurts and my body aches a little. Aren't you all afraid I'll spread it to you?"

"Strep went through half the building already. The only people who don't and haven't had it are the prisoners, visitors, and those who have been ordered to take special precaution," George answered.

"We're still working on the wiring of that new program we've designed together," Agent Won said.

My energy was fading fast.

"This was a good session. Good job, Belle. Your homework assignment, as it were, is to write a letter to General McChrystal, the chief of forces in Afghanistan with as much good advice as you can think of."

"Overnight?"

"No, I'll be back early next week."

"Alright. It will be ready for you," I confirmed. We all stood and the General and George left me with Agent Won.

"How's it going?"

"I'm a little scared. Maybe the fever will hurt the baby. What about after the birth? Are my baby and I going to live in that little room? I'm trying, so hard I'm trying to focus on the work: to use my experience and knowledge to push through and make a difference on this side of the fence."

"You are making a difference. You are," she came over and held my hand. "Tell me," she said softly, looking behind my eyes.

"I didn't count those six men in my figure. I've executed two dozen people. One here, three there, six in one night, two by poison, one looked like a suicide—hanging by window ejection—ten in battle, possibly more."

"Tell me about your first."

"West Bank, in gray areas. I was in Israel as a courier for Kabala threads. I noticed the man twice; he had a satchel around his shoulder but he was rolling a basket of groceries around. The bag looked heavy. He looked edgy. He reached into the bag and yelled those stupid words drilled into their heads by the twisted unholy leaders. Jihad! God is mighty so I will now kill innocent people, some of his own," I stopped and drank the mixed soda she had brought me. "I didn't even think. Suddenly my gun was in my hand, and there was the noise and the impact of the shot, it was like it was in slow motion. I thought I saw his eye lift in reflex just before the bullet blew into his skull, leaving a little red dripping dot less than an inch above his eyebrow. And he fell down and he was dead and people were screaming and running and shouting in Hebrew and Arabic and they were alive. Israeli street soldiers took me without handcuffs: they just kept a gun to my head the entire time. They're crazy drivers you know. It's true. That was my first kill."

"The next one?"

"Almost an accident. That was the knife throwing victim. I really can't throw knives: I was just trying to get his attention so someone else could shoot him. Hezbollah cell: I was working for Israel. It was in a box of knives they use to behead journalists and teachers. It wasn't even a proper throwing knife, I just threw it as hard as I could, and I…" I started tearing up, "it went straight into his chest. There was…it was just blood everywhere. Hot shooting blood, spraying, gushing. It was awful. I puked. I felt a little better when I saw the hostage we had accidentally rescued."

"Did it get easier?"

"Yes. The third, fourth, sixth and seventh were in conjunction with Israeli intelligence. The fifth was a woman, sort of my evil counterpart. I didn't know how to kill a woman, so I put the tetrodotoxin in her wine. By that time I was fairly independent and well connected. Number eight was an arms dealer to the terror world. I had sex with him and snapped his neck. Number nine was a nasty piece of work: he's the false suicide victim."

"What number was the Algerian?"

"Lucky number 13. Ten and eleven were bombed via grenade, and twelve was sniped. The Algerian was a bomb, and you know about 14. I did a little traveling after that, picking off men when I found it necessary," I fell silent.

"So them, plus the six and four more."

"Direct kills, yes. I can't account for what all has happened." A tear rolled down my cheek. "Sometimes I think it's far too many for me to have possibly killed, and sometimes it seems like a drop in a bucket. There are still some very bad people out there who have nothing to fear from law or order. At least I made some of them a little sweatier, looking over their shoulders for a bullet."

"You're a one man war on wheels. You may have done more for the war on terror than the entire CIA," Won handed me a tissue. "Come on, that's enough of this serious stuff. I have four seasons of Will & Grace you can borrow: talk about mindless entertainment. Is it warm enough in your cell?"

"I think so. I haven't really noticed," we stood and headed out.

"Let the guards know. Hang in there another few days."

"Thanks Agent Won. I guess you should go sterilize so you don't get the strep."

"Hey, I'm a computing pro. Viruses happen."

"God, I'm so tired," I said as she and the guard joined me in the elevator down to the cells. "I haven't done anything all day and I'm still exhausted."

"Strep sucks. You'll feel better in the morning," she stayed in the elevator while I stepped out and we started through the layers of security to get to my cell.

"Light reading for you," Benzion said at my cell door and handed me a packet. The door wasn't open, so I stood and looked at him. He grabbed the ear thermometer. "One more reading and a cup full of pills. Alright, oh, back up to 101. Well, swallow these," he handed me a cup full of pills. I slugged them down. "DVDs are on the table. Goodnight," he opened the door and I returned to my yellow cell.

Chapter 8: Friends and Foes

Five days later, Wednesday, my throat was still tender but the virus had been conquered. I sipped a cup of hot tea in Director Goode's office, waiting for her in the company of a guard I learned to call 'Officer Foxtrot'. He was not a Marine; he was Army. His Marine counterpart waited outside the door. I sat in silence. Finally, he spoke.

"They said you were talkative," Foxtrot said.

"If I'm not even allowed to know your name, I assume there is no point in trying to chat. Small talk is rather difficult when someone is protecting sensitive information," I replied politely.

"Good point."

"Thank you. They're in the hall," I heard the subtle noises. Soon Director Goode, General Jackson, Agent Tomopolis, John, and a woman I had never seen before swarmed in and joined us at the conference table. The new woman was kind looking, long dark curly hair and soft features. The Marine also stepped inside.

"How are you feeling?" John asked with a smile.

"Better. I may even eat solid food tomorrow," I joked.

"What's incredible is that she's been working the last two days," George added to John.

"Lying in my bed making adjustments to things on a laptop does not count as working," I stated. "Although it was clever to tape those interviews and let me watch them from the cell. I think that was productive."

"Belle, this is Leona Hampshire," General Jackson introduced me to the woman. She smiled and extended her hand. I shook it.

"Ms. Jones, it is a real treat to meet you. I am the new representative from Homeland Security," she introduced and we all sat. Even her voice was soft.

"Good to hear. I'm afraid your predecessor was an asshole," I replied.

"King James?" John asked George, who nodded. John turned to me. "I haven't heard this: what did he do with you?"

"Threatened to torture me and grabbed my arm," I replied and looked at Leona. She appeared sympathetic but not shocked. "That doesn't really work for me," I informed her.

"Didn't work well for him either," George stated. "She's a master at martial arts."

"Yes, I read the files I was sent. Well, I'm not here to torture anyone; our agency does not condone it. Actually, Miss Jones, I'm not even going to try to question you. The FBI, CIA, and DIA seem to be doing their jobs very effectively. I'm here to provide resources, back up, and to just keep an ear to the ground. I'll admit, you're such a fascinating person, I'd love to just chat sometime, but in a strictly casual, non-work related manner."

Director Goode steered the conversation away and gave out the good news. "The chatter sifting and highlighting program designed by Ms. Jones and Agent Won supported by FBI and CIA resources was successfully tested and appears to be a great tool for the anti-terrorism front. A full briefing is in progress. The DIA, CIA, Homeland Security, and the leads on our Marine security guards here and the General's staff are on the first wave of communication."

"What exactly does this do?" Jackson asked.

"It finds needles in a haystack and decides which needles are important and who they belong to," I explained.

187

"Really? We can do that?" Leona said.

"You can now," I replied and went back to my tea.

"I know this is going to knock NSA on their butts, but while they're transitioning, military intelligence is ready and able to start implementing this technology as little as four months from now," General Jackson stated.

Jurisdictional hullabaloo ensued. Director Goode eventually regained control.

"Alright, everyone go back to your people, talk it over and we'll go from there. General, are you good for the 1600?"

"Yes ma'am," he replied.

"Alright. I'll see you then. Thank you all for coming," she dismissed but the Army guy put a hand on my shoulder.

General Jackson saw this as he was gathering and getting ready to go. "Son," he told the guard, "Just don't." The hand was removed and Foxtrot followed him out. Soon it was just me, the guard, and Director Goode.

"We would like to thank you for your recent work by adding another cell to your living quarters," she came around to sit with me. "There is an adjacent space we can utilize without compromising security."

I mentally configured the floor in my head. It didn't make sense.

She saw my face. "It would make the space deeper, not wider," she explained. "We could add a couch and television, and it would give you more space for when the baby comes."

"Could we maybe put in a washing machine with the new water hookup? I really miss washing my own clothes. I know that's a little weird," I requested.

"I'll take it to the team, but I can't make promises," she replied. "If it's feasible and safe, I think you've earned a washing machine. Anything else on your mind?"

"Are the men I interrogate housed in this facility?"

"There are some prisoners in this facility. It's not a permanent base for most of them. Your security runs both ways."

"Yes ma'am, I had noticed. Well, if they're smart enough to keep me in, I guess they know what they're doing. I'd really like some more time in that cyber closet. I'm dying to check the feeds from the transmissions."

"Well, I can tell you that the one in his house is still active. I wish we had a camera in there."

"I wish we had me in there," I added. "This is so…frustrating! Probably because I spent the last six years doing whatever I wanted and now I get an escort to the bathroom."

"You are alive, taken care of, and in comfort," she pointed gently.

"True. This is considerably better than many of the places I have been. Sorry I'm whiny."

"It's alright. Alright, show me what you've got," It was a short show-and-tell presentation. "Would you like to sit down and have tea with Ms. Hampshire?"

"Do you advise it?" I replied.

"She's an old colleague of mine. Leona is just curious: she used to work on counter espionage training and command. You are a living prototype for her."

I nodded slowly and finished my tea. "Of course. I would love to meet with her and spend as much time as she feels is helpful giving her whatever she wants."

Her eyes said everything. This was an old friend of hers, the topic was uneasy ground, and I had given her more than

189

she had hoped for. She put her hand on the table in front of me. "Thank you," Director Goode almost whispered. "We'd like to run you through cyber first, and give you a break. I'll ask Leo if she would like to meet you this evening. What kind of food are you in the mood for?"

"What kind of food does she like?" I asked back.

"She likes everything."

"Maybe some burgers? Some kind of red meat. Honestly, just not chicken or noodles," I replied.

"I'll see what we can do," she told me. "Natalie!" she called out the door and the nervous girl poked her head through the door. "Thank you, Belle," she dismissed me and I exited to see Agents Kmetz and Tomopolis.

"I want time in the closet," I greeted.

"Not today," George replied.

"Agent Won of the DIA wanted to run our latest by you," Agent Kmetz said and we started walking. No one said anything else until we were back in the lab. "We're bringing in a specialist in this type of coding, but,"

Agent Won interrupted him. "I thought you should have the first crack at it. We can cover our entrances, but we could, I think, tag the intercepted communications."

"Follow them home," I understood the concept. "There's no cheap and dirty way to do that, at least that I've seen. When I did it, I had to do it manually. It takes days and multiple transmissions."

"To find the originator, yes. However, it only takes a split second to give it a STD, or I guess a cyber-transmitted virus…CTV? Anyway, we give it a little something; code that into our systems, and instant glowing bad guy."

"If they knew how to do this, or even that it was possible: this could be a terrible weapon," I realized.

"Fortunately, that's not the part you're here for," George stepped in and handed me a bottle of water. "Is it possible?"

I sat down and no one said anything for a few minutes. "What kind of levels are still getting through the seventh layer? Thousands, Millions? Billions?"

"Thousands," Agent Won told me.

"Apparent originators?"

"13,384."

"Estimated actual originators?"

"By cell or by person?"

"Cells."

"Less than 1900."

"That's a lot," I shook my head. "Too many. How many of those are in direct intercourse with Waldo?"

"We're not sure."

"Okay. Bring in a specialist: a virus writer. Get them to put a hide on this thing that prevents it from spreading until it receives a signal. The last thing we need is a world full of glowing dots."

"That's another thing I wanted to talk to you about," George segued and the three of us sat at the central table. "What does the name Uri Vletsko mean to you?"

I blinked for a few minutes. "Ari Hansen," I replied. "He's not on my hit list."

"Good to hear. The Brits captured him," George informed me.

"He had some interesting information for them," Agent Won added.

"Your name came up."

"They gave us a call."

"There was a meeting and we came to an arrangement with Great Britain. If we can use him to bring down Al-Zahrani, we can retain full custody of him."

"He's a good man, as far as my crowd goes," I fit the puzzle pieces together in my head. "He's going to need Natasha if you want him to write this piece."

"Who is Natasha?" George asked.

"It's his super computer. If the British haven't destroyed it, they should send it along. I set up the security mainframe on it, so unless James Bond was paying attention, Natasha may be dead," I explained.

"Fortunately, I was," a British male voice came from behind me. "And the name is Hartcastle, William Hartcastle."

I stood slowly, controlling my normal surprise reflexes. "I'm Bond, James Bond," I used my very best worst accent to mock him and his Ian Fleming nonsense. "But you might know me as The Angel," I faced him and mentally sized him up. My guard appeared to be doing the same.

"I have instructions not to come within five feet of you," he replied dryly.

"Someone likes you," I informed him.

"You designed this creature?" He lifted his steel briefcase a bit.

"Only the fail secure and other data control features."

"Well you didn't muck about," Hartcastle stated.

"We don't have the luxury of mucking about," I replied.

"You must be Agent Won," he ignored me and turned to her.

"So is Ari here too?" I asked George.

"I am speaking!" Hartcastle admonished me like a school child.

I let my initial outrage simmer for a second. "You have instructions not to come within five feet of me. I have no instructions regarding foreign citizens. Usually I do whatever I want with them," I walked toward him slowly, advancing to within four feet. "I advise you to step back, because whoever issued your orders was probably well informed."

"Alexis," my guard said and I recognized the 'you're-about-to-push-the-button' tone. I returned to the table and took a seat.

"Why is your prisoner not restrained?" Rudecastle asked.

"Believe me; she is exercising a great deal of restraint." John appeared in the doorway behind the Brit.

"I think I should go," I told George.

"I'll walk you out," Agent Won jumped on the opportunity and wrapped her arm around me as we passed through the door. Two British escort soldiers were waiting in the hall, facing down two Marines. She guided me through them. "Hey, listen," she said quietly as we passed them, "I know we usually do this together, but he's not exactly playing well. I know what you're thinking right now, so drop it. He is all mine. Okay?"

"I'd like him looking over his shoulder for the next week, if that's at all possible," I replied.

"We'll see," she gave me a squeeze and left me in the atrium of that area.

I turned and watched her return, checked out the soldiers again, and reflected on the situation. The guard didn't seem in a hurry, so I just looked for a minute until my lips pushed themselves into a small, tight smile. Then the doors opened and George walked out. He looked like a president for a moment, walking in the row of soldiers.

"Good work in there, Alexis," George came to me.

"Thank you, sir," I replied.

"You have some down time before 1700. Thanks for meeting with Leona. She's a good egg."

"Please don't place me in a room with that pretentious boob again," I requested loudly enough for the soldiers to hear.

"Please don't attack the British visitors," he replied. "Gentlemen," George called over to them and gestured. The Brits came. "This is Alastair Deacon," he waved at the first, slightly wider man with a strong build and absolutely no sign of the ability to smile. "He has a high rank and lots of medals including their version of the Purple Heart and the Silver Star. This is Seamus Dougherty. He has a slightly lower rank," he said of the taller, thinner man who could still pass for a Marine in a wrong uniform. "He's a sharpshooter, and he's worked with British and NATO intelligence on counterterrorism efforts. Care to make some observations? It might amuse them."

"Alright. You're left handed," I told Alastair, "you were shot on your left side: I'm guessing your left arm or shoulder. It forced you to become ambidextrous. I know because," I pulled my collar out and showed off the bullet mark. "And you're a little bit like me," I told Seamus. "Not really a people person, probably very talented and very smart. You want to do your thing, and orders can get in the way, at least in your head. I interested you enough to make you volunteer for this mission. I think my body count is higher than yours, but I can't be sure," I returned to Alastair, "You have been totally shocked at the idea of someone like me, but you're getting used to it now that you've seen me in person. Neither of you is totally comfortable with the idea that I may have saved your unit some lives if you were in a battle zone at the right time. I think that's a good start."

"Do you have what you need?" George asked me pointedly.

I rolled my eyes. "Are they guarding him or it?"

194

"Now that the transfer is over, just him."

"Fine. If he doesn't touch me, I won't touch him. Out of respect of these two gentlemen, I will refrain from expressing my feelings toward that twit in a nonverbal manner," I redirected myself toward the Brits. "That's at least partially on my mental calculation that you would probably tackle me with some of that wrestling training," pointed at Alastair, "or the Marine would react in a painful manner. You, sir, can tackle me any time you want," I said salaciously to Seamus. "We should really talk sometime. I drink tea."

"Goodbye Alexis," George called.

"Never let me have any fun," I muttered and left with my escort.

Shortly after 1700, which is 5 p.m. to the part of the world that isn't European or military controlled, I entered a large office. It was almost as big as Director Goode's. There were distinct feminine touches: a flameless candle on the table, the scent of grapefruit in the air, and the lighting came from bulbs instead of tubes. Two padded chairs were set at about a ninety degree angle facing away from the window.

"Ah, hello," she entered. Her voice was naturally quiet. "Dinner is still cooking. Thank you for agreeing to meet with me, Miss Jones."

"Please call me Belle," I felt my own voice soften a little.

"Thank you; please feel free to call me Leona. Does he have to stay?" she was close enough to me to just point a little. "Is there a procedure? I don't want to step on anyone's toes."

"Yes ma'am, I have to stay. I can be as discreet as possible," Benzion replied.

"They don't really leave me with people," I explained apologetically.

"No, it's perfectly alright. This is not an interview, let's sit," we sat and she continued. "This is not a formal interview, there's no recording devices, no questions you have to answer, I would have brought wine but I heard you were pregnant."

"I am. I guess I'm toward the end of my first trimester. I don't think I'm showing yet," I replied.

"I brought some Preggie pop drops and some ginger cookies for you: they really helped my sister through her first few months along."

"Wow, thank you. You didn't need to do that."

"I can't even imagine what you're going through. I've seen a containment cell here and it's just impossible to think of that as 'home'. And you're sick and pregnant and chasing down Al-Zahrani."

"Well, I've been hunting him down for a long time," I explained. We chatted for some time: I learned that she was a counterterrorism expert who had been mentored by one of the CIA Bin Laden taskforce members in the 1990s. I also found out that she was friends with one of the men in the unit in Afghanistan where my brother was when he was killed in action. She spoke some French and pretty decent Arabic, but hadn't spent any time in the Middle East. I showed her some of my scars; she showed me her tattoo, which happened to be in one of the places I had a scar. Dinner was brought in: perfectly done steak with green beans and rolls.

"Oh, this is so much better than what they feed me downstairs," I exclaimed about halfway through the plate.

"How is the prison food?"

"Well, I get a lot better than the rest of the inmates down there. It's usually not that bad. Kind of like cafeteria food, I guess. They have a nutritional guide with what I have to eat, and they give me pills every day, like vitamins," I explained. "To be totally objective, I'm treated very well. I give cooperation, aid and information, and I receive rewards as seen fit. I've never given false information to try to get a treat because it doesn't work like that. I just do the best I can because that is why I came here."

"Do the guards rough you up?"

"Not for a while now. I respect Marines in general, and these guys are top notch. There was a small altercation a long time ago where I was overly expressive of my frustration and anger, but everyone walked away. The same guys gave me pain killer as requested for my face and ribs. They're good men and good women."

"I heard they don't really use the restraints on you anymore," she led as we finished the meal.

"True and false. I'm rarely handcuffed or whatnot, but I do have a special anklet that they can use to shock me. It hurts quite a lot and makes that leg less useful for a while, and that's on the lower settings. I'd rather not find out what full-blast feels like, so I generally behave."

"They shock you like a dog with a bark collar?"

"I'm a very dangerous person, Leona. They don't use it unless they really have to, and I get a warning first. I think it's brilliant. I feel like less of an inmate."

"What does the warning sound like, 'hey, I'm going to shock you now'?"

"Usually they'll just say my real name. I have a few seconds to stop whatever I was doing and comply. This afternoon; that meant not beating the hell out of an annoying British snob. He said 'Alexis' and I returned to the table. End of issue."

"What do you think your biggest benefit is here?"

"Well, that's a two-parter. One, I'm safe. Two, I'm dramatically advancing American troop capabilities, fighting terrorism from multiple fronts, and I have a roof over my head."

"Wow. It's just…wow. Would you like a brownie?"

"Oh god yes."

She laughed and lifted the lid. "Alright, now remember you don't have to answer these questions. Alright? Okay. What would you like me to know about Israel?"

"Oy," I commented and started on the brownie. Two more had disappeared by the time I was done with that monologue. Her eyes showed enrapture.

She hesitated for a while and we sat in silence for several minutes. "Okay," she snapped out of it. "I think I understand a few more things now. So, what do you feel is the worst part about being here?"

"It's not too bad. I have no control over my schedule, but they're pretty considerate. The food isn't always good but that's not guaranteed anywhere. I didn't like having the camera in the cell, but in my new cell it doesn't wander around. That's just creepy to me. Different people are more or less friendly. I'm almost never outside, but I understand that. I guess the one thing that bugs me the most isn't even the lack of independence; it's that everyone knows who I am. I've gone through the better part of my life as anonymously as possible and now I'm surrounded by people who know who I am and a good deal about my life: much more than anyone else in the world ever has."

"I think the whole captivity thing would bug me more," she reflected.

"You get used to it. Plus they keep me pretty busy. I miss some other little things that I never thought about before they caught me: like washing my own laundry, flirting with people, getting lost…silly things."

"Can I see your cell?" she asked curiously.

"I have no idea. If Director Goode approves it, then it goes to security, then if they approve it, it's their call."

"Let me make a call," she pulled out her phone and stepped away. "Doesn't look like it's going to happen," she returned.

"It's not much to look at," I consoled her.

"This has been a great meeting," Leona said. "We should do this again, if you'd like that."

"I would," I assured her.

"Excellent. The goodies I brought you are with security, and somehow I'll let you know when we can schedule our next chat."

"Thank you."

"Thank you," she returned. I took a cue and exited with the guard.

We were on our way back to the cell when Lt. Sullivan intercepted.

"We need to borrow you," he greeted.

"Tonight?"

"Right now. The Algerian guy, the one you opened? He's gone mental."

"As in…" I asked as we entered the elevator.

"Self-inflicted damages."

"Has he been helpful? Given us good intelligence?"

"Yes, very cooperative but now he's trying to kill himself: he's ranting about how you're going to come kill him anyway and so on."

"Okay. I'm going in," I said as he stopped at the interrogation room door. It opened and I stormed in. Two soldiers were holding the chained man in his chair. I motioned them away and the prisoner's red, teary eyes opened and recognized me. "What in hell are you doing?" I asked in Arabic. "I get a call, in the middle of the night that you went cracked in the head because apparently, I'm going to come kill you. What did I say? What did I tell you?"

"Please, for the mercy of God, just do it!" he wailed.

"I told you that if you gave them what they wanted, I would not kill you."

"I have given them everything!"

"They know! And if I can convince them that your brains are not baked, you'll be out of here in a few days. Alive, and heading for a place where you can see the blue skies and feel the breeze."

"Out?"

"Out. You need a medical clearance to transfer, so you'll have to stop trying to kill yourself."

He was calmed, relieved, and sane again, crying and catching his breath. "Many blessings of God have reached me," he uttered.

"May God in his mercy go with you. They will take you to a restroom where you can wash and calm yourself. A medic will come treat your wounds and they'll take you back to your cell to rest. When it is time, you will go."

"Thank you."

"Behave yourself, and you'll never see me again," I informed him in Arabic. I switched to English. "Could you take him to the bathroom, let him clean himself up please?" I asked the guard. "He won't give you any more trouble. I told him restroom, medic, and back to his cell."

The Marine looked at me and what had just happened. "Right. We'll move when you are secured."

"Thank you," I said genuinely and exited. Lt. Sullivan and the rest of my escort met me in the hall.

"That was effective," he stated. "Okay, you're done for the day. Thank you."

"Okay, goodnight," I yawned and the guard directed me toward the cell block.

In my cell I found the materials Ms. Hampshire had brought. Officer Morgan tapped on the open door and joined me.

"So you met with Homeland Security and didn't hurt anyone."

"Yes ma'am. Ms. Hampshire is much more pleasant to work with."

"Could you put your foot up on the table please?"

"Okay…" I guessed she meant the anklet-bearing foot. She examined the device, pressed a little probe to it, and was satisfied.

"Great day. Get some rest; we'll have another great day tomorrow." Officer Morgan exited and the door sealed for the night.

Boring days passed until one morning they put me through a doctor's visit, a therapy session (traditional), and left me in my cell for three hours. I discovered that if I sat on the ground near the food tray slot, I could actually hear a decent amount of squawk on the radios. I gleaned that they wanted me secured for a specific purpose; that there was a transfer in progress; and from a phone call I overheard George telling someone that the British were not to be present when they 'moved'. I was hardly surprised when I was summoned from the cell and warned to behave myself later in the day.

"Alright, something is going down so let's just be very quiet," Agent Starr greeted on the interrogation floor. I nodded and we crept through the halls stealthily.

"In here," John opened the door for us and we slid into an observation booth. This one was directly behind a fake mirror: usually they used cameras in the cells and watched from those. It took me a minute to identify Ari: looks can change quickly, especially in prison. The British man Alastair was in there with George. Ari was sitting with his hands cuffed to the table. He didn't look scared, just uncomfortable and annoyed.

"Do you know where you are?" Alastair asked.

"Al-Amrik," he replied in accented Arabic. "The land of the free."

"Don't worry, Natasha got here safely," George added and sat across from him at an angle.

"Natasha,"

"That is what you call your super computer, isn't it, Ari?" George queried.

"At least, that's what she said," Alastair added. They played well together.

Small beads of sweat started to form on Ari's forehead. "Oh dear God. She who? She her?"

"She remembers you."

"She is here?"

"You knew she was in American custody," Alastair admonished.

"Belle is going to kill me. If you want anything from me, you must protect me from her!"

"Why would she do that?" George asked.

"There are things she doesn't…didn't approve of, and I might have done business with some people for some project which might have resulted in a certain Asian power temporarily hacking into certain American websites to stretch their feathers about cyber capability."

"Why would she disapprove of that?" Alastair asked.

"Have you met her? Don't touch Americans, don't touch America or she will take you down," he explained emphatically.

"Is that all?"

"Yes. That alone, I mean, I didn't even deliver the goods until I heard she was halfway across the world."

I stepped away from the glass and fist-bumped Agent Starr.

"Given her sense of values, would it make it up to her if you went and did something great for America?" George prompted.

"Possibly. I mean, I'll do it, it's a great deal, but that woman...she is extremely good."

"What if, in theory, we took this to her and let her decide whether she can forgive it or if you'll have to work separately," Alastair offered.

Ari took a couple of breaths.

"She wants this to happen. She liked the idea of bringing you into the project. The project was partially designed by her. You help her and I have a feeling she will forget all about China and The New York Times," George coached.

"You're not going to leave me alone with her, are you?" Ari checked.

"I guarantee that," George offered. "Deal?"

"Yeah alright. Just make sure she doesn't...hurt me."

"We'll take this to her," Alastair and George stood and exited in unison. George then poked his head in long enough to gesture us down the hall into a conference room.

"Well?" I asked as we gathered.

"Care for a cookie?" George opened a box and sat.

"Now we wait," the Brit informed.

"You're letting him stew? That's just mean. I hate when you do that," I took a cookie. "So this is what, you two taking the matter to me?"

"Sure," George shrugged.

"So do I get to play or what?" I asked after munching a cookie.

"What would you do?" George asked and I thought about it for a few minutes.

"Confirm his cooperation," I finally said. "So can I play with him or what?"

"Yeah, okay," George put his tea down. We walked down the hall, opened the door and George entered first. Ari looked alarmed to see me.

"Could I borrow some restraints?" I asked George quietly and let Ari watch him hand over the cuffs. "Thanks. Can we be alone for a minute?"

George left and I stepped over and sat down opposite Ari. To his amazement and the observers' amusement, I snapped a cuff around my left wrist and chained myself to the table, just like him.

"Hello Ari."

"Er, hi um, how are you? You look great."

"Not too bad, considering where we are."

"So I guess escaping isn't an option?" he checked with light humor. "Seeing as you're here…"

"Not an option. Look: this is a break for you. This is good; as good as it gets. You know how many warrants there are out on you."

"Not half as many as there were on you," he replied.

I smiled. "Well, my work is a little more high-profile. I could be persuaded to ignore some of your more recent, high-profile work if you help me with what we're working on now."

"Yeah, that's why they brought me here. What are you chasing?"

"Not important. I just need you and Natasha to provide me with something I'm pretty sure you've been working on anyway."

"Like?"

"I want a code condom."

"For?"

"Tracking very specific entities. Can you do it?"

"Yeah, little time. I don't have it…can you help? I might need some help on one of the platforms."

"You'll get help; they're very competent in cyber. After handling my laptop, they're well prepared."

He cracked a smile. "So, are we supposed to do this chained to the table in here?"

"No, of course not," I produced George's handcuff key and unlocked myself. "Oh, some guidelines from experience: don't fight them, don't lie to them, and for your own sake be nice to them. They're smart, they're well set up, and they will kill you if needed. Plus, if you don't behave yourself, I'll kick your ass."

"Like Monaco or Crete?" he asked the first referring to an actual fight and the second an amorous encounter. "Monaco," he read from my expression.

"They won't leave us together often. There will be no Cretan activities here." I caught the guard behind me looking at him with a protective stance. "Okay. So I have to go now. Just cooperate with them. It pays," I stood. "Oh, and they definitely know how to make life miserable, so go with them."

"That's good advice." Agent Won came in, uniformed in a custom gray suit and with her hair in a bun. She was very strong and intimidating. She made eye contact and tilted her head slightly to the door. I left without another word.

"May I go?" I asked George in the hall. The rude British man stepped out behind him. "Oh god," I exclaimed loudly with disgust.

"I was going to ask if she was ever locked up, but now I'm beginning to understand," The Brit said with a little respect in his eyes. Alastair and Seamus stepped out to flank him. "I believe I owe you an apology," he said civilly.

"I accept," I said and remained the distance required.

"He wasn't afraid of us," he stated.

"All due respect, sir, I believe I am scarier than any British person I've ever met. It helped, of course, that he had no reason to fear you: he knew what your limits were. He knows only some of what I can do, and that is sufficient."

"If you ever do get tired of the Americans," Hartcastle offered.

"No place like home, sir," I refused. Things became very loud in Ari's room. Furniture was moved, voices were raised, and an additional soldier went in. The Brits disappeared and I moved without thinking. I heard Ari yell,

"Not your slave!" and various other voices gave orders. I was stopped physically as I stepped toward his room. The Marine grabbed my upper arm, nearly wrapping his hand all the way around. I looked at him.

"About face," he directed me quietly. I placed my foot and pivoted as soon as he let go. He kept his arm on my shoulder as we exited the area. As soon as we were to the elevators, he let go. "Thank you."

"Sure," I replied, feeling only a little resentment. We got into the lift.

"Is he your friend?" the soldier asked.

"No, just a coworker. He's not a bad character though."
We reached my floor and exited, beginning the stages to get
to my cell. Someone confirmed that I was there on his radio,
and I was sealed back into my little apartment.

"Can I have the cleaning supplies?" I requested.

"Coming right up," A woman's voice said. The door
opened and Agent Starr was holding a bucket. "Mind if I
watch?"

"Come on in," I gestured. "Want a soda, water, or juice?"
I pointed to my fridge and accepted the supplies.

"I'm supposed to tell you it is laundry time too," Starr
offered.

"Excellent. I'll strip my bed. Same cart as last time?"

"Cart," she requested and the door opened again. Soon
everything was loaded in and I was scrubbing the shower.
"So how did this morning with the doctor go?"

"He said I'm going to get my bump soon; that I was
about fifteen weeks along. How long have I been here?"

"Less than two months; it's mid-October now. Are you
still getting sick in the morning?" she asked and I rinsed off
the walls.

"Not really. It's kind of nice," I scrubbed the toilet with
the wand.

"Me neither. It really is a relief. Men have no idea what
they're missing."

"Tell me about it," I washed my hands in my now-
cleaner sink and dried them on my pants.

"Hey, I almost got to go into the field yesterday. They
needed a sniper for a hostage scene but they changed their
minds. Now that they know I'm pregnant, I can barely get
into the field."

"Yes, I guess that would suck," I joined her at the table.

A small smile spread on her face. "Okay, now I feel like an idiot. Complaining about restrictions to,"

I cut her off, "a like-minded person. To me, it doesn't matter 'how' restrained you feel, it's that you feel significantly restrained. When I look at the big picture, I've got a pretty good set up here. Sure, there's a device attached to my ankle that could drop me to the floor in pain and I live in a cell, but I have been in worse places. I did amazing things but it came with a high cost."

"I like you," Starr confided honestly and quietly. "Is that weird?"

"I like you too Agent Starr. It's hard to find common ground with most of the people I interact with. I think I've reached a mutual understanding with the guards that I'll obey and they'll respect, but that's hardly grounds for a friendship."

"What name do you prefer call you by? Alexis? Ali? Belle?"

"Belle Jones is the name I took when I started becoming who I am. Ali Johnston drowned in Lake Michigan several years ago. So if you had shot someone yesterday, what would that have made your total?"

"I'm a professional," Starr excused and evaded for a minute. "Thirteen: it would have been fourteen kills or 23 wounded: I just prefer to incapacitate if possible."

"I don't count wounded."

"So higher or lower?" she asked me, "Total?"

"Ben-Adat made twenty-four. Oh, my new sheets are here," I accepted the package through the food window and began making up my bed. "So why are you here? What do you want to talk about?"

"I just wanted to chill. You want me to go?"

"No," I set the bucket back next to the door. "Sorry, I'm just," I stopped myself.

"Oh my god. You haven't had an actual conversation since you got here, have you?" she suddenly realized.

"I haven't had an actual conversation since…right about fifteen weeks?"

"So he knew you in more than a biblical sense."

"He knew enough."

"Agent Starr?" the speaker box squawked and the door opened. "Sorry," the guard stated and handed her a radio. She spoke for a moment.

"I will confirm. Over," she turned to me with an annoyed air. "Would you like to talk to the British?"

"All of them?"

"Tea with Seamus Dougherty?"

"I accept," I grinned.

"Alright then," she relayed the message. "1830. I should get back; I'm processing all the fun international paperwork. See you later." She took the bucket and left.

"Two hours to go…and it is naptime," I said to myself and sprawled out for a nap.

He met me in an office which was clearly not in use. Seamus and I sat face to face over the desk, which had a pot of tea on it, as well as plates and utensils.

"I ordered Thai food; I heard you liked it," he greeted me. "Thank you for coming."

"What can I do for you?" I smiled with charm.

"This meeting is totally off the record. The other two gentlemen are at another facility and they think I'm doing paperwork. This meeting, for Great Britain's record, never happened. I believe Director Goode will disguise it as well. As an expert in counterterrorism, and as an admirer, I just wanted to have dinner with a beautiful, intelligent, and totally amazing woman."

"Interesting. So, no wires, no microphones?"

"I swept the room when I got here and didn't find any."

"Alright. Assume we are being overheard," I cautioned him lightly. "So you want to get to know me?"

"I do. I was extremely impressed with the impact the mention of your name had on our prisoner. I wonder if there is a British counterpart to you somewhere, secretly protecting us."

"His name was Henry O'Toole," I informed him. "He died in 1999 in Afghanistan. I discovered him only through channels: through the underground in Afghanistan. He left maps, names, totally outdated information in a cave tunnel I stumbled across. I believe he lived there when he died. He almost got Bin Laden."

"What town?" he asked and I told him. "Amazing. Is he the only one?"

"No, there are French people everywhere. On my side of the fence, yours, the French; they'll do whatever. Now that is a system worth looking over again. Rogue French operatives...I knew at least four. Israel is a whole book of operatives on every side of every fence."

"I believe you. Did you have to engage in much criminal activity?"

"I don't know if I can answer that question."

"Britain has no jurisdiction; we don't even have proof you ever entered our country. I'm just getting ideas for a more effective method. You don't have to answer."

"If you placed an operative to do some or all of the things I did, you should expect him or her to engage in quite a lot of criminal activity."

"Good answer. So, murder, theft, cybercrimes, rampant identity fraud, smuggling, torture, explosives, espionage, drugs, guns and all that lot?"

"I never tortured; not real torture anyway. The rest sounds pretty accurate. Listen, Seamus, not to offend, but this will never fly with the British."

"I'm pretty sure it didn't fly with the Americans either. That's why we call them 'black ops'. Did you work in Britain?"

"Briefly, at times. Normally I avoided places like that: modern cities with modern police. Too dangerous for someone like me."

"And how do you see yourself?" he sipped the tea.

"Retired, I suppose. Young, scarred, well-experienced; not the best credentials in the world but I survive." Someone brought in dinner.

"You are right about the French," he admitted while we ate our Thai Pad.

"Do you really think I'm pretty?" I asked after a silence.

"Both beautiful and sexually attractive. If I wasn't British, and a gentleman, and if you weren't as dangerous as sleeping with an asp, I think I'd lift you onto this desk and initiate intercourse."

"My guard will shoot you," I replied demurely.

"Him too," Seamus added to his botched pick-up line.

"I guess I am a little fierce."

"You shot a man in the head on the streets of Tel Aviv!"

"He was a suicide bomber. It's not like you were there."

"No, I wasn't. I also wasn't there when a terrorist broke out of his cell here, found you, and entered the room shooting. I know the guard shot him," he read my face a little. "I also know that you're the one who killed him."

"I lose no sleep at night over him," I saw approval in his eyes. "Just like you don't lose much sleep over the civilians you accidentally killed."

"Where did you read that?" He hid his agitation, but not well enough.

"Your face," I replied quietly and leaned toward him. "That's the price of war," I almost whispered.

"Dead civilians?" he whispered back.

"No," our faces were inches apart. I could smell his aftershave. "Dead civilians are the price of violence. The losses and gains of this war are measured in our souls. Every death, every birth, every saved life leaves a mark on us. Perhaps I have my shadows and stains, but there are also auras and little stars."

Suddenly we were standing chest to chest.

"I didn't know you were a poet," Seamus said very quietly. His face, his shoulders, and his eyes all said he was going to kiss me. "Do you think he'll shoot me?" he asked in his slightly Scottish accent just before his lips closed the distance. It was long. It was wet. It was fierce. It was so much better than I thought it would be. When he stopped I opened my eyes, almost wondering why. In those few seconds, a hand wrapped around my right forearm and pulled me away from him firmly but not harshly. It was a good move, I discovered, as there were guns pointed at Seamus. The guard who had moved me put his weapon away as another man with a much larger gun came in. The action was silent and incredibly clear: it felt like I was dreaming. The clicking of the cuffs broke the spell as the Marines took him.

"Come on, Belle," The guard with me said.

"What, why, I don't," I uttered in short, quiet bursts as the man took my arm and half-guided me to my 'office', which was just down the hall. I didn't even realize I was crying until I sat in my chair and a tear fell on my hand. "I don't...why did, we weren't doing anything!"

"I'm sorry," The guard said and shut the door. I knew he wouldn't say anything else, so I just stared at him in bewilderment and then at the frosted window. The sun had set; the window looked like a decorative candle jar with an unlit wick.

I wasn't left for very long. George came through the door with a familiarity as though he lived in that complex. My eyes were dry by then.

"How mad are you?" he asked before he even sat down.

"I'm not mad, I'm just really confused. Okay, so maybe a little mad."

"Alright. Cut and dry version: you're not in trouble. Mr. Dougherty did something he was not allowed to do, he was viewed as a serious threat, and he was removed."

"Nice. I'd like the wet and sloppy version now," I crossed my arms.

George smiled a little. "I don't have the text of what you two were saying before the kissing: no one does. Things became awfully hot pretty fast. He allowed you access to himself and his weaponry, and the idea was that if you joined forces, things could become very bad security wise."

"So you just came in and pulled me away and held a gun to his head while slapping on some cuffs? What is this, Russia?" I regained my ground. "We were just...talking! He brought up the shootings, and I picked up his own little guilt trip, and we were talking about the price of war and violence and he said I was a poet and then it just kind of happened. Blame the pheromones."

"Alexis, consider that he might have been playing you," George suggested as I settled.

"Consider that I might not have been playing you," I retorted. "I don't need allowed access to his weaponry. He is a good man; he's not trying to pull a Bonnie and Clyde on you."

"You actually felt something?" George surmised.

"No, he's just a really good kisser. Do you know how hard that is to find? Man, it ranges from dead fish to large dog, and the good are hard to find."

"Relax, Beauty. We're not going to shoot him," he shot a verbal tranquilizer dart at me. "The whole thing was off books. We'll scare him a little and he'll go back to Great Britain in a few days. And before you ask," he cut me off, "I seriously doubt it. You will definitely not be alone with him. That is security's call."

I kept my mouth shut until my inner temper tantrum dialed down.

"I'm sorry. You liked him." George said.

"We understood each other. That's all. A little compatible company. I'd like to go back to my cell now."

"It is being viewed right now by Homeland Security."

"Leona," I remembered. "You know, if you treat me like a wild animal, I'm going to start acting like one."

"You liked him," George nodded to himself and got up.

"I liked his life. His character. It bothered him that he might be responsible for civilians dying. In my life, I've found an awful lot of people it doesn't bother at all. A lot of people," I kept talking until he closed the door behind him. "He's probably one of them," I muttered to myself.

I went quietly when the guard finally signaled for me. He didn't feel the need to cuff me, so I didn't feel the need to stomp on his toes. Leona had left by the time we got down to the zone. The guard patted me down, which was a little unusual, but given the circumstances it made sense. Clyde could have slipped me something. Officer Morgan was there.

"You seem…calm," she said cautiously.

"Well, ranting and raving doesn't get me anywhere," I replied.

"I'd be madder than hell," she said as she opened the door.

"Hell isn't mad, it's just hot and crowded," I imparted the wisdom and stepped in. "Ma'am."

"Ma'am," she replied with a little twinkle in her eye. "Look under your pillow," she said quietly and closed up.

I lifted my pillow carefully and discovered a minor treasure trove: literature! Two highbrow geek magazines, an issue of TIME, and Vanity Fair lay stacked in a small mountain of reality. As I browsed the pages I realized that they had been gone through and edited with black-out ink in certain areas. I didn't care, it was in English and it was the first interesting thing I had read in weeks. Seamus flew out of my head and I stayed up and read until I fell asleep.

The next day was good. I worked in cyber all morning, had lunch with them, and only saw Ari by accident. He wandered into the room from the side room they had him working in. I was almost pleased to see the butterfly suture on his face.

"What happened to you?" I asked in English.

"I learned a new word," he replied. "How does this work?"

"We work. Just do your thing and be nice. I don't have my weapons or contacts or access to explosives or poisons, so you're safe."

He smiled ironically. "No one is ever safe in a room with you."

"You're still afraid of me. Smart man," I clapped my hands and returned to my desk.

"They have guns: why should I be afraid of you? I'm not scared of you!" he denied a little too loudly. "You aren't scary in here." He took a few steps toward me.

I faced him. "Let me tell you something about al-Amrik. It's the land of the free and the home of the brave."

"I'm fucking sick of America!" he switched to Arabic. "I hate Americans, and I hate America! They can't just shove me around like a carpet! I'm tired, I'm angry, and I feel extremely unhelpful right now!"

"What's he saying?" Agent Won asked someone, but he was way too close to me.

"Kill me. Fucking kill me," he begged in English very quietly.

I then did something totally against my nature. I lifted my hand and gently touched his face, helped him to a chair, and held his hand.

"Agent Won, he really doesn't work well if he hasn't slept. He's a little jet lagged and apparently he's already finding the guards interesting. Could we maybe give him some aspirin and let him get some rest?"

"Yes," she handed me some tissues, which I handed to him. "Fried tech syndrome. I think we're going to move him into the cell we had you in. It's nicer."

I turned to him and switched to Arabic. "They're going to place you in a different cell, where it is quiet and there is a real bed and a curtain for the bathroom. They will let you rest. We want it, but I want a perfect product, you understand me?"

He was ashamed to speak, so he just nodded his head, tossed the tissues, and walked out in cuffs with the guards.

"Alright. They'll take care of him," Agent Won stated. "Now, this didn't work," she pulled something up on her screen and I saw a clearly failed search op.

"Okay," I analyzed it. "Let's narrow it down…a lot," I took over the controls and let the program run while I grabbed a notepad. "From here, take it down to just these, then this to here," I directed and a nameless drone in a t-shirt took over riding the circuit.

"You think that will work?" Agent Won asked and handed me a water bottle.

"Yeah. If not, we try again. Ari will come around."

"I hope so. I don't enjoy his escort."

I smiled to myself and wondered if I would ever see him again.

"Of course, the entourage is more interesting than Mr. Pomp and Circumstance. I think if you had decided to go to England you might be in Seamus' hands. He knows what he's about."

"You think?" I asked with a little innocence.

"Yeah. Luckily, you're all ours. You know, he used to chase after some of the same characters you did."

"Well, intelligence makes for bedfellows," I botched the quote.

"So we agree he's hot?" she guessed and we both giggled.

"I think this might be something," the drone announced and I let Agent Won go see. She returned.

"You know, from an intelligence standpoint, it could be valuable to the team if we gained some of Mr. Dougherty's expertise on counterterrorism," I made my first strategic move. "Maybe we could get him to share that with us?"

"Interesting," Agent Won mulled, "It might be interesting. I'll mention it to the rest of the team. It's not really my area: John would be more into this. Let's find out where he is and see what he thinks." We crossed the hall into her designated office and I played it cool while she checked her calendars. "Perfect," she picked up the phone and hit a button. "John? Lisa Won. I have Miss Jones here. Do you have a moment? Great. Yes, Belle is trying to play us so she gets some time with that British hunk. Thoughts?"

I had to laugh. I was busted. Their information network was vastly superior to my listening to radio blurbs.

"Great. Okay, see you then," she hung up. "Do we need to have this talk, or do you get it?"

My face burned a little. "I get it. I really just wanted to see him again," I said apologetically.

"C'mere, pull up the chair and shut the door all the way," She sat with me and assumed an open position. "I know about the hot and heavy interview. What were you two talking about?"

"Okay, so here's how it went," I gave her the conversation almost verbatim, which wasn't difficult as it had played through my head about a hundred times. "And he was here and I was there and it was really good. Then suddenly I was pulled away and they arrested him. Do you believe me?"

"Yes, I do. I believe you because you're being honest. I trust you because there actually is a recording of that conversation."

"He said he swept the room: did he miss something?"

"Honey, he was wearing a wire," Won broke the news gently. "He handed the tape over when they arrested him last night."

"Oh my god, he was playing me," I concluded.

"I don't think so. I think he was covering his six, and possibly taking notes. Did you know he was wired?"

"I knew someone would record it somehow. I just…well that resolves things a bit. No harm, no foul."

"Do you still want to see him?" she asked.

"I don't know. Could I spend time in the closet soon? I want to check on all of my plants."

"Soon. Maybe tomorrow," Agent Won stood. "Want me to step on his toes 'accidentally'?"

"No," I smiled and stood. "I'd like a pair of stilettos, and then I'll do it myself."

"That's my girl. C'mon, I have a surprise for you," she pulled a box from her desk. "Here, let's set you up in here so you can review what Uri was doing earlier. This," she opened the box to produce an MP3 player with headphones and a little speaker, "is all of the music from your computer. Rock on," she grinned and left me there in the segregated cube. I turned it on and played with the new toy for several minutes before turning to Ari's work. I was still lost among the rhythms when the guard shift changed and we had dinner. George joined us just as we were clearing the food.

"I want you in interrogation," he entered and addressed me. "Take her to 54B please. Go with it, honey."

I raised an eyebrow but followed the directions. I found Lt. Sully and some man named Agent Kensington waiting for me in the observation room linked to a cell with a fake mirror.

"The Brits leave tomorrow, so we're just wrapping things up," he explained. "Mr. Dougherty thinks he's going to interrogate Ari again."

"What's going on?" I mused.

"You and Seamus can see each other again without compromising security. I flip this switch," he pointed, "and he can see us. Ready?"

It began with George and Seamus entering the room mid-conversation.

"Unfortunate run-in," George was saying.

"Well I got what I needed. I've had worse evenings," Seamus replied casually.

"Bastard!" I whispered to myself.

"So, the prisoner is on his way?"

George looked at the glass and I nodded Kensington's confirmation. He hit the switch.

"She's right there, actually," George gestured.

"Mike on," Sully clicked.

"Hello, lover," I did a little wave and picked up a piece of paper with nothing on it.

"Ms. Jones! Er, good evening. How are you today?" he stalled.

I mimed reading the paper. "Sir; it may be of great utility of tactic to gain information regarding the British officer with a background in counterterrorism. He and I have pursued the same targets and he may have information regarding our targets of current interest which could prove helpful. I am certain I could extract information from him in a private exchange if I am given a little leeway. I await your decision. Respectfully yours," I set the paper down and looked at him knowingly. His face was suited for poker.

"You made that up. I set up the meeting," he replied calmly.

"Did you?" George asked him and took a seat.

"You're sure?" I asked him coyly and turned to Sully. "Could you hand me...there. Yes." Sully handed me a notepad with some illegible scrawling on it. "This is a draft of what I'm sending up later. I thought it only fair," I shrugged. "Ma'am: This email is to inform you that our operation with the British visitor was a success. I can

220

confirm that he is overly informed as to our operations here: particularly knowledgeable regarding the Ben-Adat incident and some of the interchanges regarding prisoners. I expected that he might know some of my past, but I was relieved to discover his knowledge was limited. As an open exchange of information, I divulged the existence of British operative Henry O'Toole, but I gave him the wrong location. I sincerely doubt he will locate him of his own initiative. Did we know about his involvement with the accidental deaths of some civilians? I can learn more with another exchange. He is sexually attracted to me, and I believe his ego sufficient to manipulate him," I put the notebook down.

"You...you're making that all up. We have a connection! I'm not using you!"

"You might want to turn your pen-microphone off for this part," I replied as we aligned with the glass between us.

"You let me have her in good faith!" Seamus retorted to George.

"Please," I said with attitude. "No one 'has' me. You viewed me as an easy intelligence source, you tried to gain my trust; get into my head. You were the actor; I was the extremely talented director that led you around."

"You are nowhere near clever enough to pull that off," Seamus' face was red.

"Don't feel bad: usually the sex card plays really well as an instant memory eraser. And I will admit you play it very well."

Seamus turned to George, "I'd like to go somewhere private where we can talk."

"Good idea."

"I can't believe that bitch played me," he muttered to himself.

"Bye!" I waved and walked toward the door until the lights had changed again.

"And we're clear," Kensington said with a grin. "That was excellent. Did you just think and do it?"

"Pretty much: let's hear it for improvising!"

Sully looked up for a second. "Uh oh," he uttered and I scrambled behind a rack of devices. The door opened and closed and someone walked in.

"Alexis?" George asked and Sully pointed in my direction.

"All clear," he told me and I pulled the wires out of my hair before stepping out. "Brilliant. Could not have been written better! I can't wait to tell John. I set up a meeting with him and Dougherty later tonight."

"He's going to want the name of the town," I informed him. "Tell him it will cost him a treadmill. I'm feeling sluggish sitting all day."

"If this causes him to give us what I want him to give us, I will reward you appropriately," George was excited. "Icing would be if you got Ari back on track."

"I've got him. He'll be in front of the computer in no time," I replied confidently. Looking back into the cell, I felt a twinge.

"You okay?" Sully asked as George went out the door.

"Yes, I'm...I'll be fine. It's just...well, I just totally screwed Seamus, and not in the way I originally wanted to. It's an ugly business. Hell, it's an ugly world."

"They put in piping, dry wall and painted the addition today. If things keep going well, you might have a nice little space down there in a week or so," he mentioned. "Kind of an odd barter system: you serve us and you kind of accumulate points that turn into rewards."

"I like getting return: I know that what I present has a monetary value, and I do work here. Weirdest job ever, but I'm flexible."

"Got to be better than smuggling porn," he observed. "Oh, Starr is waiting for you in your cell. She said to say 'chocolate'."

"See ya," I headed out of there and proceeded down with my escort.

"Question:" the guard said in the elevator. "Did you actually write those emails?"

"No, I was playing him," I replied as we reached our floor. "That was the plan, I think," I waved to the guards and proceeded through my open cell door. Starr was sitting at my table. She looked a little tired. She was also not carrying her guns.

"Okay, I lied. I have no chocolate," she admitted as the door sealed. "The vending machine is out."

"I thought chocolate was a code word for 'I need to see you immediately'. You need some?" I kicked off my shoes and opened the little rubber container I kept food in.

"No. Maybe. I don't know. I need your help again, and I don't have anything to offer you."

"Okay. Do you want to lie down?"

She did. "No, that's really sweet,"

Oy, Americans. "I'm afraid I only do under the table nonprofit business while lying down. Come on up here, plenty of room." We got situated quickly, fitting side by side easily. "Alright. Comfortable? Need a blanket?"

"I'm just fine, thanks," she smiled and looked over at me. "Okay, so what's the protocol for doing this kind of business?"

"Well, when we're comfy, you take a deep breath and stare at the ceiling while telling me the situation. Together we identify the issues, and then I solve the problem."

"Is there a catch?"

"Always. In this case, I would request that you keep visiting me sporadically, as a visitor. I like it. I can fix it upstairs if that's needed."

"You're a good woman, Belle."

"Okay, so spill."

She explained how things had gotten a little soggy in her personal life and how that had inevitably spilled into her work life, and she was afraid that her current supervisor would give up on her and recommend early maternity leave.

"Besides being a shooter, you're also a profiler, right?"

"How did you know?"

"All good snipers are profilers. Did you like the whole ethnic changing thing?"

"It was great for me, yes."

"So The Man liked that?"

"Yes."

"Have you done a lot of interagency work?" I latched onto an idea.

"Not as much as I would like."

"Alright. Here is what we're going to do. Your current supervisor is a guy: he hears the word 'pregnant' and sees a giant ball and chain attached to you. So we're going to knock him out of the picture and get you transferred to George's team of interagency superheroes. I'll take care of that. From you, I need a profile work up of the new prisoner Uri Vletsko. I will give you most of what you need for that. We're convincing them that they need an analytical insider: a profiler like you who can handle the big ugly world. To be honest, we probably do. We're going to play the personal connection between us very lightly, at least at first."

"Why are you being so nice?" she asked with affection in her slightly teary eyes.

"I'm a sucker for a blue eyed girl. Okay, look, I haven't had a real conversation with anyone in a really long time, and I feel like I might be with you. I feel like I can talk to you."

"Would it be okay if I just stayed here for a while?"

"Of course," I got up slowly and turned the lighting down a little. I tossed a throw on her feet and grabbed a notepad before returning to the bed. "Right," I snuggled down a bit and placed my dolphins. "Uri Vletsko, or as I know him, Ari Hansen or Ali al-Shedan, was born in Afghanistan as the bastard of a Russian and a native woman. He speaks Russian, Arabic, some Pashtun, and of course English. His formal education took him through the Swiss schools and he graduated from MIT in 1998, early. He had to go big on everything. That didn't take him far in corporate America, so he went underground. That worked extremely well for him, with unlimited opportunities and resources."

"Unlimited until he met you. I overheard his sudden pro-American feelings," she smiled and took over note-taking.

"There are plenty of fish in his sea. Helping China hack an American website is small compared to some of the things I know he pulled off. Let's just say he owns a Grecian Island."

She stayed for about an hour; then left me to a warm bed.

Chapter 9: Rage

I woke up before the artificial sunrise and showered. Breakfast came and they let me out around 8. Agent McEwen was waiting for me in my office.

"Well, quite an interesting affair with that British hunk," he began the conversation dryly.

"Yes, I suppose it was," I returned with caution.

"So did you mean what you said about people having value and souls?"

"Does it matter?"

"And then you stared him in the face and told him it was all a ploy."

"Don't act surprised. You know what happened."

"You shot a man," the agent shrink began and I knew it would not be a pleasant conversation.

"At least one," I replied. *Where is he going with this? He knows my number of kills, and it's universally known that I've shot several men, first to last.*

"You were carrying a gun in your purse. You shot rounds out in the Canadian wilderness until you were good. You cleaned it every night. You pulled it out and aimed it at his nose and pulled the trigger."

"I heard the noise, I saw the blood. I shot him," I retorted defiantly.

"Cold blood."

"Hot explosives," I verbally shot him.

"And the man you ax-murdered?"

"That was an accident. Almost."

"How old were you?"

"Young."

"Eighteen?"

"Younger. Murder is nowhere near as horrific as it seems on paper."

"Assassinations," he phrased. "Execute, hit, kill, neutralize."

"Blast into oblivion."

"So, no guilt?"

"I sleep just fine, thanks."

"Even after having sex with total strangers?"

"I never sleep with total strangers! I've screwed God only knows how many, but I'd never fall asleep with them. No, I make sure they're out, take their data, and move along so I can shower. They always used condoms."

"So that's how to be a whore without consequences."

"The best women in history are whores by someone's definition," I got cocky.

"Where did you find O'Toole?"

"Kandahar. I never found O'Toole's body, just his bank — you know: the stash we keep around."

"How do you know he's dead then?"

"Spy. Not a long life expectancy. Plus, his stash was ancient."

"His 'bank'?"

"No, hashish. Apparently he liked a good smoke. I don't blame him."

"Spies use weed?"

"It's a stressful job."

"What does Ari like to use?"

"Absinthe, on occasion," I remembered, "and the liquor with the worm in it."

"Last question: did you enjoy watching him squirm last night?"

"Not particularly. I just felt good that I pulled it off. I'm not a sadist: he just pissed me off."

"And I don't? I just called you a whore!"

"You're just another drone to me right now. You're clearly trying to provoke a reaction, and frankly it's being done so immaturely it's not worth much more than an eye roll," I gauged his reaction. He was pleased and trying to hide it. "You know my history; I was 'ax-murdering' people at an age when most girls are trying to get a prom date. I've lived independently for eight years in a lot of countries doing some very mature work," I shrugged.

"Very good Belle. You've learned how to sufficiently control your temper when provoked."

"Very good, Dr. McEwen: I think you've mastered the art of sounding like an idiot," I smiled serenely. "I'd like to talk to Director Goode today regarding the Waldo affair."

"Bring it up at 0930 when she meets with you regarding the Brits."

"That's in six minutes!" I realized.

"Then you better scoot," he replied and I walked out without him. I passed Natalie just after I caught my breath and straightened my jacket.

"She's here," Natalie told her phone.

"Come on in, Belle," Director Goode called and I walked in with my guard. She appeared to be answering emails.

"Good morning," I greeted and niceties were exchanged. "When we're finished with what you'd like to see me about, could I run an idea by you?" I tested the waters.

"Of course," she said and pushed her computer away. "About the British," Director Goode spoke to some extent about what had happened with and without my knowledge. She finally got to the juicy bits. "Were you harmed in your interaction with Seamus?"

I blinked on that one. "Uh, no," I replied unconvincingly. "No," I tried again and it sounded more definitive.

"You didn't know he was wired."

"I was sure that somewhere there was a recording device. It all turned out alright, didn't it? You now know I wasn't trying to bust out of here with him, plus he now thinks we have his number. Winners all around."

"Well, we won all around. I was just concerned that your heart might have suffered a loss."

"Don't be silly. Did we get the information we wanted from the Brits?"

She smiled knowingly. "What did you want to talk about?"

I pulled myself together and made my pitch. She listened, but showed no feedback. I decided to play the XX card. "Honestly, a man sees woman in his force and hears the word pregnancy and all he sees is a big old ball and chain. It's ridiculous. If I wasn't here, I would be out there doing what all I do, probably up until the last few weeks."

"I'll discuss it with Agents Tomopolis and Starr."

"She's a good profiler, and we could use that when we start putting faces to coding sequences," I pointed.

"We do need more women on the team. No offense, but you present difficulties."

"Regulations," I nodded empathetically.

"Well we can only break so many of them. Why don't you go to cyber for a while, I think Uri or Ari is up and running again. Keep an eye on him: he allegedly tends to get physical."

"It's alright ma'am, Agent Won and I can take him."

She smiled. "Why didn't Agent McEwen come up with you?"

I turned to her in the doorway. "Apparently, I'm an ax-murderer," I said lightly and shrugged for a touch of comedy. Her eyebrows demanded an explanation. "He did his very best to offend me this morning; childish, actually. He was nearly as rude as the British were, and when nothing happened he probably retreated to figure out why. Men."

"Nothing happened?"

"No ma'am. I'm a well behaved murderess," I winked and left.

At the lab, I entered to see Ari spazzing, which was normal, and Agent Won and the guard fencing the situation nervously. Ari gets very sensitive when he's working; if an interruption ruins a really good line of thought he can be very angry. Then he gets mad at himself for getting angry and wasting the time.

"Agent Won," I entered the room.

"Get out Belle, we're having a little showdown here," she called.

"No, it's okay, he does this," I explained and approached Ari from the side.

"Make them get out!" he shouted at me. I smacked him with an open palm, just above and behind his right ear. Like a hypnotized subject, he snapped out of it immediately. "Oh," he uttered and sat back down. The three pairs of eyes left in the room were giving me an odd look.

"Wait a minute," I said quietly and waited for part two.

Ari started rocking back and forth in his chair and muttering curses. This time I palmed the front of his head with less force.

"Ari," I said calmly.

"Thanks Belle."

"Reboot and start again," I told him and left, leading the pack behind me.

"I didn't know he was autistic," Agent Won said when we were safely out of range, "Is that autistic?"

"That's not autism. That's just Ari. Super computer geniuses tend to be a little…off. Mentally, his circuits overload and lock when he's pulled out of his weird little world," I explained his method to her as well as I could.

"So you just smack him?"

"Gently, with just enough force for him to feel it. Preferably the back of the head. Don't hit anything below the jaw line because he's not operating in that body," I tried to explain.

Agent Won thought it over quickly. "Alright, let's go with that," she decided and the guard nodded. "Are you on a mission?"

"No, they're just keeping me out of my cell so the workers can work," I explained my interpretation.

"Okay, well…" she looked around. "Closet?"

"Closet," I agreed. I was eager to reconnect with the cyber world.

She led the way. "Same deal as always, he's going to see everything you see. Be nice. Actually, can you find and tag someone for me?" she wrote down the name and a few details. "That would be huge."

"Iran? Okay. Why not: I'll go through Russia," I muttered to myself and got comfortable. While I taught the boy in the other room some very seedy tricks of the trade, I developed an incredible hunger. Finally I set up a program insert and pushed away from the desk. "Agent Won," I called and she came in a minute.

"Hungry?" she poked her head through.

"Starving," I replied, still watching the screen.

"Let him take over," she said and a blue eyed man of some Nordic descent came in and swapped places with me. "He's been shadowing you. Come on, we have food."

"I'm just so hungry," I said apologetically.

"Yeah, so was Ari after seven hours. Finally I just got something warm and good smelling and set it near the door. Effective, if odd," she replied. "Babe, it's three o'clock."

"Is that fried chicken?"

"KFC, pastries, and a salad. Knock yourself out," she told me and I dug directly into it.

A few minutes later I was interrupted. "Wow. You eat like a pig in prison," Ari observed and joined me, sipping a Mountain Dew.

"Shut up," I aptly replied and placed the last bone back in the box before wiping my mouth and shoving a cherry turnover into it. As food entered my system, I slowed the onslaught down to a civilized level. By the time I munched on the salad I was polite society again. "So, how's it coming?"

"It's not easy," he admitted. "Who is responsible for the bed and the cell that doesn't reek of urine?"

"That's just how it works," I replied and sipped water.

"Liar; it was you, wasn't it?"

"I may have said that it would improve your working ability. I'm saying now, behave yourself and keep working, because there are plenty of urinated on cells with bad beds."

"Break it up," a Marine ordered and Ari stood up and walked several steps away without saying anything. Agent Won came in with another Marine, and they took Ari away.

"I need to take you back to your room," she said apologetically. "It has nothing to do with you. You did great work: Vlad can take it from here."

I dumped the trash and followed her curiously.

"I need to show you something," she explained as we passed into my dwelling. I noted the cracks in the walls immediately. "They're coming right along, and eventually this wall will come out. But while you were hacking China or whatever, some of my guys were working on something special. Behind this wall is a full length electrical fence. All you have to do is pretend this wall is totally immovable and not touch it. Right now the paint is drying: they'll take out the wall before putting in the floor: you'll have a big sheet of plastic then. Next few days are going to be a little crazy in here, and rule *numero uno* is security."

"No argument."

"You want to sleep?"

"I'm good," I began to reply when Lt. Sullivan poked his head into the door.

"Doctor time, not naptime," he informed and I grabbed a decaffeinated soda. They made the switch away from caffeine and I could definitely tell.

"You know you could just hang a sheet of plastic there and lock the other door," I suggested to the guard as we exited.

The doctor did a sonogram and I saw how the wiggle worm had evolved into a fetus floating around in my uterus. I had grown half a cup size and the hint of a future baby bump was evident when I lay down. Afterwards, they took me to my cell and let me come to terms with my imminent motherhood. That took a long time. I studied how they had sawed through the grouting on the stones beneath the drywall, creating a puzzle-like pattern in the yellow wall. The line across the bottom of the floor and at the top of the ceiling showed signs of the remodeling they had done on my finished room.

I closed my eyes and was about to drift into sleep when I heard a familiar voice.

"Alexis, are you decent?" George called from the hall. I sat up as the door unsealed. "Belle?" he called.

"Yes, yes, I'm up. What's wrong?"

Officer Morgan came in first, followed by George. The door resealed.

"How's it going?" he asked as he took a seat at the table. "I want to talk about this morning."

"Which this morning?" I asked, sitting on the bed.

"All of it."

"Fine. I went and annoyed Dr. McEwen first: he called me a whore and questioned my abilities. Then I met with Deputy Director Goode; we discussed several things. Afterwards I went to the cyber department."

"How do you feel about Agent Starr joining my team?"

"I think it's a shame you didn't have her on from square one: you might have caught up to me faster with an accurate profiler on your team. She's observant, a good listener, and not being employed to her fullest ability in her current position."

"You like her."

"She's easy to work with," I replied.

"I'm inclined to agree. I told her the news over lunch," he informed. "So, are you going to kill Tom or what?"

"I told Director Goode this morning that I was a well behaved murderess; you aren't suggesting I do otherwise, are you?" I ran my fingers through my hair.

"They did warn you about the wall, yes?"

"It seems like overkill, but I have no intention of pushing out that half-ton of bricks in a seriously lame escape attempt."

"Alright: tomorrow you're scheduled to work out at 9, interrogation at 11, free time after that until 3: we have a team meeting."

"Tonight?"

"You and Ari in an interrogation room; we'll be watching behind the glass."

"Oy. What time?"

"Now."

"Did you want something in particular?" I asked and pulled my jacket on as we marched out of there.

"Yes, expose him to us," he said in the elevator.

Grand. What the hell does that mean? I thought as I entered the room where Ari was sitting.

"So, are you one of them or one of us?" Ari greeted me in English. "I've been thinking. I never would have believed it then, that you might be a deep cover American agent. Then again, you could probably pull it off. So?"

I immediately knew I couldn't answer that question. "How is it, exactly, that you know when I'm lying?" I responded and took a seat at his right.

"You get this 'shit!' look behind your left eye. It's very subtle, and I'd believe that you might be able to fake it. You are one of them."

"Ari could one of them, deep cover or not, be able to do some of the things we did on Crete?" I sidetracked the point.

He smirked to himself in a memory. "That night we broke through and planted our transmitter was a real moment for me."

"I went out and got dinner for us, and you were cussing at the computer and typing superfast when I returned. You looked up," I recalled the scene, "you looked up at me and I knew."

"We never actually ate that dinner."

I smiled and blushed a little.

"So, friend or foe?"

"It doesn't matter anymore," I sighed. He reached out his hand and slid it gently over mine. I signaled the guards and they stopped their advance.

"What's going to happen to me?"

"You won't be here forever. We'll finish what we're doing, and maybe if there's something else, they might keep you on as a sort of employee. It's not fantastic, but it's better than that Turkish prison.

"Slavery instead of imprisonment," he stated.

"Think of it as a badly paying opportunity to help a good cause," I played with his hand.

"I do like the facilities," he admitted. "They're up to speed technology wise. Of course, with you working for them, they probably have all sorts of things."

"With you working for them, we will have all sorts of things," I assured him and withdrew my hand. "Tell me, is there someone I should contact? A wife, children?"

"The only family I have is my brother and sister. Don't worry about them. She's in Russia and last I heard he was in Ukraine."

"No one waiting for you anywhere?"

"No, I haven't worked with a partner since you left. Then they captured me. Fucking Interpol."

"The people here are going to get to know you and your little quirks; they'll do whatever they can to get a good working environment going for you. You just have to communicate."

"I sleep a lot better when it's dark. I need a clock that I can see and read or I'll get disoriented. You know not to interrupt me when I'm working. I haven't seen daylight in weeks. Just a glimpse, it's just so…stale in here," he rambled.

"I know what you mean," I empathized and he continued.

"The guards are so rough and these chains hurt, and what is with these clogs? Do they have shoes here?" he added.

"I'll find out," I offered.

"One thing confuses me," he changed course. "Were you undercover when we…on Crete? Was I working for the US then?"

"You were working for me," I replied and the lights flashed. My guard touched my shoulder and I got up and left with him. I joined George, the colonel, and a few others in the control room. "By the way, no one told me what to say so I just went along with it."

"For the most part, that was exactly what I wanted," George praised.

"What were you doing in Crete?" The colonel asked confused.

"Pages 34-42 in the Karma Sutra," I informed him. He went very red in the head.

"God, Belle," Lt. Sullivan chided.

"Well not literally!" I defended. "So what's my story here? Am I me or am I me as you?"

"I don't know yet. He's going to be hard to convince otherwise at this point. We could take any angle from here and be alright."

"He's not stupid," I cautioned.

"We don't do anything tonight. Put them both back in their cells," he decided.

"George," I said with a note of irritation.

"Goodnight."

I scowled at him until the guard took my forearm gently.

"Hey, am I going to need these?" the soldier asked and flashed a pair of steel restraints.

"One moment, please," I requested calmly and turned my attention back to George. "I don't think this is a wise decision."

"You're one of us in make-believe world, Alexis. In the real world, you're a very pampered prisoner."

"I'm an asset and a resource!"

"You're a security nightmare and an intelligence quandary."

"I hate you! I'm so done," my closest guard seized my right arm and started to pop the cuffs on, "with your stupid games!" I turned and exited with the soldier.

The gang back at the cell block was slightly surprised to see the bracelets, but I didn't say anything and I stepped right on in when I was released. The door was sealed, dinner was on the tray and I pulled it in before anyone could deny me any other basic rights.

The next morning I went to the gym and got a little rage out before they sat me in an interrogation room and left Tom in there with me.

"You are grade-A pissé," he observed and got comfortable in the very uncomfortable seats.

I said nothing.

"You're not going to say anything," Tom concluded after a few minutes of contained silence.

"What was it? Who was it?"

I smiled knowingly.

"George, the guards, me, the doctor?"

I gave him no response.

"I didn't really want to be that mean to you yesterday. It was an exercise," he excused, but received nothing. "You're not a whore. You're a business person," Tom tried and received eye contact briefly. My body language told him I was not impressed. "I heard that George called you a very pampered prisoner. Personally, in your circumstances, that would totally piss me off. I wouldn't be talking to an interrogator either." He finally shifted the focus off my body and onto my brain. "Did he tell you that he didn't think you were good enough to be one of the team, that you were his little puppet to come in and do things under his dictation? That would be a huge blow to the sense of identity I expect you are forming. And it's just mean! Is that sort of what he said to you?"

I let him know silently.

"How rude is that? Here you are and your imprisonment has never been clearer to you. You see Uri in the same conditions you were in just a few weeks ago. You see Uri and the sacrifices you made flash vibrantly, they can't be ignored. And constantly, constantly you find yourself with and against the team that is with and against you; they work together without you and you don't have a chance to play that card on them. They work together with you and you get paltry thanks. You have no certainty, none. But the games don't stop."

I closed my eyes *diamonds in the sand, diamonds in the sand* I tried to visualize instead of tearing up.

"You are frustrated and angry, and maybe even a little scared. The rational part of your brain says to just stay and bear it, the part of your brain that has shaped some of the best times of your life says to bust the hell out of here at any cost, but it hits a barrier when you realize what that cost might be. You've been on your own since mid-puberty: you didn't have the normal social rites of your peers. But you realized what 'growing up' meant and you took on those responsibilities at far too young an age. Now you have another responsibility; you've come to the peak of maturity with this one. You'll be in charge of your own child. Having a baby doesn't mean maturity to everyone, but for you…this is a major milestone. You're twenty-four and you're a very well-seasoned veteran at life. So yes: it's okay to be angry that someone treats you like a child. You're not a child. You're a legend."

Even after that performance, he got nothing verbal. He took it in stride. "You should perhaps know that he only said what he said because of military pressures. The colonel was there, and we're catching heat from the Army." He stood up to leave.

"The next time you see the colonel," I finally spoke, very quietly, "remind him that 'ARMY' is an acronym for 'Aren't Ready for Marines Yet'," I stood up and popped my neck. "And if he sends men to get me, they will not return. I agreed to be held here, by these people for this cause. Anything else will result in brief but exciting activity."

"I'll pass that along," Tom replied with a hint of a smile in his eye. He was gone only a minute.

"You have something to say to me?" the colonel blew in, followed closely by Tom.

"That depends on what you're ready to hear," I said coolly.

He judged the situation. "Yes, you would," he decided and left.

I looked at Tom and shrugged. "What? I would."

"Yeah you would," he added and opened an arm to me. "Come on, I'll buy you lunch."

"Thai?"

"How about Mongolian barbeque?"

"Yum."

"Go on to your office; I'll be there shortly." He left and the guard closed the door behind Tom.

"Hang out for a minute," The guard directed.

"Okay," I said apprehensively and sat down. A blond male agent with delightful chiseling and a cleft chin walked in.

"I'm Agent Kensington. I work with our security forces here," he introduced.

"I know. We've met. You're a former Marine: you were at my arrest."

"Army Rangers," he corrected, "and good memory."

"Thanks,"

"I'm here about the construction work."

"I'm not going to attempt escape; I know all about the electric wall."

"That's gone, it was a fire hazard. Eventually the door will be sealed and built over. You'll have workers entering through your working door. I like your attitude: it's much better than I expected."

"Clearly you missed that little incident with the three guards," I forced a smile.

"No, I expected that. The shooting of Ben-Adat was a surprise though."

"Imagine how he felt," I joked and he laughed. "So, Agent Kensington," I gave him a dramatic once-over, "if you're here about the weapons of mass destruction in Iraq, I really can't help you much."

He gave me a mostly fake laugh. "Ironically, I am here about Iraq."

"It's not really my area."

"Roshad, as you knew him. Mossad's taking credit for wiping him out. Who did he play with?"

"They're all dead," I shook my head. "If that ring is still going, it's second generation. I don't have anything on them."

"Where's the body?"

"From what I heard," I phrased it carefully, "his assassin placed him in a steel vat with battery acid and Egyptian drain cleaner. I saw the results two days and then seven days after. There is no body. There isn't even a bone left. Then the factory was bombed."

"Now that's thorough," he stated.

"I call it overkill. Why is Mossad claiming that hit?"

"I can't tell you."

"Ah, Middle Eastern intelligence. Lack thereof. What else?"

"So you did not kill Roshad?"

"No, I did not. I was there, Aron shot him about five times."

"Roshad was born on American soil," he explained.

"Well, then I still haven't killed an American," I shot back at him.

"Body?"

"No body: look, I watched it happen! Aron killed him, Mossad was there and they shoved him into a small vat and poured the acid on him. We left, and a few days later I went back with a Mossad agent who wanted to show me something. I nearly puked: he poked the soup with a stick and caught a bone. There was this smell; it was the worst smell I've ever smelled. I went back a few days after that to see what had happened. They poked it but nothing poked back. I never understood why they blew the factory up though."

"They found out who he was and covered their tracks," he explained. "You'll be happy to know that of the masses of people you've killed, none were Americans."

"Twenty-three bad men and one seriously evil woman are not 'masses', Agent Kensington. They weren't even decent human beings. You've bombed thousands or millions of people indiscriminately: I just snuffed out the lives of a few poisons to the human race."

"Poetic," he said sarcastically.

"Have you read the observation notes on me? As if I would turn myself into you here after killing a citizen? I did my homework."

"I know. So did I. That's why we're taking you out of your cell and placing you in an alternate location until the work is finished."

"Did Director Goode approve this?" I said in disbelief.

"Yes. Don't worry—you aren't going far and we packed your laptop and dolphins."

"Where am I going? Another cell?" I asked as he gestured me out the door and we walked.

"Come on, I'll show you." we marched briskly to my office, where two Marines were pushing furniture and wiring the window.

"Make a hole!" someone called and we backed up against the desk. A futon was brought in: a wire bed with a red futon pad.

"Welcome home!" Tom called in the door. "Seems a little busy in here."

"Little bit. Let's eat out here," I replied.

"No," the soldier said.

"Uh, let's eat in the conference room," Tom offered.

"No."

"Let's go back to interrogation," he tried again. No one shot that down, so we went.

"Smells good," I said.

"They're going to be a while. Here, in here," we ducked into a deserted small conference room. "So you're having a little sleepover," he handed me a plate and we scooped the food out.

"How long?" I asked.

"Just tonight. There are a zillion rules with that— essentially, don't do anything without asking first."

"Great. Jumpy guards," I said sarcastically.

"Chopsticks?"

"Of course,"

"It won't be that bad."

We ate in silence and had finished when Captain Stover walked in.

"Alright: we took you out so the workers can finish, but the only place we were allowed to put you was your office. You can shower at the gym, you know the bathroom there, and we're locking down the area. Knock on the door before you open it. We're not going to shoot you; I put my best men on this detail. The night shift has two women on it. Now, when this meeting is over, I need to take you upstairs to wait in Director Goode's office until the 1500 meeting."

"Alright. Let's all play ball. We're grown-ups; you're doing your job, I'm doing mine. Let's make this nice and smooth and then we can all go home," I yawned. "Hope she lets me borrow her couch. Shall we?" I stood up slowly.

Captain Stover gestured and we left Agent McEwen to go upstairs.

"Good day?" I asked conversationally.

"Weather's miserable out there," The captain replied.

"It seems so cold here; I guess that's what I get for hanging out in the Middle East."

"We shouldn't have to house you in the alternate location more than one night; they put your dolphin blanket in there as well," he replied.

"Very considerate, thank you," I replied as the doors opened. The office was empty and I was snoozing in a few minutes. Director Goode had even left a little throw blanket for me.

I woke but remained still as I recognized voices.

"Maybe we should let her sleep, the poor thing," Leona from Homeland Security said.

"Why does everyone look so innocent when they're sleeping?" John wondered in the same hushed tone.

"We'll be finished with her cell unit very soon." Director Goode said.

"Her intelligence and the material she produces with her former contact Ari are invaluable to our effort. Her designs are incredible: I'd swear she was the one who went to MIT," I recognized Agent Won's voice.

I decided to stir. "Tai Chi?" I asked in feigned confusion.

"Great art." George greeted as he came in.

"Let's get started," Director Goode sat at the table. I joined them for a boring display of bureaucratic efficiency.

"Alright, it's Friday. Everyone go home. I'll see you on Monday. Belle, you should be back in the room tomorrow afternoon."

"Some of my techs are working this weekend; I told Kmetz you might help him," Agent Won added.

"Agent Starr is on duty Saturday and Sunday shifts," George assured me, "perhaps you two could catch up on her analyses."

"See you later," John said and people started exiting until it was just me, the director, and Leona.

"Do you get lonely on the weekends?" Leona asked.

"Lonely or bored; same difference really. May I have access to the gym this weekend, ma'am?" I asked the director.

"Yes; the security staff has a list of privileges for you. Your temporary cell is totally set up now."

"Thank you ma'am."

"What do you do on the weekends?" Leona asked.

"Sometimes people are here, sometimes they aren't. Days all look about the same. When it's quiet I read, or write, or draw or watch DVDs. I'm fine entertaining myself, ma'am; I've definitely had the practice," I assured her and exited.

The evening began quietly. I ate dinner at my desk and I folded out the futon to reread the magazines again. When I needed to use the ladies room it was tense, but we handled it like grown-ups. It seemed like I had just gotten comfortable when they knocked on the door.

"Present," I called back and they opened the door. Officer Belot, the other female MP, came in with a buddy.

"This is highly unorthodox, but Officer Morgan is a friend of mine," she began.

"She's a nice person," I agreed.

"Your friend is holding her hostage."

"I'm going to kill him," I stood up.

"She requested we try you first. I respect her, but," she had doubts.

"Ma'am, I've kicked his ass," I pointed to the buddy guard, whom I had previously kicked in the throat.

"You have less than two minutes," she said and we moved on down to the cell.

"I need at least one and a half," I said before she opened the door.

"You will give me what I want!" Ari shrieked in a crazed voice. He threw Officer Morgan toward a far corner.

"Yeah, I'll give you what you want." Fury drove me as I rammed into and then over him. "What the hell is wrong with you?" I kicked him a few times in the general torso. "How dare you do that, she's a woman!"

"They're coming to get you. They're coming to get us all. I had to see you before they turn the gas on. They're just like the Nazis; they've got a big furnace for our bodies! I love you Sarah!" He was raving mad and in and out of Arabic and English. I put him on his belly and looked over to Officer Morgan as the cell filled with soldiers.

"Everyone stand down!" she directed. "He's raving mad, out of his mind."

They bound him anyway in a burrito-like device that totally restrained him. I stood on the wall, a few feet from Morgan, who was still in a corner. A guard had a hand on me, but I was fine.

"Come here, Belle, let her come Sammie," Morgan directed, a little breathless.

"You need a medic, ma'am," I told her and she wrapped her arms around my shoulders.

"Thank you," she said sincerely. "Alright, let's get out of here. Where the hell is the medic?" Morgan kept an arm around me until we got to Sammie, who picked her up and evacuated her. I followed and soon we were all sitting in a break-room style room. "I knew you could handle crazy people," she answered my unspoken question. "But I didn't know if you would do it."

"I would have killed him, if it had to be done. He's totally bananas: snapped or something. But yes, I would have done it. Depending on where those kicks landed I may have done it," I suddenly realized how cold it was and then realized I was in my pajama pants.

"You would have done it for me," she was amused.

"Ma'am, I'd have done it for any of these people. That's what I've been doing all along. But yes, especially for you."

The medic came in and people started making plans and taking orders and all that military hoo-ha they do so well.

The blood on my clothes was from him and I only appeared to have a few rough spots from the encounter. Officer Belot showed up again and took me back to the cell, where Lieutenant Shapiro, the man I had once wind-piped, high-fived me.

"Could you please put your clothes in this bag, we have a change for you in there," he handed me a plastic evidence bag. I provided him the clothes and went to the bathroom. They cautioned me to not get too comfortable when I returned to the office and I figured that all hell would likely break loose any minute. I waited for an hour, but I fell asleep anyway. There is no sense in wasting perfectly good time waiting awake when you can be sleeping.

I was sound asleep when my door opened, instantly waking me up.

"Belle," Captain Stover said my name and I caught my breath.

"I'm up."

"Take it easy, sorry I woke you."

"Is she alright?"

"She'll be fine. Are you dressed?"

"Yes, what time is it?"

"It's around 0200. Agents Starr and Kensington are on their way; Agent Tomopolis, the CIA man John and probably Director Goode will be here in a few hours."

"How did this happen? Ari's practically a weenie."

"We think he was drugged and when the drug stopped coming, he went into withdrawal."

"Possible," I agreed and smoothed my hair. "There are a number of drugs the British may have been using to make him compliant. I've seen it before."

"From the British?"

"It's fairly common in Asia and the Middle East. Any counterterrorism specialist would know about it."

"The tox screen will be in soon."

"He was definitely tripping," I decided for myself and stood up to a sharp pain in my ankle. "Hey! Huh?" I reacted as I realized that it was not my buzz-kill device: it was the other foot entirely, and a glance showed swelling. "Okay, I'm going to need some ice."

"Dawes," he called into the hall and a face appeared. "Let the medic on duty know that we're headed that way. Sprained ankle," Dawes, previously known as Sammie, disappeared. "I wondered if you hadn't twisted or broken something during your smack down session."

"Ah, you saw the movie?" I made conversation.

"How do you not notice that?" Captain Stover gestured to my ankle. A wheelchair arrived. "In," he pointed and I didn't bother arguing.

"Hell's bells Captain; I don't really notice anything short of a gunshot these days," I replied as each wrist was cuffed to the wheelchair arms. We wheeled quickly down and out and after a brief and absolutely freezing jaunt across the compound we entered the entirely too familiar medical center. They popped the cuffs off immediately and I was allowed to shiver in peace for a moment. "It's not that bad," I offered to whoever was listening.

"Howdy there," Susan greeted and wheeled me in to X-ray. A lot of lead and some very uncomfortable poses later, I was wheeled into a patient room where Officer Morgan was sitting in a bed, fully awake.

"Ma'am," I greeted and hopped into the chair next to her.

"You're hurt!"

"That's a relative term," I reminded her. "How are you doing?"

"They're keeping me overnight for observation," she said. "I wish they'd at least give me back my gun."

"I don't have one, but I have an extra dolphin in my office. You can borrow her if it makes you feel better."

"Thanks, but keep the dolphins. Is it broken?"

"Nah, it just got all puffy and drama queen. What about you?"

"Iodine and band aids," she said bravely. "Assuming they don't fire me."

"You engaged the enemy in battle and you found yourself in a moment of disadvantage. That doesn't make you a bad soldier: it makes you a soldier that survives."

"I broke protocol. I'm an idiot, and I almost got killed."

"Were you breaking protocol when you came into my cell alone?"

"No,"

"The officers and their balls may disagree, but I'm a hell of a lot more dangerous than Ari is. Your expectations were reasonable: he's a nerd for goodness sake!"

"You did beat the crap out of him," she reasoned to herself as Susan came in.

"Looks like a sprain," Susan announced. "Wait, you did - " she pointed down the hall to what I assumed was Ari's space.

"She had to," Morgan replied.

"I really just contributed," I shrugged and let her roll up my pants leg and wash the flesh in alcohol. "Come on, it's not like anyone should be surprised at this point," I exclaimed.

"How's it feeling, Isa?" Captain Stover.

"Body's fine," she replied.

"Captain, am I more deadly than Ari?" I interjected and winced as my foot and ankle were wrapped.

"Definitely."

"Remember that for a while," I muttered.

"Oh, I get it. Good point. Not exactly apples and oranges anymore. Well, you're a lot tamer!" he objected.

"You want to see the movie again?" I pointed out.

"Isa, you're on 48 hours of Medical leave as of 0900," he said to his officer. "I'll let you know what they decide. Firecracker here makes a pretty good argument. I'll use it in your defense."

"Remember that she's one of the few guards I'll talk to," I added, and I think he chuckled internally.

"Relax Sparky. This is our job."

"I'm just saying that the male/female thing shouldn't determine so much. He's not the Hulk; he just went a little psycho."

"Duly noted," he said as Susan sat back and rolled my pant leg down. "We may as well settle here until Starr and Kensington arrive."

"Ice pack," Susan returned and with a little help I hopped into the cot next to Officer Morgan. "And elevation," she added and placed a strange boxy pillow under the foot.

It was very quiet for a few minutes. "Captain," I finally said in a small voice and he came and stood next to me. "Is she going to be alright?"

"Belle, she'll be fine. We have to do these reviews every time someone farts; nothing much usually comes of it. They'll take down the facts, decide what happened, figure out how to keep it from happening again, decide if the persons involved acted badly, and we'll all move on with a little more ink in our record books."

"I bet my record book is bigger than yours and hers combined," I joked but I was relieved.

"I bet if they had a record book on you it would stretch from here to Alaska," he quipped.

"You're secretly a sweet person, aren't you?" Officer Morgan turned to face me.

"Quiet, you'll blow my cover. Sorry, I get quite goofy at 0300 in hospital wards," I yawned.

"What's the deal?" Agent Starr walked in the door, immediately followed by Agent Kensington.

"They briefed us about the attack, what condition is Ari in?" Kensington inquired and Susan took them back there for a few minutes.

"Why do I feel like I'm in the principal's office?" I asked Morgan as Captain Stover went back, probably to show them the video off of his phone. Everyone returned except Susan.

"I'll take Officer Morgan," Agent Kensington said. "If I could just get your statement, ma'am."

"I'm a lot more mobile than she is; we'll move," Morgan offered and tottered off with the agent. Starr pulled up a chair and watched Stover's film again.

"Is he going to live?" I finally asked her.

"Yes, most of his damage is temporary. You showed decent restraint," she replied. "I need you to tell me what happened, every detail you can remember," she pulled out a pad and took notes despite the tape recorder I was speaking into. When we got up to the present, I paused.

"Is your ankle broken?" she asked.

"No, x-rays showed no fracture to the bones. It appears to be a sprain."

"Why didn't you report it immediately?"

"I didn't notice it until Captain Stover woke me. Adrenaline: it was a very adrenal night."

She clicked the recorder off and set her notes down. "What you did was very brave."

"No, what I did was very angry. It was protective, possessive, and really pissed off. Trust me, I've been brave before and this was nothing like it," I closed my eyes.

"Can you put weight on it?" Agent Starr asked me.

"Not for 24 to 48 hours," Susan replied for me. "It was the size of an orange when they brought her in," she set a pair of crutches to lean on the wall.

"Have you ever used crutches?" Starr asked.

"Not conventionally," I replied. "And they make crappy weapons, especially that kind. Aluminum foil could do worse than those, and it's about the same thing."

"Good," Starr stated. Kensington and Morgan rejoined us. Officer Morgan's eyes were a little red. "Do you want to...?" she asked Kensington on a leading note.

"Yes, I'll stay with Officer Morgan," Kensington replied and they had an understanding.

Captain Stover rolled up the wheelchair. "Come on, we've got to return the chair anyway."

"Grand," I muttered and hopped into the contraption. I held my crutches and we wheeled back into the freezing cold, back into the secure building, and slowly weaved our way through the building and up to my office. With the ice pack wrapped around my ankle and my dolphin blanket wrapped snugly around the rest of me, I fell asleep.

I awoke with my pillow half-covering my face and the door opened. I hadn't even sat up fully when Director Goode stormed in. "What the hell were you thinking?"

"I can take him down alive. I did," I replied. "Everyone walked away. You're welcome," I sat up and pulled the ice pack's remains away from my foot.

"What if you had killed him?"

"I doubt this is American soil, and he's not an American. I'm good," I wiggled my toes a little and regretted it.

"Why do you have all the answers?"

"International superspy: I'm trained to pull answers out of my," I started the response but George interrupted.

"Alexis, is it broken?" he asked from the doorway: there wasn't much room in the office.

"I don't think so. They x-rayed it but it's just a sprain."

"I've never seen this expression on your face before," he noted and held up a clip of me attacking Ari.

"That must be my 'someone's going to die' face. I don't spend a lot of time looking at mirrors."

"Why did they ask for you?" Director Goode asked and took the coffee George offered her.

"You have a bomb, you call the bomb squad," I replied and George handed me a big plastic bottle of greenish tea. "I'm a professional."

"Just promise you won't do it again."

"Yes ma'am. I also won't attack anyone with my crutches."

"And you'll follow the medic's directions regarding your ankle," she prompted.

"And I'll be good," I sighed.

"Right. Agent Tomopolis, did you want to stay with her for a while?"

"Thank you ma'am," he replied and sat on the desk.

"What time is it?" I asked as Goode left.

"About 6:45. Do you want some painkiller?"

"Yes please. I'm starving, can I have food?"

"Oatmeal and pastries are on their way," he replied.

"I would kill for a donut."

"Glazed?"

"Yeah. If I'm really good, can I have a box of Krispy Kremes?"

"See what I can do," he beeped his phone. "One dozen Krispy Kreme donuts, hot," he muttered and hung up. "Tylenol®, oatmeal, and peppermint tea," he observed as breakfast arrived.

"Best breakfast ever," I yawned. "Really long night."

"You can sleep later."

"Probably ruined your weekend," I popped the pills and started on the oatmeal.

"Donuts are on their way," George informed and I set the wrapped raspberry Danish aside.

"Oh bother. Can you hand me the crutches?" I figured out how those worked and hobbled my way through bathroom rituals. I smelled donuts immediately upon exiting the lav. I tripped over my crutches in my eagerness. The guards caught me and I hopped back to my cell.

"You're going to have to use those eventually," George commented, but I was face-first into a box of donuts. Almost six donuts later, we wiped my hands and I got the hang of the hop-swing motion of the aluminum crutches. We went down the hall and back a few times, stopping to wash the sugar off of my face, and I wore off my sugar high.

"Alright," I returned to the bed.

"Ice pack," George handed it to me as he activated it. "Get some sleep."

"Hey, can you check on Officer Morgan for me?" I asked as he headed toward the exit.

"She's fine. Be good," he replied and the guard closed my door and turned off the light. I tried to wiggle my foot but was unsuccessful.

"Girl knows how to wrap," I observed to myself and returned to sleep, dolphins in my arms.

Chapter 10: Operation Waldo

No one woke me; they just left the sandwich and apple for lunch on the desk. I must have been exhausted because I didn't sense the intrusion. When I did wake it was grey and rainy outside and I heard the tings of rain on the well frosted glass. I reached over and flipped on the light and ate the sandwich with the rest of my tea. A bottle of water was on the table, and the donut box had been neatly closed. *Why do I binge eat donuts? I should go to the gym. Eh, it's raining and icky out there.*

A very timid tapping came from the door.

"I'm decent!" I called and Jim Kmetz opened it a little. He was shooed by a guard, who swung it wide open.

"Do you have the time to just take a look at this?" Kmetz asked and handed me a stack of papers showing the action behind a halfway decent hack attempt. "You see where we're flat-lining."

"I know this sequence. Where's it from?" I studied the last frames. "Wait, don't say anything. Let's go," I pushed up and handed him the papers before I grabbed the crutches. "Don't ask about the gimp," I instructed him. "Could you grab the water and apple for me, thanks," the guards seemed amenable and Kmetz grabbed the supplies. I was back into Operation Waldo.

With roller chairs and a hard floor navigating the cyber department was actually very easy. Kmetz and I were elbow-to-elbow for such a long time we started over-reaching. It was shocking to me when the male medic called my name from the hall.

"You really should try eating," he said and I saw a microwavable soup sitting on the table.

"Be glad I'm drinking," I replied and finished off the last of the forty ounce bottle of water. "I'll eat, what time is it?"

"It's six," Kmetz answered. "But we got a lot done."

"Yeah we did," I was proud as the screens blacked out per Kmetz's command as the medic came in.

"Great. Roll on over and hop up on the table," The medic replied, unimpressed. He set his bag down and I complied. "I understand your idea was to drop the other man without killing him," he made small talk as we got into place.

"The opportunity came, so I took it," I replied.

"To protect a guard," he unwrapped the ankle carefully after folding up my pants leg. "Now that is a sprained ankle. You didn't feel this right away?"

"It hurt a little; I had a lot of adrenaline going."

"This definitely hurt more than a little. Then again, you seem to have a high tolerance for pain."

"The bullets were definitely worse," I informed him and glanced at my colorful swollen right ankle. He handled it as carefully as he could as he checked my range of motion, and he actually got me to squeak in one particularly painful direction. "Don't do that again," I commanded him and kept a clench on the table's edge.

"Okay," he began to wrap it. "At least another day with no weight on it at all: keep it high, cold, and still. If you're lucky, we'll get you partially walking by Tuesday. We'll pop you into a walking cast or an air cast when your ankle is ready for it. Hope you like crutches."

"I hate crutches," I announced and received no sympathy.

"Try this," Kmetz slid a low round padded stool on wheels. I got down from the table and perched on it, kicking and steering with my left foot.

"No," Agent Starr said as I was starting to have fun with it. She handed me the crutches. "Come on, you can eat in your cell, while that thing is iced and elevated," she sounded motherly and I submitted.

I hopped through the door of my newly redone cell and noted the clear plastic bag with all my effects in it sitting on the table. The desk had been moved so it was facing the wall between the two doors, placing it so I could also watch DVDs lying on the bed. The bed was in the addition, foot to the door. The rooms didn't mesh perfectly: the addition was about two feet in from the right and about that much from the left. The red futon couch had been installed in the wall behind the table perpendicular to the food tray and there was no room to fold it out. Overall, it was a generous growth of my space. It was very apartment-like.

"Are you there?" Director Goode's voice through the speaker on the wall asked.

"I'm here!" I replied and sat in the nearest chair.

"What do you think?"

"The room is incredible. Thank you," I replied and pulled the other chair up to prop up the ankle.

"What did the medic say?"

"Apparently I did a grade-A job of spraining my ankle. I might start walking again with the crutches early next week, if the swelling goes down," I replied.

"Alright. Take it from here Starr," The director said and hung up.

"Wow," Starr observed, looking around the room. "Are you hungry?"

"Starving," I said and she took the soup can.

"I'll be right back," she said and dashed out.

"Donuts," the guard placed them on the food table and I hopped over on my good foot. It was a short distance, and I set the donuts on the table and pulled things together so I could put my ankle on the couch while sitting at the table. Starr arrived and came in with a spoon and a napkin. One of the guards stepped in with her and stayed in the door corner after it was sealed. I figured it was new policy and began to eat the hot chunky soup.

"Have a donut," I offered Starr and she relented after a second's deliberation. When it was finished she washed her hands in my sink and began to pull things out of the plastic bag. She made my bed and put the laptop on the desk and set the dolphins right and finished about the same time I did. Starr rejoined me at the table.

"They evacuated Uri Vletsko this afternoon," she informed me cautiously.

"Because of what I did, or because he's nuts?" I asked.

"He needed medical attention we couldn't provide here. The chemicals did some damage. His right fibula snapped, which is also the same time you hurt your ankle. He also fractured his wrist and there's a little tissue damage. That's all going to heal: I just don't know if we'll get his brain back," she had emotionally distanced herself.

"I'm sorry I had to hurt him, but the alternative solution was death. He owes his life to Officer Morgan's quick thinking."

"He let her go, physically, when he saw you," she mentioned.

"She was hurt and in danger and he was clearly out of his right senses," I replied.

"He was your friend."

"He was a coworker and a one-time sex partner, not my friend."

"Am I your friend?"

"Yeah, I'd say we're working on it."

"You gotta teach me that move," she conceded.

"What, so you can sprain your ankle?" I deadpanned. "There really wasn't a 'move'; I just kind of hurled myself at him."

"Uh-huh," she half-believed me.

"Trust me; this is not worth the technique," I pointed to my ankle and she handed me an ice pack from the mini freezer in my little fridge. "I know: high and cold."

"So you're okay?"

"Yeah, actually I'm going to take a shower. Don't worry; I can definitely wrap a sprained ankle on my own."

"Considering your surgical experience, I believe that. Be good."

"Thanks for unpacking. It would have taken me forever hopping around."

"Are you going to be okay in the shower?"

"Sure, it's standing room only. I have been one-legged before you know. This is going to be so much easier than the bullet wounds or burns: the shower is a vast improvement on a bucket and there's no flesh that has to stay dry."

"While you're laid up, you should really write a field guide to medicine and surgery. I'd love to read it," she stood up and the guard knocked on the door. "Goodnight Belle."

A very interesting thirty minutes later I had showered and climbed into the new pajamas and I sat on my bed wrapping my ankle. There had been a considerable amount of cursing during that half hour, most of it in French, and I had finally caught my breath as I began to set and wrap the apple-sized ankle.

It was 8:15 when the door opened again and Captain Stover entered. He looked a little tired, but he seemed upbeat.

"Do you like it?" he asked as the door sealed behind him.

"Ankle no, room yes," I replied. I had the apple-sized lump in question elevated and iced. "Could you please bring me the laptop?" I requested and he brought it and a chair and came to sit at the foot of my bed. "Thanks. Agent Starr wanted me to write something for her," I remembered the no-guy-without-a-girl rule and looked at him questioningly.

"Why am I alone?" he asked.

"You all seem to be pretty big on rules," I shrugged.

"Well, you're incapacitated and we're not really alone," he pointed to the speaker. "We should not have involved you in the issue about 24 hours ago."

"Let me tell you something that I knew and you didn't," I leaned forward, clutching the pink dolphin. "Ari is pressure sensitive. If you had gone in there and created a threat he wasn't able to process, he would have escalated. It is just not that hard to kill a person. He can process me. He knows me, and he has a mental process set up for me. I very seriously doubt he had set up a mental process for anyone else here." I couldn't see any reaction on his face, so I continued. "There's a pretty decent probability that Officer Morgan had sensed that he was threatened; that might be why she went in there alone."

"Why do you say that?"

"She has a gift to get a feel for people. Also, being female gives her the ability to relate on an emotional scale."

"Men can't relate?"

"It can be taught, but no, it's not natural."

"Officer Morgan was cleared to go in there alone," he told me. "This was a black swan."

"There are a lot of those in this line of work."

"How did you get around them?"

"Keep your lines tight and a knife in one hand in case you need to cut them. It's a high cost."

"Do you think you're going to be alright?"

"I've definitely been in worse jams," I replied and adjusted the ice pack. "I think I'm getting used to it."

"The shrink wants to talk to you tomorrow. She'll come here," he stood up and pulled the chair back to where it was.

"I'll be here," I sighed and opened the laptop. *Field surgery 101...*

I found myself listless as the evening passed and the stars came out on my false window. I typed out my various exploits into the medical field, along with the horrors I had seen. They gave me more pain medication around 10, and when it kicked in I decided to try and get some sleep.

A medic I had caught a glimpse of, an older man named Paul came and checked my ankle around 8 a.m. One of the guards stood by as we conversed.

"That is one beautiful sprain, if you don't mind me saying," he made medical small talk as he examined the injury. "Try moving it around a little."

I showed my range of motion. "We're at around 30 hours," I told him.

"36 hours from the injury occurring, right?" he asked and checked his chart again, "Right about."

"Well, you saw the other guy."

"Alive, yes. Surprising: from what I heard."

"So what do you think: how much longer am I without right foot?" I changed the subject.

"If this doesn't start looking a whole lot better, you're going back to the medical center for a CAT scan. You may have torn some tendons."

"Not possible. I didn't even notice it until it had swollen up six hours later," I resisted the notion. "I've felt tendons tear before: trust me, I'd recognize it."

"What'd you tear?" he asked as he began to rewrap the ankle. I replied by pulling my right arm into my pajamas and out through the neck hole, displaying my right shoulder. I lifted my right arm a little and he dropped the bandage. "Holy shit."

"It came out through here," I turned so he saw my underarm. "Lucky shot."

"Was your arm up?"

"Yes, of course. I was shooting at someone."

"Yeah, I'd say you know what a ripped tendon feels like. We're still going to keep an eye on that." He picked up the bandage and wrapped the ankle up. "Same deal: high and cold and don't try to use it to walk. I can't recommend a walking brace until those tendons start looking better. Maybe tomorrow," he packed up his bag and left. Less than an hour later the shrink was in. It started pretty normally.

"So, how do you feel?" the therapist asked. I had moved over to the couch and propped up my leg.

"You know, I don't have to be proud of everything I do," I was defensive.

"Tell me what happened," she leaned back and took her cup of tea.

"I was in the office, camping out while they were working on this," I explained. "I was just reading. The guard came in and said they wanted my help; that Ari had attacked Officer Morgan and that she had asked for me. I became very angry."

"Angry at who?" she asked.

"Ari, then I realized he was nuts. He wasn't just attacking a guard, he was attacking an American and he damn well knew better. He knew it when he came here: I watched him squirm in fear of retribution."

"And maybe if he's willing to do it, to dare your 'system' you had spent so much time and work on, maybe other people out there are doing it too?"

"I hadn't really gone there. She's a good egg. She didn't deserve to be attacked or terrified. They, they would have killed him. They do, you know. They kill prisoners. I couldn't let Ari get killed by a stranger. By an American. Not after what we've done. Not after what he's done: I couldn't let them kill him."

"Why?"

"That would make the targets 'right'. Even if no one knew it but us, it would totally destroy the grounds I've been fighting on. This is mine," I blew my nose. "You know, I've seen a lot of death. In some places of the world, death is the only way to preserve life. This isn't one of them. Death here is a punishment, a tragedy, retribution, senseless violence. Sometimes it's an accident, sickness, or, on fairly rare occasion, a murder. We don't have warlords here, and the American 'war on drugs' is farcical when compared to parts of the world where drugs really are an issue. That's why America is the world's policeman, their standard. Terrorists are the ones ruining the states over there, they're the disease. Ari wasn't a disease. He was barely criminal."

"Like you?"

"No, I'm fairly criminal. I'm just a really good criminal."

"So why couldn't you let them kill Ari?"

"It might be wrong. I think it's wrong to kill an insane man unless you absolutely have to. Ari's not all there, you know? Computer genius. Slightly nutty."

"So to you, America is the 'good guy'," she discerned.

"Something like that, yes," I replied.

"And really, you're the one who suffered," she observed and sipped her tea. I took a drink of my own.

"Listening," I replied, avoiding eye contact.

"Ari snapped, and Officer Morgan got a little scuffed up, but what's your situation?"

"This is a nice apartment. I lived in something smaller than this once in Israel," I returned combatively. She let the silence drill for a minute. "I'll be running again in a few weeks. It's not that serious," she looked at me like my mother used to. It got to me. "Fine. I'm trapped. I said it, you're happy? I'm finally trapped. In my life of using violence and chaos, I built a very good system to make sure this wouldn't happen, and it did and now I'm actually here. Maybe they know it too. They may very well be having a good yuck over it. I'm disarmed, I'm very vulnerable and they can just play with me like I'm Superspy Barbie® or something: take me out of my little box and put me in the cyber lab or the office or interrogation or just leave me somewhere for a while, maybe forget about me," I flopped back onto the pillows. "God dammit I have no tissues!" I was in tears and therefore in snot.

The woman handed me a packet of tissues and I cleared my sinuses. I composed myself.

"Sorry, that must have seemed really crazy," I sniffed.

"Not at all," she said, scribbling notes. "We will talk about Superspy Barbie® some other time. I think you have some very valid difficulties, and I am so very pleased with your progress here. You did something today that most people will never be brave enough to do."

"Snot fest?" I asked.

"No dear, you acknowledged your own vulnerability. I guarantee you that any one of these men guarding you would rather run a mile in the snow in their skivvies than talk about those kinds of emotional boundaries and structures."

"That was an option?" I joked half-heartedly. She laughed insincerely.

"Well, I think I'll tell the Marine he can take off his earphones now," she said of the man standing by the door with the special noise-eliminating headphones on. "But I should leave you with this: no one is laughing," she signaled the soldier and placed the cups on the food-tray for me. "Could we maybe talk tomorrow?"

"I'm okay with it," I replied and crawled over to the fridge to re-freeze the icepack. They exited and I scooted over to the bathroom.

The day mostly involved scooting, hopping, or crawling. I typed a little, did some drawing: I mostly drew all afternoon. I had a great emotional outpouring into a scene; it took hours to finish to my satisfaction. Agent Starr came in just after dinner while I was still at the table. I was doing clean-up work on the sketch.

"Hi," I greeted and took my foot off of the other chair.

"How's it going?" she returned and the guard shut the door and stayed. "Wow, I had no idea you could draw so well!"

"I don't usually show my art," I pulled it toward me. "It's personal. I'll probably have to destroy it when I'm done."

"Destroy it? It's amazing, why would you destroy it?"

I put it on the table and let her see.

"The detail, the expressions, the…emotion of the drawing. This is real. Don't tear it up. It's like a movie poster but much more refined. Did you study art?"

"Agent Starr, I can't let anyone see this. I know what they'll do. They'll look and comment and pass it around and then jokes will start; and they'll know that I draw and they'll exploit that, or they'll tell me I stink. Even worse, maybe the director will keep it around in her office and show visiting hot-shots, oh this is the artwork from that prisoner I told you about…she's got a real talent but god only knows what she was thinking. She must feel really 'blank'" I threw the pencil at the wall. It bounced: pencils always do. "Starr, don't you think I'm exploited enough? I can't just keep it: anyone and everyone comes through here. I couldn't have a safety pin without someone posting a bulletin on it."

"You must feel really awkward, with everyone staring at you all the time. I think I would feel really…" she struggled.

"Exposed. Seriously grade-a celebrity exposure, but you can't do whatever you want."

"That must suck."

"Like a vacuum," I replied. She looked at my drawing with a longing in her eyes.

"If you had a way to keep it so you knew it was safe, would you?"

I looked at the graphite shapes and shades for a second. "How would I know it was really safe?"

"Well, you're alright showing your art to me, right?"

I watched the wheels turn in her head. "Yes."

"And you can tell if a sealed envelope's been tampered with?"

"Yes."

"We put it in an envelope, seal that, and then put that in a special Restricted folder in my files, which no one else can get into."

"And I could see them?"

"Any time you want: I'll bring your envelopes down, you can check them out."

"You're a good friend Agent Starr."

"The medic is coming at 8: I'm going to go get an envelope, if you've decided to not destroy that." She smiled and left.

I got up and took the pain pills the guards left for me on the food tray. I also picked up my pencil and sharpened off the broken tip with the child-safe pencil sharpener I had been allotted. I emptied the shavings into my little trash bin and got a refrozen icepack from the fridge. Starr and guard came in as I was resettling. She sat down with me and started labeling the envelope.

"I didn't really have a normal childhood," I opened up a little. It hurt, so I took a breath. "My mom died and dad was crushed. Then he was angry. Then he was just inebriated. By then my brother had been deployed to Afghanistan. We got the news that he had been killed two weeks after my 16th birthday. That's really when the drinking started," I slid the page into the envelope. "We become who we are, and we are who we become."

"So you took up art?" Starr pressed gently.

"No, I already had art. Art took me up, really. All of my school notebooks are soaked in ink or covered in lead. Hey, I have that report on field medicine if you want it," I changed the subject.

"That would be great," she fetched my laptop from my bed and got the file off of it. She also plugged it in so it could charge. "Thank you."

I checked the time. "I could use a quick shower. If you want, you can catch a cat nap."

"Sounds good to me. We have about twenty minutes," Starr replied and sat at the desk to read my report. I crawled along until I got to the bathroom. The bathroom was small enough that I always had a surface to hang on to. I felt better after a quick but productive shower, and I had changed into my pajamas before draping the wrap around my neck and using the crutches.

"Do you like it?" I asked Starr, who was almost finished reading the report.

"How long did you have your hand on that guy's...you know."

"The leg wound? That was...well, first I had to compress the artery, then when they had stitched up the main wound, I had a hand on it and a hand on the artery. Hard work in odd positions. He pulled through though."

"I got a laugh from the 'rear view mirror' story." She smiled.

"If you have to treat your own backside, standing in a jeep and using the rear view mirror is very helpful. Cars also give you good position options."

"That's genius."

"It is much easier when the car is parked."

She raised her eyebrows and got a short laugh out of that. "It's almost eight, why not just elevate it? He'll have to unwrap it anyway."

"Sounds good," I said and parked myself on my bed. The wiry medic was there momentarily.

"Ma'am," he nodded to Agent Starr.

"Long shift, huh?" I greeted him.

"Standard weekend work," he replied and set his bag on the bed next to me. "That actually looks a lot better. You've been staying off of it. Good girl."

"Don't kill him," Starr cautioned and I leaned back on my elbows.

"Let's test that motion range. Point and flex please?" I complied. "I didn't mean anything..." he attempted an apology.

"No worries. How is that?" I rolled the ankle around slightly.

"Not bad at all," he pushed a little on the heel. "How is that?"

"Smarts," I told him honestly.

"Let's stand on it. Okay," he talked me through it and we slowly and carefully let the foot down. It didn't stay on the floor long. "Alright, too soon. No walking, we'll try again in the morning to see if we can stand on it. Clearly you know how to get around on one foot."

"Will she be able to walk on it tomorrow?" Starr asked as he began to wrap the ankle in an ACE bandage.

"Even if it continues to heal at this rate, I don't anticipate walking on it this week. There was a lot of damage sustained. I've seen comparable cases," he finished the wrap and grabbed his bag. "I believe she has shredded some of her tendons slightly. Those cells take time to repair. The baby will also slow the healing process slightly. It could be as little as four to six weeks; possibly walking with the crutches part of the time in one or two weeks. From there we expand."

"That's ridiculous!" Starr gawked.

"That's soft tissue," I recognized. "Come on, what do I need to walk for? I mean, the guards should like it," I attempted humor. "Now they know I can't run!"

Her eyes gave me pity. His eyes were amused. I felt a very odd sensation then. Apparently my face gave it away.

"What?" Starr asked and the medic turned around.

"It itches like mad!"

"The wrap?" Starr asked.

"The ankle," I replied and the medic nodded.

"Good sign," he assured. "That's a very good sign."

"What?" Starr was puzzled.

"Itching is really just little dashes of pain," I explained. "My ankle is knitting itself back together."

She subconsciously put her hand to her belly and had an expression of revelation.

"See, I'm used to my body doing horrible things because of the horrible things I've done to it," I smiled in the shared maternal moment.

"Any questions for me ma'am?" The medic asked Starr.

"So it could be weeks before she walks?" Starr asked.

"Independently, yes. Soft tissue heals slowly. There's an air cast we can put her in when the swelling has been gone for a few days: that will be quick and easy to remove and she won't have to sleep with it on. When she can stand on her own we'll move on to walking. Fortunately, we have a physical therapist onsite who has been approved to come in on this in two weeks," he directed his gaze to me "keep it still and high: that's the fastest route to recovery," he turned back to Starr, "Goodnight ma'am."

The guards let him out.

"That really sucks," Starr sympathized.

"The baby is starting to move around. Sometimes I think its twins: I'm getting bopped in every direction," I revealed.

"We'll know the genders soon," she nodded. "Yes, I have a future soccer star in here," We both laughed a little. "I should go."

"Get some rest. Hopefully no one else will have to get up in the middle of the night for ridiculous reasons," I replied. She left with a pitying expression and the guard gave me a suspicious look.

I slipped into melancholy late Sunday evening, after Starr had left. I set the weather window to rain and crawled into bed with my sketchpad. Monday I crutched over to breakfast and picked at it. Agent Won's voice came through the door.

"Good morning, are you ready to come to the lab?"

"No, not really," I replied wearily. She came in with a guard.

"You sick?"

"Eh," I lunged over and put the half-eaten bowl of goop back on the food tray.

"I heard it was a very eventful weekend."

"Yeah: Ari tried to kill Officer Morgan, I almost killed Ari, and my ankle is now nine kinds of broken. Agent Starr discovered my talent in art, the director got out of bed at four in the morning, and George got me a whole box of hot Krispy Kremes," I shrugged.

"You look tired," she assessed. "It's okay if you want to come later."

"Thanks," I stood and crutched back toward the bed.

"Yeah," she left and they sealed me in again. I turned off the lights and stared at the fake rain. It was slightly chilly and I found myself wrapped in sheets and blankets and I quickly drifted off to sleep.

I was woken abruptly when I heard George's voice. "How's it going?" he burst into my world via the speaker.

"What's wrong?" I asked from sheer instinct. "Oh, hi George."

"Everything alright?"

"Well, I won't walk for several weeks, one of my former colleagues is nuts, and I'm tired of being imprisoned, but otherwise…"

"So you're not really in a good mood, are you?"

"Just, leave me alone for a while. I'm pissy and hormonal."

"Fair enough," he hung up. I went to the bathroom and sat down to eat lunch and in walked the shrink Cyndy.

"Are you cold?" she asked.

"Freezing," I admitted.

"It is cold in here. Just a minute," she went back out and had a few words with the guards. "They'll turn the heat up, that might help you out a bit. So, how's it going?" She plopped onto the couch and I set the empty food tray on the ledge. "You look like you're having a blah day."

"Do you think there's a God?" I crutched over to the bed and wrapped myself in the blanket. "Because if there is, I'm mad at him."

"Because you feel that your life has been crappy?"

"Because he's sending her into a crappy life, and she's not even born yet," I pointed to my bump. "She doesn't deserve this."

"You know it's a girl?"

"All babies start out as girls so yes, right now, it's a girl. If the testes drop, it becomes a boy."

"Ah."

"How am I going to carry her if I'm wearing handcuffs? What if they shock me while I'm holding her? The current will go through her too! I don't want to give this child up for adoption: she is mine and I won't let anyone take her away from me. She has a wonderful father; I want her to know him."

"You know, Sacajawea led the expedition team across mountains with a baby on her back." The shrink pointed. "Surely you've seen similar things across the world."

I nodded silently.

"Tell me; it's been about three months you've been here: haven't things evolved?"

274

I traced the fuzz on my dolphin blanket and looked around my little apartment and nodded. "This is definitely not my original cell," I admitted. "No bruises on the wrists, very little tension between me and the guards, and I have really nothing to complain about with the Agents."

"Take away the bad food and the cold cell and you could be having a really good time here," she poked with a little humor.

"The food isn't horrible," I managed a small smile and slid the blanket down a little. "The heat does help. I guess I should stop moping and get back to work."

"No, take a day off. You had a traumatic weekend and your ankle needs to be up anyway. Hit them full force tomorrow."

"Do you think things will continue to 'evolve'?" I asked her.

"Have you seen them stop evolving?" she replied with a twinkle in her eye. She left shortly and I straightened myself out and sat around for about twenty minutes before grabbing my crutches and asking the guard to take me to cyber.

Agent Won met me at the door and guided me into her office.

"So, rough weekend?"

"Well it wasn't boring," I replied.

"We looked over what you and Agent Kmetz did this weekend. Very good work," she looked at me. "How bad is it?"

"It's bad," I replied, avoiding eye contact. "They hope to have me walk a few steps in ten to fourteen days."

"That's bad."

"Yeah."

"What'd you do?"

"Ari took a guard hostage. I was emotional: furious; and I didn't really think. They think I did this at the same time that I...snapped his leg bone, the small one. He's in a loony bin now. I'm just having trouble picking up the pieces."

"Come on, you can play in the closet. I need a pathway cleared anyway."

"I can finish what he started," I offered as she stood.

"I have a specialist doing that. What I need from you is your experience in the Saudi communications networks."

"Harder than Iran but with older technology," I nodded. "Iran has better technology, but it spies on its own people. With a structure like that already into place I once hacked the entire country for thirty minutes and twelve seconds."

"That's pretty good time."

"Someone beat it?" I was dismayed.

"Forty three minutes, thirty one seconds; voluntary withdrawal," She winked at me as I turned with my crutches.

"You suck, you know that?" I hopped behind her.

"I know. Elaine will be working with you. Keep that thing elevated," Agent Won let me into the closet where a young woman with big gray eyes was staring at the screens.

"So, what's the first system you ever hacked?" I asked Elaine conversationally.

"Oh, I don't really 'hack', it's kind of illegal."

"Fine, what's the first system you gained unauthorized access to?"

"I don't um..." she balked, "I heard you really like dolphins?"

I smiled at her innocent change of topic. "I do, yes."

"Did you used to swim with the dolphins? I did that once," she shared and we entered a new threshold of programming.

"No, I've never swam with them," I focused on the screen and started typing. She watched me in awe. I sat back when I had a break. "Did you follow all that?" I called to the window I knew someone was watching us through.

"Yeah, we got it," a male voice replied.

"That was some really fast typing. You really know what you're doing," Elaine realized.

"Yeah, it's one of the things I'm good at. Lots of practice," I replied and stared at the screen. "Come on, how long does it take? You're only six thousand miles away!"

"What are you going to do when it comes back?" she asked.

"Depends on what comes back. If it's tainted, I'll know one thing. If it's only a little squished up, I'll know something else."

"What are we hoping for?"

"In this case, I'm crossing my fingers for 'totally tainted'. That means that the same system is up and I know exactly what to do with it," I explained. The message came in: REJECTED.

"That's the right one, right?"

"Exactly. Now I need to wait an hour or two, but I can go on and write the program for you to bust through without making a ripple. Actually, I need my old laptop. The program is on there, it just needs to be tweaked."

"Roger that," the bodiless voice said.

"Miss, it's time to come out," the guard told me and I wheeled over to the crutches. The artificial lights stung my eyes a little as I returned to the real world. I sniffed an aroma: Thai Pad!

"I have Thai food," Agent Won called from the other room. "Then you'll need to go back to your apartment so the medic can hurt you."

"Ain't that the truth of it?" I hobbled over.

"Did you get through?"

"Yeah, it's all set up. The program takes six to ten hours and it's not exciting," I opened the take-out container and grabbed the chopsticks. "Um, when is the next time you'll see Director Goode?"

"Tomorrow. Actually, you'll see her first for the weekly progress report. 0900. Captain Stover is going to take you."

"Thanks," I sucked noodles.

I returned to my cell with a renewed feeling of purpose. The medic, Susan, frowned at my ankle but offered no hope, and when I turned out the lights I ducked under the sheets and gave myself a mind blowing orgasm. They were probably wondering what the sudden giggling was about, but no one asked.

I was up, showered, dressed, fed, and ready for them at 0840. They almost insisted that I use the wheelchair, but I talked my way out of it. George met me in the elevator lobby on the top floor.

"Shalom," I greeted him.

"You're pretty perky," he replied. "Susan is in there now, we can go right in."

Susan the medic was indeed in Director Goode's office, showing her the medical reports and my x-rays. I hopped right in as she was finishing her explanation.

"Morning Belle, Ari is responding to treatment," the director greeted me. "Sit on the couch; I want to see your ankle."

I decided to be comedic and kicked off both shoes and bared the left ankle, showing my bracelet.

"Other ankle," she replied with a smirk. "The Commander has just finished telling me that your flight risk has gone down for the next few weeks," I bared the ankle for her inspection.

She peered at it, "How bad is the pain?"

"Bearable, as long as I don't try to stand on it," I replied.

"Soft tissue damage sucks. Did they run a CAT scan on this?"

"No ma'am," Susan replied for me, "the tissue healing rate and swelling have demonstrated no signs of a severed ligament."

"You've done this; do you think something's ripped?" the director turned to me.

"Shredded, but nothing that should require surgery," I rendered my assessment. "Bloody stupid thing," I added under my breath.

"I see a baby bump," the director announced. I hadn't really noticed it; I just thought I was constipated or something.

"Yeah, it moves around a lot," I smoothed the fabric over my stomach. "What are we going to do when the baby is born?"

"Well, you have options. Thank you Susan," she dismissed and pulled up a chair. "When our effort here is over and a new identity has been created for you, we fully intend to release you into your new life. Of course you'll be monitored from a distance; you won't need to work for a living and you and your child can live your lives happily ever after. If you choose, we can make arrangements for you to see the father and talk it over with him. Legally, adoption by him or by a total stranger is an option. If you want to keep this child though, Belle, I'm going to make it happen."

"How long do you think it will be? Operation Waldo, I mean."

"I'd say that's partially up to you, me, the President, and a few odd companions," Director Goode took my hand. "What do you think?"

"So what am I doing this week?" I asked and she smiled.

"I have a new prisoner; someone who worked with Waldo in Afghanistan two years ago. His file and a few tapes of interrogations are in your apartment. Scour him: I'm waiting for your report before we start interrogations."

"I'm on it," I replied and she stood up and reset the chair. I huffed and puffed and hopped back to the cell, where I was surprised by Officer Morgan. She was inside, sitting on the futon with a Readers' Digest in her lap.

"Hi. How bad is it?" she greeted me and I hopped to sit at my desk.

"I've done worse. So, you're back at work?"

"Finally. Medical leave, then the paperwork, then the shrink: I think they should do the shrink before the paperwork: it's enough to make anyone nuts," she replied with an insecure smile. "Hey, I just wanted to drop in and say," she took a breath and I interrupted.

"That you're glad I did what I did, but you can't let those feelings compromise your duties as an MP," I filled in for her. "Officer Morgan, you're a guard, I'm in your custody. I know that just because the guards and I have built a relationship doesn't mean that you wouldn't shoot me in the heart if I escaped and you couldn't catch me in time. As weird as that is, I respect you for it."

"I was going to say that the behavior we've seen lately demonstrates an acceptance on your part of your role here, that I'm very pleased you have come to that place, and that it can only be good for the mission."

I nodded as deeper meaning sunk in for me.

"So, how bad is it?" she returned to topic.

"Let's just say you don't need to worry about me escaping any time soon. Actually, I have no incentive to escape. This is where I wanted to be; this is where I am safe. This is where I am going to take him down."

"You tell 'em Belle," Agent Starr's voice came over the speaker. "I heard you have the tapes. Can I sit in?"

"Yeah, come on down. Two profilers are better than one," I replied.

"Great. Go ahead and start and I'll be down after I win an argument," she replied and clicked.

Officer Morgan patted me on the shoulder and stepped out, leaving me to the DVD and my laptop. I got comfortable on the futon with an ice pack and began the marathon.

The ice pack had gone limp when Starr arrived with a bowlful of popcorn.

"Sorry that took so long," Starr apologized and placed my icepack on the food tray. I saw Officer Morgan in the still open doorway.

"Mind if I crash your party?" she asked casually, but I knew.

"We need a guard presence, and I thought maybe she wouldn't mind," Starr confirmed.

"I have M&M's®," Officer Morgan was closed in with us.

"Too bad this isn't a chick flick," I replied. "Here, this is kind of a small screen," I scooted to one side of the futon.

"Yeah, I thought of that," Agent Starr smiled to herself as she heard a clunking roll in the hall.

"Clear for entry?" a man called.

"Affirmative," Officer Morgan replied and the door opened. The guard came in, set the flat screen monitor on my desk, and left. Agent Starr hooked us up, plugged me in, and started the video. We settled so that Officer Morgan was sitting in a chair a few feet away and Agent Starr and I shared the futon.

Sometime later, we decided to take a break.

"Not exactly," Starr tried to comment.

"He has anger issues," I added. "The agent, not the terrorist."

"Yeah. Focusing on the terrorist," Starr directed. "Unresponsive to machismo."

"Correction, unresponsive to Western masculinity. He's Middle Eastern: you want to insult him you don't imply his penis is small; you just show him the bottom of your shoe and touch his face with your left hand. I believe that in his mind, he will not give out information to those he considers 'beneath' it. It's not about the terrorism, it's about the social mores he was taught. Never stoop: if someone is beneath you, do not bend to them," I crutched over to the bed and flopped.

"You okay?" Starr asked.

"I know how to make him talk to me," I closed my eyes and began to knit my ploy. "We're going to need a few things. First, a tanning bed and some hair dye. He's going to know me as the beaten up, knocked up wife of one of Omar's bodyguards. I'll need a name and profile of that man: I know a few if you want to dig that up."

"Listening," Starr wrote.

"You're going to make yourself Middle Eastern?" Officer Morgan asked.

"Yes. I would have had Osama as the baby daddy, but it's really too much. The man has ethics; he'll relate with me as a victim of the American infidels, as a wife to one in the cause, and as a battered woman. It's going to take some acting and logistics. I can't just walk into the room and sit down with him."

"What do you recommend for the other interrogators?" Starr asked.

"Be polite. Introduce yourself; explain to him why he is here and what you want from him. It doesn't have to be the truth, but it gives him something to center around. Try being nice first. Have a designated 'nice' character. Ask him the same questions over and over, jumping over time periods. He has some education, and he thinks of himself as being an upper class person," I divulged.

"Strong or mild character?" Starr asked.

"Mild. Male. Tom could do it; or John. They both have the acting skills." We were distracted by the door.

"Clear for entry," someone said outside and Officer Morgan responded. It was the medic and George.

"Thank you Agent Starr," George dismissed and she gathered her materials and left. One of the guards took the big screen while the medic looked at my foot. George pulled up a chair and straddled it. "You are a real mixed blessing at times."

"You're getting what you want," I replied to him.

"You have no idea how lucky you are, do you?"

"Anyone who wants to call me pampered again is looking for a knee in the face," I replied, returning his vibe. "You know what I learned just before I got shot the second time? There's no such thing as luck. There's only life, and you just hope it goes well for you. That's what I learned when I wasn't killed in this explosion," I pointed to my ribs, "or by this man, or this woman, or even by Ben-Adat. You think I'm so damn spoiled; you look at your life. Got parents? Family? Friends? You went to college and your parents paid for it. You probably had the opportunity to decide what your career would be and what you would do with your life. Lucky my ass."

"Stay off of it," the medic concluded and left.

"You really are a mixed blessing," George said with a different intonation. "You know, I came in here to tell you off about hacking Iran."

"Iran is still an enemy," I replied. "It was a clean hack; it traces back to China. Actually, almost everything I do traces back to China: it's the technique I was taught."

"Israel?"

I smiled and shook my head. "I don't tell you all my secrets."

"Does it still drive you nuts to not have a gun under your pillow?"

"Not really. With the baby kicking and the door sealed and with all of this security, I guess I just don't think about it as much. I'm sure there are times, but then I sit up and realize where I am. In prison."

"You know as well as I do that you have been here willingly, or I'd have a few dead bodies and you'd be gone. You'd also be dead within a month or two. You have made many enemies."

"You know, George, you are exactly like I had pictured you. Did I surprise you?"

He smiled coyly. "I don't tell you all of my secrets."

"I surprised you," I concluded. "Was it the baby?"

"No. You did surprise me once, in interrogation with the terrorist who tried to stab you."

"Fierceness?" I replied.

"Quite the opposite; you showed restraint, even compassion. The pattern kept repeating. You're secretly a very nice person, for a femme fatal," he stood, "By the way; you're no longer here voluntarily."

"For now," I met his eyes.

"Until we release you, I'm afraid. You're a legit target now."

I let it sink in. "You really like rubbing it in, don't you? You may be slightly more of a bastard than I thought."

He went over to the counter and was given a freshly frozen ice pack. I watched as he wrapped it in one of my shirts and then tucked it carefully around my ankle, covering both sides. Without a word he set the laptop up so I could view it and then turned back to me.

"Do you want to watch something, or read?"

"I'd like to draw, actually," I heard myself say quietly. He brought me the kit and a magazine to use.

"Soda?"

"Please," I watched him move. He handed me the soda and then pulled the throw blanket from the futon and covered me so my icy foot wouldn't freeze the rest of the body. I lay back on the bed a little, feeling childlike. "So I'm legit now? What did I do to Uncle Sam?" I asked in a small voice. *When did my voice get so small?*

"You crossed the invisible line that made you a critical part in the war on terror. You're also off of about 25 nations' "Most Wanted" lists. As crappy as it seems right now, this is going to be good in the end."

"I trust you George," I looked away because my eye started leaking.

"Thank you, Alexis," he replied and handed me a tissue. "I like to use them as bookmarks." He turned away and left.

I noticed as the door sealed that Officer Morgan was still standing by it. I had a silent conversation with her before she spoke.

"He's telling you the truth," she finally said.

"I know. But it doesn't really make a difference to me. Of course, it does to you, but your job doesn't really change. I'm just too smart to leave."

"I think it's something else. I think you have too much honor and loyalty to leave. You nearly killed your former lover and friend for me; I walked out without a scratch and you're..."

"I also kicked a few butts and caused a few bruises on the agents and guards here, Officer Morgan. Believe me, I don't feel bad about it either. Don't go all soft and mushy on me now," I checked her eyes for comprehension. "This could just as easily have happened during an escape attempt, or in interrogation, or sparring with Agent Won, or falling down the stairs. Okay, I saved your skin: you're protecting me against things much worse than Uri Vletsko."

"You make a point," she turned to go.

"Thank you. And thanks for being the one to come supervise today. I'll admit I'd rather have you than some of the guys."

"No problem."

I couldn't see her smile, but I knew it was there. She left and the door sealed. I leaned back onto the pillows and ran my fingers through my hair. I mentally began a familiar conversation.

What if I had stayed? It was horrible, but it was home. I left him alone; well, not alone, he had his bottle, which he preferred over me anyway. What if I had stayed, what would I have done? Continued to take care of someone who didn't want me there? I would have finished high school, maybe gone to the prom. I probably would have gone on to college; the fund was sufficient for a very good school. Ha, I might have worked here! That's rich. I didn't have to kill that man. I could have just ducked: but I was fed up with it; fed up with men being destructive. I was done being the victim as soon as I started shooting up those tree trunks in Quebec. When I stole that gun, when I crossed that border: I was going to live life my way and to hell with everyone else.

I'm glad I shot that bastard. I'm glad the Israelis caught me, trained me: it's actually better than I had ever hoped. I was doing things: I was making things happen and ending lives and ending tirades of terrorism and tyranny. I don't regret it, any of the deaths. Except the second: he got the short end of it but I didn't know what I was doing. Eh, he was trying to kill us all anyway.

I'm tough. I've slept in trash cans, watched a man dissolve, and applied first aid in a moving jeep. I've been shot twice, and no one is ever going to understand the pain of being shot if they haven't been. That bitch. Ouch! The baby kicked me in the kidney. *She'll probably come out fighting. Good lord, what am I going to tell her about the scars? The truth is out of the question; it will probably be classified long after we're all dead and buried. And the biggest what if: what if I hadn't gotten pregnant? What if I chose to fake my death, where would I have gone? Somewhere remote, or in a city? Chicago? Montreal? Brazil, Argentina?*

You've had this conversation before, Belle, you know. You'd be right here, living just outside the city, sending in packages of data to the same people that I'm working with now, until they came. And they would have come, probably with a SWAT team. Maybe sooner, maybe later, but I would probably end up being right about where I am now, minus the sprained ankle. Eh, if something is going to happen, it's going to happen. I sighed heavily. "I need to be with people."

As if by magic, the door opened. "Pencils down," Shapiro entered. His height made him tower over me on the bed. My drawing set hadn't been opened so I just pushed it over to him. He counted them through the clear top and then set it on the table before flipping up the blanket.

"Good thing I'm wearing pants," I muttered as he bared my left foot and pressed the electronic probe to my zapper.

"Good," he replaced the sock and blanket.

Visitor, I decided and it proved to be correct. The door opened again.

"Clear for entry," Shapiro called redundantly.

Officer Belot came in, immediately followed by Director Goode. The door sealed shut, leaving me with two women and a man in a rather small apartment. I pushed myself around in bed so I had my back to the headboard.

Director Goode surveyed the scene briefly. "It is kind of chilly in here. How are you?"

"Apprehensive, at the moment," I replied. "Would you like a seat?"

"Yes, I think I will," she pulled one of the chairs from the table over and sat near the foot of the bed. "I have a question and I want an answer. Al-Zahrani uses four bodyguards with suicide vests on at all times. What would it take to ensure that he is captured alive?"

"Okay. Idea one: mess with the vests so they don't explode: the wiring is pretty straightforward, and the vests could even be swapped out one by one when the person bathes. Idea two involves an O.Z impersonator that the guards think is him: we could do this by convincing him an attempt will be made so he hires the double and we strike in just the right time, or we can swap him out in the toilet stall. Idea three is a series of snipers taking out the four guards and then a cobra strike. Speaking of cobras, at least four of the eight men who guard Omar are scared silly of snakes. Nice little factoid. Best shot, metaphorically, is a combination of one and three. The best time is at night: he walks in his garden at night and the guards are farther away from him. Like I've said, it's hotter than hell there."

She nodded and looked contemplative. "I have another question and I want an answer."

"You don't have to say that, you can just ask me the questions," I replied.

"Don't be smart," Shapiro directed.

She waved at him to pipe down. "How are you doing?"

"I really don't want to answer that question today."

"Tough cookies, answer me."

"I'm not suicidal. Actually, considering the circumstances, I think I'm doing pretty damn well. I think my baby is a prenatal karate king, my ankle is just plain stupid and before GI Joe there came in and confiscated my pencils, because you know, I might do something terrible like draw you, I was just thinking to myself about the mess I've gotten into here. Those classic what-ifs that everyone has. What if I hadn't walked out on my drunken father at 16? What if I hadn't fired that first deadly shot? What if I hadn't gotten pregnant? What if I had chosen to fake my own death instead? I went through it all again and came to the conclusion that I would still have ended up here. I know me: I wouldn't have stopped sending the data packages and eventually someone would have tracked them back to me and you'd have come then. Why? Because of all the moral constraints I have shed, honor is still hanging on strong. Killing, stealing, explosives, spying, smuggling, the list goes on; I still have my honor. I never lost my honor, my respect of legitimate law and order. It's a funny little quirk, but I'm a strange girl."

"If you had been able to, would you have taken him alive?" she redirected.

"My gut says yes, but with no guarantees of what condition he would have been in when I turned him over to U.S. Forces."

"You really hate him."

"I really do. I hated him then, I hated him more as I dived into the world, and I hate him now. I hate Bin Laden too; sometimes I have fantasies where I shave off that horrid beard or I alter the voice recordings of his releases so he sounds like a midget."

The director busted out laughing and I joined her for a moment.

"I just...goodness, that mental picture," she gathered herself. "Are you dressed?"

"Except for my shoe, yes," I replied suspiciously.

"Bring it in," she directed Shapiro, who went to the door. "I want you to come with me, but you have to be polite."

They entered with a wheelchair and wheeled it next to the bed. I hopped in obligingly. Officer Belot used a strap to make a sort of non-optional seatbelt and they slipped my wrists into soft straps which connected loosely to the wheelchair arms. I was able to set my hands in my lap, which I did.

"We're just going up to my office. You will be good, right?" She gave me a steely eye in the elevator.

"Absolutely angelic."

Chapter 11: Cast the Net

A few minutes later I waved at Natalie, who waved back. The director went in to the office and we waited outside for a few minutes until Natalie was summoned via buzz. Shapiro wheeled me in and then set a hand on my shoulder as though I needed a reminder that I was strapped into a chair.

The man was in his mid-fifties with a military background, battle experience, and grey eyes that looked right through me under bushy brows. He appeared to be of Irish heritage, had an average build and I guessed his height to be around 6 feet. He had indications of being a chronic smoker, including the rasp in the voice. He took a seat and I was wheeled forward again to sit facing him.

"Hello Beauty. I should warn you; I know almost all of what you can do," he stared straight into my eyes. "I wondered how they would transport you. Is it true that you normally walk around with nothing but that shock band to stop you?"

"That, and good manners," I answered evenly.

"You know those are usually used for the insane, yes?" he pointed to my wrists. "Normally, people can't get out of them. You probably could," he leaned back in his chair. "You look good," he traced a finger across his own cheekbone to mirror my scar. "It'll heal. You don't need any more scars. Actually, I brought some scar cream I thought you might like."

"Thank you," I replied, continuing to soak in his essence.

"I like your work. I like your style," he continued. "I liked your style before; you let the Israelis train you but you never changed teams. I've seen your work here, your art in cyber and interrogations, I even know about the British man. I know about locker KR142."

I locked in as he came to his point. His eyes asked.

"The locker itself is not rigged. The box is. The clock is the key," I replied. "If you turn the hands to 9:35, the box will open without the explosives."

"Why 9:35?" Goode asked.

"Multiples of seven," he answered. "She likes them. 21:35. Am I right?"

I nodded. "Seven for Germany, yes. 142, one plus four plus two. Seven."

"It's your stash, isn't it?" he asked.

"Identities, money, background stories, maps, two guns, a knife, two grenades and a smoke bomb, if I remember correctly," I spoke even as he flipped his phone open. He relayed the instructions in German, and then again in English.

"Good, we will speak later," he finally said and hung up. "I apologize for the phone call, but business can be pressing."

"I expect it is for you."

He smiled very slightly. "You know me?"

"Are you deuce or trey, sir?" I added the 'sir' for Director Goode, whose eyebrows went up.

"It comes and goes," he waved away the insignificance. "I suppose you know who you are in the game?"

"I expect I'm around the eight of spades: no one really wants me but I can be convenient," I replied and Director Goode attempted to hide that she had no idea what we were talking about.

"Someone might say that. But you're really the joker, the wild card. You're the game changer. I want to use you."

"I want Omar Al-Zahrani arrested, exposed, and humiliated," I replied, leaning back into my chair. "Those are my terms of contract."

He nodded very slightly, focusing over my shoulder into space. "I don't need an assassin. Your official name is Rhonda Perry; you're a per diem specialist on Operation Waldo. Your wages and benefits will be held until after your release. In the real world, your world, nothing has really changed."

"And the Queen of Spades?" I asked with a gesture toward Director Goode within my limited scope.

"She is on the team for Operation Waldo. She seems to work well with you, and I think we can all do business together," he stood and faced Director Goode. "Very nice," he shook her hand and turned to me. "Beauty?"

"We have a deal," I replied. He moved to shake my hand, but I froze in place. "They don't let me touch people; I may have put Homeland Security through a table," I said apologetically.

He offered his hand more dominantly and I stretched my bands to grasp it. He walked around me and out of my sight. "Get rid of those stupid things, she looks like Hannibal Lector. You'll get my note," he added as he left. The guards moved quickly and my hands were freed.

"What's with the cards?" Director Goode asked as soon as the door was shut.

"I avoid Iraq religiously, but during Operation Iraqi Freedom, while Saddam Hussein was being pursued…" I stopped because she had caught on. "Counterterrorism code names; every rank and title means something different. I'll write it out for you, but generally the ace is the highest, followed by two and three. Then it flips and things get better, like normal cards. So a four is a peon. Oh, but keep in mind that there is no Queen of Hearts. Ever."

"Why?"

"No idea," I replied. "Did that go well?"

"I don't know yet. You were, for you, very polite," she looked thoughtful for a moment. "What if Omar is wearing a belt? Sometimes he does."

"Not often in his own garden, but if it's a concern, drug him. Trust me, it's not hard."

"All the answers," she muttered to herself and sat at her desk. "Oh, that was fast," she read from her computer screen silently. "Alright then," she seemed pleased, "the guards will take you back home, and they've turned the heat up. Do you like stacking washer-driers, or the side-by-sides?"

"Top loaders, definitely. The sideways ones get funky. Glad I could help, ma'am."

"Thank you," she dismissed and they rolled me away.

The elevator doors opened and Tom McEwen was waiting for me. "Hello beautiful."

"Do you meet everyone in the elevator like that?" I asked as the guard rolled me in.

"Only when they've just pulled off a slam-dunk for our team," He followed along as we transferred elevators. He squeezed my shoulder as we loaded into the other lift. "Wow, you're tense. I'll make you a deal. I'll make your back feel amazing, and all you have to do is listen." We hit the first checkpoint and he was paused as the guard rolled me through. He followed me in without his jacket or sidearm and Officer Belot joined us for observation. I transferred from the wheelchair to straddling a chair and Tom stood behind me.

It didn't take me long to realize the man had talent.

"You have a whole mess of knots back here," he continued to work with gentle strength.

"You've done this before," I said and let my upper body relax on the back of the chair.

"Thank you. I heard Director Goode was a little rough on you in here earlier."

"Not really. You know how I feel about feelings and emotions and all that mushy stuff."

"I used to," his hands pressed firmly on my shoulder blades and lifted them. "Now I'm not so sure."

"Mmm, what are you talking about?"

"You're just not the same girl we hauled in from a memorial building. You've become a different person, on the inside."

"There's someone growing in my inside!" I pointed. "I've just adjusted to this climate. You really should have expected that."

"When was the last time you did something violent?"

"Um, Ari?" I replied with a tone for the obvious.

"Before that."

"Ah...there were those guys, the ones in the office."

"When was the last time the guards had to cuff you?"

"Ten minutes ago?"

"Non-optional."

"I don't know. When George pissed me off? I can't keep everything straight. So what's your point? I grew tame in captivity? Makes me sound like a polar bear."

"No, I think, my little Belle, that you are beginning to morph out of Belle Jones, femme fatale, and into something new and different."

I thought about that a while as he continued to rub my shoulders. Suddenly I felt a distinct bump on my lower abdomen. I thought for a moment that I was going to wet myself, but it passed.

"What happened?"

"I think the baby just kicked! That was so weird!"

"Maternity is very weird. Wait until milk starts pouring out of your breasts and you can't see your feet."

I giggled a little. "That just…for some reason that reminded me of a temple I was in once in India."

"Call, sir," a man outside announced. Tom and Belot left and I hopped over to the bathroom. I had just realized it was about dinner time, so I sat on the futon in anticipation.

Dinner was a frozen meal, served with the slashed plastic sheet still intact. I'm not all that particular: actually I'm good with a meal as long as it doesn't consist of insects, vermin, or anything I've had to kill myself. The shrimp pasta dish was surprisingly good: if it had been served in a bowl I would have been impressed.

"Incoming medic," someone called and I set the bowl and fork back on the tray and got onto my crutches as the door opened for Susan and Shapiro.

"How are we doing?" she greeted as I settled on my bed.

"It amazes me that we have the technological advances that we do, and no one has invented a better pair of crutches," I responded.

"They're called wheelchairs," she replied as she bared my ankle. "Very nice; you're ready for an air cast. Let's see your range of motion," she watched as my foot flopped around. "Excellent. It's healing fairly well," Susan fitted the cast and let me put pressure on the foot for the first time. It hurt, but I could stand briefly.

The evening was relatively calm after that. I got music playing on my laptop, folded my newly cleaned clothes and put them away, and slid around the cell in my rolling chair.

I was in my pajamas reading a magazine in bed when a click came on the intercom.

"We had a breakthrough," Agent Won said urgently. "Come up as fast as you can."

The guard opened the door; I fitted the ankle brace back on and hopped into his wheelchair. I didn't even have a jacket. We rolled quickly through the obstacle course of security. When we got there, the cyber unit was buzzing. Some people were wearing gym clothes, others wore business attire, and one guy still had his coat and hat on as he typed frantically on a keyboard.

"Good. Belle, I need you in mapping," Agent Won greeted me; "We're doing it right now."

"Now?" I asked, despite not having any idea what she was saying. I looked up to a screen and realized what was going on even as I wheeled myself over to a station. Al-Zahrani or someone from his camp had sent out a communiqué of sorts to the major leaders, which would then send it to their people. Agent Kmetz was next to me, eyes never leaving the screen.

"We missed tagging this guy, but we got his third in command. We need to back-trace it," Kmetz said and I joined him at the keyboard.

"These people have good firewalls," I joined the massive team effort. Personally, I hunted down six people, tagged their computers, locations, and identities. The software that Ari had started to create helped us slip the virtual Lo-Jack® into the cyber network of Al-Zahrani's closest followers. By the time I sat back and took a breath, the second wave of people had arrived and they began mining information intensely from the little tags before they could be discovered or dismantled. I was exhausted. Someone wheeled me back to the main table, and I ate a bagel with strawberry cream cheese. When it was gone, I looked back up at the screens.

"We're missing at least two. No, three. Ba'artis out of Liberia, Fossil out of France, and I know there's someone in Turkmenistan."

As the words sunk in, another light came on the board: it was Ba'artis. It was two other lights which drew everyone's attention though: one coming out of Ohio and one in Northern Virginia.

"Dibs on Ohio," I called and began to propel myself toward a computer. Agent Won stopped me with a hand. "They've got it. Marilyn, Vlad, and Kim: I want every breath monitored on those two," she took control of my chair and rolled me over to the wall. "Stay there. Don't say anything, just stay there," she directed and my guard appeared to enforce her command as she whirled out of there to her office.

From my angle, I could stretch my head and see the main screen. Instead of having a hissy fit, I took a breath and looked at what we had just accomplished. Twenty-five points of light on a global map were scattered across every continent except Australia, the Antarctic, and South America. More agents arrived and quickly set to work. Some of the points of light had begun firing off to their second in commands, unwittingly exposing them as well. My gut told me that within twenty four hours, there would be more incoming data than even the CIA could shake a stick at. Agent Won reappeared. She did a basic roll call of who was covering whom and then returned to me.

"We're having a little difficulty with a protected network in Switzerland," she said apologetically.

"Know the network?" I asked and yawned. She rolled me over to the man in question and set me up at his station.

I told him the program I would need and he got it for me. The next twenty minutes went very quickly, but I broke through the system and he returned to 'driving' so he could smooth over my rough hack and get into the system.

I slid out toward the bagels again to find donuts, coffee, and energy shots on the table. Agent Won and Director Goode stepped out of her office around that time and entered the main room. Director Goode's eyes were on the screen, but they scanned across the room of worker bees and found me. She looked at my pajamas pointedly.

"Ma'am," I greeted.

"I think she was in bed when I called her," Agent Won said. "Actually, I think a lot of these people were in bed."

"Well it warranted a midnight call-up. Excellent work. Really excellent."

"Did you get that wire through?" Won asked me and I nodded tiredly. "You are so great. Do you need anything before they take you back to your room?"

I grabbed two donuts and wrapped them in a napkin. "I'm good. I hope I don't have any morning appointments." They brought the wheelchair over and Agent Won helped me transfer. "But if you need any help with the trouble spots, you wake me up."

"Thank you," she whispered in my ear and the guards wheeled me away. I slid a chocolate covered piece of heaven into my mouth while they got me downstairs. I finished off that donut and the glazed before I fell into bed. I licked the sugar off of my fingers but never got around to taking off my brace.

I slept hard and had vivid dreams. I was so far asleep I didn't wake when someone opened the door and turned on a light.

I woke to George's voice.

"Wow. She is out," he said quietly.

"We can do this without waking her," I heard a familiar but strange voice reply.

"Too late," George said in a normal voice as I gathered my sheets and sat up.

"I just wanted to see where you lived. I was here anyway," the man who was either Deuce or Trey said quietly.

"Normally I'd be up, but we had a long night," I replied and unstrapped my cast, which was really starting to hurt.

"I know," he said succinctly.

"Did you really come in your pajamas?" George asked good-naturedly.

"It was like, 2200 or 2230, I don't know. I was in bed and they needed me so I went. I put on my cast and my shoes and then we hopped into the chair. I think Director Goode was impressed."

"I'm very impressed," Deuce said.

"Hell, I'm impressed," I admitted. "Did I miss breakfast?"

"No, they can bring you breakfast," Deuce said. "What do you want?"

"Sometimes they have the oatmeal that has bits of apple in it, it's really good," I replied and George sent that on. "How many have we tagged so far?" I asked Deuce.

"Well, it's been a few hours. You know how the chains work. How many do you think we'll have by now?" he turned the question around. Magically, George produced a bowl of oatmeal and a cup of tea. He brought the tray to me in bed and retreated to the table.

"Every B has two or three C's, which might lead to five to nine D's, then it gets ridiculous. I would guess about one to five hundred. Twenty five B's, plus seventy five C's," I

300

stopped to shovel large mouthfuls of apple oatmeal, "plus about four hundred D's. But, the technology isn't perfect. It might tag non-involved parties; we'll have to wait for the data to be sorted and sifted out. God, that's going to be a pain in the ass," The oatmeal was finished and I sipped my tea.

"And how many B's, C's, and D's have you knocked off?" he asked and cleared the tray away.

"At least one," I replied. If he wouldn't answer me, I wouldn't answer him. "I think we missed Paris and Turkmenistan," I added. "I didn't see the lights."

"Don't worry about it," he said dismissively. I had a hunch. "Can you sleep?"

"George, can I have some painkiller and two of those sleepy pills?" I requested. He produced the required medications in a little plastic cup. In the meantime, Deuce had a look around.

"Get some rest, we won't need you too much today," Deuce said cordially. "Last question: where'd you hear about Turkmenistan?"

"I performed a hit there, but I really got into it in Afghanistan," I replied.

"Why do all roads lead to Afghanistan?" George exclaimed.

"Because Pakistan has nukes," I replied in a matter-of-fact tone before snuggling into bed. George and Deuce exchanged a look and left.

In my dreams, I saw a woman who looked like a mixture of my mother and the gypsy in The Hunchback of Notre Dame. She took me into a tent and started to make tea.

"You have to be careful, Ali," she told me with a relaxed air. "If they can get what they want, they won't need you anymore."

"But I want to help them get Al-Zahrani!" I explained to her and realized that my hair was much shorter, like it used to be.

"What do they do to the others who help them?" she asked and the back of the tent disappeared to reveal a pile of corpses; one of them was the Algerian. "Just drink your tea, Ali," she soothed. I looked at my tea and it was blood. I dipped a finger in it to be certain. The thickness and texture confirmed it for me.

"Why aren't you drinking?" my mother asked.

"It...that's blood," I told her.

"Of course it is. What did you expect?"

"But it's blood. No one drinks blood."

"No one?" she asked in a very strange way. "You are no one. No one in the books, no one in the pages, just a phenomenon that the world will eventually forget, especially after they've killed you and buried you with the others."

"They're not going to kill me! George is not going to kill me."

"Just hold on," she whispered as a gust of wind burst through and blew her and the tent and the body pile away, leaving me standing in the air, hanging onto the current.

"This isn't real," I announced. "This is a dream!" I shouted and the wind calmed down, and I was standing on a table in a diner.

"Yeah, we've all got dreams," my Israeli benefactor shuffled up to me, speaking with my father's voice. "Dreams, hopes, ambitions. But you have to fight for what you want, and you don't get it anyway half the time.

"No, you don't exist, and this is a dream," I retorted.

"So, where's your weapon?" he asked me.

"I don't have any; they took them away."

"Bullshit, Ali. I know you. I've got your number." There was a moment of blackness and then I was awake, sweating in my prison cell bed.

The baby did jumping jacks in my stomach, but the real movement was in my head. "Weapons," I muttered to myself. I instinctively smoothed my hands against my sides, looking for the once-familiar tools of survival. "Hell!" I pushed myself out of bed and forgot about my ankle until I stood. "Shit! Fine," I hobbled to the bathroom and hit the shower.

Come on. Dive deep. They wouldn't do all of this for me if they were going to kill me. I know too much. I know too much; they're going to kill me. Wait, I'm not an insurgent, I'm not a terrorist: those were terrorists. Terrorists; the ones in the U.S. Al-Zahrani. Bomb belts: you know it would be really damn funny if they blew themselves up on a false alarm. Look, it's a Marine BOOM, oh, wait, it's just some dude in body armor. Oops. My bad. I laughed and got out of the shower. *Ok, focus. Weapons!* I dressed in the bathroom and grabbed the crutches. *Definitely not weapons,* I thought back on some of my experiences. I had not relied on traditional weapons during the last few years. *Computers, programs, my hands, my feet, that curling iron, bag of potatoes, oil, ice, glass, the electrical cord off of an alarm clock,* I strapped my brace on. *Yeah, this could do something. Hey, idiot; you have a presidential pardon, what are you freaking out about? I'm an American citizen. Oh, what now?* The speaker clicked at me.

"Hello Belle," Dr. McEwen's voice came.

"Hello Tom," I replied.

"Care for a little chicken Caesar salad a la me?"

"Fine," I answered. "I'm ready when you are."

"I'll tell the guards," he replied and clicked off. The door opened and I grabbed my jacket and sat in the wheelchair.

We didn't speak, we just went. They took me to the office that Leona had used once. Tom was waiting at the little table there with two to-go containers of the salad with the lids still on. I transferred into the chair opposite him, and the guard escort returned to the door.

"Hello," Tom said warmly.

"What do you want?" I asked in a normal conversational tone and opened the dish.

He laughed a little to himself. "How was the overnight blitz?"

"It was fine. We were very successful," I replied and we ate for a few minutes in silence.

"I know you're upset, but I'm not sure why," he announced after I had inhaled my plate.

"God you are just like my mother," I muttered before I thought.

"We're closing in on Al-Zahrani, so maybe your vigilante efforts you associate with your mother are coming to an end?" he guessed.

"Stay away from my mother and out of my head," I replied shortly and drank the bottled green tea.

McEwen evaluated me for a moment. "Okay. Fair enough. Do you want to let me help you?"

"They're going to kill me," I reported.

"We're closing in on Al-Zahrani, so you think they'll kill you when it's done?"

"You're closing in on him, I bloody found him. I could have spit and hit him."

"Bitterness…okay,"

"What happens to the people I've gotten information out of here?" I posed to him.

"The terrorists? They go back to their holding units."

"Not all of them. What do they do with the bodies?"

"Bodies? You mean that man who died after he tried to stab you?"

"Tom, I'm too smart to play these games."

"Belle, Alexis, we are not going to kill you. I see your logic. I do. But we're not going to kill you. Not when we find him, not after he's in prison, not after that. We're invested in you. You have a presidential document. You have a false identity on our papers. You're going to live a semi-free life when this is all said and done. Look, have we treated you fairly?"

I kind of nodded.

"You have good living conditions, a little laptop, movies, human interaction; we don't interrogate you for hours on end in harsh conditions?"

"Yes."

"Your cell construction gives you a decent environment and protects you from outside forces; you have medical attention and you are able to practice your job skills doing something you love to do?" McEwen checked.

"Yes," I was more convinced.

"And you have a presidential guarantee that we will never prosecute you in the United States as long as you don't try to escape? Belle, I want your life. You have no bills, you have no real chores, you get to do lots of different things and meet lots of characters. You have a really sweet take on life, and we wouldn't go to the trouble if we were just going to flush you. With the terrorists, we just need to contain them and get information which saves lives. It's that straightforward: get them so they can't kill us, and get their friends so they can't kill us. We don't ask them about strategies or things they might have overheard because they were spying on someone: that's not their thing. They're peasants, you're a princess."

The logic snapped onto my mind like a rubber band. "That makes sense."

"That's actually a really good analogy," Tom congratulated himself. "Not bad for free flow speaking."

I smiled at him, amused.

"Come on, let's get comfortable; I want to talk about what happened last night and I'd like you to share what triggered this little panic," Tom helped me up and we transferred to plusher furniture for a long chat.

Sometime later I watched the sun set through the slats in the window blinds.

"I'm still concerned about the two missing men on the trail we have," I admitted. "Turkmenistan and Paris. The French may have gotten Paris."

"I don't know exactly how much I can say, but don't be concerned," Tom replied.

"The Iranians may have tracked down the guy in Turkmenistan; that would make sense," I added. "I think I know what happened in Paris. You're right. I shouldn't worry. What I should do is set up a kind of a filter for our little terrorist-tracking program."

He looked at his phone and grimaced. "The CIA is here."

"Should I hide?" I asked sarcastically.

"No use, they are the CIA; but it would be amusing. No, better off not to," Tom considered.

"Nice of them to wait until the sun set: shroud of darkness and all that," I added and he failed to stifle his laugh. "If that redneck jackass is here, I still owe him a broken arm."

"Oh, be nice, I don't think they'll bother us," he said and his phone dinged. "They're bothering us."

"Called it!" I pushed my hair back as I saw the shadows of men in the hall.

"I'm working here!" Tom called as John poked his head in. John poked his head back out.

"You're going to need to disarm," he told his colleagues. "And I wouldn't go in there if I were you."

"She's laid up and knocked up, what harm can I do?" A horrid twang asked.

"John, if you let him in, he's going right out the window," I sang out.

"Yeah, you stay here," I heard John instruct before he and a tense short man with a gnome-like beard came in. "Hello Belle, Dr. McEwen, this is Fred. He's a systems engineer. We'll be brief, and we're sorry to interrupt."

"Hello Fred," I greeted politely.

"Good evening ma'am. May I be direct?" he asked and his face reddened. I nodded and he continued. "The system coding you put together on this program is amazing. Stealth code that's sort of virus and sort of worm? You're a genius!"

John got Fred a chair.

"I don't work alone, Fred. A friend of mine did most of the leg work on it," I replied calmly.

"We're here to set up shop and try to sort and sift the actual terrorists and the accidentally tagged people in the program that ran last night. Fred's one of the best. He's seen several pieces of your work and he wanted to bounce a few ideas off of you during this project. First, of course, I wanted to do introductions. I already explained to Fred that if you don't want to work with him, you won't. Oh, and he's always this polite; it's not an act."

"I know," I said and leaned back a little. "What's with Huckleberry Hound?" I thumbed toward the hallway.

"He's a great code morph creator. I know you hate him. You two will not work together."

"He threw me up against a wall. He doesn't speak to me, doesn't come near me, I don't even want to be in the same room with him. I owe him a broken arm from before, and I'm not sure how much I can contain myself."

"Okay, I'll keep him away from you, and you don't kill him. Deal?"

"Deal. And Fred, don't worry: I'm really a very rational, level-headed person."

"That's what the people in cyber said. Agent Won thought I would be fine with you," Fred squirmed as he spoke.

"I hope you don't mind being hawked over: it comes with the territory," I cautioned him.

"I'm sure you'll be fine," Tom added with a note of finality. "So what now?"

"Well, we're heading to the lab," John led.

"Well then I'll let you go on ahead and set things up and maybe I'll join you when Dr. McEwen and I are finished," I smiled unemotionally and the men took the hint.

"Yes?" Tom asked when the coast was clear.

"I would like to speak with Director Goode. Do you think she's still around?"

"I'll make a call. Is it urgent?"

"Possibly. It is terrorist-related," I said as I made up my mind. He found the desk phone and dialed 952666.

"Good evening ma'am, Tom McEwen. Yes, great. I just had dinner with Ms. Jones. She would like to speak to you," he paused "I'll check. Belle, will the phone do?" I nodded. "Yes ma'am. I'll put her on," he handed me the phone.

"Ma'am?"

"Yes?"

"I've been thinking about it, and I really want to help take out the Virginia terrorist."

There was a pause; I could hear faded voices in the background.

"Is it a no or a maybe?" I asked.

"Could we go for something in between those two? It's a highly complex matter; and I will discuss that with you later. Right now I have to dash in for a meeting."

"Yes ma'am. Thank you," I replied and she clicked off. "American," I stated and rested back into the chair. "No good using me if he's American or on American soil: bloody constitutional rights. Life is much easier for criminal activities when the whole law-and-order thing doesn't get in the way."

"Do you know Dick Cheney by any chance?" he asked.

I smiled just a little. "Good times."

"What would you do, theoretically?" he asked.

"Profile," I answered without any thought. "Maybe a honey trap; maybe just good intelligence. Evidence,"

"You would do that? You would sleep with a man just for an arrest?"

"I once slept with a man just to plant a bug. I slept with another to get access to kill someone. I had intimate relations with a very interesting woman a few times. For about two years she was indispensable to my effort: information, supplies, equipment, she knew the very pulse of the organization I was taking apart."

"What was her name?"

"Genent; it means beautiful."

"Was she?"

"Of course. Plus, I killed the man who killed her brother and father. She loved them. I guess love inspires a lot more than it gets credit for."

"How many women have you been intimately involved with?"

"Just three. Genent, Arida, and Clarisse."

"Are they still alive?"

"Genent was killed by her husband. Arida died after a suicide bomber attack. Clarisse had leukemia when we met. She died earlier this year: maybe a few months before my capture."

"You knew she was dying," he observed.

"We're all dying. You're a doctor, you should know that. I've been living in this world, this manic now-or-never-land where long term plans are a fantasy and every morning is one more night you managed to steal from the people trying to kill you. I was starting to feel smug every sunrise; I got a little cocky toward the end. And then the baby; and then it was time. Then I had time: I don't steal or borrow days or nights in here. They're just there. They're mine to deal with and sometimes it's boring as hell. It's a totally different mentality."

"Being a mother?" he probed.

"No, Dr. McEwen: being a person in a real social culture. I'm not just a demon anymore."

"Do you like to read?" he asked in a strange turn of conversation.

"I did, at one point. Why? Do you need something translated?"

"No, it's all English, and all for fun. I just thought reading might help pass some of your down time here."

My mother's spirit haunted me briefly in a flash of memory.

"What's wrong?" *Of course he would notice.*

"My mother," I tried to explain and my nose smarted.

"Memory?"

"You know; every bastard I killed; ever man I got arrested or shot or whatever, I thought it would help. That first time, it did. I stopped a random act of terrorism; I stopped some innocent people from being blown to hell. It's not like I expected that it would bring her back. I just…" I gasped for air. "I just had this rage, the injustice, the wrongness and I couldn't do anything…so I did what I did and I don't even know if it helped at all. She was just gone! First missing, then missing turned into uncertain death. She was in the first tower. No one had any warning; just," I stopped talking because I had started crying. "I never went into that city again. She was there on a business trip, coming home on Friday. Whatever is left of her and the other thousands of people is all ground in with the rubble and the dust and whatever steel or concrete building left in what they call 'Ground Zero'. I'm sure they hauled it all somewhere by now."

"You still love her deeply," Tom said and handed me a box of tissues.

"I think she would have liked what I did with my life. Strange thing to say considering that I've taken more lives than most serial killers, but she loved to take the initiative. Push forward, push the boundaries away and grow. Knock down the walls; move mountains one rock at a time. That was her philosophy."

"We're going to get him. We are going to get the man who murdered your mother," Tom promised.

"I should have shot him when I had the chance."

"Why didn't you?"

"My gun, I was only carrying a small gun, and it was on my back, and I was hanging from the ceiling, these are the excuses I say. Really, I wasn't ready. I wasn't really…prepared to pull the trigger and hopefully kill him and almost certainly die myself. I just wasn't ready. I didn't know I would actually see him when I snuck into the house."

"You did the right thing, Belle," Dr. McEwen reassured me.

"Maybe. But how many more people is he going to kill between that day and the day he is stopped?"

"With your help, that day is coming a lot sooner than it would have. Just remember that, Belle. You look tired."

"I'm totally exhausted," I realized aloud. "I also really want a Poptart®."

He laughed to himself. "Any flavor?"

"Anything. I just have this yen for something made of lard, flour, sugar, and fruit paste. You know, Americans are probably the only people in the world who would eat that on a daily basis," I added as I slid into the wheelchair. "Give Fred my regrets."

"Take her downstairs please," Tom requested the guard who had come to hover over my chair. I was pulled backwards and rolled out the door.

Back in my cell, I had changed into pajamas and I was hop-gimping from the bathroom to the bed when I saw Tom place a silver packet on the food tray.

"Sugary lard, blueberry flavor," he called and I smiled appreciatively. He was gone in a blink. I carried the pouch to bed with me by biting it and I got comfortable with my dolphins and a Sudoku puzzle book. I suppose it was an hour later when I heard the guards stirring.

The door opened: it was Shapiro. "Pencil down please," he directed and I set the mechanical pencil down toward my feet. Director Goode came in with an air of total exhaustion.

"How's the foot?" she asked and pulled a chair over.

"Getting there; I can't wait to walk. These crutches are killing my lower back. How's the world?"

She smiled. "Getting there," she nodded to herself. "I wanted to talk about what you said on the phone."

"I know, I've thought about it a little more and really I guess I'm useless. It's not like I could testify in court, considering that I really don't exist."

"If there's a way to add you into the operation without risk, I'll keep you in mind. The FBI is the main agency for this; it's on our soil and we want to make certain that these men are prosecuted and convicted of everything we can get them for. I appreciate your enthusiasm. I also deeply appreciate what you did last night: not just the staying up all night hacking but the overall program. You're inspiring some of my staff."

"Thank you. I met with some of the CIA group tonight," I mentioned.

"Not..."

"With Dr. McEwen; John introduced me to the analyst Fred. We'll work fine together. The hick was advised to stay in the hall."

"I may ask Captain Stover to have a word with him. I don't want an incident, and I don't think you should be subjected to his more colorful moments."

"Perhaps a little video presentation?" I half-sincerely suggested.

"Not a bad idea." The gears turned in her head. "You know, I'm going to miss you when this is all over. I may have to come visit you at your second start location. I don't know where it's going to be, but it will be very comfortable."

"It's funny to think of it all being over. It's been...I've been doing this so long."

"John was part of the team tracking Al-Zahrani before 9/11. He's been doing it about a decade longer than you have."

"I would have been about 5 when he started," I realized.

"Where does the time go?" She stood up and put the chair back. "Get some rest, and don't be afraid of taking rest breaks. You're pregnant and you need extra care. Plus, if you don't start taking breaks, we'll have to start making you take breaks. There aren't too many all-nighters in your future."

"The baby is very draining," I admitted. "I'm starting to walk a little though."

"Good," she sat back, focused on something outside of the room.

"Penny for your thoughts?" I said after a moment.

"Which video clips to show Jason," she divulged.

"Wide variety to choose from. Me and the three guards; me and the unfortunate man; me and that jackass from Homeland Security, me and Ari, or you can just show the file photos you have of the people you think I've killed. That's been effective in the past, with Israel. Then again, with them it was more like bragging…"

She smiled a little, possibly with pity.

"Or you can let me have him for two minutes," I offered.

"Belle, do me a favor: do not touch him. For me, give him a two foot bubble."

"Radius or diameter?"

"Two foot bubble, radius, from the heart: the cone covers his whole body."

"Yes ma'am," I submitted as Captain Stover slid through the open door. "I will give Jason a no-touching immunity bubble of two feet: but that will end the second he touches me. That bastard threw me against a wall, and I'm a lot more pregnant now than I was then."

Just then my senses sprang up. A hoary twang came from down the hall outside.

"Yoohoo, j'a git the pussycat all caged up?" he laughed.

"'at's it," I leapt out of bed "I got your pussycat!" I started saying as I painfully headed for the door at a surprisingly good clip. Captain Stover caught me up in a merciful yet effective backwards bear hug. My heart and senses slowed down enough to hear Stover speak quietly as he held me in place.

"Detain that man, not gently," he instructed someone. The door slammed and locked the four of us in: Captain Stover, Director Goode, and another guard joined me. "Take it easy," he softly said in my ear. He had my arms crossed over my chest, holding my hands. Breathing became harder when the tears started leaking involuntarily. "You're alright, good girl," he told me. "Bring that chair over," he told the guard. We eased me into a straddle on the chair, keeping my hands on top of the back. "There we go, hang in here with me Belle," he rubbed my back. "Ma'am," he directed to Director Goode, indicating that she should leave.

"Belle?" she called and I lifted my tearstained snotty face from my hands. "He is mine now, and believe me, I'm going to take care of him," she had a vaguely murderous look in her eye.

"Incoming," Susan called.

"Outgoing," the man with Director Goode said. Stover just kept his hand on the back of my neck. They made the exchange and I was lifted backwards onto a gurney with straps. Once I was appropriately secured, Susan came around and took my pulse.

"You with me?" she asked.

"Yes. I'm fine."

"Okay. Well I'm going to check you out, especially the ankle, and then someone is going to talk to you, and then we should be able to get you off this table and back into bed,"

315

she explained even as she started checking me out. Stover left for a few minutes and someone replaced him. Stover returned with Dr. McEwen and Susan left.

"First of all, thank you for not killing him," Tom greeted. "He's not going to give you any problems; they've locked him up." Tom started un-strapping me immediately. "Any other sources of rage or perceived threat?"

"I just want to go to bed," I replied.

"This all falls into normal, even healthier than expected behavior," Tom declared and handed me the box of tissues. "The man threatened and provoked her, and she actually showed some very impressive restraint."

"Actually, he showed the restraint," I corrected Tom.

"Perhaps, but he was wearing a gun. Either direction, she's not in a mental break so there's no reason to further observe or restrain her. I recommend lots of rest, light entertainment, chicken soup, and a total ban on the jackass." Tom helped me gimp to the bed and he set me up. "You're doing great, Beauty. Let me know if you want to talk tomorrow. Goodnight," he left, but they left the door open and Captain Stover shot a glance my way.

"Thank you," I said quietly. "For not hurting me," I explained.

"I have sincere doubts that you would have killed him," he replied.

"You're right," I tilted my head and pondered. "It was different from when I launched on Ari. But I really would have enjoyed kicking his ass. I suppose I wanted to see the fear in his eyes. It always comes, every time they see it coming, there's a moment that a man realizes that his defenses are chicken shit and he is totally exposed to a force he can't protect himself against. I wanted to see that from

316

him. But you're right; I don't think I would have carried through."

"I know," he turned to go. "Here's the real riddle: is my firearm loaded or clear?"

"The one on your right side is empty," I replied without batting an eyelash. "But you always keep two spares, and I'd guess that the one on your ankle has a round or two in it," he scrutinized me for a few seconds. "I survived the jungle, desert, ambushes, explosions, Al-Qaida and two dozen death matches," I shrugged. "Choosing not to be that person anymore doesn't change my past and it can't erase my memory or learned instincts."

"You're welcome," he returned to the origin of the conversation. "Now get some sleep and stop trying to kill rednecks."

I laughed at the phrasing and delivery and the door sealed shut. The lights switched off and I had my bedside light.

Minutes after I had turned that one off, I heard Starr's voice.

"Belle?"

"What?" I replied.

"Are you okay? I heard there was an incident," I determined that she was using the telephone.

"I'm good. I wasn't hurt, and I didn't even get near the other person. Can we do this tomorrow?"

"Oh, gosh, you're asleep aren't you?"

"Yep,"

"Sorry. But no one's hurt?"

"If they are, I didn't do it," I replied and flopped onto my stomach.

"Okay. Sleep well," she replied.

I did.

Chapter 12: Bloody Hands

I slept long and hard, ate a nice hot breakfast, showered, and I was wheeled over to the cyber department around ten a.m. Fred was just leaving; he looked exhausted.

"Good morning miss," he greeted as he slid a jacket on.

"That's a long night!" I replied.

"Yes, well, lots to do. I caught a quick nap around two. Agent Won started reading in on my work around 8; she'll be able to brief you."

"Sounds good. Do you know when you'll be back?"

"Should be tomorrow afternoon: they're switching me onto a day shift, which is great," he replied earnestly.

"That's probably my fault: they told me that I'm on a restricted schedule," I replied.

"Well I certainly appreciate it. Look forward to seeing you tomorrow," he said and exited.

I wheeled myself forward to Agent Won and got into the day's activities. It was very strange to me when her watch beeped and she got to a stopping point and stopped.

"Good work."

"What's wrong?" I asked and looked up to the room's clock. "It's only been three hours; we can pull this through."

"We have a meeting," she replied and took over my wheelchair's steering. She wheeled me into her office and took a set of trays from her assistant. "It's a lunch meeting."

"Do you want the stir fry or the noodles?" I asked as I examined the two frozen dinners, now steaming and ready to eat.

"Whichever," she sat on her side of the desk and produced eating utensils. I gave her the noodles. She started eating so I just took her cue. The food was gone in minutes.

"Two cold root beers?" her assistant delivered and closed the door on his way out.

"Awesome. So here's the poop," Agent Won leaned back and I knew she was about to set the facts out for me. I love this about her. "What?" she caught my expression.

"I love how you just tell it like it is. No nonsense: I like it," I replied.

"Well it's a hell of a lot easier than being flowery. So here's the deal. One, I don't know what you've heard about the incident last night, but you'll get that straight from the director. Two, I have a new set of regulations for working with you. I know it's going to be counter intuitive for you and it's going to be a little annoying because I know you, and you like to see things all the way through. Thus, the beeping watch. Look, this is new to me too, but these rules are how it has to be," she was struggling a little.

"Director Goode said last night that I was going to be on a more restricted schedule," I informed her and it seemed to help.

"Okay, good. Just to give you an idea; you can only work in cyber for 6 hours a day. You must take breaks every three hours. You must rest for at least one hour for every four hours engaged. Food on a regular basis, etc."

"So I'll work here for six hours plus breaks, and then what? File my nails?"

"No, you can be used up to fourteen hours a day which includes the breaks. It just says that you can work in cyber for up to six hours per day. You can work in analysis up to eight hours a day, or in…God, where's that list?" She tapped wildly on her keyboard and the screen evidently satisfied her. "Okay, six for cyber, eight for analysis, eight for translation, four for interrogation-related activities, six for sharing methods and tactics and then there's a director's discretion category with a big fat unexplained asterisk. The rest is up to the director. That was your three-hour mark 'break', now it's off to the director so she can get in an hour before your mandatory hour-long rest break."

"This is nuts," I observed.

"Welcome to the government," she locked her computer and rose. "You're wonderful."

"Thanks for lunch," I said and secured my bottle of soda before I wheeled around to follow her out the door. From there, the guards took me up to see the director, although I wheeled myself. It's a hell of a lot easier than using crutches. The door was slightly open, and I eavesdropped as we waited.

"Well you had better be damn sure because if anything remotely like this happens again, you're going to be answering to one step short of God. That's coming straight from the top. He's also making the call on when and how I'll release him to you, so don't bother coming here," there was a pause. "Good. I know you will Stephen. Your standards are better than this, so I know you'll take care of it," her voice was gentler toward the end. "We'll talk then. Thank you," she hung up. "Come in," she called louder and the guard helped me wheel in. "What part did you hear?"

"Short of God," I replied and transferred to a regular chair at her signal. "Shall I forget it?"

"Not a bad idea. How are you feeling today?"

"I haven't tried anything fancy with my ankle; it didn't appreciate me walking on it last night."

"I thought about that afterwards. That must have hurt like hell."

"It's about a four on my pain scale, but I've been shot twice. Is this about my new schedule?"

"Partially. Could you take off your shirt?"

"Yeah, okay," I sat forward in the chair and took off first my jacket and then pulled off my blouse. She hit a switch and it became brighter in the room.

"Can you rotate?" she asked and I spun around to show her my back. "Thank you. You can put your shirt on, but not the jacket yet," Director Goode directed. The shirt slid on and I went ahead and presented my forearms for inspection. "So I guess I don't have to explain," she regarded me warmly before turning her attention to the skin.

"No ma'am; and I don't expect any bruises from last night. Captain Stover was very gentle."

She seemed satisfied and dimmed down the lights to a normal level. "Yes, I thought he handled that very well. I assure you, he was not quite as kind with the antagonist," she swallowed and I drank from my bottle. "Well, that man is gone. You won't see, hear, or smell him again. The CIA man Fred is going to start working days so your schedules will align. Your working schedule is going to be slightly more limited. We put in structures recommended by pre-natal health care specialists, psychologists, and pediatricians and they also align with the OSHA and various other regulations. You're not going to like it, but if you work with us, there's some wiggle room and we might be able to make some adjustments," Director Goode pushed a chart toward me and we went over the time restrictions, the definition of a 'break', and so on.

"Finally, you do need to exercise. How do you like swimming?"

"I'll need a suit and some goggles, but I think it'll all come back to me. That's probably our best option right now."

"I agree. Last note; keep thinking cooperatively, one hour of therapy twice a week minimum."

"Dr. McEwen or the woman?" I asked.

"Either."

"Agreed."

"Appreciated," she stood and Natalie came in with the aluminum crutches. "Exercise by crutches. It burns tons of calories and if you do it for at least 30 minutes a day, it can satisfy your exercise requirement."

"Good thinking."

"Thank you. You're off to your unit and hopefully a nice mid-afternoon nap."

"Thank you ma'am. When is my next activity?"

"Later," she replied and I resigned myself to my crutches, tentatively putting a little weight on the injured foot.

Once back in my sunshine colored cell, my first observance was that someone had come and cleaned. The sheets had been changed, the bed was made, the floor was clean, and the faint smell of citrus cleaning chemicals lingered. The noise of the door sealing behind me broke my train of thought, and I saw the papers from Director Goode. The guard had placed them on my desk. I glanced over the documents before tossing them on the bed and hobbling my way to the bathroom. I found a surprise hanging on top of my towel.

There were two bathing suits: one as a one-piece and one was a sports bikini which had a modest top and room for a stretching belly. A sticky note on the mirror gave me a message: "please try these on for size." It seemed like a reasonable request, so I did. The one-piece had a little pooch in the front: room for growth I figured.

"Okay, they fit," I climbed into my pajama pants and put my normal sports bra and shirt on. "They fit great, if anyone's interested," I called out the food slot before setting the crutches so they wouldn't fall; then swearing at them when they did fall over, and I turned off my light.

It was four o'clock when they gave me a bag and told me I was going to the gym. I changed into my swimsuit and put a fresh set of things in the bag so I wouldn't be wet and cold. I guess it was about 4:20 when they showed me the pool: short of Olympic, but still extremely large. I sat on the bench and started stripping.

I heard George come behind me just before he spoke; I recognized his scent. "Never have been much for modesty, have you?"

"I have the basics covered," I replied as I unstrapped the brace. "I'm going to need goggles," I reminded him and he produced a brand new set of Speedos, still in the plastic. "Thanks."

"Black is all I could find."

"There's nothing wrong with black," I replied and shucked my pants.

"I'd like you to do some live-feed analysis later: sit in the booth while someone else does the interrogation, and give hints through an earpiece."

"That's a lot of trust. Someone here is willing to do that?"

"Any reason they shouldn't be?" George asked and took the packaging from the goggles. "Enjoy your swim. I'll join you for dinner."

"What's for dinner?" I asked as I grabbed a crutch and started heading for the water.

"Fresh fruit, roast beef au jus, vegetables and lemon meringue pie if we're lucky. Listen, I want to talk to you about something later," George replied and moved in to replace my missing crutch. "It's okay; you can put that down Alexis."

At the water's edge we turned to face each other. I handed him the crutch. "The last time you said that, you were arresting me."

"I was trying to keep you from getting hurt."

"Worth it?"

"I think so," he let go and I sat down to slide into the water. When I came up to put the goggles on, George was halfway out the door.

The cold, deserted swimming pool was mine for the taking. I rapidly discovered that my ankle injury did not mesh with swimming and realized I would need to only use my arms. After a few false starts, I got into the stride of a childhood sport. I hadn't swum competitively since I was twelve, and aside from survival I hadn't swum at all in five or six years. The chlorine in my sinuses, the water in my ears, the incredible silence gave me a great rush of sensations. I pushed through the water, sometimes diving deeper to the darker waters, where the slight increase in pressure hugged me before I soared up for air and a dramatic splash. A shrill whistle called me out of the water, and Agent Starr was there to hand me a towel.

"That was awesome," I walked pretty well for a few steps before my ankle reminded me that it hates me. I crutched to the showers and talked to Starr while I rinsed off and did a quick shampoo.

"Good swim?" she asked on the other side of the tile.

"Yeah, it was great. I haven't done it in years," I replied. "Hey, whoever thought of putting in little soap and shampoo dispensing thingies in here was a genius!"

"No, the person who put them in was kind; the person who went back and got the two tubes labeled was a genius,"

Starr replied. My head went underwater for a minute so the next thing I heard was "I've ever known. They really do come in and bleach the floor every day," I turned the water off.

"Yeah, it is very clean."

"If you've shampooed your hair, I thought you might like it blow-dried," she said as I pulled my clothes on and strapped on the brace. I wrapped my wet hair in the towel. She sat me down on a bench and slowly blew out my hair. When it was dry and shiny, she gently pulled back a few strands and braided them around my head, attaching with a little rubber band.

"Sorry, I just haven't played with hair in a long time," she said apologetically.

"I look angelic. Weird, but I like it. Thank you," I replied sincerely and let her spritz on some hair spray.

"Are you ready for dinner?"

"Sure, I'm not that hungry. Looks like nausea is coming back into style," I joked.

After dinner, I found that I slipped very quickly into the world of live interview support. I had a headset with a microphone and I felt totally involved, despite being outside of the room.

I did this for a few days for a few hours at a time; they kept me out of cyber for four days straight and I was about to start asking questions when Agent Won dropped by one evening to explain that they were all very deeply involved in the American terrorist hunt and I couldn't be on the floor.

I satisfied myself with what I could do; working about half out of my cell and half in observation rooms. Director Goode came to me for our weekly sessions and something was definitely bothering her. It was the middle of a week, twelve days after the original injury, when I saw Halloween candy in the observation rooms.

"Is it Halloween? I thought we had another week or two to go?" I asked Fred as we passed in the halls.

"Stores in the U.S. start stocking Halloween stuff after Labor Day, Miss Jones," Fred replied nervously. I had decided by then that if Fred could find some balls I might just keep him. I looked extra hard for clues as to the date once I was back in observation for the mid-afternoon interrogations.

Not all of my tips provided gold, but several did. A few hours in, we had gotten the terrorist past the denial, the lies, the stories, the accusations; he was tripping over himself. I guided the team to his buttons and prompted them on how to push them. The technician flipped a few switches and my feed went dead.

I turned to him as the door opened and Agent Powell joined us.

"You're done," he greeted.

"I'm on a winning streak here!" I objected. "Tell him how well we're doing!" I told the tech.

"I know how well you're doing. You've had him by the balls a few times, and I have to admit I like watching you go, but you're done."

"One more hour?"

"No."

"One hour and I'll take two naps tomorrow," I bartered.

"Belle, they can take it from here. Please get in the wheelchair. You're out of hours today, and if you don't get in the chair," he annoyed me so I just got up, hobbled over with the crutches, and sat in the damn chair.

"Rules are stupid," I grumbled to Powell.

"Deal with it," he replied dryly and wheeled me away. I realized quickly that we were alone; there wasn't an accompanying guard with us.

In the last elevator, I spoke again. "I am good at what I do."

Agent Powell didn't respond. We left the elevator and then he stopped at a dead spot in the hall. He put a hand on my shoulder very carefully; lightly but positioning his fingers and thumb to potentially hit pressure points.

I left the arm go loose: tensing up only makes pressure point reactions worse.

"I have a question to ask you while we are alone."

"Okay," I said quietly.

He stayed behind me. "The night we arrested you, I took you out of the building and into the vehicle. I've gone over it in my mind dozens of times, and there was an eight to twelve second window where I didn't really have a close back-up agent."

"Seven seconds with no second agent within thirty feet, three with no second agent paying attention within thirty-five feet and two where only two outside agents were paying attention," I corrected him.

"Had a feeling you would have noticed."

"I can't help it. What are you asking?"

"You had a window. Most people wouldn't have been able to use that situation as a window of opportunity, but you are not normal. What happened?"

"You are examining the situation with a set perspective. In your head, it goes 'hauling prisoner away, prisoner had chance to escape, nothing happened'. Change those words to 'taking operative to car in my custody, chance to escape occurred, operative did not take the opportunity'. See what happens," I advised. He removed his hand and resumed wheeling me down the hall.

I smirked to myself as I heard someone from the secure area walking toward us and talking.

"Charlie twelve, retracing steps," a man said somewhat quietly. He came into view and reached back for his radio. "Charlie twelve, egg is okay."

"Something wrong?" Agent Powell asked as we entered the secured area.

"We expected you seventy-two seconds ago, sir," Benzion replied. Agent Powell shrugged and gave me a look before he left. I wheeled myself up to my cell entrance area and stood up.

"What happened?" Benzion asked, backing me against the wall and staring into my eyes. He wasn't touching me, and he wasn't about to hit me. I was turned on.

"After the last elevator," I started. *God he's so hot. Focus!* His eyes were green, and he was leaning down slightly so we were at level. "It wasn't me."

"Belle," Benzion held his position, and kept a patient tone. "I need to know what happened."

"We got out, he was pushing the chair, and he stopped. He stayed behind me, put a hand on my third and fifth upper torso pressure points and asked me a question." Falling into his eyes was pleasant, so I did. "I answered his question, he removed his hand and we resumed walking. We ran into you. I don't think I can tell you what the question was."

"Did you touch him?" Benzion wasn't accusatory. I like that.

"No."

"Did he hurt you?"

"No," I replied but my eyes darted away from his to check my surroundings. It was brief, unintentional and a rookie mistake but I truly didn't care. It was as if I actually trusted Benzion; a total impossibility.

"Belle," Benzion said softly. I forced myself back into his eyes, "You said Agent Powell stayed behind you and put a hand on a set of pressure points. The ones on your shoulder?"

"Yes. Right shoulder near the neck. He didn't apply pressure or anything."

"Is there anything you would like me to know?"

Whatever wildness is in my soul awoke as I processed the situation mentally. I set my healing foot down and stood gingerly on my own two feet. I looked right into his eyes and showed my hand. "I was isolated, at many disadvantages, and I did nothing to reassert my space boundaries. I was relieved to find that someone was tracking me. I know that he wasn't out to harm me, and I know I still could have taken him. He didn't hurt me; he just creeped me out a little. The only problem I have is discovering that I have devolved into someone who feels vulnerability."

"Are you feeling vulnerable right now?" Benzion asked without missing a beat.

I considered it. "No."

"You're not vulnerable, Belle," Benzion slid his hands around my waistband and up, performing a gentle but thorough search. "On this side of the street," he continued the conversation and the search, "it's okay to let someone have your back."

My mind took a left turn without me.

The hot, dusty streets were narrow, and the noise of the street market covered the sounds we made. I was in Aswān,

Egypt to spy on someone; a Sudanese someone who had come to the famous markets. According to my Israeli friends this was a major pusher of the genocides.

The Mossad didn't give a damn about people killing their own people: it was hardly a threat to them as long as no Jews or Jewish interests were threatened. Nearly all of the Jews had gotten out of Sudan, as far as I knew. I took the mission because the thought of genocide kept me up at night.

I was in or near the city for three days prior to that day and I hadn't slept for any of them. Just before the mission, I made my way down closer to the border with Sudan. It wasn't possible to see far into the country, of course, but it felt like I was watching the slaughter anyway. I had seen the pictures. I had heard the voices. Both haunted me; it was all I could think of during those few days.

I saw the mark. He looked healthy, happy, and comparably well-off. The mission was to confirm the Arab contact. I took the pictures Israel wanted, tucked the camera safely in my bag, and ducked behind a barrel. I don't remember making a decision: I really don't. There was a loaded gun with a silencer on it in my hand, and as the men said their goodbyes, I fired two shots...

A voice came from the direction of my ten o'clock. "Belle?"

I zoomed back and discovered that I was still standing in the hall. Benzion had stepped back and both guards were looking at me strangely.

"Flashback?" the other guard offered.

"That was weird," I felt a little dazed as I gathered my wits. I took a crutch and walked into my cell and they sealed the door.

I puttered with the computer, but then everything stopped suddenly as my moderate cramps became very immoderate. Sharp, stabbing pains hit my gut and I flopped forward in the chair. "Oh my god!" I exclaimed and for some reason I reached for my groin. It was wet. The black pants didn't show it, but I pulled my hand back and it was blood streaked.

"Hey! Oh God!" I took a few short breaths. "Medic! Call the medic, I need," I couldn't finish it, but they were already in the room. I showed them my hand. There was lots of talking into radios and someone pulled the desk out of the way. I hadn't felt pain like it in my life: it was like someone had stuck several hot pokers into my bowels and my body had liquefied and was now heading for the exit.

I was lifted onto the gurney after a quick examination and on the way out I saw the fresh imprint of blood on my chair.

They rushed me to the medical center and examined me four different ways. They hooked me up to saline and used psychiatric straps to tie my hands to the bed.

"What is it? The baby: is the baby…" I asked the medic Paul as he prepped something on a metal tray.

"The outside doctor will be with you in a few minutes. I'm sorry," Paul replied and left me there with Officer Morgan.

Morgan was one of several people who just mysteriously came out of the woodwork in that twenty-four hour period between me collapsing and the final prognosis. She stayed with me and even held my hand as we waited for the doctor to arrive and read the charts. Around midnight, the doctor came in and introduced herself before getting down to business. She was middle aged, African American, and had the bedside manner of a coroner. Between my legs she 'mm-hmm'ed and went through countless sponges before shaking her head and pulling out. She listened to my gut, to my chest, and back to my gut, all while totally ignoring what my mouth had to say. Finally she got some sort of diaper-like thing set to catch the blood, and left the room without a word.

George showed up at some point and they let him in to see me then. He immediately went into an attempt to calm me down.

"She can't be deaf; she was listening to my stomach just fine!" I vented.

"We don't know what her orders were. Just hang in there," George tried to calm me.

Susan came back in and glanced at the monitors. "Okay Belle, try to stay calm; keep your heart rate down. We're going to give you a sedative because we need your heart and blood pressure to stay stable for the baby. We're still getting life signs, and we're taking you to a civilian hospital for some prenatal checks to be certain we're still playing with two."

"The baby's okay?" Relief flooded me.

"I've got a heartbeat and an outline. We'll know more after the hospital obstetrician examines you. Now," she came up and held my hand, "you're going to hear it from security too, but I'm speaking as a medical professional. If you run, if you try to escape, even if you somehow make it out alive you will definitely lose this baby," she squeezed my hand gently and left.

"Alexis, we're doing a lot to help you out here," George reminded me as Paul prepped the sedative. "Keep in mind; these guards still have shoot-to-kill orders."

"George, I am so not thinking of that right now!" I berated him and tried to take some deep breaths. "I've

333

weighed it all, trust me, and right now with a bum ankle and a baby on the way; a dozen very powerful people who probably know roughly where I am and want me dead; and a perfectly good deal guaranteed if I don't run, honestly how stupid do you think I am?!!"

Susan injected the yellow sedative into the IV someone had installed and then she went on to pop the nasal oxygen drip into my nose. George stepped aside as someone brought in a paramedic's gurney and Susan and a guard transferred me onto it. The drug worked quickly, but I watched them remove the padded restraints and cuff my right hand to the metal hand bar before they tucked me in with sheets and a blanket and strapped me to the bed. I think I might have started a flashback, but I was chemically overwhelmed.

My body was stiff and cold when I woke up to bright florescent hospital lights and an annoying beep.

"Coming to," a familiar female voice announced quietly. "Take it easy," Susan instructed me as I surveyed my surroundings.

I was in a hospital bed, in a hospital room. My mouth was incredibly dry. There was one Marine standing next to my bed staring at me like it was his purpose in life to count my breaths. His uniform told me he was Staff Sergeant Andrews. Another Marine with what might have been an M50 stood guard near the closed door. Both men had MP armbands.

"We're going to call you Jane here," Susan told me and she picked up a cup. "We've been giving you fluids, but I thought your mouth might be dry."

I reached for the cup with my right hand and realized that it was cuffed to the bed frame. I tried my left, which was free, and took the ice chip cup from her. The man to my left stared at me extra hard as I moved in slow motion.

It was quiet for a few minutes while I froze into a giant ice chip, but then there was a tiny buzz in the earpieces and the door opened. A beautiful Hispanic woman came in; she was probably in her mid-thirties with a lab coat and the traditional stethoscope around her neck.

"Hello Jane, I'm Dr. Morales. Call me Gloria. I'm an obstetrician; my specialization is in difficult pregnancies."

I liked her instantly. "Hi, I'm Jane."

"First things first," she segued perfectly, "It is way too cold in here. Are you cold?"

"Freezing,"

"Okay," she set down a tablet and typed in something. "Great; that should get the room temp up a little," she flitted over somewhere behind Andrews and reappeared with a blanket, which she covered me with. "While you're warming up, I just want to check a few things. This is your first pregnancy?"

"Yes."

"Any STDs?"

"No; they tested."

"Great. You're about five months along?"

"I'm not sure. I tested positive August 15th but I can date conception down to a two week period mid-June."

"Great, so that's right about 18 weeks. When was the trauma to your foot, and what else was injured in that incident?"

"It was two weeks ago," Susan cut in. "She had minor abrasions and some bruising, but there was no full body effect or direct blows to her abdomen."

The doctor asked me a dozen more questions: stomach pain, vomiting, blood in anything, my bowel habits, and whether or not I have stiffness anywhere. She gently checked my lymph nodes, abdomen, and my healing ankle. By that point the room and I were warm and she pulled up two machines and popped out the foot holsters.

"Commander," Doctor Gloria said expectantly and stared at Susan.

"We're ready," Susan nodded and pulled the curtain around to block the man at the door's view. "Exam stance, staff sergeant."

That man rotated his body ninety degrees so he was facing my head. His eyes remained fixed on me, but now his view would be blocked from my genitals. Doctor Gloria did an inside and outside sonogram and showed me a really good outline of my baby. It looked like a lizard until she reminded me that the baby was the white part.

"You see how nice and high she is? You have irritation around the bottom of the uterus and the cervix; that's where the blood's from. It's going to be just fine. You're not ectopic, it's not molar, it looks like you got an infection and irritation and the body just reacted. We're going to give you something for the infection and give you cranberry juice and something for your yeast. You're going to be fine. Now, you do appear to be anemic, but we'll check the vitamins you take every day. Take it easy for a few days, and you'll be one hundred percent."

They finished and let me scoot back up on the bed. I was relieved, exhausted, and slightly annoyed at the chain. I closed my eyes and drifted off and when I woke up, several hours had passed. Andrews was still right there and he spoke briefly into a radio as I opened my eyes and lifted my head.

"I need to use the bathroom," I announced quietly. Andrews repeated the news into the radio and I smacked my forehead with my left hand. "Oh great, who heard that?" I muttered embarrassed.

"Nurse is on the way," Andrews informed me.

A perky young woman in scrubs came in and balked at the sight of the really big gun at the doorway. She held her badge up for inspection and I could feel her fear.

"Really big gun," she muttered briefly and then smiled for me. "Hi, I'm Sara, how are we feeling now?"

"I need to use the bathroom," I replied. The matter was becoming slightly more urgent.

"That's great; shall we try for the toilet?" she came over and pulled down my blankets and sheets. "Sir, can we unlock this please?"

Andrews didn't move at first.

"Sergeant, I am about to have an accident," I looked him in the eye while blushing. "I promise, if I make it past you, he can shoot me."

Andrews unlocked me with keys that the other man had. I noticed that the other man knocked twice on the outer door first. I would have rolled my eyes at their procedure, but I really needed a toilet. Sara came around and asked which leg was the bad one and she supported me on my way to the bathroom. She partially closed the door for our privacy and as I sat I could hear a conversation and some noises outside. Someone sounded antsy and it wasn't Andrews.

"How are you feeling?" Sara asked and distracted me.

"Better," I answered honestly. "Did you already start me on antibiotics?"

"Here we go," she helped me up and stood by while I washed my hands in the sink.

"I think I'm good," I told her and took a few ginger steps on my own. Once the door was open I saw the source of the ruckus as no fewer than three guns were pointed at me, plus a Taser had a laser beam on my breast.

"EEK!" Sara shrieked.

"This happens a lot," I told Sara dryly in an attempt to calm her down. "Hello, Homeland Insecurity," I greeted the strange men.

"Two steps forward!" the man with the laser demanded and I obeyed slowly. "Get your hands where I can see them! Step to the left. Step to the left," he adjusted his angle as I moved back toward my bed. "Get in the bed, don't make any sudden movements."

With my face toward Andrews and my back toward the idiot I rolled my eyes and sat in the bed. Andrews' lip twitched and I knew he wanted to smirk.

"Hands together, interlace the fingers!" Laser-man dictated and I played along. The other new man, who had held a gun in each hand like an ersatz cowboy, put his weapons away and pulled out a new set of handcuffs. He slapped them on me in short order and then linked them to the bed.

"This might be overkill," Sara stated in a not-at-all cheerful and bubbly way. She was standing in her corner by the bathroom with her arms crossed. Not much was said and no one moved significantly in the next few minutes until Susan came in with a clipboard and a temper.

"What the -- get the hell out of here. Now!" Susan almost shouted. "Did you cuff her? Who the fuck told you to do that? Get out here," Susan pointed and the new boys slunk off into the corridor. Susan watched them out but pointed at Sara. "Name?"

"Sara Smith I work here!" Sara replied with at least a little courage.

"Badge!" Susan ordered and Sara produced the cards for inspection. Susan still looked plenty pissed. "Nurse, would you give us a moment please. If those idiots are still out there, tell them they step one toe in here and I shoot."

Sara nodded her comprehension and glanced over me again before stepping out.

"Commander, what is it?" I felt my inner woman tug in an empathetic direction.

Susan just shook her head and after pacing for several minutes she collapsed into the chair. She started to cry and I looked around to the other soldiers trying to not look incredibly uncomfortable.

"The baby?" My voice broke.

Susan shook her head and heaved a few breaths. "I'm sorry. Belle, you're fine but…I'm so sorry. He's gone."

The truth sunk in and I wanted to curl up and die. Everything we had accomplished had gone up in flames and Al-Zahrani was in the wind.

Time to go.

*****

Belle Jones' story continues in *Killing Waldo,* book two in the Belle's Revenge Series.

*****

Works by Victoria Helen Rose:

Transatlantic (2014)
Beauty, Fury, and Lies (Belle's Revenge Series) (2014)
Killing Waldo (Belle's Revenge Series) (2015)

*****

Thank you, thank you, thank you for reading this book. My readers absolutely astound me with their energy and enthusiasm and I feel so privileged to entertain you.

If you enjoyed this book I would greatly appreciate it if you took a moment to review it online and recommend it to your friends and family members. I would also love to hear from you: find me on Facebook as Victoria Helen Rose.

*****

www.ingramcontent.com/pod-product-compliance
Lightning Source LLC
Chambersburg PA
CBHW050919250626
47155CB00001B/305